H

“L

“Refreshingly different, with an almost classic fantasy flavor . . . an exceptional literary debut.”
—John Charles, reviewer, *Chicago Tribune* and *Booklist*

“A fresh new voice in fantasy romance. . . . I loved the characters and mythology!”
—Alexis Morgan, bestselling author of The Paladins of Darkness series

“An exciting new fantasy world!”
—Ellen Higuchi, Borders Romance expert and bookseller

“A fabulous read, cover to cover.”
—*New York Times* bestselling author C. L. Wilson

“Unlike anything I've ever read. A brilliant adventure with tremendous heart. You'll love this book.”
—*New York Times* bestselling author Marjorie Liu

“A remarkable new voice and a stunningly original world. . . . An amazing start to what promises to be a truly engaging series!”
—Jill M. Smith, *RT*

THE SUMMONING

Shaking, the prince walked to the altar. White-faced and trembling, he never looked at Solie. His fear had nothing to do with killing an innocent girl, she saw, and she glared at him with terrified contempt.

A circle appeared in the air above them, a sphere of shining energy. The priests chanted, their sonorous words filling the room, and the sphere went from gray to green to red to black. A wind was blowing, whirling into the circle with a strange roaring sound. The fire sylphs darted back, leaving the circle in shadow, and Solie realized that there was something looking through that gateway, assessing them all. It was looking at her, nude and helpless on the altar. It saw her and wanted her.

"Now!" the king shouted. "Kill her now!"

The prince started, gasping, and raised his knife. His arms trembled as he brought it up over his head. At the same time, Solie broke through her bonds and sat up, thrusting her tiny blade deep into the prince's arm. . . .

L. J. McDONALD

THE BATTLE SYLPH

LEISURE BOOKS

NEW YORK CITY

I'd like to dedicate this book to my editor Chris Keeslar and my agent Michelle Grajkowski, who both believed in me, but most of all:

To my husband Oliver, without whom this book wouldn't have been possible.

A LEISURE BOOK®

March 2010

Published by

Dorchester Publishing Co., Inc.
200 Madison Avenue
New York, NY 10016

Cover art by Anne Cain.

ISBN 10: 0-8439-6300-X
ISBN 13: 978-0-8439-6300-7
E-ISBN: 978-1-4285-0817-0

Printed in the United States of America.

10 9 8 7 6 5 4 3 2 1

THE BATTLE SYLPH

Prologue

They brought the sacrifice in before dawn, while the streets were mostly empty and the roads still dark. Only the castle and its inner environs were lit, the fire sylphs mostly concerned with keeping the buildings warm in the frigid winter air. Keeping the streets outside the walls lit was less important.

Devon watched them bring her in from where he stood on the ramparts of the castle, huddling in his cloak and waiting for the ship that was soon to arrive. At least, he assumed it was a sacrifice in the cart driven through the old back gate, three armed men sitting inside before something covered in canvas. Whatever it was, it moved. There had been whispers that another battle sylph was to be summoned. The prince was of age, and no simple sylph would ever be considered good enough for him.

Devon sighed, glad that his sylph at least hadn't needed anyone to die before she could be bound to him. He could feel her, hovering incorporeal in the air around him, waiting as he did. When she wanted, she could take on solid shape, as all sylphs could, but she preferred to be invisible most of the time, dancing on the air that she could control. First summoned by his grandfather, she'd been passed down to him through his father for a gift of music, bound to him for the rest of his life. She didn't mind. Devon felt her contentment in the back of his mind. It was said the men bound to battlers felt nothing but their sylphs' hate. Certainly everyone near them felt it.

The breeze was cold, enough so for an autumn night to

make him think unhappily that soon it would be snow blowing across his body as he stood there, huddling deeper against the lee of the castle. "Hey, Airi," he called, teeth chattering. "It's freezing. Can you do something about the wind?"

Her presence grew closer, a face forming out of the air. *It's a big ship,* she reminded him.

"I don't think keeping me from freezing to death will use up too much of your energy," he replied, and the wind stopped around him, the air not quite warm but not so bitterly cold anymore either. "Thank you."

A silver laugh answered him, and Devon shook himself, straightening his cloak and looking up. Where they stood, there was a wide space a hundred feet across, easy for a ship to land on. Usually they docked during the day, but this wasn't a standard trade ship. It was rumored it had been bait for pirates instead. Three ships these brigands had attacked so far, taking the cargo and releasing the crew, but the king wasn't known for tolerating anything, and this latest craft had gone out armed with two battlers.

Whatever they'd found, they were on their way back now, damaged. Devon's job was to use Airi to help Tempest, the ship's official air sylph, land. His superiors hadn't told him when the craft would be arriving, however, and he'd already been out half the night, waiting.

He wouldn't complain, he admitted with a sigh. The same as he wouldn't ask what had happened to damage the ship, or about that cart he'd seen. Air sylphs were easy enough to get, as were those of earth, fire, and water. Someone like him could be replaced if they started questioning too much, and it had happened before, especially when battlers were involved. *They* were rare. Fortunately. Devon didn't like to think about what kind of damage even one could do.

Despite knowing better, and though he had just finished reminding himself how expendable he was, he looked back down over the ramparts at the cart now vanishing inside. A ship sent out for bait with *two* battlers on it? A sacrifice brought in to summon a new battler for the prince? That upset the normal world Devon was used to, where he didn't have to worry about anything but his work and Airi. Devon was happy being an air-sylph master. He didn't want to think about anything else. He felt sorry for the girl who was going to be killed, though.

"Do you sense Tempest yet?" he asked.

No.

Devon sighed, leaning back against the rampart again. At least he wasn't cold anymore. He closed his eyes, trying to catch a bit of rest. Late night or not, he would still have a full day tomorrow. Airi would wake him if anyone came. Sylphs rarely slept.

They're here.

Devon looked up. Enough time had passed while he dozed that dawn was starting to break, and on the skyline he could finally see a ship floating toward them. It was huge, its hull rounded on the sides like an ocean-going vessel, but the bottom was flat and the sails rigged to the sides. The only waves this ship sailed were those of the sylph who bore it. Tempest was a major sylph, one much more powerful than his little Airi. Devon was almost envious as he watched the thing glide silently in.

I'm just young, Airi told him, though she was almost a hundred years old. Sometimes that made him wonder just how old creatures like Tempest were, or how long Airi would live. He'd never asked her. In a lot of ways, Devon just didn't want to know.

"I know," he soothed, not wanting her upset. An upset

sylph was nearly painful for its master. He didn't know how the battlers' masters handled it. "If you weren't, we'd spend all our time on a ship." He'd hardly see his father again.

The ship slowed to a stop overhead, and he felt Tempest's winds beat harshly against him as Airi went to help her fellow sylph. Together, the two lowered the vessel toward the stones of the castle and lifted a ramp up to it.

As he walked forward, Devon noted that the ship's sides had gaping holes and one of the sails was torn. It was no wonder extra help was wanted to land her. He looked at the burn marks and felt a cold that didn't have anything to do with the weather. A man came down the newly set ramp, pulling his coat closed. In his wake stomped a behemoth in full armor, light gleaming out through the eyeholes of his helm. Recognizing both, Devon bowed deeply.

The man swept past without slowing. He was dressed like a dandy, his face pinched with pride, and he didn't even see Devon: Jasar Doliard, a minor landowner and one of the courtiers in favor with the king and the council. Enough in favor at least to win himself a battle sylph, the second figure, who Devon hoped would ignore him as well. He wasn't that lucky. Immediately, those glowing eyes within the helm locked on him. At least, it looked like a helm. It was very probable that the armor was physically a part of the battler and not separate at all. Devon could feel the hate rolling off the creature, yet Mace didn't do anything, not without his master's command. Mace usually didn't do anything other than hate. He just stood near his master and looked impressive. It would have seemed a waste of a battler if the creatures weren't so horrific when they did act.

Behind Jasar came the second battle-sylph master. He was a well-built blond man, though nowhere near the size of Mace, and his sylph *did* go into battle. Leon Petrule had been the king's head of security and lead battler master for years. Leon's battler took the form of a red-feathered hawk, perched on his shoulder, and Devon felt its hate as clearly as he had Mace's.

Ril's loathing was sharp, and the bird's grip tightened on his master's shoulder when he saw Devon, talons cutting into the leather. Devon bowed deeper, not wanting any attention. The only thing battlers knew how to do was hate. All they were good for was killing, and he was beyond grateful no one ever suggested he master one, though a man could only be master to a single sylph at a time, and the Chole family already had Airi to care for. Even if that weren't so, he didn't have the spirit for it. You had to have a certain hardness to your soul to hold one in thrall. Leon had it. For all his frilly clothes and brownnosing attitude, Jasar had it. Devon wondered if the king's pansy son would, and found himself doubting it.

Airi flowed around him, taking shape as a whirlwind of leaves, when Leon, to Devon's dismay, stopped before him. Ril shifted on Leon's shoulder, looking at Airi out of one eye. Devon bowed again. "My lord."

"You didn't see anything tonight," the king's battler master told him. "Understood?"

Devon bowed even deeper. "Yes, my lord."

"Good."

The battler master continued on his way. Devon waited until he was gone before straightening. His hands were shaking. "Airi," he managed. Her attention focused on him, a breeze in his mind. "Tell no one about tonight."

There was no argument. That's what it meant to be a master. She was beholden to him, unable to disobey. Should Devon and his father both die, she would return to the otherworld from which she came, never to return, unless he passed her on to a new master first. If Devon died before his father, Airi would return to the old man. She'd been his father's and his late grandfather's before him, and the old bonds still held, but Devon owned her loyalty now. She'd still obey any former master, though. Once someone owned her, they would always do so. Even the battlers followed that rule.

Devon shuddered, turning back to the ship to help unload as the crew started to emerge, but as he did, an explosion shocked him to his knees. Gasping, he scrambled to his feet and ran to the edge of the castle ramparts. Looking down, he saw a massive hole blown out of the side of the keep, near the base, and heard the cry of something inhuman. It was an outraged scream, like one he'd heard only once before, on a day that he still couldn't forget in his dreams. A moment later, a winged cloud shape shot from the hole, wings stretching out as it angled upward. Devon gasped as he felt its hate.

The lightning-filled cloud flew up into the sky, already vanishing in the early-morning light. It was carrying something with long red hair and pale limbs, something that shrieked with fright and clung to it.

"Airi," Devon gasped, not knowing what he was thinking or why he did so. "Follow them."

In a moment his sylph was gone, chasing along after her quarry through the air currents. Devon stood alone on the ramparts, staring after the escaped pair and wondering how any girl could manage to handle a battler.

Chapter One

Solie had an aunt named Masha, a woman who had never married and was known for her temper. She had refused to wed and lived on her own, running a bakery and working long hours every day. She'd forced the people in her town to accept her, and finally they had. Even now they bought her bread, when she was old and her hair gray. Solie had been born with Masha's red hair, if not her temper, and had been adored. Masha spoiled her niece, giving her presents and, more importantly, her time. Solie had lived for these visits, preferring her aunt's life of freedom to the marriage and certain servitude her mother promised. Her aunt's best present, however, was a knife that Solie could wear in her hair, hidden in a barrette.

"You'll never know when you might need it," the old woman told her. "And to know you have a weapon is to have a sense of security that shows in a woman. Men go after weak targets. Never present them with one. Your carriage is your greatest defense."

Solie took to wearing the barrette daily, with its green butterfly, and though she became known for it, she never told anyone what was hidden inside. It gave her confidence, and pride, and she snubbed the boys who came to court her, as well as the older men who thought a slim redhead might make a good wife. Her mother felt she was too picky, but her aunt felt she didn't have to choose at all. So when her family tried to arrange a marriage for her, Solie refused, leaving the same night with everything she owned shoved into a pack.

Masha will take me in, she decided, as she headed down the road out of her village. Her aunt lived only five miles away, on the other side of the crossroads in the next village. She had started out at dusk, sure her family wouldn't even realize until dawn that she'd gone out the window. She wasn't going to stay, though. She was seventeen years old and was not going to marry a forty-five-year-old fat man, no matter who told her she must.

Confident, frightened, and rather excited at her sudden freedom, she headed down the dirt road, the sun setting on the horizon and shrouding everything in darkness, which she rather welcomed. The dark didn't have anything in it to frighten her, her aunt assured her, only men did, and they were as dangerous during the day. As long as she kept her wits about her, she would be fine. So Solie walked along the road she'd taken so many times in the daylight, her pack thrown across her back, and whistling to prove to herself that the growing darkness wasn't making her nervous at all. She didn't run, quite, but she walked quickly and looked back a lot.

The night grew both dark and cold. It was late in the fall and the trees were already skeletal, their leaves lying in wet piles beside the road. The chill in the air was bitter as well. Solie pulled her cloak around herself and struggled onward, wishing her parents had decided to marry her off in the summer instead.

Time passed, the moon rising overhead, and she sighed in relief as she finally reached the crossroads. She hadn't seen a single person on the way. She'd come from the south. West, the road led to towns she'd only heard of, and turned eventually south itself. Three days' ride, she'd been told, and the kingdom of Eferem ended. Other kingdoms lay beyond, and more past them, carrying on until the world ended. She'd have to go that way eventually, she supposed, though that idea was still too remote for her to dwell upon. East was the capital, where the king lived, and she could see the lights of the fire sylphs who lit the castle, even from here. North lay her aunt's village, and then the road continued northward again in a route she'd never taken, even in play. That way wound through forests and other towns before ending at the dead Shale Plains, which had to be skirted to reach the kingdom of Para Dubh, their nearest neighbor. Here, though, the road was just a worn-out crossroads, the ruts deep and solid.

Solie crossed, jumping over tracks that were almost deep enough to trap a wagon. That was when she heard a horse snort. Startled, she looked up to see three men in the king's red and black livery on horseback, riding from the east. They stared back at her, equally surprised to see anyone out so late at night.

The lead rider grinned. "Looks like this will be easy," he said.

Discretion over bravery, her aunt always said. Solie ran. Immediately, she heard hoofbeats coming after her and tried to scramble off the road into the brush, but the men were trained. She barely got twenty yards, struggling across a pile of leaves, before one of them grabbed her by her long hair and hauled her back, also yanking her upward. Letting go of her hair to get a better grip on her shirt, he threw her across his saddle before him.

"Let me go!" Solie screamed, struggling.

He struck her across the back of the head with his mailed fist. "Don't," he warned. Then he ordered his companions to get her pack and spun his horse, cantering back the way he'd come, one hand still gripping the back of her shirt.

Her head spinning with pain, Solie could only hang on, feeling as if she would throw up whenever the horse's movements dug the saddle into her stomach. The soldiers soon galloped as a trio back toward the capital, laughing and congratulating themselves on their success. They'd been searching for a girl, she realized, and fully expecting that they'd need to break into someone's cottage to get one. She'd gone and made it easy for them.

She nearly panicked, her terror so great that she could barely breathe at all during the horrid ride. If the soldiers wanted her, there was nothing anyone could do to help; not even her aunt would be able to save her. She'd just vanish and never be seen again. She'd heard about it happening before. Her parents had always cautioned her that it could happen, and that she must be careful. Her aunt had said to never make herself look like an attractive target. Apparently, walking alone at night did.

"Please let me go!" she wailed. "What do you want with me?"

The man who held her laughed roughly, slapping her backside and making her cry out. "We don't want *you*, girl. We just want female bait. There's a battler coming for the prince tonight. You'll like him." The other men laughed as well.

Solie's heart froze. A battler? They wanted her for a *battler*? Like everyone, she'd heard stories of sylphs, spirits bound to serve human men with their magic. She'd grown up on those stories, distantly wishing for one herself but knowing it would never happen. Only men bound sylphs, and then, only men with more rank than her family had. Battlers were the horror stories of the sylphs, though: evil creatures born only to destroy. The safety of all Eferem was based on them, but they were cold and cruel, and according to the stories, to gain their services required the sacrifice of a virgin girl.

Solie started to scream, trying to buck off the horse. That made it shy, whinnying nervously. The soldier who held her cursed, and he threw her down onto the ground. Solie tried to scramble to her feet and run, but the man dismounted and grabbed her again, pinning her easily into the dirt while the other men bound her hands and feet.

"Gag her as well," he snarled. "She's damned loud."

They shoved a rag into her mouth and pulled her upright. Her wrists bound together, Solie could only move her fingers as she was hauled back across the saddle. The horses started to move again.

This wasn't supposed to happen! All the confidence her aunt had given her was gone, and she cried into her gag, her face pressed against her bound hands. Then she touched her barrette. Blinking, she felt the butterfly under her fingers—it had slipped free during her struggles. She unhooked it from her hair, keeping it hidden. The soldier didn't notice, shouting something to his companions about getting a wagon.

They were starting to canter on cobblestones now, which clattered loudly under the horses' shoes as they entered the city that surrounded the king's castle, passing through a side gate in the main wall and swerving their mounts down back alleys where no one could see them. Finally, they pulled up at a barn, where two of the soldiers dismounted. The man holding Solie stayed on his horse, one hand on her back, while his companions readied a cart. Solie twisted her head around to look pleadingly up at him.

"Too bad the battlers prefer virgins," he said, leering down at her. Solie shuddered and looked away.

They transferred her to an old cart that smelled as though it was used to carry vegetables. Its wooden boards were cold and hugely uncomfortable, but the men put a tarp over her that blocked the increasingly frigid night air. Solie was doubly glad of it; the three men sat on the seat ahead of her, probably looking back, but they wouldn't be able to see her under the tarp. Solie couldn't see in the darkness either, but she could feel her barrette.

She carefully worked the butterfly out from her palm to the edge of her fingers, careful not to drop it—she might lose it in the darkness if she did. Trying not to shiver as the cold seeped into her from the bottom of the wagon, she managed to point the tiny weapon toward her wrists before pushing on the little latch that would release the blade. This eased out—barely an inch long, but enough to convince a man to leave her alone, her aunt claimed. Solie took a deep breath and bent her fingers as much as she could, bringing the knife to the rope and starting to saw. It was hard, agonizing work, but the blade was sharp, and she nearly wept as she felt the first strands part. Yet the rope was thick and it took time to cut through.

The sound of the horses' hoofbeats changed, sounding hollow, and she realized they'd gone inside the castle. She resisted the urge to scream or work any faster. She'd only drop her knife if she did, or make too much motion and give herself away. Her chances of escaping were slim enough as it was. She tried not to think of that, just focused on cutting her bonds one strand at a time.

The cart turned a corner, descended, and finally stopped. She heard the men dismounting but kept sawing until the last second, palming the knife again just as they threw back the tarp. Blinking away tears, she looked up into a terrible brightness. They had a fire sylph, something Solie had never seen up close before. She saw it clearly now, floating above everyone in the form of a ball of light, illuminating the area as bright as day.

They were underground, in a cavern, and she whined behind her gag as the soldiers yanked her off the cart and held her above the ground between them, one gripping her under the shoulders, the other under the knees.

A man dressed in white frowned at Solie. "She'll do," he decided. "Everything else is ready. Come." He turned with a dramatic sweep of his robes and strode off, leading the soldiers down a corridor cut out of solid rock, the walls shiny as glass and reflective—the work of an earth sylph, since there weren't any tool marks.

Solie stared. Her reflection was better than anything she'd ever seen by glancing into a puddle or a lake, and she blinked at her first clear view of herself. She looked awful, her curly red hair a mess and her face covered in dirt and bruises. Her eyes were heavily shadowed, her skin blotchy from tears. She looked broken and ugly, and she tried not to sob again. She had to be strong—she *had* to be, or she'd die. She probably would die anyway, but her aunt would be ashamed of her if she cowered like some weak little girl. For that reason, she closed her eyes for a moment. When she opened them again, they were hard. She could feel the knife between her palms, and the ropes were a little looser, the innermost loop mostly sawn through. If she could cut the rest of the way, she'd be able to free her hands. Then she might have a chance.

The men dragged her into an underground cathedral, its high arching roof lit by more fire sylphs, whose masters stood along the walls dressed in red with their heads bowed. More men armed with swords stood closer to the center of the room, as did a group of priests in robes and one man in ermine.

Solie shivered, recognizing the king. He was heavyset, his beard turning gray and his eyes like chips of flint. She had seen him before in the paintings they hung in inns, and once inside a carriage at a distance. He didn't even look at her, speaking harshly to a young man dressed in expensive yellow silks that didn't match his skin tones. The young man was shaking, staring at her as she passed as though he'd never seen a woman before.

"Pay attention!" The king slapped him across the face, and the boy flinched.

"Yes, Father," he apologized, his eyes still tracking Solie

for a moment as she was hoisted up onto a dais and stretched out over an altar, her rope bindings passed over restraining metal hooks. She started her muffled shrieking again as the white-robed man started to cut off her clothing.

"The priests will open the gate," the king told his nervous son. "They swear there's a battler on the other side." He shot them a glare that had the men surreptitiously cowering. "Once it crosses over, kill the girl. Don't hesitate or it won't be bound to you. The second it turns to you, name it. That will complete the binding."

Solie gasped for breath on the altar, shaking over what she'd heard. They were going to kill her. The soldiers turned away, leaving her there, and she fumbled her barrette knife out again, praying no one saw it as she resumed sawing at her bonds. No one did. They didn't even look at her.

"What do I name it?" the boy whimpered, twitching.

"Name it whatever you want," the king snapped. "Just don't pick a stupid name, as you can't change it later. Don't fail me in this, boy. The king has always had a battler. You'll be a target for your enemies otherwise." When the boy squirmed, the king slapped him again and laughed harshly. "He won't let me smack you around anymore—though if he tried to stop me, my battler would go after him. He'll be your constant companion, as Thrall is mine. The only time Thrall is away from my side is in here, or when I'm with a woman. So be prepared to get used to it."

The prince looked down, obviously not thrilled with the idea. Solie sawed desperately at her bonds, none too pleased herself.

The white-robed man bowed to the king. "We're ready, my liege." The king nodded and stepped back, preferring to watch from the entrance to the corridor through which they had arrived.

Shaking, the prince walked to the altar. White-faced and trembling, he never looked at Solie. His fear had nothing to do with killing an innocent girl, she saw, and she glared at him with terrified contempt. Still, if he didn't look at her, he couldn't see she had cut halfway through her bonds. Solie hoped he maintained that unthinking dismissal of her even as he swallowed, shifting both his stance and his grip on the ornate dagger he held.

A circle appeared in the air above them, a sphere of shining energy. The priests chanted, their sonorous words filling the room, and the sphere went from gray to green to red to black. From there it went to a non-color, and the prince gaped at it in amazement while Solie squealed and hurried, nicking her own fingers in her haste. The wounds hurt but the blood helped, greasing the rope even as it threatened to make her drop her knife.

A wind was blowing, whirling into the circle with a strange roaring sound. The fire sylphs darted back, leaving the circle in shadow, and Solie realized that there was something looking through that gateway, assessing them all. The prince sensed it too, and she saw his eyes widen even farther. His Adam's apple bobbed up and down.

The presence looked through the gate, assessing, deciding whether to cross. Solie felt its attentions shifting, focusing . . . and suddenly she knew it was looking at her, nude and helpless on the altar. It saw her and wanted her, and she hacked through the last bits of rope as it appeared, huge and shadowy, not yet taking any distinct shape.

"Now!" the king shouted. "Kill her now!"

The prince started, gasping, and raised his knife. His arms trembled as he brought it up over his head. At the same time, Solie broke through her last bonds and sat upright, thrusting her tiny blade deep into his arm. The prince shrieked, dropping his knife and falling backward off the dais. Still bound at the feet, Solie yanked out her gag and looked up . . . straight into dark red eyes. She yelped and dropped back against the altar, hands raised in surrender.

The battler landed on the altar, bracing itself atop her, a beast formed of smoke and lightning, staring downward. She felt its emotions, its interest and its curiosity. Its eyes stared into hers, and she blushed as it slowly looked down the length of her body and then back up again. It purred, bent its head, and licked her from her navel up across her breasts and along her neck. Solie couldn't see its tongue, but she could feel it and squealed, frightened, cold, and somehow hot at the same time.

What had the king said? Name it.

"Hey, you," she managed, barely able to speak at all, she was so frightened. She swallowed, trying to get her tongue untied enough to ask its name, and it breathed warm air on her.

Heyou, it repeated softly, the sound echoing in her mind.

Had she just named it? she wondered, and suddenly became aware that there was shouting. Startled, she looked away from the beast to see that the priests were backing away in terror, the soldiers moving in with real fright in their eyes, but still determined.

"Kill the girl!" the king bellowed, even as he ran up the corridor and away from them all. "Send it back, now!" The prince sat at the base of the altar, staring up at her in shock.

"Help me," she begged the battler. "Please!"

The battler ducked its head, nuzzling her again, and then it rose up, roaring. Solie could suddenly feel its hate as it focused on the men, and half of them backed away—which didn't do any good. Something like an arm lashed out, and a wave of destruction rippled from the altar, blowing into soldiers and priests alike and tearing them apart. Fire sylphs dove to try and protect their masters but were obliterated as well, flashing for a moment and then vanishing. Everything inside the chamber vanished except the altar, and Solie screamed, terrified.

The arm came around her, lifting her up against something warm. She felt it move, and abruptly they were flying, sweeping across the room and out the way she'd come, arching up the passageway. At the top, the king ran away, bellowing for help as the cart horses screamed and reared. Heyou growled, but the king had reached what looked like a short, slim man with a bald head and unblinking eyes. The king's battler looked at Solie and Heyou unwaveringly, and it was Heyou that flinched back, turning away.

The creature holding Solie blew out the corridor through which she had been carted into the castle, making the stone passage suddenly fifty feet high. He swooped outside through the gap, and Solie felt the cold bite into her as he struggled for altitude, lifting them both up over the castle walls, and headed toward the dawn. Solie screamed, freezing and terrified, until black smoke wrapped around her, warming her, and then she fainted, unable to deal with any more. The battler looked down at her in concern, but she was still breathing.

Heady with her scent and his own freedom, Heyou flew on.

Chapter Two

Heyou flew into the dawn, arcing high over farmland as he made his way toward the mountains, the girl held close. He'd never seen such a place as this, but the air currents felt familiar enough under his wings. Not quite settled on a solid form yet, he stayed in his natural shape: that of a dense cloud of black smoke streaked with flickering electricity, his eyes red spheres of ball lightning, his mouth full of teeth formed from pure energy. Wings made from the same smoke stretched out to either side of him, the tips fading to nothingness. Normally incorporeal, he still kept enough shape to carry her as he searched for somewhere safe to land. That place certainly wasn't where the gate had been. He would have destroyed everything there if it weren't for the need to keep the girl protected. Plus, there had been another male there. Heyou was young and untried. He could sense the other's age and didn't want a fight. Not with a female in his arms.

He still reeled at the wonder of it. A low-level guard for his home hive who never even saw the queen, he hadn't known what the gate was when it appeared. He'd only investigated to ensure the safety of his queen and hive. When he saw the female on the other side, though, there had been no way to resist crossing over to her. Now she slept in his arms and *she* was his queen, or something so close it didn't matter. He could feel her ownership of him and wanted to scream his triumph.

Instead, he flew. She was small and delicate, locked in flesh and, from the look of her, prone to the cold. He surrounded her with his warmth and looked for a warm place to land, finally settling deep in a mountain valley southeast of the gate, where steam rose up through vents under the lakes, heating the water. It felt safe there, hot and moist, and he landed lightly on the edge of a hot spring, lowering the girl gently to the ground.

She stayed unconscious, her long hair fanning around her face, and he studied her body. He wasn't really familiar with her shape, but he understood the concept of *female*. She smelled right to him, overwhelming, and he shimmered, taking on a form that he hoped would be pleasing to her: the male of her species. He'd seen enough of them, destroyed enough of them back at that place. Hating men, he became one, standing nude over her for a long moment before kneeling at her side, reaching with human arms to touch her soft skin.

She'd named him. *Heyou.* The sound of it echoed in his mind, binding him, but he didn't care. To be bound, to be owned . . . most of his kind never were. They stayed drones, serving the queen, wanting the queen, fighting and dying for her but never touching her. Only a tiny few did, each of them named. He'd never thought he would be so lucky.

"Heyou," he whispered. It sounded good. "Heyou." He trailed a hand gently down, touching her lips and feeling her breath against his fingers. Down her neck, feeling the pulse and delighting in it. Down her chest, where her heart beat, and over the rounded softness of her tiny breasts, which would hold milk. He groaned deep in his throat and explored her farther. Her belly and womb, untouched, the mound of soft hair, and lower, where the source of her femininity lay.

He wanted her. He wanted her so badly he could take her right there . . . But she was the queen. He lived on her whim, and he would wait for her. He instead let his hand linger for a moment, learning her scent, the feel of her skin, and the essence of her mind. It fed him, fueled him in this energy-poor land, and he let himself pattern that energy into his own mind. He would recognize her anywhere now, find her anywhere.

Finally she stirred, and he settled back on his haunches, not sure how she'd feel about his forwardness. He was ready for her, though, as her eyes fluttered and opened, looking up at him.

The girl screamed.

Heyou was so surprised that he turned to smoke, wings flaring as he spun to see what the danger was. Nothing. Just a few birds with no minds, a few insects, and an air sylph that was female but sterile. He returned to human form and twisted back to her, wondering what she was frightened of. Belatedly, he realized it was *him*.

Solie stared at the battler, so shocked she couldn't speak. When she'd woken, she'd looked up at a man with no clothes on and panicked. He'd been very . . . erect, and looking down at her with an expression she had no doubt about. She'd screamed and he'd turned to smoke. Now he was in the shape of the man again, looking at her uncertainly, still nude and—she peeked down—yep, still interested. Solie looked down at herself to see she didn't have any clothes on either and squeaked, wrapping her arms around herself.

The battler looked disappointed.

"Don't look at me!" she gasped. "I'm naked!" He blinked and she waved at him wildly. "Turn around!" He did so, presenting his back. He didn't look bothered by his own nudity at all, but Solie didn't think she'd ever stop blushing. There was no clothing to get dressed in and no sign of any people at all. She looked around at the steaming springs and felt lost.

"Where are we?" she wondered aloud. The battler looked over his shoulder. She glared. He snapped his head around again.

"Away," he said softly, his voice deep and resonant. "I don't have the words."

"Oh." She bit her lip. "Just don't look at me, okay?" She ran a hand through her tangled hair, wincing, and looked down at her still-bound ankles. Quickly, she started working on the knot. "You, you're the battler, aren't you?"

"Battler?"

"The battle sylph." She clawed at the knots, but they were too tight. She couldn't feel her feet anymore, she realized. "You came through the gate?"

"Yes. I am Heyou."

So she *had* named him. Solie shook her head at the inadvertent joke of a name and sighed. "Um, can you help me?" He looked back at her, and she gestured at her feet while trying to keep herself covered. "I can't get them off."

Heyou stared at her feet and frowned. Turning completely around, he reached out with one hand, hooked a claw through the rope, and pulled. The rope shredded and Solie gasped in pain as feeling rushed back into her feet.

"What's wrong?" he asked, his eyes widening.

"My feet. They were tied too long." She rubbed them frantically, trying to get the pins and needles to fade and very aware that the battler was still watching her. "Can you turn around again?" He did. "Um, thank you for saving my life."

His back muscles tensed. "Why did they try to hurt you?"

"Don't you know?"

He shook his head, his short hair shining with drops of water from the spring. She'd never liked hair that short, and he was really rather skinny, his features plain and unremarkable. For someone who could change his shape, he'd certainly picked a boring one. Then again, she'd never seen a sylph who looked so human. She wasn't sure, but she didn't think it was legal.

"I saw a gate," he said. "I saw you. I came to you."

Bait. Solie rubbed her feet harder and tried not to cry. She'd survived, that was what was important. She felt horrible, though, and so grateful to him, she was nearly sick to her stomach. "Yeah, well, I was a lure for you. They were going to kill me and make you the slave of the prince."

His head swung around, his form shimmering and a look of such horror and rage on his face that she cringed.

"What?" he screeched, his voice suddenly so high-pitched that she had to giggle, her fear gone. He'd saved her life, she reminded herself. He didn't have any reason to hurt her.

"That's what they always do to battlers," she told him. She paused a moment. "Why did you save me?"

Confused, he turned his head away from her again. "You're my queen. You named me."

She frowned. "Does that mean you're *my* battler?"

"Yes."

She felt giddy suddenly and wanted to giggle again. He belonged to her? She had a battler? Women weren't supposed to have battlers. Women weren't allowed to have any kind of sylph. "Oh, wow," she said, and he looked back over his shoulder again. "Don't look!" He snapped his head back.

"Why don't you want me looking at you?" he asked plaintively.

"Because I don't have any clothes on." She paused, realizing he was a sylph. He probably didn't care that she was naked. "It's just a rule here. You can't look at a woman when she's naked, not unless she says you can." She frowned. "If you're my battler, don't you have to do what I say?"

"If you make it an order," he admitted. "Yes."

She thought she had. Maybe she had to be more deliberate. "I'm ordering you not to look at anything but my face when I'm naked, understand?"

"Yes." He turned around and sat cross-legged, staring at her face and nowhere else. His expression was calm, but his face was a little creepy, too much like the soldiers who'd kidnapped her. "I don't know what I'm supposed to do with a battler," she admitted. "You look like an ugly guy."

"I do?"

"You didn't notice you looked like a guy?" she asked dryly.

"I didn't notice I was ugly."

"Well . . ." She shifted. "You're kind of skinny and your hair's too short."

"Oh." Suddenly, his hair lengthened, tumbling down his back in yellow waves.

Solie squealed, delighted. "That's wonderful! Can you change the color?"

"Of course."

"Make it darker," she begged, and it darkened to black. "Less dark, more brown." He obliged, changing the hair color. "Make it straighter."

Forgetting her nudity at least a little, since his gaze hadn't shifted a bit since her order, she directed him in changing his shape, making his chest and shoulders broader, his legs longer, his face more angular and symmetrical. He let her, delighting in her enjoyment as she turned him into her ideal mate. He became a stunning young man only a little taller than herself, the kind she was sure even her aunt would sneak a look at in the streets, and she moved a little closer, not afraid of him anymore, as she directed him in the details. It was expected, she told herself. Sylphs looked like what their masters wanted. If she was going to have a battler, he had to look human or everyone would know what he was. There was no reason he couldn't be someone attractive.

Someone *very* attractive. As she directed him in the specific shade of his eyes, Solie realized that she was kneeling right in front of him, her face up close to his so that she could see the details, and she was feeling much warmer than the hot springs really should have caused. She shivered, suddenly wondering if those lips she'd had him shape tasted as good as they looked.

He inhaled deeply. "I like the way you smell."

Solie turned beet red, covering herself even though he wasn't looking. "Turn around!" she screeched, and he obediently did so. "Why don't you have clothes on anyway?"

"You don't have any."

"That's because they cut mine off!" She looked down at herself. "I need clothes. Can you get me some?"

"And leave you alone? No."

Solie frowned. "Why not?"

"I have to protect you."

From what? She looked around. "Well, I can't stay here forever, and I need clothes. I can't go into a town without any."

"Why not?"

She blew out a breath, wondering what kind of place he came from that he didn't know about something as simple as that. "People don't go around naked. Not unless they're . . ." She blushed again.

"Not unless they're what?"

"Never you mind!" she snapped. "You have to obey me, don't you? Well, I'm ordering you to go find me clothes! Girl clothes," she added, "that aren't taken off some girl! And don't hurt anyone while you do. And don't give yourself away as a battler!" Was anyone looking for them? she wondered in terror. She hoped not. No one knew who she was, and they certainly wouldn't recognize Heyou now.

The battler sighed, accepting the order as he rose to his feet and shimmered, turning into black, winged smoke. He rose into the air, flying away, and Solie sat staring after him, suddenly nervous again at being alone. She'd forgotten to tell him how soon to be back.

Heyou headed in the same general direction he'd come from, though he was careful not to return to exactly the same place. He still remembered the other male he'd seen, the other "battler," as his queen called them, and the scent of several others. He did not want a fight. Not with them. The rest of the males he'd been able to sense in the cavern and below him when he flew were all weak things, like the ones he'd destroyed at the gate. He thought about destroying them too, but she'd told him not to hurt anyone. Besides, he could smell females around many of the males and didn't want to risk hurting them. They weren't part of his hive, but females were inviolate. The males could quite happily die, for all he cared.

Heyou landed outside a small hamlet on the edge of a forest. Shifting back to his human form, he strode in, sure he wouldn't be recognized as a battler. A girl came out of a hut and saw him, and he was simply smiling at her when she screamed and ran back inside. A man came out a moment later, blinking. His face showed shock, and he grabbed a pitchfork from beside the hut.

"Get out of here!" he yelled. "Freak!"

Heyou looked down at himself. He still looked human. Glaring at the man, he felt the loathing inside himself, the blinding hatred for any male not of his hive. It boiled inside, reaching out, and the man blanched as he felt it. A woman stepped out of the hut behind the man, and Heyou's hate was tempered immediately with interest and his queen's order to be discreet. This woman had children. She smelled wonderful.

"I need clothes for my queen," he told her.

"You need clothes for you," she replied.

"Don't talk to him!" the man hissed, and Heyou snarled. The man went white and backed up.

From the rest of the hamlet, more people started coming, the men armed with whatever farming implements they could find, the women standing back and chuckling appreciatively. Heyou delighted in the shape he'd taken and smiled winningly at the mother.

"Do you have clothes?" he asked.

She shook her head in amusement, obviously trying not to laugh. "Some old and worn ones. What happened to you? Were you robbed?"

Heyou thought about it. "Yes," he decided.

That seemed to settle it for her. "Your poor lady! She must be devastated." Then, while her husband stared in amazement, the woman vanished back into her hovel and returned with some folded pieces of rough burlap.

Heyou took them thankfully but stared at them, not knowing what he was supposed to do. The mother laughed and helped, showing him how to pull an itchy tunic on over his head. The cloth was so worn in places it was barely holding together, but it covered him from his neck to midthigh.

"You must be used to far finer clothes," she commented, and he didn't disagree.

"Thank you," he told her.

She waved the thanks away, blushing. "I'm just sorry I don't have shoes for you."

"He doesn't need them," her husband growled.

Now that he was decent, the women all moved in, chattering and introducing themselves. The men held back, recognizing the danger, but for the women he was too appealing to ignore. He had to fight his instinct to put his protection around them, the same as he fought his hate for the men. A little leaked out anyway, and the women all loved him, while the men were afraid.

"You'd better go to your lady now," the mother told him at last, and Heyou nodded.

"Thank you." Turning, he strode back into the woods, the women waving good-bye and a few children—all female—running after him. He let them follow, waiting until he had outwalked them all before shimmering back into smoke and returning to his queen.

Chapter Three

Airi watched the girl and the battler as a drift of sun motes on the wind. The battler was young, barely more than a hatchling. A seasoned battler wouldn't have let her come so close to his master. This one had left the human girl alone, and without any spoken warning to Airi. It wasn't as though she would hurt the girl—not even with a direct order from her own master—but battlers were extraordinarily possessive.

She watched him go and wondered what to do. Devon hadn't been too detailed in his instructions. Follow them. She had. Should she stop now? She wasn't an unintelligent creature, but she was a minor sylph. Her duty was to obey, whether in her original hive or with her master here. Independent decision-making skills weren't something strongly encouraged in her kind. That lack of independence was what the humans used to bind them, but she really didn't mind. She had one master focused on her alone. No one back in the hive she hatched in had that kind of attention. More, Devon gave her greater freedoms than most sylphs could dream of.

Unlike battlers, elemental sylphs in Eferem weren't usually bound into a single shape, though they were limited in what forms they could take. That of a human being was forbidden. Like most air sylphs, Airi preferred to stay incorporeal and invisible, rarely acquiring solid form, since she could use wind to lift whatever she needed. Unlike most others, however, Devon let her speak. That was forbidden to every other sylph, but he'd given her permission, so long as no one else heard. That was a gift and she knew it, for she'd never been allowed to talk to either of the masters she'd had before him. But she spoke to Devon, chattering at him, asking questions, asking him to play his flute for her, and thanks to their bond, she didn't need to speak aloud. She could whisper her words directly into his mind, where no one else would hear, just as she would have to other sylphs back home. Trapped in silence for fifty years after her arrival through the gate, she still reveled in speaking and knew how rare her freedom truly was.

She saw this battler had the same freedom she did—and more. He was locked into a shape of his master's choosing, but he certainly didn't seem to mind, and she hadn't ordered him not to shift back. Airi watched him soar away as a pattern of energy that was both familiar but alien. He wasn't from her hive, but he looked to be from the same one as Mace. At least those two wouldn't fight if they met up . . . unless their masters ordered it.

The girl watched the battler go and stood, looking around and making her way to the hot springs, testing their temperatures until she found one she liked. Airi watched and wondered if she should speak. In the end, she decided against it—Devon had made it clear she wasn't to reveal to anyone that she could talk. Besides, the battler would be back soon. He might not like Airi being too close.

She swirled in the steam, dancing on the hot air as she decided to wait a bit longer. The human girl couldn't stay here forever, and her battler would return. She'd wait to see where the two went, and then she'd return to Devon.

The redhead slid into the water with a sigh, unaware of Airi's presence, and the air sylph floated back into the steam, well clear of her but close enough that she could do anything required.

Screaming invectives, King Alcor of Eferem hauled off and struck Thrall across the face as hard as he could with his mail-clad fist. The battler's head snapped to one side and then returned to its original position, looking at him. The eyes were unmoved as always, the hate as familiar and even as ever. Thrall loathed him, the king knew that. The creature would kill him if he could, but he was bound to obey. It was the extremes of that obedience Alcor protested at times.

"Why didn't you kill that thing?" he thundered, even though he knew Thrall was ordered not to speak. A battler giving voice to its hatred could drive a man insane. "My son is dead because of you!"

Thrall didn't react, his face not changing at all, but Alcor could almost hear the laughter. The battler had been his slave for decades; he knew when the monster was amused. Cursing, he hit Thrall again. It did no good. He could hit him all night, and he was the only one who would suffer for it.

"You'll pay," he growled at the battler instead. "I'll make you pay."

Thrall had done nothing, nothing at all. He'd let that battler kill his son and he'd let him escape. He hadn't disobeyed, though. If Alcor had ordered him to fight instead of protect, he would have. But he hadn't needed to do any protecting. Instead, he'd just stood there and let the battler escape, leaving his king looking like a coward.

"Your Majesty?"

Alcor turned, gasping for breath and far too hot in his ermine cape. His son was dead, turned to ash by a battler he should have controlled. He would have killed those priests if they weren't already dead. How had that slip of a peasant girl got free? How had she been armed? Now she had the battler. He just hoped the thing killed her.

Jasar Doliard stood behind him, dressed resplendently in a black suit with white lace at the collar and wrists. The dandy had actually found time to change in the face of all this. Alcor felt rage, but Jasar was a major controlling force on the council. The other council members stood behind him, waiting nervously for his favor. In the corner, Leon Petrule stood quietly, his arms crossed.

The battlers of the two men waited outside. Only Thrall was allowed in these inner chambers, just as only Thrall was permitted to look human. Alcor stomped to his chair and sat down, leaving the others standing. Leon seemed as though he could wait all day, but Jasar looked irritated—and felt such irritation was safe, Alcor realized angrily. Jasar thought his battler would be able to protect him. He had no idea how fast Thrall could move, though. If the king wanted, Jasar would be dead before Mace even got into the room.

Somewhat mollified, the king gestured at the other chairs around the table, none of them as ornate as his own. Thrall took a place at his shoulder, staring at the assembled men without blinking. All of them sat, except for Leon, who remained in the corner.

"You know what happened," the king growled, leaning on the wood. "The crown prince is dead and a battler is loose." He was still furious. He hadn't loved his son. The boy was too weak for that, but he was the only son he'd been able to get. His daughters couldn't wear the crown when he died, and he wasn't as young as he used to be. He'd never admit it to these fools, but he hadn't been able to get it up for years. He'd have to find someone suitable to wed his eldest daughter, and from the smirk on Jasar's face, it was clear who *he* thought the best candidate was.

The remaining men weren't quite so obvious in their ambitions. "We grieve for your loss, Your Majesty," the oldest said, bowing his head, as did the others. Even Leon did, his face showing a regret Alcor thought might actually be genuine. Born without any land or titles, he wasn't a member of the council and didn't owe his authority to politics, but instead to a ruthlessness Alcor had recognized in him years before. It had tempered over the years into a calm efficiency that the king still appreciated whenever he needed to get things done.

"Save it," he snapped. "There'll be time for that later. The succession is in doubt. I want to make it clear"—he paused to stab a finger on the table—"that *I* will decide who is to succeed me. I don't want any suggestions. If anyone makes one, I will give him to Thrall." This was a blatant threat. The men of the council stared uncertainly at the battler, even Jasar, and Alcor leaned back, pleased. "For now, I just want to know what happened."

The assembly stared at him, silent, none of them confident enough to speak.

"Surely one of you has talked to the priests!" Alcor snapped.

"They're all dead, Your Majesty."

Jasar lifted his head. "Not all, Your Majesty. I spoke with Father Belican before I came here. He's too old to attend the rituals, but his mind is sharp. I took the liberty of filling him in on what happened."

"And?" the king growled.

"He says nothing like this has ever happened before."

"Of course not!" Alcor thundered. A woman gaining a battler? It was unthinkable.

Jasar shrugged, amused. "While it has never happened, Belican could theorize. Somehow, the girl used magic to snare the battler, magic we've never heard of. Perhaps she was planted by our enemies, sent for just this reason."

"Bullshit." Everyone looked up as Leon Petrule pushed himself away from the wall and walked toward the table. "The girl had a blade up her sleeve. She palmed it before she was stripped, and no one searched her." He tossed a butterfly-shaped barrette onto the table with a one-inch blade sticking out the end. "I found this on the altar. She cut her rope and stuck His Highness, the prince, before he could stab her."

The king flushed red. "The bitch . . . How dare she!"

His head of security shrugged. "She was saving her own life. I admire that. But the timing meant she ended up with the battler, instead of His Highness. She must have named him."

There were murmurs of discord. "A woman can't control a battler," one old man protested. "They don't have the strength!"

Leon shook his head. "I don't think strength is what they need."

"What do you mean?" the king asked.

Leon bowed. "With your leave?" he asked, gesturing toward the exit. When Alcor nodded, he went to the door, opened it, and whispered to the servant outside. The man bowed and hurried away.

"This better not take long," Alcor growled.

"It won't." Leon paused. "Ah, they found one already. Wait a moment," he ordered the servant and held out his arm. "Ril!"

The battler appeared, folding his wings and landing on Leon's forearm as he was brought into the room. The council gasped at the presumption, and even the king tensed, but Thrall merely tilted his head to one side, quietly regarding the other sylph. Ril stared back at him and the familiar aura filled the room. The two battlers hated each other, and they hated the council. The antipathy was palpable. Even after thirty years, it still made the king want to pull his cloak away from his neck and get some air. He resisted.

"You feel it?" the head of security asked unnecessarily and looked at his battler. "You despise us, don't you, Ril? As you despise Thrall. And he'd kill you too, if he could." The bird blinked, glaring at him out of one eye, and Leon smiled at the council. "Ril is my glory. He's worth the danger a thousand times over and I don't regret him. But I'm a simple man. I live in a small house when I'm not working, surrounded by my wife and daughters, and I've noticed something interesting."

He nodded toward the door. A serving girl in a white and black uniform came into the room, curtsying nervously. Alcor raised an eyebrow. No woman had ever been in the council room, not unless it was empty and she was on her knees cleaning it—or perhaps on her back on the table. Alcor watched the girl enter visibly shaking.

Leon took her arm. "Hold it out," he ordered, and to everyone's surprise he transferred Ril to her. The bird settled down, feet lightly gripping the servant's arm, and bowed his head, his attention on the girl. She stared back in fascination, obviously not knowing what she held.

"Does he scare you, girl?" Leon asked.

"N-no, sir," she managed. "He's a pretty bird."

The council guffawed, Alcor joining in. They laughed at the girl, who smiled uncertainly as she held the battler on her arm and tentatively scratched his bowed avian head. Alcor would have thought he'd rip her arm off. He'd seen the thing mutilate a spoiled courtier's son who'd tried to touch him.

"Do you feel it, my lords?" Leon asked.

The king frowned. The hate was there, the same as always, but it was lessened. Ril was actually ignoring them in favor of the girl. Alcor looked over his shoulder. Thrall was staring at the servant as well, his expression rapt.

"Ril plays with my daughters," Leon told them seriously. "He's never harmed them. Look at his feet. He's dug into my leather pads so hard that they cut me. He's not even touching her with his claws. Look at Thrall. I bet if we brought Mace in, it would be the same."

Jasar started in surprise.

"Ril, come!" Leon commanded. Shrieking, the hawk spread his wings and flew back to his master's shoulder. The creak of the leather guard as the bird dug in its claws sounded clearly to all the men at the table.

"Go, child," Leon added. Swallowing, the servant girl curtsied and left. The king shot a look at Thrall. The battler was staring at the council again, as disinterested and hateful as ever.

"Battle sylphs like women, for some reason," Leon continued. "Probably because they're no threat. I have no idea what it means for one to be bound to a girl, but it makes me nervous."

Alcor frowned. Given what he'd just seen, the situation made him nervous as well, and he had enough other things to worry about. "Find the girl. Have her killed."

Leon bowed, not questioning the difficulty of the order. With the girl dead, her battler would be banished. Turning, he went out the door, Ril swaying on his shoulder.

The king turned back to his council. Some of them looked upset, others thoughtful. Jasar was smirking to himself, about what, the king didn't want to know. He had his uses, but he was perverted. Alcor didn't care too much about the fate of his daughters, but he didn't want to see any of them married to the man unless it became unavoidable.

To change the subject, he commanded, "Tell me what Para Dubh said about our trade proposal."

Out in the hall, the serving girl shivered, rubbing her arm where the bird had sat. His feet had been warm against her skin, and he'd been so much lighter than she expected. She shivered again, almost missing him, but the servant who'd taken her away from her wash bucket flicked his fingers at her, dismissing her before he returned to his post across from the door. She knew better than to disobey.

Curtsying, she hurried down the hall and around the

corner. On the way, she'd had to pass the alcove where battlers waited during the council. Always before, she'd nearly run past. Now she slowed, looking curiously inside.

Ril's golden perch was there, empty, while beside it stood the seven-foot suit of armor that was Mace. She knew his name—everyone knew his name. He stood there, staring down at her, and she gaped in return. The hate she'd always felt before near the battlers was gone without his master. She felt . . . safe. Somehow, this massive creature, whose waist she barely reached, made her feel safe. She hadn't felt so secure in years.

Slowly she stepped toward him, reaching out a hand to touch his leg plate. It wasn't metal she touched, though. It was warm, and it trembled under her touch. She peeked up at him.

"The armor's you, isn't it?" she whispered.

Silently, he nodded.

The servant girl stared, licking her lips. Something about the battler made her very warm, and protected, and daring. "Mace," she said, trying out the sound of the name.

He shivered again.

"Mace," she repeated, stroking his leg and sliding her hand around it. There was no hate, but she could feel lust in the air, filling her, and she didn't know if it was coming from him or her. It was there, though, more than she'd ever felt from the lords who had the right to take her whenever they wanted. She'd rather *he* took her.

She whimpered. Mace reached down and lifted her, and she didn't resist, his desire as deep in her mind as his hate was to men. He lifted her skirts and pulled her bloomers off, and then he was inside her, holding her along his forearms as he entered her body, her legs spread wide around his hips. She cried out softly, wanting to scream but not daring to let anyone hear her, not even when no one would pass the area for battlers if they could at all help it.

He was surprisingly gentle, his size just enough to stretch her without tearing, to fill her without harming. He seemed to know what she wanted and he gave it to her, even as he kept the desire firm in her mind. It did come from him—his need penetrating her mind until he overwhelmed her inhibitions—but she'd invited him, just as all those serving girls and courtiers who sneaked to his side did, entranced by his danger and his size. His master had only told Mace to wait when he was busy and come when called, nothing more. Nothing about not letting women come to him. And come they did, all keeping the secret of his attraction, as he knew this one would, for her own safety if not for his. She wasn't a queen to him in the way the girl who'd died to lure him through the gate would have been, but she was enough to keep his sanity intact in this place. He didn't know how Ril and Thrall and the other battlers kept theirs, but this was how he maintained his: in the bodies of any women he could reach without his master finding out, many of whom returned to him repeatedly.

He plunged into her as deeply as he dared, bringing her to orgasm over and over again before finally letting himself finish. Then he shook, there in the alcove, holding the girl to him like all the others and wishing one of them could be his queen.

Chapter Four

Heyou landed by the edge of the hot spring to find his queen sitting in one of the cooler pools, her head reclined against the side. She was asleep, her breasts poking up through the steam. Remembering her order, he tried to look at her face without seeing the rest and finally had to stand with his back to her, holding out at arm's length the clothes he'd brought.

"I'm back, my queen," he told her. Predictably, she shrieked, and he heard splashing behind him as she fell into the water. He sighed. He really didn't understand queens.

"Th-thank you," she managed, coughing, and snatched the garments out of his hand. He heard rustling, and finally she told him he could turn around.

He did so. She stood before him dressed in a tunic made from much the same material as his, though hers was a faded green instead of brown and reached to her ankles. Her dress had no sleeves, but she had a worn blouse on under it, the waist tied with a rope belt. Her hair was a tangled mess and her face still dirty around the ears, as was the neck where she'd missed when she'd bathed.

"How do I look?" she asked.

"Beautiful, my queen," he told her truthfully.

She blushed. "Thanks. You know, you don't have to call me your queen. My name is Solie."

She'd told him her name. Heyou's eyes widened in gratitude. "Solie," he breathed.

Solie blinked, not sure about the tone he'd used, and glanced around. "Um, now what?"

Whatever she wanted.

"Can you take me to my aunt's house?" she asked.

He didn't have the faintest idea where that was. Nonetheless, he said, "Absolutely," and reached for her. She flinched back and he frowned. He pointed out, "I have to carry you."

"Oh, right."

Laughing nervously, she stepped into his embrace. It nearly undid him. She smelled so good, so female, so much his queen that he shuddered, wanting nothing more than to take her in his arms and . . . His hands closed around her slim form and he swallowed, afraid to look into her eyes and show it. She didn't want him that way. At least, he didn't think she wanted him. He didn't want to see the fear in her eyes, so he held her and changed form and rose up, flying over the springs with Solie cradled gently within him.

The air sylph from earlier tracked them, following a distance back. Suddenly suspicious, Heyou blasted his thoughts at her. *What are you doing?*

Following, following, she answered immediately, not stupid enough to try a denial. *Only that. My master demands it.*

Why?

Curiosity, I suppose. It didn't sound as if she knew.

Heyou kept flying, thinking. Solie had said not to harm anyone. That, to him, included sylphs, but this one wasn't from his hive. *Well, stay back,* he decided.

The air sylph increased the distance between them.

Heyou rose up over the mountains, looking downward at slopes of trees and rocks. It was cold up here, but Solie was warm, cradled in his embrace. She couldn't see where they were going, surrounded by his darkness, but while she was nervous, she handled it well.

Where is your aunt? he asked, sending the words directly into her mind, the same as he'd spoken to the air sylph.

Solie jumped. "Um, northeast of the castle where you

found me. There are crossroads there. She's north of the crossroads in the first town, at the bakery. Can you find it?"

Probably, though he didn't like the thought of going close to the gate again. There was nothing for it, however, so he banked his turn, headed back in that direction. "I can find it," he assured her. He'd have to.

He flew slower than he had when searching for clothes, not wanting to risk her and content just to hold her anyway. Carrying Solie felt strange, but she was light, and there was a sweet aura of energy around her that he knew he could drink from. It tasted soothing to him and good, unlike the rest of the foul energies in this place. Those, he knew, were inedible to him, poison. Only Solie had energy that could sustain him.

Below, the mountains and forests were replaced by farmland, and he saw the castle he'd taken her from, surrounded by its walls and city. East of that, the road she'd mentioned led away in a snaking line, crossed by another road after a few short miles. Heyou glided far above these, following the northern fork into a shallow valley surrounded by fruit orchards. A small town lay there, the streets cobbled and the buildings made of clean stone.

He swooped in, keeping behind trees, where no one would see him. He sensed no new sylphs. Most of them seemed to inhabit the castle, which was another good reason to avoid it. The air sylph still followed, keeping about a league back. He thought about it again and decided to keep ignoring her for the moment.

Landing behind a copse of apple trees long since empty of fruit, he shifted, settling Solie on her feet and reluctantly letting go of her. She looked around herself, eyes widening at the sight of the orchard. Pushing her way through the low-hanging branches, she looked down the slope at the backs of the houses.

"This is my aunt's village! It took so little time to get

here!" She turned, throwing her arms around him in thanks, and Heyou immediately embraced her, his face buried in her neck. Solie froze, her breath catching in fear.

Heyou closed his eyes and breathed through his mouth against her throat, his hands flat and open against her back. He fed on his queen's energy, and the taste of it only increased his desire. He could feel her heart beating with increasing speed against his chest and pulled her closer, his body pressed against hers from chest to hips. She shivered, and he pulled his head back to look at her, eyes heavy lidded. Her own pupils were immense, shaken by a need she wasn't ready for, despite the bond between them. Heyou couldn't let go, though—not without her order. It was all he could do not to push forward into her. Such was his desire.

"Wh-what are you doing?" she whispered, and he heard the longing in her voice.

His mouth was only inches from hers. He could taste her breath. "You're my queen," he answered, his hands moving slowly up and down her back. "I'm yours."

"We shouldn't be doing this," she gasped, her nipples hard against his chest.

Oh, he thought they should. Her body thought they should also. "Please," he whispered, and licked her neck. "Let me."

In answer, she shoved him back, gasping. Her face was flushed and beautiful. "No! I hardly know you. Women . . . we don't do that! Not when we don't know the man." She stared at him. "You're not even human!"

"I'm human enough," he tried, but she shook her head.

"My aunt is waiting," she told him. "Come on." She headed off through the orchard, nearly running.

Obediently, Heyou followed.

Solie shuddered at how close she'd come to doing something she never would have imagined of herself before. She'd looked at boys, certainly, and daydreamed with her friends, but she'd barely known Heyou a few hours and she'd nearly . . . She blushed red and tried to tell her body to forget the idea. None of the stories she'd heard about battlers mentioned behavior like *this*.

She didn't dare look back. She didn't know what she was going to do about Heyou—maybe she could get him to leave? But she knew one thing: she was *never* going to touch him again, even to pass him anything. Some aspect of him woke too many things inside her, and that was one storm by which she had no intention of being swept away.

Breathing hard, trying to settle her mind, she found a little bit of peace as she made her way out of the orchard and along a back lane into town. She'd been here hundreds of times during her childhood and knew the way very well. Her aunt's bakery was only a short way off, and there was no one to see them as they crept down the road except children like the child she herself used to be, playing in the bushes and the trash and staring at her old clothes and tangled hair.

They were only children, but Heyou moved between them and Solie, intently watching a group of tow-headed boys. "They're fine," Solie told him, almost reaching out to touch his arm but stopping herself. He relaxed slightly, but still kept an eye on the boys, who ended up screaming and running off.

"What did you do to them?" Solie asked, confused.

"I don't like men," he snorted, his eyes narrow.

"They're children!" she protested.

"They're male." That seemed to be enough for him.

That was something Solie had heard from the stories, actually: battlers hated men. More specifically, she'd been told they hated all people and other sylphs like themselves. "How do you feel about women?" she asked him.

He smiled. "I like them."

"But you hate men."

"Yes."

She shook her head. "You're very strange. I think you'll like my aunt's bakery, though. If she lets you in." Solie hadn't actually thought about that, but her plan had never been to show up with company when she first left home. With a pang, she wondered if her parents knew she was missing yet. Surely they did. They might even be waiting for her here.

She wondered how Heyou would react to her father. She didn't think it would be good.

The back of the bakery appeared ahead of them, the door painted a vibrant blue and the rear wall stacked with firewood. She could smell fresh bread, and smoke poured up the chimneys. Her mouth watering from the smell, Solie hurried up to the back step, bypassing the well, and knocked on the door.

It opened to show a middle-aged woman with her hair tied back in a kerchief. She looked at Solie and her eyes grew large. "Child! What in the world happened to you?" She swung the door wide. "Get in here. Your aunt will catch a fright!"

"Thanks, Mimsy," Solie said, stepping past. The baker went to close the door behind her, but Heyou squeezed through, hurrying to Solie's side.

"Hey!" Mimsy called, startled. "You can't come in here!" She was staring at him, and Heyou smiled in return.

"I won't leave Solie," he told her cheerfully.

"Mimsy, p-please," Solie stammered. "Um, it's a long story, but can he stay here? I'll explain everything to my aunt, I promise."

The woman looked Heyou up and down. "It doesn't look like a long story at all," she commented, and stomped away. "Wait here and don't touch anything. You're both filthy. I'll get your aunt."

Solie exhaled once the woman left, and looked around

the room. The kitchen took up half the main floor and was scrupulously clean: the counters shone, and the wood table they rolled the dough on was scrubbed until it glowed. Huge ovens stood against the back wall, two of them filled with rising bread. Fresh loaves were stacked on the table, ready to be transferred to trays and taken to the front store to be sold.

Masha's other helpers, two girls from poor families, stared at Solie and Heyou. They'd seen her before, but not with a man. Not with a man like *him*. Solie found herself blushing and tried to look uninterested, but Heyou seemed right at home. He wandered over to the girls, smiling, and he started chattering, that strange aura of his both comforting and familiar. The two girls relaxed immediately and responded. Solie almost felt jealous, but he didn't touch either of them . . . and then she frowned at the realization that she was feeling jealous at all.

A moment later, the door swung open and her aunt Masha came in. A tall woman, her face pinched and stern, she'd always been kind to Solie. Her long gray hair was bound up into a bun, streaks of red still showing in it, and she wore an apron over her flour-spattered dress. Masha always helped with the baking.

She looked at Solie, hugging her back when the girl ran into her embrace, and sighed. "I really hoped you'd be smart enough not to come here," she said, and Solie drew back in surprise.

"Your father and your fiancé are here," her aunt went on regretfully. "They've come to take you home."

Chapter Five

Heyou looked up as he felt Solie's sudden fear. He'd been talking with the two other girls, enjoying their happiness and pleasure at meeting him, but at her sudden gasp he forgot them, his attention shifting to her and his aura flexing. He almost changed to his real form, ready to attack or defend, but the only new development was the appearance of a woman with a face similar to his queen, and Solie didn't seem to be afraid of her, only of what she was saying.

"They're upstairs," the woman explained. "I told them you weren't here, but my brother isn't a stupid man. He figured you'd come this way." She glanced at Heyou. "He's not going to be happy."

"But I don't want to get married!" Solie wailed. "He can't make me."

"I'm inclined to agree," her aunt said, "but the law is on his side. Your grandfather let me choose to stay single, but your father isn't quite so . . . noble. He's entitled to marry you to any man of his choosing." She practically spat. "He thinks Falthers is a good choice."

"He's old," Solie complained. "And fat. Father just likes him because he owns the grocery."

"And Falthers likes you because you're a young redhead."

Heyou didn't know what marriage was, but he was starting to think that he didn't like the idea.

"Can't you do anything?" Solie begged.

Her aunt looked at her and sighed. "Go out the back. Run to the old widower's house on the edge of town. I bring him fresh bread every day. Tell him I sent you. I'll try and convince your father you're not coming, and once he goes, I'll see about sending you somewhere he can't find you. You do realize you're giving up your family, don't you?"

"I don't care," Solie whispered, looking down.

"On your head it is, then." Masha appraised Heyou. "Who's your friend?"

He smiled. "I'm Heyou."

"He helped me," Solie added, looking at the battler with tears in her eyes.

He ached to hold her, but she'd told him not to. Only, she hadn't really ordered it. She'd just said not to. Was that enough? He wasn't sure.

"He's my friend."

"Just don't let your father see him, or the wedding really will be off—in ways you won't like." Masha sighed and pushed her back. "Go now. And make sure you have a bath when you get there. You're filthy. And your hair! I'll send decent clothes for you when I can."

Solie nodded, thanking her aunt and hugging her tightly. Turning, she hurried past Heyou, and he followed without being ordered, shadowing her to the door. They slipped outside and she returned to the back path, heading down it in the same direction they'd come.

The boys he'd threatened with his hate were back, yelling insults, and Heyou snarled, letting his hate flare briefly. They shrieked and ran.

A window opened. "Hey!" a man's voice shouted. "Stop!"

Solie gasped and Heyou looked upward, ready to obliterate the entire second floor of the building. A man with Solie's red hair leaned out through a window, shaking his fist. Heyou hissed angrily, but his queen grabbed his hand, dragging him with her as she ran down the path. Heyou allowed it, happy to be touching her. She'd told him not to kill anyone, he reminded himself. He'd have to ask her if that applied to direct threats. The red-haired man disappeared back through the window.

Noticing Solie wincing as her bare feet came down on pebbles in the dirt, Heyou scooped her up into his arms, his own feet impervious as he ran. "Where do I go?" he asked, ready to take her anywhere. The hot springs would be nice.

"To the end of the lane," she told him instead. "There's a house with a blue rooster weathervane on the roof. We have to hide there."

Heyou nodded and increased his speed, blurring down the lane. They blew through an intersection, making a cart horse rear, and then they arrived. Heyou vaulted the waist-high fence.

Solie clung to him, shaking. "I didn't know you were so fast," she gasped, her fright sufficient to keep his ardor down, at least long enough to put her back on her feet.

"Sorry," he apologized.

Solie stumbled a few feet off, shaking, and the door at the back of the house opened, an old man shuffling out with a pipe. Heyou growled at him. The old man started, nearly dropping his pipe as he was hit with the full force of Heyou's hate. But he was male and near Heyou's queen. He was a threat. He needed to be destroyed.

Solie slapped the battler across the back of the head. "Stop that!" She hurried forward. "Please, Mr. Chole, you have to hide us!"

"F-from what?" the old man stammered, staring at Heyou in terror.

"Please, there's no time," she begged. Heyou had moved like the wind, but he had probably attracted attention, and someone could easily have seen them come into this yard. Also, the bakery wasn't far away. Her father might pass here and see her while she was standing and arguing.

Heyou looked at her and back the way they'd come. He could feel the man they'd fled approaching—easy to destroy, but his queen had given an order. He swallowed his hate and turned to the old man. "Please let us in," he said.

It helped, the softness of his voice. The old man looked between Heyou and Solie, at first confused, but then he relented. "Come in," he sighed at last, shuffling back.

Solie hurried past, brushing his arm as she did, and Heyou stepped up into the doorway to stop and stare at the man. He held on to his hate for his queen's sake, but the old man saw the challenge in his eyes and shuddered, looking away. Heyou nodded and went inside, mollified for the moment.

The interior of the cottage was tiny, the furnishings worn but well maintained. Mr. Chole closed the door and came in, careful to keep well clear of Heyou and, Heyou noted with satisfaction, Solie as well. "What's going on?" he asked uncertainly, eyes downcast. Heyou glared at him and glanced to his queen.

She rubbed her hands together uncertainly. "My aunt sent us here. Masha? She runs the bakery." The old man nodded in recognition, and Solie took a deep breath. "She said you'd hide us. My father is looking for me. He wants me to accept an arranged marriage."

Chole looked like he wanted to laugh, but a glance at Heyou dissuaded him. "You can hide here," he grumbled.

"Thank you!" Solie gasped. "Thank you so much!" She went to hug the man, but Heyou growled. The old man jumped back. Solie glared. "Calm down, Heyou!"

Heyou decided he had liked it better at the bakery, with all the women.

Chole offered Solie his attic, there being a tiny straw tick there for her to use, and Heyou the floor in the main room. He then went out to see what was happening with her father, leaving Solie in the kitchen with a washbasin of lukewarm water and an old comb.

Sighing, she looked at the tepid water and slipped off her dress. She'd bathed at the hot springs but hadn't washed her hair and had fallen asleep before doing a really thorough job. That hot water was missed as she knelt and wet a cloth, using it and a bar of soap on her body. Starting on her hair, she found it horribly tangled, and she couldn't help a short sob as she pulled the comb through, yanking tufts of hair loose to drop on the floor. Everything else started coming down on her then: yesterday's marriage announcement, which she hadn't even been warned about first, the kidnapping by the king's soldiers, the ritual where she'd nearly died and Heyou killed everyone else, their flight, coming here, finding out her father was after her still . . . She put her hands to her face and wept, sobbing disconsolately on the worn kitchen floor.

"My queen?" Heyou appeared and knelt beside her, looking only at her face as he put a hand on her shoulder, turning her toward him. His eyes were wide and worried, and a touch confused as he stroked the tears on her cheek and looked at his fingers. "What is it?"

He was the only one not against her, the only one who seemed to care what she wanted, the only one who listened to her. With him, she was the one in control, since he'd do whatever she said. She had the power over him that she'd always been told men would hold over her. And she'd be dead now without him. Looking at Heyou, Solie started to cry harder, throwing her arms around his neck and burying her face against his chest. She didn't care about her earlier resolution not to touch him. She wanted to be held.

Heyou's arms came around her and he made some sort of keening sound in sympathy. It cut through her, and she lifted her head, pressed her mouth against his. Heyou drew back, obviously confused, and she pulled away, burying her face against him again, weeping. He tightened his arms around her and just waited, letting her cry herself out. It took a long time. The water in the basin was icy cold and her skin dry before she felt as if she could move again.

Heyou held her throughout, not trying anything. She could feel how bewildered he was. That only made her feel worse, but eventually her tears stopped. "Thanks," she murmured at last, pulling away. "I . . . um . . . I have to wash my hair."

"Yes, my queen," he breathed. Standing, he moved back into the main room, a puzzled look still on his face.

Blushing, Solie washed her hair in the basin of cold water, wondering why in the world she always ended up naked with him. Or why she'd kissed him. His lips had tasted so sweet, though, and she did feel better for the hug and the weeping.

Solie sighed and finished scrubbing her hair, combing it out again wet and drying it with a towel. That done, she pulled on her blouse and dress just as she heard Heyou growl from the other room. His familiar hate flared again, and she wondered how any man could stand to have it directed at him.

"Wait!" she yelped, running out. Mr. Chole stood at his front door, shaking. Heyou was hissing at him, ready to attack. Running up behind, Solie put a hand on the battler's shoulder, and he relaxed immediately.

"Sorry," she told the widower. "I'm so sorry. He's not used to people. He's just scared. He's a really nice guy, though."

Chole snorted. "So you say." He shuffled inside, leaning on his cane, and went to sit in one of the chairs by the window.

"Behave!" Solie whispered into Heyou's ear. "Got it? Stop trying to scare him!"

"Yes, my queen."

Mr. Chole settled down and laid his cane on the floor before looking again at his two guests. After glaring at

Heyou a little fearfully, he smiled at Solie. "I saw your aunt." He produced a loaf of bread. "She tells me your father is going door-to-door looking for you. He's quite worried."

Solie tensed. She loved her father, but he was a strict man who wanted the family to be wealthier than they were. For him to give her in marriage to a man she didn't love . . . Well, it didn't surprise her. It hurt, though, and she didn't want to see him. She didn't know if she could forgive him, and he'd only try to make her feel terrible again. She didn't want to marry creepy old Mr. Falthers. He'd always leered at her once she grew old enough to have breasts, and the thought of letting him touch her . . .

She looked at Heyou, remembering his kiss. She didn't even know how to guess how her father would react to *that.*

"I don't want to see him," she managed.

The old man shrugged. "So your aunt says. It's up to you. I'll tell him I've never seen you if he comes here." He looked briefly at Heyou, and then away again. "You can't stay here forever."

Meaning, Heyou couldn't stay. And she doubted she'd be a welcome guest for too long herself. Solie nodded, forcing her fear down. She'd figure something out. It wasn't as if anyone could hurt her with Heyou at her side. So she tucked her hand around his arm and led the battler away, thanking the old man as she went up into the attic.

Heyou looked at her curiously as she flopped down onto the tick. "What's happening?" he asked finally. "Who is this man you're afraid of?"

Solie shrugged, wishing things were different. Still, he deserved to know. "My father. He wants me to marry a man I don't even like. So I ran away from home. That's when I got kidnapped and ran into you." She started gnawing on a thumbnail. "I thought I'd be okay if I went to my aunt's house, but he came after me."

"Oh." Heyou paused. "I can kill him for you."

"No!" she gasped. "I just want him to let me live my life!"

"Yes, my queen." Heyou sighed and settled down near her on the hard floor.

Solie lay back on the tick, exhausted and sad. Even though it was only mid afternoon, the day had been long and all she wanted was for her aunt to just come and collect her. It didn't seem like that was going to happen though.

Heyou sat and watched her fall asleep, not needing to sleep himself. He watched Solie's breathing deepen and thought about this father who threatened her. He wanted to hunt the man down and kill him, obliterate him so that his queen couldn't be hurt again. She hadn't specifically ordered him not to, but she certainly hadn't told him he could. He'd have to wait and hope the man stayed away, he decided, because if the man threatened his queen again, he would be dealt with. Heyou wouldn't have Solie afraid, no matter what. He thought again of when she'd pressed her mouth against his, and he shivered. He'd liked that.

Outside, he sensed the air sylph who'd been following them. She swooped away, vanishing, and he felt one of several tensions deep inside him ease. He looked back at Solie. She was safe for now, as safe as he could make her, and he'd keep her that way. He still wanted her physically, but that desire was tempered by a deeper urge to protect her—and by an awareness that she was giving him choices, not just ordering him. He didn't quite know what to do with those choices, but he was pretty sure he liked them nearly as much as the kiss. As long as she kept him by her side, he thought he would always be happy.

Hours later, as the sun started to dip toward the horizon in late afternoon, he heard a knock on the door and the old man going to answer it. Heyou walked to the window and looked out and down to see a red-haired man standing at the door. He growled immediately, recognizing him. Another stocky man was present as well.

Solie still slept. Heyou glanced at her, thinking. She'd told him not to kill when she sent him to get clothes, but she hadn't specified that rule as applying all of the time. She'd told him not to hurt her father, but she hadn't ordered it. That must mean he could make up his own mind.

Heyou decided to frighten the man away, to convince the villain to leave his queen alone. He headed for the stairs, grinning cruelly as he went.

Chapter Six

Leon went home before he headed out of the city, unprepared as he was for any coming long journey. He rode his horse to the small stable of his manor and dismounted, holding Ril up out of the way of the stableman who stepped forward to take the horse. Ril glared, but the stableman was used to his hate and bowed to both the battler and Leon before the hawk was shifted to Leon's shoulder and Leon headed toward the house.

His estate was on a patch of land inside the city that was barely half an acre in size, surrounded by a huge stone wall. The house was made of the same material, square and forbidding. It was centuries old, originally from his wife's family, as his ancestors had never had any money, and he loved it. It was home.

As he walked, he planned out what he would have to pack and take, and where he would look for the girl. He didn't know much about her, but she wouldn't have been brought from far away, and with a battler she'd attract attention. She shouldn't be difficult to find. It was getting past her battler that would be the hard part.

The front door of the manor opened at his approach, and a trio of girls ranging from three to twelve ran out, yelling for both him and Ril. Leon had no doubt that Ril loathed him most if not all of the time, and he'd always regretted that, but he couldn't begrudge his daughters their affection for the battler. The hawk shifted on his shoulder, wings spreading, and Leon chuckled. "Go to them, Ril."

The bird immediately took flight, swooping over to the

girls. He arced around them as they danced in circles, laughing, and finally he alighted on the eldest daughter's arm, cooing. The three converged on the bird, gently stroking his wings and back.

"No hugs for me?" Leon asked. Giggling, the girls ran over to hug him as well, the twelve-year-old walking with exaggerated care so as not to disturb Ril. They hugged him and Leon laughed, letting them lead him into the house.

His wife, Betha, waited there, smiling at him and stroking Ril's head when her oldest daughter held him up. "I wasn't sure when you'd be home," she murmured, leaning forward to kiss her husband.

"I'm afraid I won't be here long," he assured her, thinking again about the girl with the battler. Home was his sanctuary. Ril never blasted out with his hate here, not once he'd discovered it made the girls cry. Leon had peace here, and he did need the break, though he wouldn't get one for long.

"Do you have to go so soon?" Betha asked with a frown.

"I'm afraid so. The king's ordered it himself." He turned and put a hand on his eldest daughter's head. "Okay, Lizzy, Ril needs some serious play. Are you three up to it?"

"Yes, sir!" she called, saluting. Her little sisters started giggling, and all three ran for their bedroom, taking Ril with them. Leon looked after them and shook his head. *A girl with a battler.*

"Sometimes I wonder if Ril thinks he belongs to the girls instead of me," he mused. "I certainly wouldn't have to worry about boys sniffing after them if he did. . . ." Not that he had to worry yet. Once he did, he'd be sure to meet them at the door with his battler on his arm. That should scare them away. Or it would prevent his daughters from ever being married, he admitted ruefully.

"Lizzy's asked for him already," Betha spoke up, and leaned her head on her husband's shoulder. "But any talk of that's years and years from now."

"Years and years?" Leon smiled.

"Decades. At least six."

Leon laughed. "Yes, ma'am." Then, putting his arm around his wife, he led her toward their bedroom, having learned years ago to take his opportunities when they presented themselves.

Ril relaxed, considering himself to be home. Shoved into a baby bonnet and tumbled over onto his back, he snatched gently at Cara's fingers with his feet, trying to keep her from cramming a little wooden pacifier in his beak. The three-year-old, Nali, sucked her thumb and pulled on his tail, while the baby cried from her crib, wanting attention.

"Don't hurt him, Nali!" Lizzy protested, dragging her sister away. The young girl started to cry, which only encouraged the baby. Cara giggled, giving up on inserting the pacifier and settling instead for throwing it at Ril's head. "Cara!" Lizzy gasped. "You're so mean!"

Stuck in this bird shape at his master's order, Ril flared his wings and started to sing. All four girls silenced immediately, staring at him in wonder. Ril had been ordered to never speak, just like all sylphs, just as he'd been ordered never to change shape. He'd never been told not to sing, though, and Leon didn't know he could. He sang for the girls alone, when his master and his master's wife were elsewhere.

Ril had been insane when Lizzy was born, lost in the horrible memory of his master killing his queen while she stared up at him in terror, her round face covered in freckles. He'd still be insane now, if it hadn't been for the child. He'd been overwhelmed by Betha's birth pains and screams, hysterical in the hall he'd been left in, and he'd crashed into the birthing room before Leon even realized how upset he really was, ready to kill whoever was harming the only female in the house. He'd been just in time to see Lizzy's birth.

He saw the babe come through that fleshy gate into this world, like his own arrival through the gate, and he'd been lost to her. She'd saved him, and he'd not wanted to leave her or her sisters' side since, and his master had been kind enough to let him see all their births and to let him be with them. Ril had to keep telling himself he still hated the man, remembering those freckles on a round face every time he was tempted to forgive Leon because of his daughters, but he was grateful for this.

He sang to the girls, singing songs he remembered from his time before the gate, before he was trapped by the hope of a queen, and he sang of her, she who'd left him before he had time to do more than fall in love with her. Cara and Nali settled down sleepily, dozing off from his lullaby, and the baby slept as well, little Ralad in her crib. Only Lizzy stayed awake, her eyes soft.

Once the other girls were asleep, she took the bonnet off Ril. "They're poopheads," she whispered, though he didn't agree. Lifting him up, she carried him to the corner of the nursery she considered hers. Opening a trunk there, she dug out the box of lettered blocks that was their greatest secret. Cautiously looking around, she dumped the lot out on the carpet, careful not to wake her sisters.

Ril stepped forward, looking the blocks over until he found the one he wanted and pulled it to him with his beak, rolling it so the correct side was pointing up. Grabbing the next, he laid it alongside, then followed with six others.

Lizzy peered at them. "'I . . . love . . . you,'" she read. "Aw, I love you, too!" She kissed his forehead and the battler ruffled his feathers. He reached for more blocks. This was their secret: that he could talk to her through the blocks, so long as her father never found out. *Be my queen,* he spelled out.

"You always ask me that," she laughed, grabbing his beak and waving it from side to side. "Of course I am!"

Ril sighed, opening and closing his beak sharply to make a clapping sound. He knew he repeated the request too often, but he always wanted to hear the answer. Her father had killed his first queen, but Lizzy had been his from her birth. He'd asked her to be his queen since she first taught him the blocks, and she always said yes. One day, she would be his queen for real, and he would love her forever. All that had to happen first was for her father to die. Then they'd both be free.

Airi soared high on the wind and back to her master, following her permanent awareness of where he was. It had been the longest she'd been away from Devon's side since she was given to him, but she found him anyway, sitting in his quarters in the barracks used by single men with sylphs and sharpening his knife. She flowed in through the open window, and he lifted his head with a relieved smile.

"Airi! You're back!"

Hello, she said into his mind, blowing around him and then forming into a face made of the loose dust balls he'd left on the floor. He never was much of a cleaner.

"It's good to see you," he told her. "I was getting worried. What happened?"

The battler took her to a valley of hot springs, and then to a village south of us. The one you were born in. Devon started in surprise. *They're at my old master's house, on the edge of the village.*

"What? They're with Father?" His grip tightened on his knife, his face frightened, and she danced a sigh, pretty sure she knew what was coming next. Devon would deny it, but he really was the type to run to the rescue. Donal Chole was an old man now, but a battler would still see him as a threat. It actually bothered Airi a bit as well, if not in the same way. As long as that battler was left alone with his female, everyone else would be fine. If someone threatened him—or worse, her—he would turn the village into a crater.

Donal had worked around battlers. He knew better than to threaten them, provided he was aware of what he had in his house. *But he might not realize he's got a battler,* Airi admitted.

That did it. "We're going there," Devon decided, standing and grabbing his pack.

You plan to fight a battler?

Devon almost gagged. "Oh gods, no! I just want to make sure Father's okay." He grabbed his sword and buckled it on. "I have time off coming to me. Let's go rent a horse." Airi could carry him if she must, but such a trip always terrified him and exhausted her. She knew he was really worried whenever he asked her to carry him.

Devon went to let his superiors know he would be away for a while. Airi drifted along behind him, dancing around a few other sylphs in the hall as she did, communicating through touch and motion, since they weren't allowed to speak. After centuries of slavery, though, they'd found ways around the rules, and she reacquainted herself with her friends, whether originally from her hive or not, before following her master out the door, headed for the main road that led east and then north.

Leon carried his saddlebags outside, his sword strapped across his back along with his bow. With Ril he didn't really need weaponry, but he'd never been a man to risk being unprepared.

The bird sat on Lizzy's shoulder, preening her hair while the girl looked up tearfully at her father. "Do you have to go so soon?" All of her sisters had been left inside, their screams of protest too loud for Leon to handle. He'd given them his good-byes and his hugs, but they were still screaming. Betha put a hand on Lizzie's back, shaking her head.

"You know I have to leave," he told Lizzy wearily, tying on the saddlebags. "Don't whine."

"But—"

"I mean it," he warned, and went to lift Ril off her shoulder.

The battler snapped at him, and Leon jerked his hand back with a curse. "Ril! Behave!" The bird hissed but let himself be taken. Perhaps, Leon thought, he shouldn't let the battler play with his daughters; Ril got more unruly each time he was taken away from them. But when Leon saw his daughter's tearful face, he relented. She'd never forgive him if he took her pet away.

"I'll be back soon," he promised her, then kissed Betha. "A few days only, I hope."

Turning, he mounted his horse and rode out the gate, waving back at his wife as he went. She waved in return.

Lizzy ran alongside her father's horse until he left the grounds, but then he coaxed the animal into a canter. With the manor behind him, Leon again felt Ril's stare and felt the hate, the blistering, terrible loathing the battler harbored for him. Sometimes it lessened. Sometimes, when they were alone in the woods and no one else was there, it was gone, and Leon could almost be sure he felt other emotions from his battler, but now it was as bright and sharp as ever.

His horse whinnied in fright, trying to leap sideways, and Leon sighed wearily. "Thanks, Ril," he grumbled sarcastically. "It's always good to have you back."

Climbing down from the attic, Heyou listened to the men's voices at the front of the house. Mr. Chole was saying Solie wasn't there, but he was a terrible liar. Heyou heard him stammer and walked up beside him. The old man yelped and jumped back, stumbling against the wall and nearly falling.

Heyou ignored the old man, focusing on the other two. Solie's father was only a little taller than himself, his balding head sparsely topped with bright red hair. The second male was even taller but overweight, nearly the same age as Solie's father, and he was frowning.

"Go away," Heyou growled, trying not to use his aura in case it woke his queen. Not unless he had to.

"You," her father snapped, pointing. "You're the one who was with my daughter. Where is she?"

The second man gaped. "She has a lover? I didn't pay your bride price for Solie to have a lover!"

"She doesn't!" the father assured him frantically. "She'd never do that. She's a good girl." He shot Heyou a hateful look. "Who the hell are you?"

Heyou snarled. It still felt good to say his name, but these men angered him. They had no rights when it came to his queen. "Go away. Solie is mine."

Both men wore identical looks of shock. It would have been laughable if Heyou was amused at all. His real form itched under his skin from an urge to hit them with the aura of his hate, to flex it the same as animals showing plumage to drive away their rivals. Their own hatred was nothing. They couldn't even be food to him. But his queen was asleep. He didn't want to wake her.

"You. . . ," the father started to say, his face flushed with anger. "You lousy little—"

"Don't," Mr. Chole gasped. He pushed himself away from the wall, clutching his chest below a white face. "Don't provoke him. He's a battle sylph."

The fiancé gawked, not understanding fully, while the father barked a laugh. "That's a sick joke!"

"It's not," Chole promised. "I felt his hate. I worked for years with an air sylph. I felt the battlers many times. She told him to hide it, but I felt it anyway. He's a battle sylph."

"That's impossible," the father snarled. "How could my daughter get a battler?"

"I don't know," Chole wheezed. "But I beg you, don't anger him."

"Saml," the fiancé whined to Solie's father. "I didn't buy into this."

"It's all lies!" Saml snapped. "He's no battler, he's some reject, sniffing after her. Well, I'm going to march in there and drag her home. I'll make her regret defying me!" He went to push past Heyou, shoving with a farmer's strong muscles, and was surprised when his opponent didn't move. Pausing, Saml blanched.

It was too much, endlessly too much. Threaten his queen? *Attack* his queen? Every instinct Heyou had flared, and the rage burst out, his aura of hatred expanding. Minor sylphs would run from this. Other battlers would prepare for bloodshed. Named males would prepare to kill. Entire hives went to war over a battler's temper, unless the queen said no.

His eyes changed from the gray-blue Solie found attractive to a searing battler red. Heyou heard the old man wailing, running out past Saml and after the fleeing fiancé, but Solie's father still gaped at him, frozen. Heyou snarled, and lightning filled his mouth as he spoke. "Stay. Away. From. My. Queen."

Saml screamed then, stumbling backward out the door and falling over the step, landing on his back in the dirt. He stared up in terror, with Heyou already losing his shape. The battler advanced and changed to smoke and lightning, his aura flashing out over the town as he himself expanded, suddenly as big as the cottage as he flared his mantle and spread his wings. His voice boomed across the village, and he felt the tiny humans in it scream with fear. This territory was his—nothing could defy him—and he roared, his scream echoing through the valley and up into the hills.

Other battlers answered, screaming their own challenges back. The gate! He remembered it suddenly. There had been other battlers at the gate, males older than he was. The gate was a reasonable distance, though. He had a few minutes to finish this if he hurried. Then he'd have to take his queen and run, before one of the others decided to take his challenge personally.

He bent over Saml, his fanged, burning mouth larger than the entire man. "SOLIE IS MINE!" he roared. There was no defiance in the human at all anymore, his rage turned into panic . . . but it would still be easier to destroy him. Solie wouldn't have to worry about her father at all if he were dead. Heyou opened his mouth wide, fully intending to devour the father whole, when he felt a touch to the edge of his mantle that had him shimmering back into his human form, reappearing in the tunic that he'd swallowed inside of himself as he changed.

Solie stepped up behind him, shaking even as she pressed herself against his back and wrapped her arms around his chest, palms flat against his body. Heyou tilted his head back, closing his eyes and relaxing. He could smell her and he purred, trying to remember there were other battlers who might be coming and that he was too untried to be sure of winning against even one.

"Don't hurt my father, Heyou. Please."

For her, anything. He moved his arms back, laying his hands against her hips. "Yes, my queen."

She hugged him, and all his anger vanished. His aura dropped and the tension that had covered the village eased.

"S-Solie . . . ?"

Snarling, Heyou dropped his head and hissed down at her father who was frozen on the ground where he'd fallen, staring up with an ashen face. There was no sign of Chole or the other man, though different villagers stood a distance away, gawking and armed with whatever weapons they could find. Heyou growled at them and they flinched.

"Heyou," Solie admonished, hugging him. "Don't." She loosened her grip for a moment and then tightened it again. "Go away, Father," she begged in a tiny voice. "I don't want Heyou to hurt you."

"B-but . . . ," he gasped.

Her arms stayed around Heyou, her body pressed against his. Heyou let his eyes close again, just relaxing against her. His queen's smell was making him drunk.

"He won't hurt me," Solie told her father. "He saved my life."

Somewhere, Heyou realized, the man was finding courage. Perhaps it was that Solie embraced him, keeping him contained. Heyou resented that the man recognized this, even as he leaned back against his queen, desiring her. He'd take her right there if she let him, other battlers be damned.

"But Solie, your family loves you!"

"I don't want to marry Mr. Falthers, Father," she told him. "I know you agreed to it, but I didn't." She paused. "And I think Heyou will kill any man who comes near me now."

At that, Heyou gave Saml a particularly evil grin. Solie's father shuddered, realizing that he'd lost, and then he scrambled back, leaving his daughter standing on the doorstep and embracing her battle sylph from behind, her face hidden against his back. Heyou saw regret in the man's eyes but didn't care; he was leaving. Saml scurried off, regaining his feet and running after the others, toward the line of uncertain men with their useless weapons.

"Heyou," Solie said "I—"

Heyou barely felt it in time: a flicker of concealed energy

spearing down at them from above, something he might not have caught if he hadn't been half expecting it even as he let his queen distract him. He spun, wrapping his arms around Solie as a hawk-shaped battle sylph dove down upon them.

The entire cottage exploded.

Chapter Seven

Devon trotted his rented horse out of the capital and along the main road, nudging it into a canter that could be maintained for some distance. The horse was one he'd used before, a dark chestnut gelding with a white nose, and he knew it was sound. The beast was also used to him, and its ears perked eagerly as it sped up. Its mouth was hard after years of being hired by incompetent riders, but the horse responded well enough to the bit, and its gait was smooth.

Airi flowed around his head, ruffling Devon's hair. It was her way of showing affection, and he tried to relax as he rode. He could only get there as fast as he could get there. His father would be all right. In fact, he'd probably already done what his son intended—grabbed his boots and cloak and made a run for it. Devon might even find his father on the road, heading for the city. That was a reassuring thought.

Mostly. It was still a fifteen-mile ride to his father's village from the city.

Devon settled back in the saddle and tried not to think about what he might face, which was just one more of too many things that weren't normal: a girl with a battler, two battlers sent to destroy pirates brazen enough to attack the king's ships, the rumor that the crown prince was dead. No one knew anything. No one knew for sure, at least. Devon suspected that if there had been more than rumors flying, he wouldn't have got his time off. There were even stories going around that the other ten battlers of the kingdom would be recalled to the castle! There were always stories about that, though. The generals and their battlers stayed at their separate keeps most of the time, and the king never called them all in at once. Not with the amount of damage their battlers could do. Devon had seen a battler's magic once, and that had only been a test. The hill didn't exist anymore. Neither did the prisoners who'd been chained to it.

Now he was going to face a battler who he knew was no rumor. Devon took a deep breath, trying to calm his churning nerves. He could feel the hate already, surrounding him and wearing him down.

Airi suddenly let off playing with his hair, rising up above him defensively. Devon looked behind. Another man was cantering up, his tall gray steed having a better stride than the chestnut. Devon felt his gut fall out from under him as he recognized Leon Petrule, the king's head of security and lead battler master. He had his arm up in a falconer's position, Ril riding on it easily. The battler glared at Devon, who winced. He hadn't expected this.

Leon cantered up beside him and slowed slightly, his gray fighting the bit while he made to match the gait of Devon's chestnut. The battler master looked down at Devon evenly, who suddenly felt as if he needed to stammer an explanation for his presence here. He didn't doubt at all that the man recognized him. Airi floated above, ready to grab him and flee if she had to. Provided she could outrun a battler. The bird looked right at her before returning his gaze to Devon.

"Good afternoon, my Lord Petrule," Devon managed. "Nice afternoon for a ride."

"Bit late for it," the man answered. "Do you always ride out so close to sunset?"

Devon swallowed, trying to look natural. His only help

was the fact that every male in the kingdom was nervous around Ril. "I'm going to see my father," he admitted—only a partial lie. "He's unwell."

"I'm sorry to hear that."

The battler master looked forward again. Ril hissed as he was jostled, his aura of hatred increasing. How did Petrule handle that battler without going insane? Devon wondered.

"And you, my lord?" he asked, dreading the answer.

The battler master looked at him sideways, and Devon tried not to cringe. "I'm looking for someone," the man answered quietly, and left it at that.

Devon felt sick. He could well imagine whom the king's man was seeking. And what if he found her? Devon looked at Ril and tried to picture the two battlers fighting. He couldn't.

"You look ill yourself," Leon noted.

Devon shuddered. "It's your battler," he said. "He's rather unnerving."

"Yes." Leon looked at his battler with something that could only be affection, hard though that was to believe. "It must be easier with an air sylph."

"Yes, my lord," Devon managed, and felt Airi dance above him.

"There's nothing else like a battler," Leon continued. "They make you earn everything."

"Yes, my lord." Devon didn't know what else to say.

They rode in silence for a time, the miles vanishing under them. It was still an hour before dusk, but the sun was getting low on the horizon. Devon tried to think why Leon was riding alongside him, but all he could guess was that the man wanted some company. Either that or he knew he'd been lied to.

Ahead, finally, they saw the crossroads. Devon said, "I go right here, my lord. My father's village lies that way."

Leon nodded. "I may as well join you. It's as good a direction to start as any."

"Yes, my lord," Devon answered, his heart sinking.

They reached the crossroads and turned, their horses trotting up onto the grass around the churned mess made by hundreds of passing wagons. Regaining the smoother northern road, they broke into a canter again, still riding side by side. It was getting colder out, and Devon pulled his cloak closer around himself.

"Do you know of any girls in your father's village?" Leon asked suddenly. "Girls with long red hair and who wear a green butterfly barrette?" He held the delicate object out on his gloved palm.

Devon recognized it immediately, and his throat went dry. "Uh—"

Suddenly, a roar. Both horses screamed, rearing, and Devon had to fight the chestnut for control—and himself as well, for an overwhelming hatred blew over him and he heard a deep voice shouting, "SOLIE IS MINE!" It echoed from everywhere, and Ril straightened, his wings spreading, and suddenly the bird was screaming as well, his hatred blasting back at the first.

As his gray reared again, Leon cursed, pulling its head down one-handed while he raised his arm to point. "Ril! Go!" As he snapped his arm down, the battler was already airborne, shooting upward into the sky. Ril vanished into the clouds, headed toward the village.

"Oh, gods!" Devon gasped. He yanked his chestnut's head around and kicked the beast forward, whipping it with his reins in the direction of his father's home. The horse broke into a gallop, thundering down the road.

Half a second later, the king's man passed him, bent low over the neck of his gray. Devon flogged his horse harder, trying to catch him. Airi wailed in terror, racing at his side.

* * *

Solie screamed in panic as the world exploded, flame filling her vision even as Heyou wrapped his shape around her, protecting her from it. For a moment she was enclosed in his warm darkness and heard him bellowing, his hate a palpable force. She could feel his protection as well, though, and his fear. Something hit him and he shuddered. He couldn't fight like this, she realized.

So did Heyou. In a moment he was human again, shadows of blackness shifting around him like ethereal wings, and he threw her clear. Solie hit the ground with a yelp and looked up. The cottage was on fire, a chasm two feet deep torn down the center of the lane toward it. The ragged earth smoked, ringing Heyou as he turned, facing away from her.

Something sparkled in the sky above, and Solie stared as a bird twisted in midair, coming round from a swooping arc to return in their direction. It went into a swift dive, its feet tucked close to its body and its wings outspread. It headed straight toward Heyou, and an invisible wall of destruction wreaked havoc before it.

Heyou crossed his arms, blocking that force, and the air itself screamed around him, shaking. A moment later the bird shot past, leveling out its flight, and Heyou turned, transforming. Massive black jaws slammed shut just shy of the bird's tail, but the hawk made its escape and arced upward for another attack.

Solie scrambled to her feet in horror. There wasn't anyone in the villages or hamlets near the main city who didn't recognize the king's battlers. Ril was locked in his one form, however, while Heyou was able to shed his entirely, leaping with a scream into the air. The bird and the black cloud raced upward, vanishing from view. She could still feel their hate, though, their absolute loathing for one another.

"Heyou!" she screamed, not wanting to see him hurt. If he heard her, he didn't respond.

The two battlers appeared again, smashing together, the force of their contact blowing down on the town and knocking people off their feet. A boom sounded a moment later, deafening Solie. It muted the sounds of the screaming and panic. People and animals tried to flee in all directions, but the sylphs were fighting directly over the town, arcing in every direction and leaving no one sure of where to run. One blast blew apart a small shop, while a second hit the orchard Solie and Heyou had first landed in.

Solie started to cry, not knowing what to do.

Heyou lunged at the other battler, lashing out at him with his energy, but the bird dodged every attack, swerving around and looping under him to try and get behind. Heyou had to flip nearly inside out to stay facing him. He couldn't figure out why the other battler, much older than himself, didn't change shape. Eventually he realized he couldn't, and his excitement surged. This was one fight where he had the advantage.

Minutes later, though, it became apparent that his advantage wasn't quite so great. The other battler might be stuck as a bird, but he was too fast to hit. He dodged Heyou's best blows, and the town and valley below paid: half of the buildings were in flames, the people and animals trying to flee. Unlucky victims lay scattered everywhere.

Some of the bodies were wearing long skirts. Heyou felt agony and shame, and a desperate terror that Solie had ended up caught in the crossfire. The other battler hadn't targeted her, though—he obviously wanted Heyou. Which meant Solie had to be all right. He felt her fear and confusion, but no pain. Had she been injured, he'd have known. If she was killed, he'd lose his grip on this dimension.

The thought of that was horrifying, and he renewed his attacks, careful now to avoid indiscriminate blasting at the other with his energy; it was too draining and too inaccurate. Instead he surged forward, trying for close combat—and screamed as the bird's talons tore into his mantle.

He was losing, Heyou realized suddenly. Desperate, he searched for his queen. They had to escape.

Leon galloped into the village, hugging his horse's neck and swearing. The village was in ruins, all rules of decency clearly discarded in the war overhead.

There weren't many fights between battlers, not like this. Every kingdom he'd ever studied had them, but they were used more as a deterrent than anything else, preventing all-out war or invasions. Actual battles between them were semiformalized, each sylph under strict control. Northward were the wide, dead Shale Plains, nearly the size of Eferem itself but stripped of most life, thanks to a conflict between battlers centuries before. They'd left nothing but rubble behind, obliterating the kingdom that used to exist between Eferem and Para Dubh. Ril had been set loose on highwaymen and pirate groups stupid enough to risk invading, but he'd only been in three formal fights. He'd won every one.

He must have thought this would be as easy, Leon realized, berating himself. But this new battler had no controls, and his shape flickered wildly as he fought. So did his powers, and the town paid the price.

Leon leaped his horse over a shattered wagon and the people who huddled behind it, searching. Ril wouldn't damage the village intentionally—his orders were clear about collateral damage—but even he could make mistakes. There was one easy way to win the fight before that rogue destroyed everything. Leon saw her a moment later, standing in shock in the middle of the street before a burning cottage, her hands pressed to her face as she stared upward. Her long red hair blew in the unnatural winds. She had no control over her battler. Not her fault, but it was true.

Leon drew his sword and spurred his horse forward. Kill

the master and banish the sylph: the king's order would be a simple one for him to obey. At least, he tried to tell himself it wouldn't be hard. This wasn't the first time he'd killed a girl for a battler.

Devon raced his hysterical horse into the town, so panicked himself that he could barely focus. Airi pressed against his back, freezing cold in her terror.

The town was in ruins, people running away down the road past him. He looked for his father, who was nowhere in sight. Devon swerved around a wagon—and saw Leon instead, his sword drawn and held clear of his body as he galloped toward a redheaded girl who stood with her back to him. Devon knew her, having seen her before when he lived in the town and she came to visit her aunt. He'd recognized her butterfly barrette in Leon's hand.

"Airi!" he screamed, not knowing what he intended to say, or what he meant for her to do.

She had to guess. In an instant the air sylph abandoned him and shot forward, a shimmer of air that raced past the king's head of security and wrapped around the girl. Flaring, she yanked Solie out of the way, pulling the girl screaming off her feet and into the air, over Leon's head and back toward her master.

Devon gasped, seeing the other man pull so hard on the reins that his gray sat down. Leon turned, looking back at him. Blaming him. Then Airi was there. She grabbed Devon as well and pulled him off his horse, crushing him against the screaming girl as she retreated, rising up over the tops of cottages, all while staying low enough not to get caught up in the fight between the battlers. Holding both humans close, she fled.

Heyou felt Solie's sudden terror and whirled, forgetting himself. She was in the air, held by an air sylph—the same air sylph he'd ignored—wrapped around a man and vanishing up the slope of the valley. She was being taken away.

Solie! he screamed.

Ril slammed into his back, tearing right through him. Heyou gasped and fell, shifting back to human as he plunged, crashing through a cottage roof and slamming into the center of the main room. Floorboards buckled beneath him and he vomited blood, in terrible pain and beaten. Above, he saw the other battler circling the building in the darkened sky, screaming in triumph.

He was dead. The other battler would kill him. Solie would be alone, unprotected, to be ordered killed on the command of that bird sylph's queen. Heyou had only one option left, the only one available to newly hatched battlers, if they were to survive long enough to grow and serve their queen: he let his rage go—all of it—and also his form. Shimmering to nothingness, he released his hold on reality and hid.

Still looking thoughtfully up the darkening slope the girl had vanished over, Leon held out his arm. "Ril."

The battler landed and started to preen, adjusting his feathers. Leon brought him around in front and checked him over with his free hand, looking for injury. The sylph was singed but not damaged, and he exhaled in relief. Ril ignored him, though he let Leon touch his body, his focus now on cleaning his tail feathers. His hate was less than usual as well. He was tired.

"Good boy, Ril," Leon whispered, stroking his back as the bird drew energy from him. Sometimes he could feel the creature do so, especially if Ril drank more than usual, and he felt it now, an oddly sensual tingling along his skin. "Good boy." Ril hit him with a little deliberate loathing and settled down, puffing his feathers up and tucking his head under his wing. A moment later, the battler was asleep.

Leon allowed it. Battle sylphs rarely slept, and he could count on one hand the number of times Ril had done so. He frowned again and looked from the destruction in the town to the slope over which the girl had escaped. The sun was down now, and he couldn't see any details, let alone where the girl and her rescuers had gone. He hadn't thought that air-sylph master would have the balls to try something like that. Going to visit his father indeed!

He turned his horse, careful not to wake Ril. It was unclear if the other battler was destroyed. It wasn't as though he could ask Ril, but he doubted the bird would allow himself to sleep if there was still a danger.

The town was in ruins, more than half of it gone, and the survivors peered out at him in terror. Leon's frown deepened. It would take hours to sort through this mess, but Devon had said his father lived here. He'd have to see if that was a lie. If not, he'd see what the old man could tell him.

Chapter Eight

Jasar rolled off the woman with a groan, blowing out a breath as he landed on his back and wiped the sweat out of his eyes. She was a minor courtier, pretty enough but a little dull in bed. She'd cried out enough times, though, and he knew he'd pleased her. He smirked: he always pleased them.

Alica sighed and stretched beside him, her breasts shining in the light of the lamp. He looked at her appreciatively. She certainly was an attractive woman.

"That was wonderful," she breathed, and rolled over, leaning her head against his shoulder while she traced a hand along his chest. "You were fantastic."

Jasar frowned, not wanting her touching him now that he was done. He shoved her off and stood, reaching for his robe. Only women wanted this hugging stuff. Once he got what he wanted, he didn't want anything to do with them.

"I need a bath," he told her. "You can go now."

Alica didn't get the hint, as most women would have. She sat upright, pouting. "But I want more. Don't you?" She shook her chest at him.

Jasar sneered. "I think not. Perhaps later." Much later. There were many other women on his list, and a half-dozen bastards already running around with his eyes. He didn't acknowledge any of them, though. There was no reason.

"Are you sure I can't make it worth your while?" Alica purred, leaning back with her spine arched.

He wasn't—not entirely. Which gave him an idea, something that had occurred to him during the council meeting.

He hadn't had the opportunity to try it out, and perhaps he should now.

"Would you like to play a game, my dear?" he asked with a smile.

She beamed. "Of course!"

Jasar laughed, wondering if she'd still think the same in a minute. Not that it mattered. She was just a minor courtier. She wouldn't have any way to protest.

"Mace!" he called. "Come!"

The door opened, the huge gray battler stepping inside. His footsteps echoed on the stone floor and Alica went white. Mace looked at Jasar, and the familiar hatred flowed.

Jasar was so used to it that he barely noticed anymore. Mace couldn't do anything to him. "Mace," he cooed. "The Lady Alica would like you to make love to her. Do it."

Mace stopped, his hatred shuddering to a halt with surprise, and Jasar laughed out loud. The shocked battler turned his helmed head to the woman, and he started toward the bed.

"No," Alica gasped, scrambling backward. "Please! No!"

"You may as well settle back and enjoy it," Jasar told her, sitting in a chair near the bed. "He's going to do it anyway."

Mace climbed onto the bed, and his master licked his lips as the battler crawled over the woman, his glowing eyes never leaving her face. She stared up at the sylph in frozen horror as he adjusted himself. Jasar leaned over, observing the details with interest. Mace moved and Alica wailed.

"At least you're anatomically correct," Jasar commented after a moment. "I must say, I thought you'd be bigger. How disappointing."

Mace ignored him, his hate barely present as he focused on the woman, the bed shaking with his movements. Jasar watched Alica's eyes widen, and laughed again as her head snapped back. Her expression had changed to a sudden grimace.

He thought it was pain—expected it to be, with something that big inside her—but then she started to pant and cried out, her entire body arching. He realized she wasn't feeling pain at all. That was even more exciting, and he reached down to grasp himself as Mace rose up, lifting the woman's hips off the bed. The sylph thrust faster, making Alica's breasts shake.

Minutes passed. However, instead of his excitement increasing, Jasar felt his ardor start to cool. Alica was screaming out of control now, shuddering and writhing on the bed, reaching up for the battler and howling, her pleasure obvious. She bucked continuously, orgasming over and over, bowing her back nearly into a C as Mace settled on his knees, pulling her against him repeatedly.

Jasar had never made a woman react like that. "Damn it," he growled, letting go of himself and rising from his chair. "You goddamned whore."

Mace looked at him, and suddenly the sylph was finishing, buried deep inside the overwhelmed woman. That just pushed her further over the edge, and she screamed until her voice broke. The battler set her back on the bed with uncharacteristic gentleness.

"Get out!" Jasar snarled. "Get out now!"

Mace pulled free of the woman and stood, leaving the room with the same heavy footfalls as when he'd entered, his hatred returned and unrelenting.

Jasar didn't care. He stood over his bed, staring down at the exhausted Alica. A tiny smile played over her face, and she lay wantonly, her legs splayed and her thighs soaked.

"My," she breathed. "Oh, *my*." A truly slaked desire was in that voice, and Jasar's rage grew out of control.

"You whore," he growled, and punched her. "You filthy whore!" She screamed, but he kept hitting her, shouting curses and almost crying as he beat her, grabbing a heavy silver candlestick from beside the bed and striking her with that. He continued until there was nothing left of her face and head, and he felt ill, sickened—not at what had happened to her, but at what Mace had done.

"How dare he," he gasped, wiping his chin with a bloody hand. "How *dare* he!" He went on to smash the room, wanting no reminder of what had happened, or of how his own slave had outshone him.

Outside, Mace stood in his alcove. The only outward sign of what he felt was his hand slowly tightening into a fist.

Devon and Solie both screamed as they tumbled through the air, falling repeatedly as Airi tried to juggle them and run at the same time. Afraid a battler would tear her apart at any moment, the air sylph swept up the hill and down the other side, skimming above pine trees before dropping down to a river where she couldn't be seen so easily. Her passengers shrieked and vomited, but she wasn't strong enough for them to be comfortable. She could barely hold them both as it was, and she was tiring. An older sylph could have run with them easily. An ancient sylph such as Tempest could have lifted the entire town and run with it, but Airi was still a youngster by her kind's standards, even though she'd been passed down through three generations.

The river ran away from the village, angling up and twisting toward the northern forests. Airi fled along it, able to feel the fighting end behind her, and she was afraid this meant a battler would be after them. She couldn't imagine the younger one not following his master, not unless he'd lost, and then the other one would give chase. Airi whimpered, but she knew her master's mind and couldn't imagine him asking anything less of her. Save the girl. Save them all.

When she couldn't go any farther, she dropped them gently down into a moss-filled meadow. She had nothing left.

"Airi!" Devon gasped, rolling to his feet and reaching for her. His hand passed through where she shimmered on the ground, and he cursed before he fumbled inside his tunic, coming out with a small, thin flute. Airi shuddered as he put it to his lips and started to play. He'd been playing the instrument since he was a toddler, learning the music style she liked and the tunes she loved, trained by his father as his father had been trained by his grandfather. He performed for her. This was the promise made to her when she first crossed the gate, and Devon had always been careful to fulfill it.

His music was healing to Airi, giving her something to focus on as she fed from his living energy, drawing it into herself. This world was both alien and poisonous to her kind, but after the binding she could feed from Devon, and his music only made him taste sweeter. She drank deeply, and the girl she'd rescued stared at both her and her master as he played, at the man and at the shimmer of air, her fear fading in the face of what she saw. Devon closed his eyes and kept playing, the high, sweet tones filling the entire meadow as the sun finished setting and the stars came out. Grasshoppers started to sound from the bushes, a counterpart to Devon's playing.

Airi started to feel better, singing along. That battler could be coming, but it wasn't important. Her master played for her alone, and even the girl they'd rescued didn't matter. At last Airi felt strong enough to take on the most corporeal of the several forms she used so rarely: a translucent female child, thin enough almost to be made of twigs—and a shape illegal enough that Devon could be put to death for allowing it. In this guise she sat on the ground, her knees drawn up and wrapped by her arms, while her master put down his flute. His expression was relieved.

The human female sat a few feet away, shivering in her old, battered clothes and watching them both warily. She was terrified, Airi could feel it, and there was no sign of her battler. By this time, Airi knew, he was either dead or defeated. Airi grieved for the girl.

"I know you, don't I?" the redhead asked, looking at Devon.

He nodded, pocketing the flute and crawling forward to put a hand against Airi's cheek. "Are you all right?" he asked in an undertone, his concern palpable.

She smiled at him. His care wasn't what held her here, but it made her happy. *I'll be fine,* she breathed into his mind. *Thank you.*

He nodded, stroking her cheek again, and turned to the girl they'd saved, his face whitening once more as he stared at her. "Yes," he told her. "I'm Devon Chole. I saw you in the town a lot when I was growing up there. You're the baker's niece, aren't you?"

She nodded. "Solie. Do you know what happened?"

She didn't? Airi supposed the human didn't have any way to know. Not coming from being a sacrifice to having a battler. Airi remembered how confused she herself had been when she first crossed the gate, and she hadn't been cheated of her prize as the battlers always were. Long ago she had communicated to a few of them about it, using the wordless language they'd developed to counter their masters' rules against speaking, and she knew how horrible it was for them. All of those battlers were gone now. Unlike other sylphs, battlers weren't handed down through generations, and so they vanished once their masters died. From what Airi knew, they were probably glad of it, for they never recovered from what had been done to them: they were forced to watch their females die before they had a chance to make them into queens, forced to serve their killers. . . . Solie's battler had been spared that, but that wouldn't help him understand what was going on here, or just how lucky he'd been.

"You know that you bound a battler?" Devon asked her. When the girl nodded he said, "That's never happened before. I didn't see it, but I can't imagine the king was happy." He sighed. "He sent a man named Leon Petrule and his battler, Ril, after you. That's who attacked you in the village." He took a deep breath. "While Ril was distracting your battler, Leon went after you. You'd be dead now if Airi hadn't grabbed you."

The girl turned white, her lower lip trembling as she raised a hand to her mouth. A moment later she was sobbing, bent over double to press her forehead against the ground. Devon looked at Airi in desperate confusion, but Airi didn't know what to tell him. *He* was the master. Finally, he crawled over and put an arm around the girl. She leaned against him, still crying, and he held her while she wept herself out.

It took a while, and Airi again faded incorporeal. She climbed wearily into the air and sensed outward as far as she could. Smoke was lifting from the village in the distance, darker than even the night sky, but she could see nothing more. There was no sign of either battler. She wasn't sure if that was good or not, but she wasn't going to go check without Devon's express order. She was no fighter, and she was too tired to run. Even having just fed, she didn't have the strength to try and hide. She needed rest.

Below, Solie spoke softly to Devon, telling him what had happened: how she'd ended up with the battler and what they'd gone through, how she'd come to feel about him. Airi didn't bother to listen. The girl was bound to the battler fully, her soul patterned inside him as his was in hers. She'd always want the feel of that bond and would suffer for being away from him, just as Devon would if Airi left. Airi couldn't deal at all with that. It was up to Devon to decide what they needed to do, and it was up to her to do it. She would wait for his order.

Wearily, she stayed on watch and swirled in memory of his music, dancing a dance that no one with human eyes could see.

Solie clung to a man she didn't really know at all and wept, trying to understand how she could be so upset about someone she'd only just met. She was, though. She missed Heyou, missed him terribly, and neither of the two who'd saved her could say if he was still alive. From the sound of it, the answer was no.

The thought of Heyou's death hurt more than she could have imagined. He'd protected her. It didn't matter how basically crazy he was, growling at any man who came near her, or how much he tried to get into her skirts. Even then he'd made her feel safe, and when she spoke, he listened. Solie wasn't too used to that, not in her family. From her aunt, sure, but the older woman still gave advice and direction. Heyou didn't try to tell her how to think at all. He might edge with giddy skill around what she directed, but he still listened, and he'd wormed his way into her soul somehow. Without him there, she felt empty.

She sniffled and wiped her eyes on Devon's shirt. It seemed impossible not to blame herself for Heyou, the town, and everything. She could imagine what her aunt would say to that. *If you take the blame on yourself, you let the real culprit get away*. But she still felt responsible.

She should have realized that the king would be after her, and she should have taken Heyou so far away they never would have been found. It wasn't as though it would have been hard for him to carry her. Instead, she'd run to the town closest to the castle and let him announce himself to the world by trying to defend her. How could she have been so stupid? Now she didn't even have Heyou at all, and she couldn't go home. Her father would never accept her, the townspeople would blame her, and she wasn't so idiotic anymore as to think the king would just let her go now that her battler was gone. He'd want revenge for his son at the very least. He'd also want her dead for being proof that a woman could bind a battler just like a man. She'd have to run, find somewhere that the king's hunter wouldn't find her . . . and now Devon would have to go with her, for having committed the crime of saving her life. He was in just as much danger as she was, he and Airi both.

"I'm so sorry," she sobbed. "I got you involved with this!"

Devon stroked her hair. "I'm pretty sure I got myself involved with no help from you," he disagreed. "Don't blame yourself."

"But you can never go home! And that man will be after you!"

"Yeah." She heard him sigh. "I'm trying not to think about that. Sometimes you just have to stand up, though." He pushed her back and wiped her eyes with a handkerchief, leaving Solie to wonder what Heyou would think about him touching her. That brought on an urge to laugh and cry at the same time.

Devon smiled, though his mouth was tight and he had lines between his eyes she didn't remember from before. She'd never known him very well, but he'd always struck her as a peaceful sort.

"We should try to get some sleep and get moving in the morning," he told her, "once we can see where we're going and decide where we're going to go."

"Where can we go?" she asked, still gulping air, if mostly sobbed out. She didn't know the land very well—not past the hamlet in which she was born or her aunt's town.

"I'm not sure. I think north. If we skirt along the Shale Plains and cross the mountains, we can go to the kingdom of Para Dubh. It'll be hard, but they won't look for us there." *I hope,* she could almost hear him adding.

"Okay," she agreed, not knowing what else to suggest. He had a cloak, boots, a flute, and an air sylph who couldn't carry them very far. She had a worn-out dress and no shoes. Still, she pushed herself to her feet and took a deep breath. "I guess we should find shelter under the trees for now. Let's go."

Chapter Nine

Twenty-eight men were dead, all of their sylphs destroyed. The harvest was lost and they'd only been able to recover a third of their livestock. At least they had enough gear for everyone to camp in, and they still had the ability to bind more sylphs as well. They could rebuild everything, provided they were left alone long enough and they survived the winter.

Morgal stood at the edge of the bluff on which they'd made their camp, staring over his supposed domain. It wasn't much. A collection of tents and fires, built on the back slope of the cliff. They had close to fifty tents, and two hundred men, women, and children, along with ten fire sylphs, eight air sylphs, seven earth sylphs, four water sylphs, and even a single healer sylph. Back in the valley, all of them together had been a wondrous thing—an invigorating thing. Now it just looked like a dirty camp filled with desperate men.

They'd had battle sylphs sent after them, two battle sylphs that tore into their tiny community, ripping their people apart and scattering them out into the Shale Plains. It had taken them days to regroup here, and cost them half their sylphs and far too many friends for Morgal to want to count, including all of their former leaders. He closed his eyes for a moment, feeling the icy wind on his face and trying not to get discouraged. He was a thin man, his face gaunt and pitted, and the shortened rations they were all on hadn't helped. His long hair was thinning on top and graying as well. His left arm was bandaged and it hurt to breathe, but the healer sylph was exhausted. They would have lost far more if it hadn't been for her, and she still had work to do. He'd have to recover on his own for a while.

Behind him a light flickered, a fire in the shape of a girl staring out over the barren plain. She looked to be made entirely out of burning embers, and was appropriately named Ash. Looking at her, Morgal abruptly tensed. "Are they coming back?" he asked.

The fire sylph shrugged. "No," she said aloud, and he relaxed. All of the sylphs were watching for attack now. They could sense each other when they were close enough, and they'd feel the battlers before anyone else. Sylphs could hide their energy, but battlers never had a reason. Morgal just hoped that "close enough" wouldn't turn out to be too close.

He turned and went back across the top of the bluff, Ash at his side, trying not to jar his injuries as he returned to the camp. Survivors looked at him and nodded as he passed, before returning to their own work. There were a lot of men left, but with their casualties they were outnumbered by the women, attached and widowed both. And there were children as well, playing among the tents as though two thirds of them weren't orphans.

We should have expected the attack, he thought—just as he'd been thinking since it happened. *We became arrogant, careless. We paid for it.*

All of his compatriots were peasants from the mountain hamlets of Para Dubh, people too poor and unimportant to earn sylphs from the king—or the priesthood, providing one could pay enough. Most of those here were newly bound, though, thanks to a rebel priest who'd joined them and given them all a reason to set out on their own. Wanting more than the class structure of Para Dubh for their future, the first men to befriend Petr the priest had started this community, settling down on the uninhabited edge of the Shale Plains in a canyon valley that was protected from the worst of the wind and snow. They should have been left alone there for years, but they'd been stupid. At their leaders' suggestion, they'd started to attack air ships coming from the kingdom of Eferem to Para Dubh. It took years off the time they expected to take building up their community, and people stopped questioning the safety of it. Then the battlers came. Morgal just prayed that the battlers' masters only thought they were killing pirates—and more, believed they'd destroyed them.

Ahead of him, a tent that looked no different than the others was pitched next to the community's collected barrels of water. Morgal ducked inside, and the women there looked up from tending the injured. Seven survivors still lay, waiting for healing. There were more than seven, of course, but these were the worst, unable to recover without help.

That help glanced up at Morgal, sniffing toward his injury before she turned back to the man she was mending. She was hard to see, vaguely female in shape but mostly formless and decidedly translucent. She'd been fading more and more as she worked alone to save the wounded, and her master watched her worriedly. Zem was a tiny, nervous man, but more devoted to his sylph than any other master Morgal had ever seen.

Zem hurried over, wringing his hands. "Let me tell her to stop, Morgal," he begged, looking over his shoulder as the healer put her hand on the forehead of the injured man. She shimmered and his breathing evened out and deepened, though he was still unnaturally pale. "Luck's going to end up killing herself!"

Morgal sighed, hoping Zem was just being paranoid. "If she stops now, our friends will die."

"But if she doesn't, we won't have her for the next injury!" Her master was nearly in tears. "She's the only healer we have!"

"Does *she* want to stop?" Morgal asked.

"You know she doesn't," Zem wailed. "She never wants to stop. She'll heal acne if she can't find anything else."

Over by the bed, Luck looked up at them and rose, drifting over to the next cot, where she sat and laid her hand on its occupant. She was healing the wounded in increments, taking a long time but using less energy. Morgal had been impressed when he first saw her strategy. He still was, even as she ignored his wounds.

"She'll be fine."

"But what if she isn't?" Zem wailed.

Morgal looked back at his fire sylph. "Ash, is Luck okay?"

"Yes."

"See?" Morgal told the man. "Ash says she's fine. She'd know."

"But she's a fire sylph! Luck is a healer! They're totally different!"

Morgal shook his head. "Just let her do her work. She knows to stop when she needs to rest. She understands how important she is to us."

He caught Luck's eye for a moment, but the sylph didn't bother to respond. She only answered to Zem—who, thankfully, still answered to Morgal. If not, they both would probably have gone. If they'd only had another healer . . . But healers were the rarest of sylphs, and the summoning ritual wasn't an exact process. The group could open a gate and their own sylphs could tell them what was on the other side, but they couldn't aim the gate at all for the type of sylph they needed. They hadn't found any other healers, nor did they have many men with the unique quality Zem had to attract one. He'd been constantly sick until Luck came through—or had complained that he was. It made her happy somehow to keep him healthy.

As Morgal stood contemplating, the sylph floated past to her next patient, pausing to lay a hand on her master as she did. He took a deep breath and shook himself. Morgal looked away.

"I leave it to you," Morgal told Zem, and headed outside before the man could get his focus back and return to complaining. He'd just wanted to check on the injured men. When he'd last been there, she'd been dealing with a dozen. Zem would argue until he went blue, but Luck would have them all healed within the week. Tomorrow, perhaps he could insist she take a break without the risk of someone dying.

Outside, the growing cold made him shiver, and Ash pressed close, warming him. It would start snowing soon, which was another problem. He didn't know what to say to these people. Their real leaders were dead. Morgal was just an assistant, yet he was the most experienced leader they had. They'd formed a new council, with him in charge. But he was also one of those who'd suggested they attack the Eferem cargo ships in the first place, use them to increase their own supplies and speed the founding of their intended new kingdom. As the only one left of that group, he felt the heavy burden of the disaster.

They couldn't afford another fight like that. Their sylphs were useless against battlers, and they would never have any for themselves. Not when a woman had to be sacrificed to bind them. None of this group wanted to kill anyone, not even a volunteer. He remembered that ship veering toward them instead of fleeing as they attacked, and that bird and armored knight both leaping down—

He closed his eyes. It was done. Most of his people had escaped, thanks to their sylphs. They'd be able to do it again.

He walked to another tent, closer to the edge of the camp. Inside, their only priest and the man who'd made all of this possible looked up from the circle he was drawing. It was nearly done, ready to be infused with energy so that they might open the gate to the sylphs. They still had men who weren't bound to one. They'd draw as many as they could, and if they were really lucky, they'd get another healer.

Morgal nodded at Petr and eased himself down onto a wooden chair in the corner. Ash floated beside him, now in the form of a ball of fire, close enough to warm his aching muscles without burning him. "Soon?" he asked.

"Yes." The priest nodded, kneeling to continue with the circle. He was bald, and his scalp was heavily scarred, as was the rest of his body. When Morgal had first met him, Petr had no tongue, though Luck had eventually been able to regrow it. Morgal didn't know entirely what the man had done to earn his punishment, but he'd been tortured and his earth sylph destroyed before he was dropped into the wilds to die. Morgal's former leaders had found him, and in return he'd given them the secret of summoning sylphs. He had no new sylph of his own, though. Morgal could understand that. He couldn't imagine ever replacing Ash.

He watched the priest work, knowing it took more than just learning the patterns to make the ritual successful. Petr had years of experience, and Morgal was beyond grateful that he'd survived the battler attack. Neither man spoke of the fact that Morgal himself had only survived the battle because he'd grabbed the priest and run, leaving the others to fight alone. They each carried their own wounds. He just sat and watched, and hoped that the sylphs to come would be enough to ensure their survival.

Heyou floated back to cohesiveness as discreetly as he could as the sun rose, sensing for the other battler with every bit of awareness he had left. He could feel his foe hovering on the edge of his perception, aura muted and resting.

He didn't bother to congratulate himself on wearing the other sylph out. Heyou was badly hurt, his form torn and his energy low. The pain was nearly overwhelming, but he didn't dare wait any longer to heal. He wasn't so sure anymore that he would. Once he would have stayed where he was and either lived or died, but Solie needed him. She was out there with that man, and he had to get to her.

Slowly, less a part of the world than a cloud of dust motes but still in agony, Heyou wafted from his hiding place and across the shattered floor of the cottage, headed away from the other battler. His aura he swallowed completely, leaving nothing for his enemy to feel or track him by. He felt nearly blind without it and as naked as he now understood Solie was when he'd first met her—defenseless. It was . . . humbling.

He flowed across the floor and out through a crack in the wall. There the early-morning sun shone down on him, warming his edges as he shadowed across the lane and into the woods. From there he fled across the orchards and the hills, following a tenuous link that took him slowly northward, in the direction his queen had gone.

It was incredibly hard, his energy cloud form disrupted so badly that it could barely keep its shape. Heyou finally had to stop and resume human shape, giving himself a framework in which to exist before he tumbled into oblivion completely.

Doing so hurt as much as the blow he'd taken from the other battler. Heyou knelt on the leafy, moldy ground and pressed his face to it, weeping from the pain, his skin cold for the very first time under his worn tunic. Physically, he looked as Solie had wished, but he could feel the injuries inside. His enemy had crippled him.

"Solie," he gasped. She would make everything better. His queen would feed him the energy he needed, and he knew he had to be with her. That instinct was still incredibly strong, if tempered by exhaustion and a strange new loneliness. He'd never been lonely before. Angry, yes, and determined, but never lonely. He couldn't defend her anymore, but he could be with her, as she could be with him. That was worth surviving for.

Heyou forced himself to his feet by sheer force of will, choking and shuddering as he did. He could feel the harsh ground under his bare feet and stumbled, falling to his knees. That hurt more.

Finally, he found a broken sapling about his height and stripped the branches off, used it to help him stand. Leaning on it, he slowly moved to follow his queen.

Deep in a dream about Lizzy, Ril twitched and came awake, his eyes blinking open as he glanced around in the early-morning light. For a moment he'd thought he felt . . . He ruffled his feathers, listening intently with something other than ears.

He'd been sure he killed the other battler—or damaged him so severely that his energy would continue leaking out until he died. Now he wasn't quite so sure. He shifted and half spread his wings, ready to race in whatever direction was necessary so he could finish the job. But he couldn't sense anything. Not clearly.

Leon, who had been talking to a frightened old man outside a crater that used to be a cottage, looked at him with one eyebrow raised. He didn't say anything, though.

Ril had seen many masters talk to their sylphs, asking them questions that they weren't allowed to answer. Leon at least had never been so stupid. He held his tongue, letting his battler search. Ril ignored him and focused, looking for that faint tinge of hate that would reveal his quarry.

He turned his head, and Leon turned as well, walking slowly in whatever direction Ril looked, carrying him forward. They traveled across the ruins of the town to the devastated cottage into which the battler had crashed, the old man following uncertainly at Leon's beckoning. There,

Leon shifted Ril to his arm and held him up, stepping carefully inside, waving dust out of his face. Ril looked down and his master knelt, lowering him. Ril gripped Leon's forearm hard.

The floor was streaked with the energy that was the other battler's blood, the colors swirling in ways Ril knew only he could see. He looked and listened and finally raised his head with a squawk. Leon stood, and when Ril looked at the back wall, he carried him there.

There was the faintest trail, just a hint of energy trickling out through a crack only an inch wide. Ril looked at it, and at his master.

"Damn," Leon muttered. Standing, he walked outside. Pointing at the old man he'd been questioning, he ordered him to stay where he was before he carried Ril around to the back wall.

The energy led to the woods beyond the town, through the orchards. Ril leaned forward and let his weight guide his master. They climbed the hill as a pair and moved into the trees, followed a thin trail of energy that finally ended in a clearing.

Ril stared and shook himself in disgust. The other battler had changed his shape, locking his energy inside a physical form. With his aura suppressed, he'd be much harder to track. Trapped as a bird, Ril's senses were so blunted, he doubted he could do so at all.

Leon watched for a moment, waiting, and Ril focused some hate on him just to express his disgust. The man blanched and shook his head. Transferring Ril back to his shoulder, he walked around the clearing, studying the ground. A moment later he started to walk slowly northward, following tracks Ril had never bothered to learn to find. The battler clapped his beak but otherwise didn't acknowledge his master's efforts.

They followed a twisting path through the trees and up

the slope. In a few spots Ril saw the ground torn by the weight of something passing, but that was it. Leon was the one who led the chase to the top of the hill and through the woods, coming at last to a cliff over a river. There the pair stood, surveying the water below in both directions.

Nothing.

Ril screamed in frustration and spread his wings, flying to one of the nearby trees. There he preened his wings and waited for his master to make his way back to the village, before he would return to his shoulder. Leon didn't order otherwise. They both felt the same. This time, they'd failed.

Under the edge of the cliff, in a hollow he hadn't known was there until he half fell over the edge, Heyou cowered against the cold clay wall and tried not to make a sound, not even breathing. He could feel the two hunters above and knew they'd kill him if they found him, and for the first time in his life, he was afraid. All bravado was gone. He had no fight left in him, not anymore. He hid instead, hoping they'd go away, and even when they did it was cold and desperation that finally drove him out.

He continued his painful journey, slowly heading north.

Chapter Ten

Twenty miles north of the town they'd been forced to flee from stood another, one grown up to service local lumbermen and trappers and those willing to risk the long, dangerous road to Para Dubh. It was a rougher town than the last, and burly men on the outskirts shouted and laughed at each other, yelling insults as often as they did greetings.

Solie eyed the place nervously, wrapped in Devon's cloak and hanging onto his arm. She didn't want to be there, but they had no choice. It was well into late afternoon the day after they fled the village, and they'd been walking since dawn. They were both getting desperate for food and clothing. With Devon's cloak she was mostly warm, but he needed something as well, and she couldn't go much farther without shoes. Her feet were bruised and cut, and she winced every time she took a step, but Airi was still too tired to carry her. The sylph hovered somewhere around her master's head, impossible to see—but there, according to Devon.

She didn't know how she would have made it without the man. He never complained or protested her slow pace, helping her whenever she needed it, and unlike Heyou, he didn't try to convince her to sleep with him. She found she didn't have any interest in him anyway. He was more like a brother.

She tried not to think of Heyou, but that emptiness she'd found inside without him was still there. She missed him terribly. If Devon picked up on her grief, he didn't say anything, and he always looked away when she wept.

"Are you sure you have enough money?" she whispered, trying not to attract attention from the town's rough inhabitants. The place was larger than any town Solie knew, and she was appalled to see that the only women visible seemed to be selling themselves.

"I should," Devon assured her. "I should be able to afford a couple of meals and a room at the inn. If they don't inflate their prices here." He sounded unsure, and she hung on to him a little tighter. They had little hope if they couldn't get supplies. It was a very long way to Para Dubh, which had become their destination.

To Solie's surprise, their entrance went unremarked. Anyone unfamiliar was big news in her home town. Here, no one paid any attention at all, and they were ignored completely as they approached a mercantile near the center of town.

"Let me do the talking, okay?" Devon said, and Solie nodded.

The shop was filled with more things than Solie could imagine, piled on shelves up to the height of the ceiling. She saw plates, dolls, bolts of fabric, tools, weapons, mining supplies, dried fruit, and a thousand other items. She'd never seen the like, and gaped like a child overwhelmed by too many presents. Devon held her hand, tugging her along behind him until he found a barrel filled with boots. Digging, he finally came up with a pair that might be small enough.

"Try these," he suggested.

Solie did, gingerly slipping her sore, cold feet inside them and finding she had room to spare. "I think they're too big," she admitted.

"Typical." He tossed her a few pairs of woolen socks. "Try them with these."

She did, and found the boots fit better, though she still felt odd dressed in the large, ungainly shoes.

Devon walked farther down the aisle and found a plain

gray cloak made of felted wool. It was almost too long, but incredibly warm. She wrapped herself in it.

"Thank you," she breathed.

"You're welcome. Next, we need some sort of pack for supplies."

After some looking, he found a waxed leather bag into which he piled a saucepan, plates, utensils, and a tinderbox. He paused thoughtfully in front of the spice shelves, but opted instead for a length of rope and some soap. Items in hand, he went up to the counter to haggle.

Solie followed, not wanting to get in the way, as he started what sounded like a vicious argument. Instead, she stood a few feet back and watched his hair ruffle, though there was no wind: Airi was playing with it. Solie watched curiously, barely able to see the shimmer that was the air sylph, and then only when she moved in front of a candle that burned on a shelf behind her.

She was so different from Heyou, Solie realized. Airi was female. But then again, all sylphs were female, except for the battlers. She rarely took on a solid shape, didn't even usually stay visible. Heyou did, and the other battlers as well. Of course, they were all locked into one form. Solie wondered for a moment if she'd passed invisible sylphs before. She doubted it. Her home hamlet wasn't of much interest to anyone, let alone a sylph master.

Oddly, she found herself missing her home and her family. They lived in a tiny house on a rocky farm, all the girls sharing a single room. Solie couldn't really blame her father for trying to marry her off, but his choice had just been so repulsive. She missed them all . . . yet she still felt better off in this mercantile in a strange town, listening to Devon try to get the price dropped on a collection of clothes and supplies.

She sighed and looked away, staring at a collection of pipes in an open box. Another pain was present: she still missed Heyou terribly. He'd pierced her soul as deeply as she had his, and she wanted him back, even with his inability to stand other men. He would have torn the store owner's head off by now in order to get what they needed.

Solie watched Devon argue over the supplies for a while longer, then walked to the main window for a view. Outside, horses pulled carts through the town, and she saw a few men riding, but she also knew they couldn't afford a horse. The one Devon had been riding had been left behind at the town, and she knew that bothered him. He'd worried that it wouldn't know how to get itself home. Solie just wished it were here. She and Devon would be walking for a long time to come.

As she watched, a man drove a wagon pulled by two old horses up and climbed down, tying the animals' reins to the bar out front. He came into the mercantile, and Solie stepped out of his way, noting as she did that he had heavy circles under his eyes. He looked nervous as well. He nodded to her slightly, not really making eye contact, and went to browse a shelf covered with bolts of white cloth. Having not much else to do, Solie watched, wondering what brought him there.

At the till, Devon finished his haggling and complained massively as the storekeeper put his purchases into a bag. He handed over a few coins and turned away, pocketing the rest. But as he took his things and walked toward Solie, he passed the man who'd just entered the store. Both stopped abruptly, staring at each other.

A strong breeze started in the shop, Airi suddenly flaring her power. Solie couldn't figure out why. Still, Airi was hovering like a sinister transparent child over her master. The shopkeeper noticed nothing, having gone into the back with his money.

Devon and the stranger continued to stare at each other, the smell of earth filtering into Solie's nose. A moment later, a rough dirt wall shot up through the cracks in the plank floor between the two men. Devon stepped back, glancing over at Solie in concern.

An earth sylph, she realized in alarm. They'd been afraid of battlers, but had some other sylph master been sent after them instead? She waited beside the two men, feeling the tension rise until she couldn't handle it anymore.

"Stop!" she cried out, moving between them, careful not to touch either sylph. They both pulled back, and the men stared at her in surprise. "I surrender! I surrender! He had nothing to do with any of it!"

The earth sylph's master's jaw dropped open, and he gaped at her. "You what? You're not looking for *me*?"

"Why would we be?" Devon asked. "I thought you were looking for us."

The man's suspicious gaze became a grin. "Cal Porter. Pleased to meet you." He extended a hand.

Devon shook, all the while wearing a bemused expression. Solie sagged, finally able to breathe again. The two sylphs faded back into invisibility.

"You really scared me," Cal told them cheerfully. "I thought you were sent by the king or something to find me, though I don't know why anyone would know to look for me here. Or for me at all. I'm nobody. I haven't told anybody what I'm doing, and no one's asked. This is a good town for not asking questions. Nobody cares what you do as long as you stay out of their way. Expensive, though. I don't know how I'm going to be able to get enough supplies, and I'm not sure what I need. I only got the one message, and that was short. Too bad Stria can't carry messages. She can't fly, plus I don't like to send her away. It gets lonely here, and I need her for the wagon. . . ."

As he talked, he hauled the bolt of cloth he'd been looking at off the shelf and carried it to the front counter. Solie and Devon shared a look, neither of them sure how the man had managed to keep any secrets at all. He left the bolt where it was and went to find other items, grabbing poultices and salves and other objects used for healing. He jabbered nonstop, talking about his horse and his sore feet and his lack of money and his earth sylph. Solie had never met anyone quite like him.

"Um . . . ," Devon interrupted. "Just a minute. Why were you afraid of us?"

Cal glanced at him and then toward the shopkeeper, who wandered into the back again, this time searching for herbs Cal had requested. Cal leaned close. "I'm from the Community," he confided in a whisper. "They got attacked a few days ago. I just found out yesterday. I'm getting as many supplies together as I can. Apparently they lost just about everything, and there are a lot of people hurt."

Solie blinked. "The Community?"

"Yeah." Cal nodded earnestly. When the shopkeeper came back, he accepted the herbs, then sent the man for salt. "It's a bunch of people who don't like how the king of Para Dubh runs everything and won't let anyone but his toadies have sylphs. We've broken off and are trying to establish a place with our own rules—up north, where no one else lives."

Solie's breath caught in her throat. Was this somewhere they could hide? "Can *we* go there?" she asked.

"With a sylph? Sure. We can always use new recruits." Cal puffed himself up proudly.

Solie peeked at Devon. He was a nice guy, but she couldn't imagine living the rest of her life on the run. She didn't imagine he could, either.

"You said you were attacked," Devon said, not looking at her.

"Yeah," Cal admitted, his voice dropping. The shopkeeper had returned, so he led them down an aisle where he poked at some blankets. "We kind of were . . . hijacking some ships, and we went after this one that had a battler on it. That's what the message said." When he heard Solie's breath catch he added, "*I* didn't tell them to attack the ships. I thought it was a bad idea, but they said it was the quickest way to get self-sufficient. We didn't hurt anyone and we let the crews go. We'd only gone after a couple, but then there was a battler, and . . . The message said a lot of people are dead."

"That ship had *two* battle sylphs on it," Devon told him flatly. "Ril and Mace. You're lucky anyone survived." His brow creased. "How could you have been so stupid?"

"It wasn't me!" Cal whined. "I said that!"

"Right." Devon looked at Solie. "I don't know that we want to hear any more. These people have their own problems."

Solie stared at the ground. "But . . . we have to go somewhere."

"I would almost bet you money that Ril and Leon are tracking us," was Devon's reply.

"But . . . but with Heyou dead . . ." Solie's voice caught in her throat, and she had to wipe away a tear. "They have no reason anymore." At least, that's what she wanted to believe. Even if it was a lie.

"Who's Heyou?" Cal asked.

Solie looked away. "A friend of mine. They killed him." She started to cry in earnest, if softly. She'd wept about him so many times, but still the tears came. She covered her face with shaking hands. Neither of the two men knew what to do. Both stared at her stupidly.

"Maybe you should come with me anyway," Cal said at last. "I mean, we're *all* getting chased by battlers."

Devon sighed. "Fine. If Solie wants to. Do you?"

She forced herself to stop weeping. She didn't care where they went, not really. Just as long as it was somewhere safe and had other people around—other women she could talk and cry with. "Yes."

"Fine." Devon shrugged. "It's settled."

They ended up buying the blankets and an assortment of other gear and medical supplies. Cal didn't quite have enough, so Devon dipped into his own money in order that they could pay for everything. At least they'd gotten food, Solie thought, as she chewed on a piece of jerky and watched Devon help load the wagon. Even after all the money they'd spent, there was a great deal of space left in it for passengers.

An hour later they were driving the animals out of town, headed north along a rutted old road through the forest. It was going to get a lot worse, Cal admitted cheerfully. Where they were going there were no roads, and they'd need the help of the sylphs to continue. A cold wind blew, but Solie was warm in her cloak. Airi blocked most of the wind, anyway. The other sylph materialized as a child-shaped mass of dirt and rock in the back of the wagon, playing with a set of marbles that Cal gave her. Solie watched the sylph amuse herself and thought of Heyou again. Huddling down in her cloak, she tried to find other contemplations, but it was hard. It was as if she could still feel him, wandering somewhere, lost, and looking for her.

She closed her eyes and pulled her hood up, determined to get some sleep as the wagon slowly moved north.

Heyou struggled through the woods, his legs covered in mud and pine needles up to his knees. He was actually getting cuts on them, and his feet were bleeding. He could feel Solie, though, somewhere far ahead, and he followed her unerringly, making a dead-straight line toward her—at least, as much as he could. Whenever he reached an obstruction he couldn't conquer, he went around it and returned to his route, faithfully tracking his queen.

He didn't know how long he'd been walking, nor did he care. He just knew he had to find her. It didn't matter how much pain he felt, or his fear. All aspects of his battler nature he kept suppressed, all except that unbreakable tie. His queen he could feel and always would.

Just as he could feel the faint touches from other members of his hive scattered throughout this strange, solid world. There weren't many, but they were there, and he reached for them desperately . . . only to feel their regret. He even felt the grief of a battler who couldn't come to his aid, much as he wanted to. He was on his own, the battler breathed distantly. Only Solie could help him, if he could find her.

Heyou was convinced he could. Find the queen, protect the queen. Nothing else mattered.

He stumbled along a narrow trail, leaning heavily on his makeshift staff. It was cold out and he wasn't used to that, wasn't used to the sensation of cold at all, nor that of dying. Heyou gritted his newly created teeth and fought for strength, head bowed low as he kept walking. Walk long enough and he would reach her. Only, he could tell she was moving herself, faster. Didn't she know she was leaving him behind?

He'd never reach her, he realized desperately, not like this. But he didn't have the energy to change shape anymore. It was all bleeding invisibly out of him. That other battler had known what he was doing.

Heyou shuddered, determined, absolutely resolute not to give up—and stumbled, falling to the ground. The world went away for a while.

It all came back with the sound of hooves. Heyou opened his eyes, finding that he was lying full-length on the ground and wasn't dead yet. Everything hurt, though. And someone was coming. He forced his head up, lifting himself on his forearms, and saw the gray legs of a horse as it made its way down the trail toward him. Dazed, he looked up the animal to the big man who sat astride, peering down at him through a bushy beard and a fur cloak.

"Isn't this a sight?" the man said lightly, and Heyou had one final moment before he passed out to curse the fact that he'd been found by another bloody human male.

Chapter Eleven

Leon's lips were tight as he strode down the hallway toward the king's audience chamber. On his shoulder was Ril, stiff with fury, his hate flaring out.

They hadn't learned anything from the old man or the girl's aunt, nor from the father—nothing more than that the girl's name was Solie and the battler's Heyou, and that he didn't seem to hate her, even as she barely kept control of him. The aunt hadn't even realized he wasn't human, and only Devon's father had recognized him as a battler . . . at least until he'd attacked the girl's father.

Leon had gathered what information he could and prepared to head out again, to track the pair more carefully this time, when an air sylph appeared with a message ordering him to report to the king. The timing couldn't have been worse. If he didn't start following the group immediately, they could escape. He was skillful, but time was every tracker's enemy. The girl was unprepared and the battler injured. Now was the moment to find them. Instead, he was being forced to dawdle. Worse, he could see the king wanting to know what he was doing, and demanding the deaths of everyone who knew what Heyou was. The girl and the battler were even more likely to escape if Leon had to waste time hiding her family.

Leon reached the sylph alcove before the audience chamber and looked up to see Mace. The battler hit him with his hate, but Leon was already in such a foul mood he didn't care—and Ril actually hissed at the enormous sylph in response.

Leon sighed and shifted his battler to the usual perch. "I'll be right back," he told Ril and headed for the door. The two battlers stared silently at his back.

A servant held the door to the audience chamber open for him and announced his arrival. Leon walked in and bowed to the man sitting on the throne. Jasar stood grumpily below the dais and glared. Thrall stood to one side behind the throne, staring at him. The hate coming from the battler was cloying.

"Your Majesty," Leon said. "I've come as ordered."

"Yes." The king rubbed his chin. "Tell me what's happened."

Leon straightened. The sooner he reported, the sooner he could get out of there. "The girl's name is Solie. She named the battle sylph Heyou and took him to her aunt's bakery in the village of Otalo, just south of here."

"'Hey, you?'" Jasar repeated dryly.

"Apparently," Leon said. "Ril fought and injured the battler, but they escaped after the fight. I know they're heading north, in the company of an air-sylph master named Devon Chole. I don't know yet why he's helping her. I'll have to ask when I find him." He fell silent, watching the king chew on a thumbnail.

Alcor stared at him for a few moments, then looked over at Jasar. His eyes again found Leon's. "Take him with you," he commanded.

"What?" both men shouted—Leon in shock, Jasar in horror.

"Your Majesty!" the dandy gasped, stepping forward. "You can't expect me to go out into the wilderness again."

"I can, and I do," the king snapped. "You shouldn't have killed that courtier. I want you out of my sight for a while."

Jasar jerked back and shot a hateful look at Leon, as though this were his fault. "Yes, Your Majesty. I suppose another trip on an air ship will be refreshing." He almost spat the last word.

The king looked amused. "I doubt Leon can track anyone from an air ship."

"No, Your Majesty. We'll have to ride."

"Ride?" the dandy shrieked again.

The king waved a hand in dismissal. "Report when you're done" was his final command.

Leon bowed and left. His face showed nothing, but he was outraged. Alcor didn't care who knew about the battler, at least for now, but his new companion was less than useless. The last time they'd worked together, to ambush those pirates, Jasar had commandeered the captain's quarters and refused to come out for anything. At least he'd sent his battler to fight the pirates when they attacked, but that was probably just to protect himself—and he'd ordered Mace back well before the job was finished. The only good thing about the trip was the fact that Leon hadn't seen much of him. Now they were going to have to travel in much closer quarters.

He went out and down the hall to the alcove, well aware that Jasar was following him; the dandy's curses were loud and relentless. Leon collected Ril and turned to his supposed partner, careful to keep the contempt out of his face and voice.

"We leave in an hour, my lord. Make yourself ready."

Jasar stared as though he were mad. "An hour? I can't possibly be ready in an hour! We'll have to leave in the morning."

Leon's eyes narrowed. "They could disappear for good in that time."

Jasar, however, was already walking away, Mace following. "In the morning," he repeated, waving. "After breakfast."

Leon watched the courtier go, and only belatedly became aware that he was grinding his teeth. Ril peered at him appraisingly, no hatred coming from him at all, and Leon stomped off toward a new destination. If he was going to be stuck here overnight, he was at least going to spend it with his family.

Heyou felt warm, leaning back against something that moved beneath him, hearing a steady thump in his ear. His feet were cold, though, and he could smell nothing but fur and animal.

Slowly, he opened his eyes. He was sitting in front of someone on a horse, leaning back against their body while they rode. They had their cloak drawn around him, but his feet dangled down below to be chilled by the night air. He could hear the person's heartbeat under his ear and could feel them breathing.

He actually felt better than he had—in pain but not so exhausted. He blinked, simply sitting quietly for a moment. The rider had an arm across his abdomen, holding Heyou on the horse, and he smelled of old blood and dirt.

He?

Heyou snapped upright, pulling himself away from the man with a gasp, but the arm tightened before he could fall from the saddle.

"Easy now," he heard a voice say. "Don't do that, you'll spook my horse."

Startled, Heyou looked over his shoulder at the bearded face of the man who'd found him earlier. Almost, Heyou hit him with his hate, but he stopped himself. He felt better, but he was too weak to change shape—and, if he was honest with himself, too frightened. He didn't know where that other battler was. He didn't want any more fights, and Solie had told him to hide himself. Heyou swallowed hard and did as ordered.

"Who are you?" he croaked.

"Galway," the man told him. "I found you dying in the woods. Figured I'd take you to the nearest town."

"Why?" Heyou paused to cough. "Why would you do that?"

The man shrugged. "I've got a bunch of kids at home, including a son your age. Sure as hell would want someone to pick him up if they found him lost. What's your name, boy?"

Heyou looked away. He hated this stranger, loathed him as a matter of course, but . . . the man had saved him. "Heyou," he whispered.

"Hey you? Weird name for a boy."

Heyou glared. "It is not!"

Galway shrugged. "Weird's not so bad. It'll do."

Heyou didn't answer, staring off into the distance and sitting so stiff that his back began to hurt. He didn't want this man touching him, didn't want him anywhere nearby, but he was too weak to walk on his own. Whatever the motive, at least this man was taking him in the right direction. He could feel his queen moving far ahead of him and still going north. He might be able to catch her now, if this man was willing to help.

He grimaced. The thought of asking for assistance made him ill, and he couldn't threaten. He was too weak to change or fight, and he didn't dare use his hate aura. He had to rely on charity.

He closed his eyes, breathing deeply and trying to calm himself, seeking to remember Solie and that he did this for her. "Can you help me?" he asked slowly. "I need to find someone."

"Oh?" the man asked. "Who's that?"

"My qu—girl. She's traveling north."

"Not much north of here, unless she's heading to Para Dubh." The man guided his horse around a fallen log. There was a second animal following them, Heyou saw, furs piled high on its back. "Why'd she leave you behind?"

Heyou nearly hit him with hate. "She just did. She

doesn't know where I am." He stretched a little, wincing at a pain in his side just so he could get a bit of distance between them. "I have to get to her. Will you help me?"

"Well . . ." Galway considered while Heyou contemplated several different ways to kill him for dragging the answer out. "I got traps up north. I suppose I could take you a ways. It's good to have company for a while."

Heyou looked away and didn't speak again, humiliated but relieved. Perhaps now he could catch up to his queen.

Devon sat beside Cal on the wagon seat, only half listening to the man ramble. Airi played with his hair while Solie slept in the back on top of the supplies, and Stria stacked blocks and played with marbles. Sometimes, to Devon's amazement, she spoke out loud to her master, something that was forbidden in Eferem but apparently normal in this community they were seeking. He'd quietly told Airi she could speak out loud, but she still only spoke to him, and then only into his mind. There was a greater intimacy that they both appreciated, and he didn't bring the subject up again.

He was intrigued by this alleged community, but still too stressed to really think about it much. He had no idea if his father was okay, and the worry over that was close to driving him insane. He also didn't know if they were being followed, and finally looked up at his air sylph, needing the truth. If they were being tracked by Leon and his battler, they'd only get these people killed.

"Airi," he whispered. "Go back to the village and find my father. Find out if he's okay and if anyone's tracking us. If you can, find out if Solie's aunt and father are okay, too. But be careful! Don't take any risks."

Okay, she answered, and was gone, sweeping away on the winds. Devon sighed and huddled deeper in his cloak, staring at the forest they were traversing. She'd be back. The distance wasn't far for her, and she knew how to be discreet. She would be fine. He'd count the seconds until her return, though.

He went back to looking at the scenery—not that there was much. The forest was made of pine trees and brush, the ground broken by ridges and low hills that had the road slowly climbing upward and winding. The horses labored, but they did get the cart through the hills, even if the bouncing eventually woke Solie and made Devon feel somewhat nauseous. Cal kept chattering on about his childhood.

As the horses went around a huge boulder to find a large gap in the road, Devon said, "Um," wondering if the man even noticed. He was rambling on about his son now, and letting the horses make their own way, not doing much more than randomly glancing at the route. The horses walked on, heading for the gap, and Devon started to pray they were smart enough to stop.

"Stria!" Cal called suddenly, then went on with his story. In the back of the wagon, the earth sylph scooped up her marbles and put them back in the bag before hopping down off the wagon. While Devon watched, she ran past them and dove into the ground, vanishing.

The gap suddenly filled, and the horses continued unhindered. It was actually the smoothest part of the road they'd been on so far. Devon looked behind them, and once the horses were over the break, Stria reappeared, scurrying after the wagon.

Devon looked at Cal. "Nice trick," he said.

Cal beamed. "That's why I got this job. There are places you can't take a horse, but Stria can get me anywhere. She's awesome." He beamed over his shoulder at the sylph, who was settling back in the wagon and reopening her marble bag. She glanced up and smiled, her grin eerily wider than a human's and with far too many teeth.

Devon looked back at the road. Sylphs looked however they wanted, he reminded himself, and wondered again how his own sylph was doing.

Airi found a wind stream high up that was going the way she wanted and floated on it, letting it carry her and do all the work. She was still a little tired, and nervous, but she was happy to be busy again. Devon hadn't said anything, and she doubted he ever would, but she'd terrified him by saving Solie. She was still sure it had been the right decision, but it had made his life much harder and she hadn't meant to do that. Thus, while she always obeyed him, she was acting more quickly about it this time. If he wanted her to find her old master, she would. It was the least she could do.

She could still feel the old man, for he would always be her master, no matter whom he gave her to. She had a newer bond with Devon, but the patterns of former masters would stay with her for as long as she lived. She could ignore these, though, and when Donal Chole had given her away, she had. She'd done the same with his grandfather. She didn't want to go back to her hive, which she would when all of her masters died, but she wanted someone to want her as more than a possession, someone who wanted her to stay with him for the entirety of his life—and who would at least ask her if she minded being handed on. She hoped Devon would do that when the time came, though she hadn't brought the matter up.

At least with him she could ask. He was the only one of her masters to give her permission to speak. Devon's father had been horrified when he'd found out, and he'd never spoken to her himself. Now he'd have to.

Airi soared down into the town, careful to watch for any other sylphs. There were none, and she hadn't sensed any as she approached. Battlers rarely had the inclination to hide, and she could only sense the ones at the castle.

Soaring around the ruins of the devastated town, she examined each of the people, searching until she found Devon's father. He sat at a small table outside the bakery, his hand shaking as he drank from a mug. *Donal,* Airi whispered into his mind, and the old man spat a gout of cofi across the table before looking in shock at the shimmer of atmosphere she created.

"Airi?" he gasped, and looked around to make sure no one else saw. "Where's my son?"

Safe, she answered, able to speak to him in the same way she did Devon. *We're heading to a town in the north. Is anyone following us?*

Discreetly, the old man shook his head. "No. The man with the battler asked me questions, but he went back to the castle."

Airi shivered with both happiness and grief. The battler had to be dead after all, if they'd given up. Still, that meant Devon wasn't in danger. Airi felt sorry for Solie, though.

What of Solie's aunt and father?

"Safe, both of them." Donal looked uncomfortable at having to speak with her.

Thank you, she said, but Devon's father waved his hand, obviously not wanting any more attention. Airi rose up, heading back toward her master and content that she could tell him they all were safe. He and Solie couldn't go home, she didn't doubt that, but no one would be searching for them. They could go to the Community after all.

She flew back, fighting the air currents this time, but she was in no rush, and Devon wasn't so far away—not the way she could move. She danced as she returned to him, twisting as she went to her memory of his music.

Chapter Twelve

Sometime before dawn, Leon went quietly down the stairs of his house, his gear thrown over his shoulder. Betha followed, carrying a lamp. She'd been pleased to see him, and he knew she was disappointed that he was leaving again so soon, but there was nothing to be done and she knew that.

He let her walk him to the door and set his gear down while a servant hurried out to saddle his horse.

"Come home soon," Betha told him. "We miss you."

"Soon as I can," he replied, kissing her softly, and took the lamp. "I have to get Ril."

Leaving her, he went quietly up the stairs to the nursery. All four girls were asleep in their beds, their breathing soft in the large room. Leon held the lamp down low and made his way to his eldest daughter's bed. She was curled asleep on her side, Ril nesting on the pillow beside her head. The battler wasn't asleep. He looked up at Leon and his eyes glowed.

"Come on," Leon whispered, lowering his fist. "Don't wake her." Silently, the bird edged himself up and onto his arm. Lifting him, Leon crept out of the room, his girls never stirring.

He took Ril downstairs and outside to where Betha stood next to his horse. Their servant held the gray's reins, yawning and rubbing his eyes. Leon's gear had all been tied behind the saddle.

"Thanks," he told the servant, and kissed his wife again.

Finally he mounted and guided the horse out through the gate, sending it trotting toward the castle.

It was only a five-minute ride, and when he entered the courtyard, he wasn't terribly surprised to see no sign of Jasar or Mace. "Great," he muttered. Turning his horse in a large circle, he waited, but there was no sign of the man. "Ril. Go wake His Lordship up."

Ril looked at him for a moment, then grudgingly spread his wings and flew up to the second floor of one of the towers. Leon suspected he was tracking Mace. At last the bird settled on a windowsill and shrieked into the room so loudly that Leon suspected they could hear it all the way back at his manor. He prayed the screech hadn't woken the king. A moment later, he hoped it hadn't woken Lizzy and the girls, especially not the baby. Betha didn't need to deal with that.

Ril had definitely woken someone. The battler leaped off the windowsill, barely flying out of the way of a large, mailed fist that shot out at him. Leon hid a smile. Mace wouldn't have attacked without a direct order. At least Jasar was awake now.

Ten minutes later, a servant in livery came out, sniffing imperiously as he walked over and bowed. "Lord Jasar Doliard of Sialmeadow sends his regrets, but he will not be able to join you for several more hours. He needs his morning constitutional."

Leon leaned down from his horse. "Tell Lord Jasar that if he isn't out here in five minutes, I'll send Ril to bring me back his balls. The rest of him can stay behind."

On his shoulder, Ril made a cackling sound. The servant blanched and bowed before hurrying off.

It took another ten minutes before Jasar appeared in a dressing robe, Mace following along behind, and the courtier was livid when he did. Accompanied by the loathing of their battlers, the two men glared at each other.

"How dare you!" Jasar snarled. "Do you know who I am?"

"I know exactly who you are," Leon snapped. "Now get your gear or mount your horse dressed like that. I don't care which."

"I'm not going anywhere until I'm ready!"

"You want that battler to get away?" Leon shouted. "You want to explain that to the king? Get your gear!"

Jasar was livid, his face red and splotchy. Leon had made his point, though, and the other man turned, screaming obscenities to a servant and ordering him to get his horse and supplies. He stormed off to get dressed, Mace following.

He didn't reappear for another hour, and by then Leon was nearly in a rage. The sun was well above the horizon, and at this rate they wouldn't find the trail anytime in the near future. To make it worse, Jasar was decked out in an entirely inappropriate outfit of lace and velvet, with high boots and an ornate cloak that wouldn't keep him warm at all when wet.

The courtier glared at Leon and mounted his horse, a delicate mare that didn't look to have any stamina. Mace, under his direction, took up the lead tether of a second horse piled high with supplies. Leon had never seen such a thing, but he also didn't care. Turning his gray, he rode forward, leaving Jasar to follow, which happened with a lot of cursing. Apparently the man thought he was supposed to be in charge. Leon had no intention of putting up with that, not after that farce with the pirates.

They rode out of the city, heading for the village where Ril had fought the rogue battler; Leon hoped to find the sylph's trail where he'd lost it at the river. But they'd only ridden for twenty minutes before Jasar called the first break.

"Are you insane?" Leon thundered. "We just started!"

"I'm tired!" Jasar snapped back. "And this saddle is hard!"

"Are you a man or a woman?" Leon shouted. "We are *not* stopping now!"

"You don't command me, commoner!"

Leon raised his arm, furious. "Ril!" The battler spread his wings, hissing.

"M-Mace!" Jasar stammered, yanking uselessly on his horse's reins. The massive sylph stepped before him, eyes on Leon.

"Do you really want to find out who has the stronger battler?" Leon asked, disgusted. "And do you want to find out what I'll do to you while they're testing each other out? You will stop whining and follow me. I may be stuck with you, but I won't let you screw up my mission. Is that clear, *my lord?*"

Jasar stared at him, his bottom lip trembling. He finally turned away. "Fine. You're the supposed expert."

"Good." Leon spun his horse and kept riding.

Jasar wouldn't have ordered Mace to attack. Not while there was the slightest chance he'd lose. Leon looked at his battler, though, his order to Ril unspoken but clear: watch them.

The bird glared in return, but his hate faded for a moment in agreement. Turning on Leon's shoulder, he perched staring back, never blinking. Jasar started whining about it soon after, but Leon didn't reply.

They arrived at Otalo close to noon. Leon saw the old man he'd questioned and the girl's aunt, both outside the bakery and staring at them in horror, but he didn't bother to speak to either; he had the information he needed from them. Leading the courtier and accompanied by the two battlers, he rode quickly through the suddenly silent town and up into the woods. At the edge of the cliff above the river he dismounted, staring around at the place where he'd lost the battler.

Damn. The trail was easy to find. The battler had been hiding in a crevice just below the edge of the cliff, and he'd left plenty of signs as he climbed back up. The sylph's tracks now led north, with no attempt to hide them.

"I have his trail," he announced, grinding his teeth. As he rose and returned to his horse, he thought briefly of sending Ril ahead, but he wasn't sure just what his own sylph would find of the other battler.

"Wonderful," Jasar said, astride his horse and staring at nothing, a handkerchief held to his nose as though he smelled something rotten. Leon rolled his eyes and remounted. With luck, they'd find the battler quickly and get this over with. Then he could get rid of this deadweight.

He put his heels to his horse and rode slowly into the woods, leaning over his saddle and staring close at the ground in order to read the fugitive's tracks. Jasar sighed and followed, Mace trailing behind with the packhorse.

Galway came out of the mercantile with a heavy pouch of coins, his furs having fetched a good price, and found that his new companion had taken off. Eyebrows raised, he looked up from where his two horses were still tethered, along the road that led to the fork to Para Dubh and the Shale Plains. The boy had been vociferous that they waste no time in town, but surely he hadn't started walking again, had he? Galway had planned to get him some shoes and a cloak, and to have the doctor look at him. The boy hadn't looked injured, but it was obvious he was sick. Was he stupid, too?

Apparently he was, the trapper mused as he untied his horses and mounted up. He couldn't let the boy make his own decisions, not in this apparently senseless frame of mind. The boy reminded Galway all too much of himself when he was young, full of attitude and idiocy. He needed someone older than him to bash him on the head and save him from himself. Galway was lucky enough to have had someone do that for him, and he'd always intended to return the favor.

Amused by how the young were always so determined everything should happen *now*, he turned his horse and sent it at an easy trot northward, the packhorse trailing along behind. He had a full pouch of money, and his traps were all checked. He had some free time. He'd originally planned to head home and see the wife and family, but they were used to him being gone. He could do a little mentoring, maybe come home with another kid for his wife to raise. It wouldn't be the first time.

The boy had gone farther than Galway expected, slogging along the road with bare feet and in a thin tunic, leaning heavily on his makeshift staff. He was already past the fork that would lead around the Shale Plains to Para Dubh. Thank the gods. Only fools went through the plains themselves.

Galway saw the kid's shoulders stiffen stubbornly as he rode up behind, and he slowed his horse to a walk beside him, looking ahead. There wasn't much to see, only scrub trees and rocks. The clouds overhead were heavy, the air cold enough to threaten snow.

"Nice day," he commented, resting one hand on his leg while he held the reins with the other.

Heyou ignored him, glaring straight ahead as he walked.

"Looks like it might snow, though," Galway continued. "Get right cold tonight. The plains are especially bad with all that arctic air coming down through the mountains. You thought of that? What with the bare feet and all?"

Heyou's lip twisted, and the boy glared at him with almost as much loathing as Galway had seen from his sixteen-year-old son. "Go away!" he snapped. "Or I'll kill you!"

"With what?" the trapper asked reasonably. "That stick? I think it'd need to be thicker."

"Don't you know what I am?" Heyou growled. He looked to Galway as though he was about to cry. "I'm dangerous! Go away! I don't want your help!"

"Well, you might say you don't need my help, but I think you do, and I'm used to danger. How about I give you a ride, since we seem to be going in the same direction?"

Heyou trembled, trying to speed his walk, though he clearly didn't have the energy to keep it up. Galway maintained the pace easily, waiting for the boy to wear himself out. He doubted it would take long. The kid was a mass of anger and emotions all spinning out of control. He'd crash soon.

"Get lost," Heyou told him venomously. "Die horribly, you bastard! Don't you get it? I don't want you near me! I hate you!" He stumbled, barely catching himself with his staff. His face was now more white than red.

Galway had seen enough. "Well, I don't hate you." Edging his horse closer, he reached down and grabbed the boy's arm, pulling him bodily up onto the saddle and wrapping his cloak around him. Heyou shuddered, trying to punch him, but Galway held him close enough that the kid couldn't get leverage.

"Why do you have to be so damn nice?" Heyou sobbed, giving in at last.

"Because you'll die if I leave you out here, and not everyone in the world is an asshole." He couldn't take the kid back home yet, not if he was going to get through to him. The boy wanted to go north, so for now he'd go north. Iyala would understand.

Galway kneed his horse into a canter, just to show Heyou they could move faster if he stopped fighting, and the boy finally sagged against him. It was probably just exhaustion, but that was a start. They cantered north, and the miles slid away behind them. Where they were going didn't matter, not yet. Just that Galway was willing to take him where he wanted would have to be enough. There wasn't anything in the Shale Plains, after all.

He was very surprised when he was proven wrong.

Chapter Thirteen

Twenty miles beyond the town where they'd met Cal, the forest ended and the ground started to slope, the path heading downward toward a plain formed of rock and shale, dotted by tiny lakes. Great mountains loomed in the far distance, covered by snow. Solie reclined on the wagon seat between Devon and Cal, staring. The horizon looked desolate and cold, lifeless. It was no wonder the king didn't bother with this land. It didn't seem as though anyone could survive here.

Ahead the road dipped, descending but not looking any better than it had through the woods. In fact, the path looked as though it disappeared completely somewhere on that plain, no one having bothered to push it any farther.

The wagon was heavy and the horses old, but with the help of the sylphs, they would likely be able to cover another ten miles before dark. Solie looked up at the clouds and hoped it wouldn't snow. It was cold enough as it was, and she dreaded the wagon's getting stuck.

"How long will it take us to get to the Community?" she asked.

"About four days, if we make good time," Cal answered. "We used to have a town built in a valley northeast of here. We'd worked the land enough that it was fertile again, and we had crops coming in. Pretty good place. Where it was, the valley walls blocked the wind. There were some really old paintings on some of the rocks there, too. We don't know who did them, but they're ancient. Horses and deer and stuff."

"Where are your people now?" Devon asked.

"Oh, sorry." Cal shook his head, recalling himself. "The message said they were at the bluff. It's this cliff with one side that's really sheer. Some of us think it was made to be that way, but no one's really sure why. No one can get to you from the front without sylphs, and the other side slopes down enough that you can drive a cart up. Kind of steep, and there's no water source for a couple of miles, but it's more defensible. I guess they're kind of thinking that way right now. You can see for absolute miles from the top. They'll know we're coming long before we get there."

Solie sighed, wondering what it would be like when they arrived, or if the Community had already moved on. She supposed they'd send another message if they did . . . ?

She rubbed her temples. Her head was aching, and her heart, since she couldn't stop thinking about Heyou. Even sillier, she kept looking behind her as though he was about to come charging out of the woods in pursuit. She looked back again, just to see, and Devon put a hand on her shoulder.

"Are you all right?" he asked, in an undertone so Cal couldn't hear.

"I . . . can't stop thinking about Heyou," she confessed. "I barely knew him, but it hurts."

"Yeah." He squeezed her shoulder. "They say when you lose a sylph, or they're taken away . . . I'm sorry, Solie."

She bit her lip. "Does it get better?"

"My father said it did, after he gave Airi to me. Eventually."

She looked away again, not wanting to talk about it. At least Devon and Airi were safe and they knew no one was following them. They all could go to the Community and make new lives.

Maybe they had a postal service there and she could get Devon to write a letter to her aunt, explaining everything.

More likely she'd have to borrow Airi to carry it. Solie sat quietly, trying to think of what she'd write, but she couldn't get past explaining Heyou. Biting her lip, she stared at her hands, finding it easier not to think of anything at all.

Galway cantered his horse easily along the road out of the forest and onto the slope leading down to the plain. What he saw made him raise one eyebrow with interest. Far ahead, a wagon traveled slowly, its yellow wheels brilliant against the gray shale.

"I'll be damned," he muttered. The boy was actually following someone. Not that he would have caught up without help. Also, provided there was a girl on that wagon.

He nudged the boy, who had fallen asleep again after swearing at him with an appalling lack of skill. "Hey, Heyou. Look at this."

Heyou stirred, sitting up slowly and blinking. Galway had to put a hand on his head and turn it in the right direction, pointing past the boy until he woke up enough to realize what he was supposed to see.

Heyou saw, and nearly fell off the horse trying to get to her. Galway barely caught him and had to put him in a bear hug to keep him from spooking his horse into throwing them both.

"Calm down!" he shouted. "You're going to land on your head!"

"Please!" Heyou gasped, reaching out for her. "Solie! Please!" He looked up at Galway, his eyes desperate and unguarded for once. "Please take me to her!"

Boys and girls. They never changed. Galway hid his amusement, knowing Heyou would be deeply offended, instead urging his horse faster. Heyou stretched taut in front of him, staring forward and so tense that he was nearly vibrating. Galway decided not to point out that the wagon might not have the girl the boy was looking for. After all, he hadn't expected to find anyone out here at all. Even he didn't come out this way. No one did, and the road ended only five miles out. Galway didn't have any idea how they expected to continue on after that.

The horses continued smoothly, able to keep the pace for hours, and so they gained on the wagon. Galway made no attempt to hide their approach, yet they came very close before they were spotted. Less than a mile away was the first time he saw the wagon's occupants moving and looking back, and then one figure stood up, a figure with long, flowing hair that he could see even from where he was.

"Solie!" Heyou screamed. "*Solie!*"

Distantly, Galway heard her shout the boy's name in return, and he grinned. He'd always loved happy endings.

Heyou thought he'd go insane. He could see Solie, could hear her shouting his name, and he felt a mad gratitude to the man who held him that was horrendously confusing. Males were *bad*. Every instinct said so, but this man had kept him alive and now brought him back to his queen.

The horses cantered forward, not moving nearly fast enough. Heyou saw Solie jump down from her wagon, running back toward them with her arms outspread. Heyou nearly whimpered, and when Galway finally pulled his horse to a stop with her beside them, he slithered down off the animal and into her arms. Unable to hold his weight, she tumbled to the ground with him on top.

Solie landed awkwardly on her back, a stone digging into a rib and Heyou's weight crushing her, but she didn't care. He was alive, he was really alive, and he was warm and kissing her and she didn't care anymore who saw them.

She kissed him back, hugging him tightly and crying, so relieved that she couldn't do anything other than embrace him and weep. She could feel his mind, his absolute joy, and that only made her cry harder. He just kept kissing her, pressing his lips against her mouth, her cheeks, her eyes, her neck . . .

Devon walked slowly over to the two, happy on one level to see the battler alive, but also badly frightened by his existence. Airi pressed against his back, her chill a sign of agreement. The man who'd brought Heyou dismounted, and he stared at Devon with placid eyes. Devon couldn't figure out how he could be so calm.

"Galway," he said, holding out his hand.

"Devon." They shook. "You found him?"

"Yep." Galway looked down at the pair and laughed. "Found him freezing to death in the woods. He said he was following a girl. I guess he was. Glad to see he was right. He's a stubborn one."

Devon gaped. "Stubborn?"

"Yeah. Bit of a temper, too, but I figured he had a good side somewhere."

Devon stared at the battler. Were they talking about the same person? From Solie's reaction, this had to be Heyou, but he couldn't feel any aura of hate from the sylph at all. Solie had said he didn't hate her, but this . . .

Considering the sylph currently had his tongue down her throat, Devon realized there was likely no hate involved at all.

Cal walked over, looking bemused. "That's Heyou?"

"Apparently," Devon said.

"I thought he was dead."

"So did I."

"Dead?" Galway asked. "Is that why he got left behind?"

Devon hesitated, not sure what answer to give, but Cal beat him to it. "Yeah. He was supposed to have been killed by a battler. I don't know how he could have got away. I can't imagine facing one of them. I think I'd piss myself immediately and start begging for mercy, though I doubt that would work. That's what I would have done if I'd been there when those two attacked the Community."

The man really couldn't keep a secret. Devon shot him a look, but Galway didn't seem surprised. He looked so laid-back that Devon doubted he would be shocked by anything, including the news that he'd rescued a battle sylph.

"Community?" Galway repeated. He looked at the heavily laden wagon and out at the barren landscape. "Guess you're heading there. Think I'll tag along for a while. I feel kind of responsible for the boy. I'd like to make sure he gets where he's going this time."

There was something very absolute in the man's words, and Devon recognized the reprimand. As far as Galway was concerned, they'd abandoned a youth to die alone, and he was going to personally make sure it never happened again.

Not knowing how he could ever tell him the truth, Devon nodded. "Good to have you."

Cal opened his mouth and then closed it again, apparently realizing that this man perhaps didn't meet the requirements the Community sought in recruits. "Um . . . ," he said, "I don't know that you'd like to come. We're going a long way, and it's not a really nice journey, and we're not going anywhere that's nice to see."

"That's fine," Galway replied. "I'm coming anyway." Turning his back on both men, he walked over to where Heyou and Solie seemed determined to suffocate each other with their passion and grabbed the battle sylph by the back of his tunic, yanking him right up off the girl. "Come on, you, there's time enough for that later."

Devon yelped out loud, tensing to run before the battler blew his top. From the look of shock on her face, Solie was feeling the same, and Heyou's expression would have been comical if Devon hadn't seen the devastation caused by his fight with Ril. There was no explosion, though, and Heyou was set on his feet, where he swayed until Galway put a hand on his back.

"You don't want to give her whatever you're sick from, anyway," the man added.

"You're sick?" Solie gasped, scrambling to her feet. Heyou smiled, moony eyed, and shrugged.

Devon took a deep breath. He didn't like this. "Can I talk to them alone for a minute?" he asked.

Galway shrugged. "Sure." He led his horses over toward the wagons. Cal blinked and followed, talking apparently about why it was a good idea for the man not to come along.

Devon braced himself and looked at the girl and the battler, hoping he could get some answers without angering Heyou. He didn't know how Galway had managed to survive.

Solie looked up at him uncertainly, her arm around Heyou. The sylph stood with his head resting on her shoulder. He looked very tired.

"I thought you died," Devon told him quietly. "We all did. We never would have left you if we knew you were alive."

The battler raised his head and glared, but the expression didn't last long and he buried his face against Solie again. "I hid," he told them softly. "When it was safe, I followed my queen."

"I knew," Solie breathed. "I don't know how, but I knew. I knew you were alive." He pulled away and smiled up at her again.

Devon frowned. "Why did it take you so long to catch up? And why are you, um . . ."

"Not scary?" The battler sighed. "I think I'm dying." When Solie gasped, he pressed himself against her again. "But I'm happy."

"How can you be happy if you're dying?" she wailed.

"I'm with you."

Solie stared at Devon with heartbroken eyes and he had to look away. He didn't know how to save a dying battler. He didn't know anything about sylph health. They didn't get sick! "Airi?" he asked. "Can we do anything?"

Not us.

He sighed and shook his head. In human form and without that aura of hate, Heyou didn't look like a battle sylph at all, just a sickly boy. "Let's not tell anyone he's a battler, okay?" Solie nodded, tears in her eyes as he added, "I don't know how any of these people would react. Come on."

He helped them walk over to the wagon. Heyou was leaning heavily on Solie. Devon wasn't sure if that was because of his condition or if he just wanted to get close to her. The pair climbed up in back, and Solie wrapped Heyou in blankets.

Devon got up on the front seat with Cal, and the wagon started off, Galway riding easily behind. Devon blew out a breath and tried not to look at the two lovebirds behind him, but he couldn't help wondering what all of this meant.

Solie lay in the wagon on top of the blanket covering Heyou. He was pillowed by a bag of rice and staring joyfully at her, his hand cupping her face.

She couldn't stop touching him either, stroking his hair and cheeks while he made a bizarre, almost purring sound. He was alive! Some strange emptiness in her was full again. Her battle sylph was with her, and she could feel how happy he was. She had to wipe tears away, and leaned over to kiss him.

"I missed you," she whispered. She didn't understand this bond between them, but she didn't want to deny it anymore either. He was hers, for as long as both of them lived.

Heyou smiled at her, his face pale. "I missed you too."

"What happened to you?" she asked. The wagon went

over a heavy bump, and he winced. Solie bit her lip worriedly.

"He was older than me," Heyou admitted. "I thought I could beat him since he was locked into one shape, but he destroyed me instead." He looked away for a moment. "He would have killed you."

"Devon and Airi saved me," she told him. "You were very brave. I never would have escaped without you." He smiled happily again. "But you're not going to die, are you? You can't mean that." Her voice cracked. "You just found me again."

"I don't know," he mourned. "He hurt me. . . . I just . . . I'll try."

Solie bent her head, pressing her forehead against his. He put an arm around her neck, and it weighed heavily on her shoulders. "Just don't die," she told him. "You're not allowed to die, got it? We'll get to the place we're going in three days."

"Yes, my queen."

"Good." She kissed the end of his nose and smiled. "I can't be your queen if you leave me."

"Then I'll never leave," he promised. "Not ever."

Chapter Fourteen

For once in his life, Leon was in perfect agreement with his battle sylph: Jasar Doliard really needed to die. And even though he was the man's battler, Leon suspected that Mace would agree.

Busy trying to follow tracks through the heavy woods, Leon kept his eyes focused on the ground and tried really hard to ignore the man riding behind him. It was next to impossible. Jasar whined nonstop. He wanted to take breaks, he wanted to ride slower, he wanted to ride faster, he wanted cooked meals, he wanted quick snacks. He wanted to stop well before dusk and go again long after dawn. If it weren't for Mace, Leon would have gutted him long ago and buried the body.

He even yelled at his battler, berating Mace constantly, which struck Leon as one of the stupidest things anyone could ever do. A battler at the best of times radiated an aura of hate that was draining to everyone around them. A pissed-off battler was a thousand times worse. Mace walked behind them, leading the packhorse and exuding a loathing strong enough to nearly wilt leaves. Leon had a desperate headache from it, and even Ril seemed affected. They were only on the second day of their travel and were still stuck in the woods, trying to track a battler in human form. It should have been easy, but Leon was in so much pain he could barely focus. The battler had been picked up by someone on horseback—he'd been able to figure that much out—but he couldn't figure out who would. It didn't make any sense, but he was sure he was following the right track.

They headed north, toward a rough town that serviced the trappers and lumbermen that worked the area. The battler had to have hooked up with one of those. But why would he? How badly hurt was he?

Behind him, Jasar was shrieking something at his battler about having a smaller penis, which was so absurd that Leon finally spun, nearly shaking Ril off his shoulder. The battler dug hard into his shoulder guard, making Leon wince and souring his mood ever further.

"Will you stop it?" he shouted. "I doubt your battler even has a dick! Stop comparing it to your own!"

Jasar's face tightened, his anger obvious. Mace walked past both humans, sullenly leading the packhorse.

"You don't know anything," the dandy told Leon coldly.

"I know you're driving me insane. Stop angering Mace. He's giving me a headache."

"Can't take it?" Jasar sneered. "So much for the king's head of security. Can't even take a little battler hate."

Leon shook his head in amazement. "How did you ever get a battler? I'm amazed no one smothered you in your crib."

"You better make sure no one stabs you in your sleep," the courtier retorted.

Leon snarled, and Ril screamed from his shoulder. He knew his battler had little fondness for him, but the sylph definitely seemed to hate Jasar more. Leon actually felt sorry for Mace, and so angry he didn't care what he said to Jasar. The dandy couldn't do much to him, anyway, not with Ril around.

"You are an idiot," Leon snapped. "And a sick bastard. I bet you enjoyed killing that woman to get Mace in the first place."

"And you didn't? I bet you loved it."

"I still have nightmares! I never would have done it if I'd had any choice!" Leon shouted. "But *you* got sent out here to make my life hell because you can't get enough of killing women!" He'd heard about the girl, beaten for whatever twisted reason Jasar had contrived to kill someone who couldn't defend herself. He'd never met such a coward. Even having Mace he was one, and a bully besides.

"Shut up!" Jasar shouted. His battler kept walking, never looking back. "Mace! Get back here!"

Turning, the battler returned, bringing with him his loathing.

Two hours later they reached the town, and even though it was only midafternoon, Leon was glad of the chance to stop. His head was pounding worse than ever, and his stomach felt sour. He missed his family so badly he felt ill, and he truly wanted to kill his companion.

Jasar was distinctly happy to see the town, not that anyone in it was happy to see him. The two battlers were in such a foul mood they cleared the streets before they were even within sight of the place, and Leon and Jasar rode down empty streets to the only place of lodging.

"They call this an inn?" Jasar said in disgust.

Leon ignored him, dismounting from his horse and carrying Ril inside. Men who had been hiding inside stared in horror as he entered and pointed at the barkeep. "I want a room as far away from that asshole outside as you can get me, and someone to take care of my horse. I want food as well, in my room. Now." He stomped wearily toward the stairs, and a frightened woman in an apron scurried ahead to lead the way.

"F-follow me," she stammered, holding up her skirts as she climbed.

Leon followed. She was a pretty young thing, a little thin but kind faced. Right now, she also looked terrified, shooting looks back over her shoulder at Ril.

He glanced at the battler. "You're scaring her." One

golden eye turned toward Leon and the hate faded, at least from him. Mace was still in a cranky mood, but he was outside, and the girl relaxed a bit, staring at Leon with wide eyes.

"He obeys you?" she gasped.

"He does when I give him no choice," Leon admitted. The girl giggled and coughed, trying to look demure again. Ril tilted his head to one side and Leon had to stifle a laugh. At least his headache was fading.

The girl led him to a room at the end of a hall. It was a plain chamber, clean and serviceable. She went to open the window, and Leon settled Ril on the back of a chair. The battler watched, his aura now as calm as when he was around the Petrule family. The girl turned to see him watching her and she started, but there was no real fear there.

"Not so scary, is he?" Leon asked. He stepped forward and handed over a penny. "For your time." He paused, his fingers still holding the coin in her palm. "My companion, the one with the big battler: warn your friends to avoid him. He's very . . . unkind."

The girl blinked and curtsied. "Thank you for the warning, my lord."

"I'm not a lord. But he is." Leon looked at Ril again. "If the man . . . pushes any issue, tell your friends to shout the name Ril as loudly as they can. Help will come." He looked straight at the battler. "Understood?"

"Yes, my lord," the girl said, and the bird nodded once.

Leon sent her out and sat heavily on the bed, resting for a moment before he pulled off his boots and set them aside. They were scuffed. He'd have to polish them again to keep them waterproof. He wanted to check his gear as well and make sure everything was fine. He didn't trust his usual thoroughness when he'd been subjected to the muddling auras of the recent journey.

"No hate?" he asked Ril. "I figured you'd let me have it

once she was gone." He lifted his head and glanced at the battler. The bird stared back at him with one golden eye, unblinking.

"What? You hate Jasar so much now that I'm looking better by comparison?"

The battler blinked once.

"Is that a yes?" Leon ran a hand through his hair, then muttered, "I must be tired if I'm asking questions you can't answer."

He thought of the battler they were tracking, who was allowed to speak—his female master didn't know to order him against it. Leon looked at Ril again. "How the hell did that happen anyway? I know you can't answer, I'm just thinking aloud. How did a woman end up with a battler, when it takes a woman dying to bring you bastards over? Why do you like women so much if you won't be bound by anything less than their deaths?"

Ril hit him with a blast of hate so strong that Leon flinched back with a cry of pain. The battler was shrieking at him, he realized, screaming so loud that the window threatened to break. Somewhere in the inn, Jasar screamed for Ril to shut up before he sent Mace after them.

Leon lay on his back across the bed, pressing both hands to his forehead to try and hold in the massive migraine. Ril had never done that before. Leon hadn't even known he could hit that hard. The battler was furious, though, and slowly Leon forced himself upright, peering at the bird through the spots the headache was causing in his vision. He'd always wanted Ril's affection and had thought sometimes he had it, in those moments when Ril seemed to forget that he was supposed to hate him. But this put the lie to any hope he'd had for that, and Leon felt a real grief in his heart at the thought.

Masters bonded to their sylphs as much as sylphs did to them, he knew, becoming in some ways closer to them than their own wives. Battle sylphs were supposed to be different, but he'd always known that wasn't true. Their masters just pretended it was, because of the hate and the deep sorrow it brought. At least, it brought sorrow to Leon to know that Ril hated him.

"What did I say to piss you off so badly?" he whispered.

Wings spread, Ril clung to the chair and hissed.

A faint, frightened knock sounded at the door. "M-my lord?" a female voice called. "I brought your meal."

Leon sighed. Ril had never given him any answers about anything. "Come in," he called.

The door opened, and the same serving girl peered in. As Ril suppressed his hate, she entered, carrying a plate and mug on a tray. She placed this on the table and laid everything out before turning and curtsying, her head down. "M-my Lord? My father runs the inn. He wanted me to ask how to calm the other battler down. He's in the stable, but he's frightening everyone."

It was just like Jasar to leave his battler outside and himself open to assassination. Leon just wished someone would take him up on it. "What's your name, miss?" he asked.

"Sally, my lord."

He walked over and took both of her hands in his own. "Well, Sally, if you want Mace to calm down, wait until his master is in his room and then go up to Mace and tell him he's frightening you. I bet he'll stop."

"M-me, my lord?"

"Only you. Not your father, not your brothers. You." He stood and walked toward the food.

"Thank you, my lord."

As Sally fled, Leon sat down to his meal, deciding to let everything else wait until later.

His suggestion in mind, Sally went outside and around to the stables, her apron twisted in her hands. Her father had immediately latched on to the direction that *she* go, as none of the others wanted to, and no one dared face the sylph's master. He'd thrown his meal at another serving girl, and they didn't know what they were going to feed him. She just felt lucky that she'd been assigned to the nice one. If only she didn't need to do this, too.

The hate coming from the stable was palpable, and it took all of her courage and fear of her father's switch for her to step inside. "Mr. Mace?" she whispered.

To her surprise, the hate turned off instantly.

Sally moved forward, nervous, intending to explain, just in case it was necessary. "Mr. Mace?"

The battle sylph stepped out of the shadows in an open stall to look at her, and she swallowed. He was huge, his eyes pinpoint lights glowing out of his helm. But without the hatred, he wasn't nearly as frightening. She pressed a hand against her breast and swallowed.

"My—my father asks that you not frighten us. I . . . you frightened me. Will you stop?"

Silently the creature nodded, and Sally exhaled, trembling. "Thank you," she breathed, then left, shaken for reasons that had nothing to do with fear.

She returned to the inn, still trembling, and finished her duties. But after everyone else had gone to bed, she returned to the stable, and didn't go back inside until shortly before dawn.

Stria the earth sylph worked furiously, drawing up the ground and flattening it, propelling along through this mad cycle the slab of stone holding Cal's wagon and horses. The contraption raced at a tremendous thirty miles an hour, making the terrified riders cling to the wagon and forcing them to blindfold the hysterical horses.

Solie wailed in fear, clinging to the hand of Heyou in the back of the wagon. It was for him that they moved so fast, leaving a trail of ridged earth behind them as they moved, Airi fighting to keep the wind from blowing them off their platform. The earth sylph was much older, much stronger, and Airi trembled as she worked, the other sylph's quiet encouragement all that kept her from giving in to exhaustion. They'd been traveling this way since dawn, when Solie woke to find Heyou had nearly died during the night.

In the wagon, he could hear them speak, could feel the fear of the men and his own queen's terror. He couldn't rise, though. His energy levels had dropped too far for that, and he didn't have the strength to draw any more from Solie. He could only lie still and gasp, feeling himself slowly fail. Solie begged him to fight, but it was an order he couldn't obey. Ril had been far too precise with his blow.

She brushed some of his hair out of his face, the soft hair he'd made to please her. He gloried at her touch even as he grieved. He hadn't even been able to love her, to create that final link that would truly make her a queen of his hive line. He was a failure of a battle sylph, losing his first fight. He wasn't worthy of her.

"I'm sorry," he whispered.

She shook her head frantically. "Don't give up," she ordered him. "We're nearly there."

"I think we *are* there," Galway corrected, hanging on to the side of the wagon right beside them.

Solie straightened. The mountains had leaped in size as the group flew across the plains toward them, becoming tall peaks and cliffs. Straight ahead was a bluff, the edge that faced them sharp and perfectly straight, sheared off by some force she couldn't imagine. Stria was turning the wagon, though, propelling it around the hill toward the back. There, the sides were the easier slope of a regular hill, if covered in short, scraggly bushes and rock. A rutted switchback road led up it, shadowed by the hills and mountains behind.

In the flat stretches immediately around the strange hill, livestock grazed on bales of hay. Horses were tethered to long lines, while cattle and sheep were watched over by men huddled in cloaks against the cold and wind.

Stria continued to rocket the wagon along, passing frightened animals and their shocked tenders. Solie gawked at them as they shrank into the distance behind them, even though some of them gave chase.

Sylphs were suddenly all around them, beings of air and fire shouting in loud strange voices that they stop, Cal shrieking back that they were friends. Solie looked down at Heyou again, grasping his hand.

"We're here, Heyou. Hold on." In answer, his eyes closed. His breathing was slow. She could barely feel his presence. "Heyou?"

"We're here!" The platform with the wagon and horses reached the top of the bluff. There it slowed, coming to a stop before a gathering of tents, and domes of rock made by other earth sylphs. People were gathering despite the cold, all of them whispering and many of them armed.

Devon raised his hands as Galway leaped into the wagon and scooped Heyou into his arms, blankets and all. Solie scrambled to stay at his side as the trapper jumped down, carrying the limp battler but not sure where to go.

"We need help here!" he shouted. "Tell me you have a doctor!"

A man with thinning hair and an arm in a sling came toward them. "Who are you?" He looked at Cal. "What have you done?"

Cal started to stammer a reply.

"No arguing," Galway interrupted, walking with authority toward the new man. "This boy is dying." Solie looked fearfully at the stranger, praying he could help.

"I don't know that you can do anything—" Devon

started to say, his hands still raised, and Solie shot him a furious look. "I don't know that a doctor can help."

"Please," she begged, not caring how weak tears made her look. "Please save him if you can." She couldn't imagine not having Heyou's presence at her side or his emotions in her mind. Not anymore. He was an addiction she couldn't bear to lose.

The armed group of men started whispering. Women and their offspring were appearing, along with more sylphs than Solie ever could have imagined, many of whom took forms reminiscent of children.

One sylph in particular pushed forward, shoving through the crowd. She rushed toward Heyou, her form adult in size but as soft and featureless as a statue after a thousand years in the wind. Her eyes gleamed as she reached for him, and Solie could feel the power in her, just as she had sensed the potency of the battler who'd fought Heyou. This was different, though, not dangerous at all.

"Luck!" someone shouted. "Wait!"

The sylph ignored the order, grabbing Heyou. Dropping to her knees, she pulled him close, power already pouring forth. She'd felt his pain while he was still out on the plains, felt the air and earth sylphs bringing him. His aura was hidden from the others, concealing what he was, but she could feel it. A battler, a battler brought to her strange, adopted hive. A battler she was bound to heal. They were always healed first, even before the queen. They protected the hive, and this one had been attacked once already. With him they would have a battler of their own—a young one, but a battler still!

She felt where he'd been torn, his mantle ripped expertly so that his energy would leak out until he died, weakening him until he couldn't even feed anymore. The mantle was still there, though, and she labored to fix it, to knit the gaping wounds. She forced everything she had left into the battler's body, hearing her master wail behind her, but this would protect him as well, and he'd never been good at orders. She kept healing and fading, tying the other sylph's body back together even as her own broke down.

Solie watched in amazement as the female sylph glowed, her brilliant light spreading out over Heyou's insensate form. Everyone else fell silent, gathering in the frigid wind and watching as she healed him. Nothing happened that Solie could see, but everything that she could feel. Whatever tie it was that she had to Heyou, it all came back. She felt his sudden pain flare up and fade away, and his strength return. Wrung out, she went limp and slumped to her knees.

At last the Healer let Heyou go, her own form so faded that there was little left of her to see but the diminutive ball of energy she'd become. Shivering, that ball rose up and bobbed over to a frightened bald man, who held her tenderly in his hands and walked off toward the tents, taking cautious steps as everyone else got out of his way.

The man in the sling watched them go. Turning back to Solie's group with a heavy expression, apparently not pleased with what the healer sylph had just done to herself for a stranger, he growled, "Who are you?" The armed men closed ranks around him, flanked by their sylphs.

"Solie?"

She looked over to see Heyou sitting up, rubbing his head and glaring at the man, though his aura remained hidden. He looked tired, but she could feel confusion instead of pain, and she scooted toward him with a wail, throwing her arms around his shoulders. "Oh, Heyou!" she cried. "You're okay!"

Happy, he hugged her back, though his eyes never left the circle of armed men.

"Don't," she whispered. "Not if you don't have to." His arms tightened in acknowledgment.

"Don't know much about them just yet," Galway spoke up, answering the other man's question, "but I'm Galway, and that's Heyou sitting on the ground there. I'm a trapper from the woods on the Eferem side of the Shale Plains. Heyou I picked up in the woods. Supposedly he's with them." He nodded at Solie and cocked a thumb at Devon and Cal.

Devon looked at the group of armed men and slowly lowered his hands. "My name is Devon Chole and the girl is Solie. Heyou's with her. My air sylph is Airi. We're . . . well, we're on the run from the king. Cal said you'd have a place here for us."

Cal grinned nervously. "I did. Um, yeah. Really."

The man in charge looked over them all, and finally sighed. "Fine. Luck apparently vouches for you. For the time being, welcome to the Community. My name is Morgal. I'm the leader of the council we've set up here. You'll have to answer to me."

Cal blanched. "What happened to Nor and the others?"

"They died," Morgal said. "They drew the battlers away while the rest of us escaped. You know of the attack on us?" he asked the rest.

"No," Galway answered, even as Devon said, "Yes."

Morgal shook his head. "It was our fault," he admitted. "You may as well know, if you plan to stay here. We attacked a couple of Eferem ships to get enough supplies to make sure we survived the winter. It won't be happening again. We don't have much, but we'll find places for you, providing you're willing to work. Devon, your air sylph will be useful. The boy and the girl can help out with the chores. That'll keep them out of trouble. You—" He looked at Galway.

"I won't be staying long," the trapper told him. "Just came

to make sure the boy would be all right. Unless you have a problem with people leaving?"

"No." Morgal sighed. "We're not that strict. Just promise you won't tell anyone where we are. They'll find out about us soon enough anyway."

"I can do that." Galway shook Morgal's hand.

Solie hugged her battle sylph gratefully. "We're safe, Heyou. We can stay!"

"What are chores?" he asked.

Chapter Fifteen

As the sylphs were busy working to create a system to bring water to the top of a hill, where it had never been before, and to dig tunnels and chambers throughout its core so that the humans could escape the ever-present cold, much of the grunt labor of the camp fell to the youngsters, partly to take advantage of their energy and partly, as Morgal intimated, to keep them all out of trouble.

Eyes wide with absolute horror, Heyou picked up a rock, hefted it against his belly and duckwalked it over to the edge of the cliff, where he dropped it over the side, just like his fellow miserable prisoner.

"Are we done yet?" he whined.

The other, a pimply fifteen-year-old boy named Relig—to whom Heyou considered he'd been very generous by not making a single death threat—glared at him. "There's a whole pile's gotta go over before lunch, or the witch won't let us eat."

Heyou looked at the pile, which had to be at least the size of the entire world, and wished Solie hadn't made him promise that he'd keep hiding his real nature. Relig slouched off in the other direction, muttering something about the latrine as he passed the stone pile and vanished. Heyou immediately took advantage of the opportunity, grabbing a few dozen larger boulders and whipping them over the side from where he stood. He was just starting on the midsized ones when he sensed a male approaching. Immediately, he grabbed a rock in the traditional manner and started duckwalking it to the edge.

He'd realized, a little grudgingly, that males in this world weren't like those of his own. Galway had saved his life, after all, and Devon had saved Solie. Cal was an idiot, but the man had helped bring them all here. Heyou had decided he could afford a little leeway and forgiveness, especially if it made Solie happy.

Around the pile sauntered a boy who pretty much made Heyou want to give up on the whole idea of forgiveness and start mass killings again. Bevan was the leader of the local youngsters, whether they wanted him to be or not, and he was also their number-one tormentor. Heyou particularly hated him, even after only a few days. He wished he could show him he was a battle sylph.

"Hey, loser," the newcomer taunted, looking at the pile. "Is that the most you've moved? I could have got rid of all of it by now."

"Go away," Heyou told him.

Instead, the boy grinned. "Aw, are you afraid of me?"

"No."

"Liar." Bevan smirked, walking right up to him. He was a little taller than Heyou's current form, and, Heyou had been told, much less attractive.

"Solie says you're ugly," Heyou pointed out.

The boy blanched and his face turned red. "Do you want a punch in the mouth?" Behind him, Relig appeared, slouching back toward the rock pile, but when he saw what was happening he ran.

"Do you want to die?" Heyou retorted, his temper flaring. It threatened to leap out of control, but the memory of a battler in the shape of a bird and his own humbling failure forced him to control himself. Solie had told him to act human. She was the queen. This time he was going to listen to her, no matter what.

Bevan got right in his face, glaring belligerently. "You better watch who you get mouthy with," he warned.

Heyou dropped the rock he'd been holding on the bully's foot.

Bevan howled. A few seconds later, he and Heyou were having a wonderful fight, pounding on each other with their fists. Bevan couldn't actually hurt him, and it did wonders for Heyou's wounded self-confidence to get to beat on someone and actually win. He had Bevan's face down in the dirt, experimenting on whether humans could breathe with dirt up their nose, when he felt a familiar hand grab him by the back of his shirt and pull. A moment later, Galway regarded him evenly, his expression showing he was unimpressed.

"Did you see what I did?" Heyou asked happily. "I won!"

"I saw," the trapper answered, pulling him around so that they were both facing the other direction. A red-faced older woman in black stood there, so angry she was almost steaming. Heyou remembered her from that morning, when she'd put him on rock duty in the first place.

"Hi!" he said to her winningly. "Are you the witch?"

Solie was used to hard work, especially after growing up on a farm. Still, she'd rather hoped never to have to peel quite so many potatoes again. Sitting down before the fruits of her labor, she sighed and pulled her kerchief off. Along with the mashed potatoes, she had a single piece of bread and a few boiled carrots.

A boy sat beside her but was immediately yanked backward onto the floor. Heyou sat down beside her instead, carrying his own plate, which he immediately ignored in favor of beaming at her. "Hi!"

Solie grinned. He really was cute, and being around him made her heart beat faster. The bond between them just kept getting stronger the longer they were together, and she was getting better at feeling his emotions as well. Either that, or he was getting better at projecting them. Whichever it was, she found herself increasingly relaxed around him, enough for most of her earlier inhibitions to weaken. Maybe she could find somewhere to take him in order to try some of that kissing stuff again. But to do that, they had to escape the Widow Blackwell. The woman watched over all the orphan children, which was about two-thirds of them, and Solie had already heard horror stories about her.

"What have you been up to all morning?" she asked.

"I moved rocks," he told her. "Then I got to beat someone up. Then I got to dig feces out of a hole." He paused. "What's a feces?"

"You don't want to know. Did you wash your hands?"

He looked down at them in bemusement.

"Go wash your hands," she ordered, and he stood up, immediately heading out.

The three girls sitting on the other side of the table leaned forward, their faces shining. Each had something to say.

"He's gorgeous! Where did you meet him?"

"Are you betrothed?"

"I'd like to take him out behind the supply tent." This last comment drew silence from all of the girls, who glanced in surprise at the speaker. She looked to be two or three years younger than Solie. "What? Like you're not thinking the same thing?" She regarded Solie. "Have you gone there with him?"

Everyone turned to Solie in fascination.

Solie turned red. "I . . ." She'd thought about it, but how could she tell them that? Heyou wasn't human. She couldn't be with him! Could she? But she'd kissed him when he found her again, and she'd enjoyed it. And he wanted her so much. Every time he came near she found it harder to remember to say no.

"Oh, yeah," the third girl decided. "She's gone out there with him."

"No!" Solie gasped as the others dissolved into giggles. "I couldn't!"

"Why not? He's beautiful. I'm Loren. Your name is Solie?" The girl extended her hand.

Solie took it. "Yes. We just got here a few days ago."

"We noticed. It's kind of a small place. These are Mel and Aneala." She indicated the others.

"I heard he got into a fight with Bevan this morning," Mel said breathlessly. "He must be very brave."

"Yes," Solie agreed uncertainly. Heyou had mentioned something about that. At least he hadn't killed anyone.

"I heard Luck, the healer, let someone die to heal him," Aneala continued. "My cousin said Brev was going to be okay, but he died this morning because she was too weak to work on him after healing your boyfriend." She stared at Solie solemnly. "No one understands why she'd help a stranger before one of us. Brev was here for years."

Solie fought off horror. Stuck in the kitchen tent all day yesterday and again today, she hadn't heard any of this. By the time she'd got back to the sleeping tent she was sharing with several other girls, she'd just wanted to think about Heyou and actual slumber. "Wh-what?"

"Brev," Aneala repeated. "He was the blacksmith. He stayed behind to help fight off the battlers with his fire sylph. They killed her and nearly him. I guess they did kill him, since he died last night."

"Hey," Mel protested. "That's not Solie's fault. Luck went all crazy. Was her boyfriend supposed to die instead?"

"Tell that to Brev's wife."

Solie stared at the ground, disconsolate.

A moment later, Heyou plopped down beside her again, grinning. "I'm back!" he said. Then he picked up on her mood as his attention focused, reading her emotions. He glared at the other girls. "What did you say to her?" It wasn't quite a threat. He wouldn't threaten a woman.

"Nothing," Loren told him sweetly, while the other two blushed. Heyou glowered at her, able to read the lie, then turned back to Solie.

"It's okay," he told her softly, and leaned forward to kiss her shoulder. It sent wonderfully warm tingles through her and she actually gasped, dissolving the other three into a tizzy of giggles. Heyou took her reaction as an invitation and leaned closer, stroking her back as he leaned in to kiss her.

It seemed like a good idea, Solie thought. It really did.

Heyou froze a moment later as a wooden spoon came down on top of his head, hard. "Do I have to separate you two?" the Widow Blackwell snapped.

The Community, they learned, was made up of two hundred people from different villages and hamlets in the mountains of Para Dubh, all of them wanting more than the kingdom's peasant class was allowed. There were a lot of women and children—more than Devon had realized when he arrived—and an unfortunate number of them were widows and orphans. Before the attack, there had been dozens more men in the Community. Now all of them were lost, including their entire original leadership base.

There were also more sylphs than Devon had ever seen in one place, even after living in the barracks. Back home, they worked behind the scenes, usually invisible, and silent if seen at all. Even in the barracks they stayed invisible or in private rooms. Only the battlers were obvious. Here, there were no battlers, and the sylphs had no restrictions. They took shapes so varied that he couldn't identify what many of them were, though most adopted forms like strange little children—and all of them talked. They chattered like birds, most of them ignoring humans other than their own masters but gossiping among each other as they worked to turn the bluff into a serviceable home, doing the tasks to which humans weren't suited.

"Is this what you're normally like?" Devon asked his sylph, a little overwhelmed. A group of water and earth sylphs were digging a tunnel under the ground to bring water up the bluff. They looked like a group of giggling ten-year-olds, except they were brown or blue, made of water or dirt, and squealed like rabbits every time they succeeded at something. Their masters moved among them like schoolteachers, helping out whenever possible.

Yes, Airi told him happily. "It's a good hive." The last sentence she actually spoke aloud as she formed herself into the translucent shape of a long-haired girl. "I like it," she added.

Devon stared at her, amazed. He'd rarely seen her take solid form, and he'd never heard her speak aloud. She looked a lot like him, he noted, as though he could be her father or uncle. It was touching.

"Hive?" he asked her.

We live in hives back home, she continued. *There aren't any in this world, but with so many of us here we decided to make a hive of our own. I'm happy. I never thought of making an adoptive hive.*

"Then there aren't any adoptive hives back in Eferem?" he asked her, curious. He'd never thought to ask about where she'd come from. No one really did. It was thought by a lot of people that sylphs came from nothingness, or from hell. Why else would they cross the gate?

No. Too many rules. We're not allowed to talk to each other, so no one could share the idea even if they came up with it. . . . This is much nicer. Can we stay?

Devon looked around at the work being done to turn the bluff into a home. "Sure." Where else were they going to go?

Thank you! Airi vanished again, and he felt her winds sweep around him. *I do like it. And they like me. I feel welcome here. Everyone talks to everyone else.*

He looked toward where he knew she was, though she stayed invisible. "Does that include Heyou?"

No. He's still hiding. Battlers don't interact with us smaller sylphs much anyway. They're different. Maybe he'll want to be our battler, though, and protect us. That would make everyone feel better.

Devon wasn't so sure of that. He especially wasn't sure that the humans in Airi's new "hive" would be happy to find out there was a battle sylph among them. It seemed there wasn't a single family that hadn't lost someone to Ril and Mace's ambush, and so he doubted they would even welcome a young battler among them. His group's welcome could end very quickly if the battle sylph slipped up and revealed himself.

"Devon."

Still considering their welcome, he turned to see Galway walking toward him. The wind blew right through Devon, despite his warm cloak. Unlike Devon, the trapper didn't seem to feel the cold at all. "Interesting place, isn't it?" the man asked.

Devon nodded. "It is. I'm impressed with how much they've been able to do here so fast. When are you heading back?"

"Not for a few more days. Running the risk of getting caught by the snow, but I kind of want to see what this place turns into—and to make sure the boy is all right."

Devon's laugh was hollow. "I don't think Heyou needs guidance as much as you think he does."

"He's young. Youngsters always need someone to watch out for them." Galway looked back the way he'd come, farther down the slope. "Morgal said they were trying for a healer. Thought we could go watch."

The two headed down the hill. Its slope was barely noticeable for the first several hundred feet, then the drop became steeper, plummeting to the plains and requiring a switchback road to get any wagon up it. As a defensible place against humans, it was brilliant. Against battlers, nowhere would work.

Before Devon, an earth sylph stood next to her master, peering critically down at the ground. She glanced up at him and grinned hugely. A moment later, she dove into the earth and Devon felt it shake. A sinkhole appeared, and he and Galway paused, the sylph's master gesturing them back. The opening widened, growing twenty feet across, and then steps started forming, creating a stairway leading down. A fire sylph dove after the earth one, lighting the way down to a chamber being widened below.

Devon gasped. "What are you doing?" He'd known they were digging into the hill, but that hole was at least fifty feet deep.

"Making homes in the hill," the man told him. "An entire underground town. It was the sylphs' idea. It'll get us all out of this damned wind." He stepped back as a lid of stone rose up above the hole, bending over it and creating an archway entrance to the stairs.

They're making a physical hive, Devon realized, and was amazed. Airi ruffled his hair again, coming up behind him. *It'll be good*, she promised. *It'll be home*.

Providing a bunch of humans could stand to live like this. Shaking his head, Devon continued after Galway.

"Don't know how I'd feel about living in a hole in the ground," the trapper remarked, as if reading his thoughts.

"Me, neither," Devon admitted.

On the edge of the sleeping tents was a larger one. Galway led the way inside, and the two men found a huge, ornate circle drawn on the floor, a man in robes with horrible scars on his face standing above it. There was no altar, but a younger man stood in its center, looking at the chanting priest nervously. He wheezed as he breathed, holding his chest.

Morgal looked up as they came in, his fire sylph a glowing brand on the ground. "Welcome," he said quietly. He'd warmed to the pair since they'd come, either disinclined or too busy to harbor suspicions for very long.

Devon nodded. "What's happening?"

Morgal gestured to the youth. "Jes has breathing problems. We're hoping he looks like enough of a challenge to attract a healer."

The priest continued chanting and raised his hands, eyes closing, and the circle glowed dimly. The ritual was nowhere as grandiose as the few Devon had seen; it was stripped of nearly all its trappings. Still, a circle of nothingness opened above the boy, and he cringed, coughing.

Devon waited with the others against the tent wall, watching, but nothing happened. They stood silent for ten minutes until at last the priest dropped his arms and the glow faded from the circle. The gate closed.

"No healer today, I guess," said the priest.

Morgal sighed. "I can't say as I'm surprised. They rarely leave the hives, so few of them are wandering around to be attracted. When Ash told me one was near the gate, we hoped she'd take the bait. I suppose she was too busy to notice. Or a battler stopped her. Lucky thing *it* didn't try to come through."

"You know about their hives?" Devon asked, still reeling from his own recent revelation.

"Some. I know the sylphs here are creating one. It gives us all something to work toward, and going underground will make up for the fact that there isn't any cover from the weather here." The man nodded to them. "If you could go see Raseb at the foot of the hill, he should have some more work for you both—and for Airi. We need every air sylph we can get."

"No problem." Galway turned and headed out.

Devon followed more slowly. As he exited the tent, a distance away he saw a group of young people being herded by an older woman in black, he supposed to their next assignment. Heyou was among them, sidling up against a giggling Solie for a kiss every time the widow's back was turned. They looked like perfectly normal teenagers with their hormones way out of control. Devon took a deep breath and turned away. As a responsible adult, he should stop them from doing anything foolish. As an intelligent man, there was no way he was going to get between a battle sylph and what he wanted. He followed Galway instead.

Chapter Sixteen

Solie's bed was a straw tick in a tent shared by three other girls, blankets hung between their beds to give them each a bit of privacy. She was glad of that, for she lay upon it, biting her lip to keep from crying out as Heyou moved atop her. He had her nightshirt shoved up to her neck and licked her nipple, making her want to scream. Apparently, all her reservations were gone. As he moved contentedly from her one small breast to the other, she realized dazedly that in another minute she'd let him have her bloomers off.

Reading her emotions, Heyou could sense where each and every sensitive spot was on her body—and he was determined to find them all. He gently sucked on her breasts, feeling her shudder under him, then moved downward, kissing his way along Solie's belly. The bed rustled but he didn't care. The other girls were asleep, and his queen wanted him. Her desire had pulled him from his own bed on the other side of the bluff and into her tent with her. Now she was letting him become one with her.

Reaching the cloth she wore across her lower body proved only a mild distraction, but as he nuzzled lower, Solie made a strangled squeal, shuddering.

Outside the tent, Heyou sensed the Widow Blackwell making her rounds, checking on the youngsters in her charge. He looked over his shoulder in that direction, then turned back to his queen. He couldn't have her here—it wasn't safe. Instinct demanded security. Back home, this would be found in the center of the hive itself, other battlers guarding the doors. Here, he wouldn't enjoy that luxury.

"Come with me, Solie," he urged.

"Where?" she whispered.

"Somewhere no one will find us."

"O-okay," she managed after a few seconds. She let him pull her up.

They went out the back of the tent, Heyou leading her unerringly through the darkness. A few sylphs floated by but said nothing, and he took her to the edge of the cliff. Gasping, Solie backed away.

"It's okay," he promised, putting his arms around her. "I won't let you fall."

He let himself change for the first time since his fight with Ril, embracing her with his mantle and stepping off the side of the cliff. Solie clung to him, shivering as he flew her down to the plains below, well clear of the horses and livestock and the men who might be tending them, moving fast before she grew frightened enough to lose interest. Landing on the plain, he lowered her to a patch of soft sand, laying himself over her to keep her warm while kissing her neck.

"Where are we?" she gasped.

"Safe." They were. He couldn't sense anyone nearby.

Quickly, he pulled her shift up and off entirely, careful not to actually look at her, as she'd commanded, even while he nuzzled her breast and returned to her nipple. Solie looked down at him, her face soft in the dim light of the moon. "You can look at me," she whispered.

He did. She was beautiful.

Reverent, he pulled her bloomers off, and Solie shivered again, suddenly frightened. What was she doing? He was kissing her again, though, sucking the sensitive skin on her inner thighs, and she collapsed upon the sand. Did it really matter, propriety? They belonged to each other, and this felt too good to stop.

"Heyou," she whispered.

He licked and nibbled, sending hot fire up her legs, and all she could do was grasp his hair and shiver. He seemed not to mind, his kisses moving upward until he was lapping at the center of her, and she wailed, her entire body shaking. Everything felt like it was exploding inside of her, and he could feel it. She could *feel* him feeling it, and his enjoyment rocked her even more. She cried out, wailing into the darkness, and unconsciously pulled him against her.

At last the fire eased a bit and she was able to let go of his hair. Heyou nuzzled her contentedly and crawled up the length of her, shedding his own borrowed clothes as he went. "Solie," he whispered. "My queen."

Her body was warm, her heart pounding, and he lay against her, his legs fitting themselves perfectly between hers. She let him, still gasping in reaction. He moved himself, pressing against that core of her, and locked his gaze on hers, never looking away.

He pushed against her. For a moment there was resistance. Then he adjusted his size and slid in easily. She enclosed him, hot and damp.

"Oh, my god," she gasped, her face going white.

He was in her, in his queen! Overcome, Heyou kissed her and belatedly remembered to move, drawing himself out and carefully pushing back in, starting a rhythm that she slowly began to match. She began to cry out, making little whimpers of pleasure underneath him as her fingers clawed his back, pulled him against her.

She felt phenomenal. Heyou started to move faster, to push harder as her heat burned all around him and her hips lifted up so that their bellies smacked together. Ecstasy! He loved her, and his mind projected both that and his passion. In return, he felt Solie's mind and her wonder, and he accepted both and understood them, and in pure battler instinct he projected them.

She was no longer innocent. She was the queen, the sovereign of all, and in this ultimate act she took her place as the unassailable ruler of a hive in need of a leader. Heyou felt it, and as her chosen, he amplified the pattern of her. Solie was queen!

Every sylph within a dozen miles, and all those of Heyou's hive line, heard.

Up in the Community they answered Heyou's call, ignoring their startled masters' orders and gathered at the edge of the bluff, staring out at the night. A queen was being chosen, the mate of the battler, and sylphs who'd come from a dozen different hives now felt acceptance of their new queen just as they would have back home. Respectfully they gathered, though none went close enough to threaten the battler. They didn't need to, and even as their masters panicked, screaming calls to arms, they relaxed.

Airi herself found peace unlike any she'd expected since she first crossed the gate. There was a queen again, and with a queen and a battler, the hive was safe.

A hundred and twenty miles away, Mace turned suddenly. He stared northward across the Shale Plain, his eyes glowing. Jasar and Leon slept, but Ril looked at him with bored incomprehension.

Mace couldn't have spoken even if he was allowed. A queen! A queen of his hive line! He could feel her ascending with her chosen, and if he could have, he would have screamed and run to protect her. There was a queen! As the other battler projected her pleasure and the pattern of her mind into him, Mace accepted both, taking that pattern into his soul, making it his own. She became *his* queen and his link to this world, and he sighed blissfully, free in his heart, if not in his form. He looked down at Jasar. Not yet.

* * *

Solie cried out, overcome. She could feel Heyou's absolute joy as he moved against her, inside her, and she could feel her own, and she couldn't tell them apart or figure out who was pleasuring whom. It didn't matter. There was a fire building in her belly even hotter than before, and Heyou couldn't move fast enough. She clawed at his back, fingers tangling in his mantle as he became half-disembodied and half-human, pushing her repeatedly into the sand. She kissed him and was kissed in return, her body drenched in a layer of burning sweat.

The pleasure grew, and suddenly it was too much. She stiffened, her scream strangled and shrill. Heyou gasped and pushed into her a final time, shuddering and clinging. A moment later they both collapsed, shaken.

"Oh, gods," she breathed. That had been magnificent. Gently she put a hand against her lover's cheek and felt his happy little sigh. "Thank you."

"You're welcome," he mumbled, his face pressed against her neck.

She bit her lip. "Um, don't tell anyone about this, okay?"

"Okay," he promised.

The collected sylphs sighed. It was done: there was a queen.

Nearby, Devon stood at the edge of the cliff and stared into the darkness, not knowing what was happening on the plains below. Around him, other men were just as frightened. Women back farther were tensed to run with the children.

The sylphs started to drift away, chattering as if nothing had happened.

"Airi!" Devon called as Galway came over with an arrow notched to a bow. "Where are you?"

His sylph swept to his side, and he heard the men around him start to relax as their sylphs returned to normal. They really were all wound pretty tightly, Devon realized. The

Community was afraid of another attack. But they had good reason, he admitted. King Alcor wouldn't want them here, even on useless land that could only be used because of their sylphs. The attack these people were dreading would indeed come at some point . . . but Devon was one of them now. He had nowhere else to go.

The men started to disperse, returning to their beds. The tension had eased. Devon stared at Airi. "What happened?" he asked.

Good things. The hive is complete.

He was about to ask what that meant, noting puzzled looks on other masters' faces as they indubitably questioned their own sylphs, when he heard a shout. The men all tensed again, but the call was angry instead of frightened, and it was the Widow Blackwell who pushed her way through the crowd. She was obviously searching for someone.

A man grinned. "Lose another kid?"

"Don't you laugh," the Widow snapped. "Two of them aren't in their beds. The new boy and girl. I am going to tan their hides!"

The men all laughed, joking about teenagers, but Devon felt cold sweep over him. He stared out into the darkness. "Heyou, what have you done?" he whispered.

"What?" Galway asked.

Staring out into the void, Devon saw the battle sylph first, saw black moving on black and a flicker of glowing eyes. A moment later Heyou was on the edge of the bluff, his mantle pulling back to reveal Solie in her nightgown as he resumed his human form. It was so quick that Devon only saw the change because he was looking in the right place, but everyone heard Solie's startled gasp.

Men who had been heading back to their beds turned and saw the pair standing there, as did the widow.

"Where have you been?" she thundered. "Sneaking out in your nightgown with a boy! What were you thinking?"

She stormed toward the couple, the men grinning as they watched. Galway chuckled, but Devon felt his heart start to pound, wanting to warn the woman, but afraid.

The widow went to grab Solie's arm, but Heyou stepped between them. Suddenly there were no sylphs anywhere. Even Airi was gone. Sensing their absence, their masters gaped in shock, their fear returning. The widow was oblivious.

"Get back," Devon warned, putting one hand on Galway's chest as he retreated. The trapper let himself be guided, puzzled.

"What's going on?" Morgal demanded from somewhere in the darkness behind them. "Does anyone have a sylph?"

"Are we under attack?" someone else shouted. "The sylphs are gone!"

The sylphs aren't stupid, Devon wanted to say. "Get back," he repeated, louder, his mouth dry.

Heyou regarded the widow, his expression flat. "Don't touch her," he said.

The widow froze, staring at him. In a moment, everyone was. It wasn't hate. It was far from hate, but the aura was huge and it promised violence. Devon was petrified with terror. Never anger the battlers, he'd grown up knowing. Keep away from them. Every fiber of his body knew that meant death.

Heyou glared at everyone. The battler had one arm around Solie, her body pulled close to his, and his attitude was obvious: no one was getting near her. Then she glanced up at him and put her hands on his shoulders, whispering into his ear. He smiled and his aura vanished.

"Heyou's going to walk me back to my tent," she told the widow. Then the pair ran off holding hands, Heyou trailing behind. Armed men parted to let them go, and they vanished into the darkness.

Devon felt his knees would give out under him. The widow stared at the gathering in frightened confusion.

Morgal pushed forward, his eyes wild. "Did anyone else feel that? What happened?" He looked around for answers, but none was to be had.

Devon returned to his tent, knees shaking. Galway followed, but saw his face and didn't ask any questions. Devon was glad of it. Someone would be asking soon enough, once everyone calmed down. He just didn't know what he was going to tell them.

Solie ducked back into her tent, Heyou following a second later. The other girls squealed at the sight of him, but he only had eyes for his queen. Solie went straight to her bed and sat down on the edge, shaken. She'd . . . she'd slept with Heyou, and oh, she'd enjoyed it. He grinned at her, picking up on her emotions. She glared at him in response.

"How aware of me are you, anyway?" she demanded.

Very aware, he answered in her mind.

She jumped. He hadn't done that before. It was a little scary, but easy to hear. She still didn't know if it was her picking up his feelings or him pushing them into her, but she could feel his happiness and contentment. More, she could faintly feel the other sylphs as well now, roaming outside the tent. They were happy, too. Everyone was happy, except for her. She was confused.

Heyou took her hand. "It'll all be okay, Solie."

She stared at him as he sat beside her, his eyes shining. Okay? She wasn't so sure. She felt different, in ways she didn't think had to do with losing her virginity. "What's happened?" she whispered. "What did you do to me?"

You're my queen, he told her.

She shook her head. "You keep telling me that, but this is different. It's not just you I can feel. Why?"

He looked down sheepishly. *I don't know*, he admitted. *I don't understand it either.*

"Why not?" she wailed. The other girls stared in puzzlement, confused by her seemingly one-way conversation. "You did this! How can you not understand it?"

He looked hurt. "I'm sorry," he said aloud.

She sagged, not able to stay mad at him. Biting her lip, she leaned forward to hug him reassuringly, and he met her halfway with a kiss. It was quite good and very distracting, making her forget her strange new awareness and that there were other girls there peeking around the corner as he pushed her back on her bed.

Unknown to Solie, Heyou glared at the girls over her body, his expression a very clear warning. Swallowing, the girls fled, and he returned contentedly to his queen, completely baffled himself by what had happened, but happy that the other sylphs also seemed to think Solie was their queen. It made this place feel like a proper hive. At the very least, they knew not to approach her, and now the humans did as well. Those girls could find somewhere else to sleep while he spent the rest of the night here pleasing his queen.

Galway grabbed the kettle from the fire as it started to whistle and poured some water into a mug, adding tea leaves. His shoulders hunched against the cold, he carried the mug back to the tent shared by most of the single men. It wasn't much warmer inside, and he left his heavy cloak on as he went to a cot partway down the right side. Devon was there, still shaking, his face ashen and one hand pressed over his mouth. Galway didn't understand what had happened, but apparently it terrified the other man.

He handed Devon the mug and forced him to take a swallow. "Are you going to tell me what happened?" he asked.

"You don't want to know," Devon replied. "Trust me, you don't. Gods, that was so close. He could have killed us all."

"Heyou?" Galway asked, puzzled. "That's crazy."

"You have no idea."

The tent flap opened, a blast of cold wind preceding Morgal and some of the men who now led the Community. All of them looked shaken and angry. Devon put the mug down, his hands still trembling so badly that he nearly dropped it.

"What's going on with the sylphs?" Morgal demanded. "I think you two know."

"Not me." Galway shrugged. He regarded Devon apprais-ingly. "He thinks Heyou is dangerous."

"Heyou?" Morgal asked. "Who's Heyou?"

"The boy who was injured," one of the other men re-minded him. His name was Norlud. "The one Luck nearly killed herself to heal."

"How'd he get hurt?" asked a third man, called Borish. "I didn't see a mark on him when he got here."

Devon ran his hands through his hair, staring at noth-ing. "He got into a fight with one of the battlers that at-tacked you. They devastated the village they were in."

The men of the Community stared. "That's impossible."

Devon took a shaky breath. He couldn't keep this secret. Someone might die if he did. "Heyou—" He choked. "Hey-ou's a battle sylph."

Chapter Seventeen

The eight men stared in shock. "He's a boy!" Galway shouted. Devon hadn't imagined the trapper could get so worked up. "Just a boy!"

Devon shook his head, his mouth dry. "No, he's not. I watched him destroy that village. I saw him blow the side of the castle out after he killed the crown prince. I felt him scream his hate from miles away. He's a battle sylph. Somehow, something went wrong when he was summoned, and now he belongs to Solie." He stared up at the men, weighing their shock. It looked severe, but they had to know the rest. "She's his master," he continued. "She's got him pretending to be human so they can fit in. Only, I think . . . I think he did something with her tonight." He gave a bitter laugh. "He's made it pretty obvious he's wanted her since I met him."

"Why didn't he kill you?" Borish asked in a shaken voice. "Or the rest of us?"

"Solie wouldn't let him. But he nearly killed my father, and he did kill a lot of other people who got in the way. I have no idea how much control she has over him."

The men seemed wholly flabbergasted. "What do we do?" asked an older man named Bock.

"What we all do around battlers," Devon said. "Don't anger him. Just keep out of his way, and stay away from her. Don't even touch her. He'll kill to protect her."

"I don't believe you!" Galway snapped. "He's a normal boy."

"You felt that aura on the edge of the cliff, didn't you?

The one that made every sylph vanish? Mine isn't even back yet. Are any of yours? That was him warning us away from her."

"But . . ." Galway sat down slowly, still shaking his head. "I found him in the woods. He never did anything to me."

"He was hurt then. He needed your help. Ril tore him apart in their fight. He might not have had the strength to be a threat before, but he's healed now."

"Why would Luck heal him?" Morgal whispered. The man was gray. An uncontrolled battler in his community, just after they lost a third of their people to two others? Devon was pretty sure he was about to lose his mind.

"Who knows. They don't think the same way people do."

"Maybe we can use him to protect the Community," Norgal suggested.

"That's insane!" Bock snapped.

"I want proof," Morgal said, causing Devon to glance up at him. "I want proof that he's a battler. Until then, why should I believe you?"

"You want to wait for him to kill someone?" Devon asked.

"Hardly. But I've seen battlers before, too, and I can't believe he's one. You'll have to prove it." Morgal took a deep breath. "We'll decide on what to do next after that."

Devon shook his head. He'd have to talk to Solie, he thought with dread, providing he could. Whatever it was that had happened tonight between the two, Heyou looked as though he was being a lot more protective. He sighed and rubbed his temples. Maybe his obliterated body would be proof enough.

Whatever happened, it would have to wait for morning, because he was not going to interrupt whatever was going on in Solie's tent. Not now. He doubted any of them were going to get much sleep tonight.

* * *

Leon had been waking up at dawn for years, though Betha complained whenever he did so at home. He liked the concept of sleeping in, but it just never seemed to happen. Since they'd left on this journey, he'd been up as the sun rose every day, getting his gear ready and preparing his breakfast, making as much noise as he could until Jasar reluctantly dragged himself out of bed and ordered Mace to make breakfast and clean up after him. He'd even forced the battler to shave him before grudgingly agreeing to move. They'd cut this ritual down to about an hour, but it still drove Leon to distraction.

This morning he woke and opened his eyes, glancing up to where Ril perched on the saddlebag next to his head. The bird was ignoring him, staring at something in the camp. Rubbing his eyes, Leon rolled over and looked.

Mace was breaking camp. The battler had most of the gear packed already, and both horses were saddled. Leon watched in surprise, wondering what had Jasar so motivated, but the other man was still in his tent, snoring.

As Leon watched, Mace stomped over, pulled out the pole that held the tent up, and started folding the fabric. This uncovered the sleeping man inside, who continued to snore. Leon raised an eyebrow. Mace carried the tent to the packhorse, stowed it, and went back. Grabbing the end of Jasar's blanket, he yanked it right off his master and started rolling that up as well. That woke Jasar. Sprawled half-naked in the dirt, he started shrieking obscenities, but his battler completely ignored him and went to pack the blanket.

It was surreal. Battlers didn't do anything on their own initiative, not unless it involved killing someone. But Mace was breaking camp. He stomped in Leon's direction, and Leon rolled out of bed before the sylph could dump him on the ground as well. Mace rolled up his blankets and took them and Leon's saddlebags to his gray. This was the first time such a thing had ever occurred.

Ril, who had flown out of the way, landed on Leon's shoulder and shot him a look that mirrored Leon's puzzlement.

"Mace!" Jasar shrieked. "You bastard! Stop putting my things away!"

Mace ignored him.

Leon scrambled to his feet, one hand on a very tense Ril. He backed off, staring at the massive armored sylph.

"Get over here!" Jasar commanded, pointing to the ground before him.

With a reluctance that would have made Leon extremely nervous if it came from Ril, Mace went to his master, who proceeded to screech at him for his behavior. "Get my breakfast!" he finished at last.

Mace returned to the horses. Pulling a handful of dried meat from one of the saddlebags, he threw it at his master—which was the act that finally permeated Jasar's oblivious confidence. He stared at his battler in fear, then looked at Leon.

"What's wrong with him?" he whined.

Leon didn't have the faintest idea. He'd never seen a battler come so close to outright defiance. He grabbed his cloak and stroked Ril with what he would have recognized as a nervous gesture, if he weren't so distracted.

"Get dressed and get on your horse," he told the courtier. "I don't feel comfortable here."

Jasar looked around at the nearly lifeless plain. They'd made camp in the lee of a massive boulder that blocked the wind, but the air was still very cold and their breath steamed. The clouds overhead were heavy, promising snow. Other than themselves and the odd gray bush, there was no life.

"Are we in danger? Is that why he wants us to go?" Absorbing the idea, Jasar scrambled into his clothes and hurried to his horse faster than Leon had ever seen.

Mace took the lead as they headed out, walking at a near jog across the Shale Plain. They had reached the end of the official road shortly before dark, and the battler followed the strange ridged line that continued off from it. Towing the packhorse behind, he set off, Jasar on his heels and already bitching about the cold now that his nerves were steady again.

Leon followed more slowly with Ril, not wanting to get close to the other battler. Ril was so nervous that he didn't reach out with any hate, staring at Mace instead. It was a very uncomfortable ride.

Solie woke up tangled with Heyou, her head pillowed on his chest. She heard no heartbeat and her head snapped up, her heart pounding.

Heyou smiled. "Morning." He looked fresh and rested.

"Did you sleep?" she asked.

"No. I don't sleep much."

She blinked and looked around. They were still in the girls' tent, crammed together on the tiny bed. She blushed, remembering the night before.

"What happened to the others?"

"They went away." He kissed her bare shoulder and she shivered, quickly sitting up and grabbing her dress. He settled for sitting behind her and kissing her back. That was distracting, but she yanked her dress on over her head.

"Hungry?" she asked.

"No. I drank some of your energy while you were sleeping."

"What?" She stared at him. She'd forgotten that she'd never actually seen him eat. He took food when it was offered, but he never actually ate. "I feed you?"

He nodded happily. "I live off the energy inside you. It's the only kind I can use."

She blinked. The stories did say that sylphs fed off their masters. "How often do you do that?" she asked.

"Once or twice a day. You never notice."

Apparently not. "What did you do back home?"

"Ate the energy the food sylphs made. Yours tastes better." He stood and grabbed the new shirt and pants he'd been given, managing to get them on before adding a pair of boots too big for him. Collecting her cloak, Solie ducked outside with him.

It was bitterly cold from the frigid wind that never seemed to stop blowing with extra force across the flat top of the bluff. Men kept their heads down as they went on their way, and Solie didn't see any of the youngsters she'd worked with the past few days. It was well past dawn, but no one had woken them. Or rather, no one had woken her, since Heyou didn't sleep. She looked around and stopped.

A few dozen feet off, the Widow Blackwell was arguing with Morgal while Devon watched, and the woman pointed frequently at Solie's tent. Solie blushed and jumped with a squeal when Heyou walked up behind her and started licking her neck.

"Behave!" she hissed. The last thing she needed was for the widow to see his action. She didn't want to imagine what the woman was going to say about last night, and she cringed as the widow stared balefully in her direction. Rather than coming over though, the woman threw her hands up and stomped in the other direction.

The two men started toward her. Solie swallowed nervously. Heyou growled.

"Don't!" she hissed in an undertone. "They're not going to hurt me!" Yell, maybe, lecture, probably. Make her feel like crap, definitely. "Be nice," she added.

"Yes, my queen." He sighed.

The two men approached, Morgal regarding her flatly, while Devon never made eye contact. He was afraid, she realized—not of her, but of Heyou. Morgal was uncertain, but fear was in him as well. Both men were focused on her, though, hoping she could give them the answers they wanted.

Solie blinked in surprise. The emotions they felt were faint but undeniable. They'd had to get within ten feet before she felt anything, but now it was clear and disconcerting. She shot a look at Heyou. She could feel him, and she'd felt all the other sylphs last night. Was she going to be able to feel everyone now?

He grinned at her.

"Solie," Devon spoke up, still not meeting her eyes. "Heyou. How are you this morning?"

"Okay," Solie replied, feeling Heyou's interest in the exchange. He didn't hate Devon; Solie could feel it. He'd gone through too much to hate so easily anymore. That was good to know.

Devon couldn't tell that he wasn't in danger, though, and his fear stayed sharp. "Good. Good! Ah, Solie. I should have talked to you first, but last night . . . last night I told Morgal that Heyou was a battle sylph. He wants proof."

Would they be asked to leave? Solie blinked and glanced at Heyou. She bit her lip and met his blue-gray gaze. "Can you show them? Um, without freaking everyone out?"

Heyou frowned and closed his eyes. When he reopened them, they glowed red. A tiny trickle of hatred issued forth, and both human men stepped back. Then it was gone. After another blink, Heyou's eyes returned to normal.

Devon choked, turning to Morgal. "Convinced?"

The other man nodded, his face pale. "What do you want here?" he asked Heyou.

Heyou scratched his head, puzzled by the question. "To protect and serve my queen. What else is there?"

Morgal pursed his lips. "If you stay here, will you protect the Community?"

"Well, yeah, this is where she is. Why wouldn't I?"

Both men relaxed a bit. Solie watched them uncertainly, but she felt that they felt content—or at least unwilling to push for more. She hadn't ever encountered anything like it. Usually people were telling her what to do.

Get used to it, Heyou told her silently. *No one tells the queen what to do.*

Solie shuddered, not sure why that made her nervous.

Soon. Soon he'd be with his queen.

Mace strode quickly across the plain, ignoring the obvious trail of ridged earth as he went in a direct line toward his queen, zeroing in on her without pause. He'd be able to feel her anywhere, just as he could feel everyone in his hive line. That line had become much larger since the queen had ascended and subsumed so many other sylphs. It was glorious.

Mace could sense the queen's battler as well, the youngster he'd sensed dying and had been unable to help. The child had done well indeed. Mace had no urge to challenge him for supremacy. Battlers didn't do that inside their hives. It was the queen's choice whom she let have her, and most battlers never did. It was the touch of her soul that was important, and they were all hatched with the need to protect and serve her. None of them had thought they'd lose that bond when they crossed the gate, but they had. Mace had never expected to find a new bond in this world at all.

Ril sent him an almost communication of curiosity about what had him so excited. Back home, they never would have interacted except to fight, being from different hive lines as they were. But Ril had no queen at all. He'd been too far away to be subsumed when this new one arose. Mace's new queen could accept him, though. Ril could be pulled in just like any sylph from a conquered hive. Those that survived were always subsumed by the victorious queen, brought into the hive line. The queen could subsume Ril now. He could become a friend for real, instead of the almost friend he'd been since they met, neither sylph having anyone else. One battler wasn't enough to protect a queen and ensure her comfort sufficiently. Three would be far better.

He had no real way to tell Ril, though. They could feel each other's emotions, but it was hard to share without their masters also feeling them, and their instincts still told them not to trust each other. That would end when the queen had them both. Then all things would be possible.

Mace would have run if he'd been allowed. Instead he had to settle for a rapid walk, giving Ril an expression of happiness to come that the other battler didn't understand. Mace almost had to laugh, especially as the miles passed by, the hive growing ever closer.

Chapter Eighteen

In the end it was decided not to reveal the identity of the battle sylph to the others in the Community. There was fear of a panic, and there were enough troubles just trying to make sure they could last the coming winter. No one on the council wanted the additional worry of potential riots. Heyou and Solie ended up excused from the labor teams, though, just in case someone irritated the battler.

Solie's feared meeting with the widow never came to pass. Instead, she and Heyou were given a small, ancient, drafty tent of their own. The older woman didn't like the new arrangements, but she had been told to leave well enough alone. She focused on the rest of the youths instead, making sure they didn't think Solie and Heyou's exceptions applied to them. The other youngsters glared enviously whenever the widow's back was turned, and Solie found few of them wanted to sit with her anymore. It hurt a bit, but she still had Heyou and his unrelenting devotion. That kept her spirits up most of the time.

"It'll be nice once the caves are all dug," she told him three days later as they made their way from their tent to the eating area for supper. The wind was getting colder and harsher, and she could smell snow on it. Some had fallen already, and she could see small pockets in places protected from the wind. But the work was close to complete. The earth sylphs had been working without pause to bore tunnels and rooms into the bluff, and the fire sylphs warmed them. The water sylphs brought water, and the air sylphs kept the rooms fresh-smelling.

Heyou had taken her down to pick out a large apartment in the middle. To Solie's shock, the sylphs seemed to agree and were working to finish that first. Most people had to wait a few more days before they could abandon the tents, but she and Heyou would start living in their room tonight. To her even greater shock, none of the adults had any issue with her taking it. Granted, she doubted anyone who knew what he was wanted to argue with Heyou.

"Yeah," Heyou agreed, surveying the area. He did that a lot, she'd noticed. She didn't know what he thought he was guarding her from, but he was determined. She'd woken more than once in the night to find him gone. Every time she searched for him, she found him standing on the edge of the cliff, just watching.

"Evening."

She turned to find Heyou already watching Galway approach, his emotions sparking toward happiness. Galway maintained a steady calm. The trapper nodded to them both and pulled his cloak close around him. Solie had no idea if he'd been told Heyou's identity, but she suspected not. He didn't treat either of them any differently, and he didn't feel afraid.

"It'll snow heavily soon," the man remarked.

Solie looked out over the plains. They were white in the distance. "You think so?"

"We might have a few days before it gets really bad. I'll have to head out first thing in the morning. I wanted to catch you both to say good-bye, just in case I don't see you again."

Heyou looked at the man intently, the emotions Solie felt from him complex and a little sorrowful. He didn't want the trapper to leave, she realized. He had a strange fondness for Galway that he didn't really understand. The feeling wasn't questioned, though, was just accepted as it came. "Do you have to go?" he asked.

"If I don't want to stay all winter, yes." Galway slapped Heyou on the shoulder and Solie decided he didn't know the truth. Not that the battler would hurt him. Even if he hadn't felt grateful to Galway, she'd truly stressed the idea of nonviolence to him over the last few days. He wasn't to hurt anyone, not unless it was to save someone's life. "I'll come back in the spring. Okay?"

"Okay," Heyou grumped, and the trapper grinned.

Nearby, air sylphs flowed past over the edge of the bluff, carrying sacks of flour from the stores below. The bags looked as though they were floating in midair. The sylphs themselves felt happy, eager to serve the hive. It was oddly soothing for Solie to sense it.

One zipped past with a bucket full of milk, and potatoes whisked by seemingly unsupported, though the air currents used to hold them threatened to tangle her hair. Galway saw but said nothing. All of them were getting used to seeing things like that.

"Have you eaten yet?" Solie asked the trapper.

"Not yet. Care to join me?"

Smiling and nodding, Solie turned toward the meal tent, hoping to get there before the hot food was all gone. But while Galway fell in beside her, Heyou didn't. She called his name. Turning, she found him half facing away from her, staring out at the darkening plains. Leaving her side, he walked slowly past the safety rope placed around the edge, all of his senses focused.

Solie felt a surge of fright as, looking out into the enshrouding darkness, Heyou started to growl.

All day the mountains had grown before them, fronted by a bluff like some kind of vanguard. It looked unnatural, as though someone had cleaved off the front and then the top as well. It was probably the work of battlers, Leon decided, from the war that had devastated the plains centuries before. Either that, or earth sylphs had made it before the war as an outpost. It didn't matter either way. All that mattered was the fact that it was occupied.

He peered through his spyglass at the cliff, seeing obvious signs of human habitation on the top, as well as livestock herds at the bottom. The raised ridge they'd been following plowed straight toward it, as did Mace. The battler was already a hundred feet ahead.

Seeing how close they were, the battler had made Jasar keep traveling despite the falling sun. As for himself, Leon hadn't minded. It would be better to attack in the darkness after all. Likely no one knew to look for them, but they'd still get a lot closer unobserved if they approached at night.

"Call your battler before he gets so close they can feel him," he warned.

Jasar looked at him grumpily, but he called Mace back. The two battlers' hate could be felt for a long distance, but they were still out of range, and everyone Leon could spy through his glass seemed relaxed. They weren't expecting an attack.

"See anything?" Jasar spat. Leon could tell he itched to have a look himself, but he'd never lower himself enough to admit it.

"Yes. I see pirates." From the same group they'd ambushed before. Leon was positive. He recognized the wagons at the base of the cliff. He grimaced. He'd been sure they hadn't gotten everyone, but their ship had been damaged, thanks to a suicide run of a dozen fire sylphs, and Jasar had ostensibly been in charge of that mission. He'd ordered a retreat, and Leon honestly hadn't minded. Turning Ril loose on anyone, even pirates, felt like murder.

He glanced at his companion, wondering if Jasar even realized they were in the same general area as before. They were less than a hundred miles from the ambush, and the landscape was nearly identical.

From his bored expression, Jasar didn't recognize anything. Then again, he'd stayed in his cabin that entire trip. He still seemed uninterested, but it wasn't him going into combat. Leon looked at Mace and wondered if they could dare loose the battler, given the sylph's recent actions. Obvious though the trail was, they hadn't followed it here. Mace had brought them.

At least Ril was okay. Leon stroked the battler and felt his hate, though Ril didn't try to stop him. He knew the sylph would never admit it, but Ril liked to be stroked. Under the hate, Leon could feel a flicker of his contentment, and the anticipation of being released.

"Just a minute," he told him. "I'll let you fight soon." Or slaughter them, he corrected silently. Those people didn't have any chance this time. If the girl who'd stolen the battler was indeed here with her sylph, she didn't have a hope. Her battler hadn't been able to fight off Ril before. Now he had to deal with two.

It didn't feel fair. Leon hadn't thought so when they ambushed the pirates, and he didn't think so now. In fact, now that the time was here, the thought of killing the girl made him ill.

"Go for the battler," he told Ril. "Kill the girl only if you have no other choice. Leave the rest of the group alone." The king had said nothing about them when he gave his orders, and surely they had learned their lesson. Leon wouldn't kill them if he didn't have to. Pirates or not, they hadn't killed the crews they robbed. If they had, he would have finished them the first time, no matter how loudly Jasar was screaming that the ship was about to fall.

The dandy looked over with disgust as Leon gave the order. "What's with you? Mercy is a waste." He waved a hand at Mace. "Kill everyone on that cliff," he ordered, "starting with the girl. Go!"

Mace took off like a sprinter from where he'd been standing, racing toward the bluff.

"Damn!" Leon yanked his startled, rearing horse around and dropped his arm. "Ril! Go!"

Shrieking, the bird was gone, outdistancing the flightless battler. Nonetheless, Jasar smiled smugly at Leon. Leon felt like hitting him.

Heyou started in surprise, his patterns freezing inside him. His senses were naturally better than the other sylphs, and he could feel them out there: two battlers fast approaching. One was from his own hive line, but silent, refusing to speak to him, and the other . . . That one had nearly killed him once already.

Nearby, an air sylph rose up over the cliff edge with a basket of dried meat. She hesitated, her energy patterns showing confusion. Then she started screaming, shrieking a warning about the battler attack. All across the bluff sylphs took up the cry and fled to their masters, desperate to take them and go into the cliffs, to hide within the hive while their battler did his job of protecting them.

Heyou spun to find Solie. Her face was white. "There are two battlers," he told her, terrified. If they got past him, they'd kill her, but he couldn't fight two at once. They were older than him, stronger. . . . "I have to go." As he turned away, she screamed his name. He glanced back.

She threw herself at him. "I love you!" she sobbed, hugging him tightly. "Don't go!"

He shuddered. That was the only order she could ever give him that he would disobey. "I have to," he whispered. "This is what I'm for."

Galway regarded Heyou evenly as Community men appeared carrying weapons, Devon and Morgal among them. Most of the Community's members had fled underground with the sylphs, some hauled bodily by their sylphs when they tried to face the danger. "Don't throw your life away, boy," the trapper said.

"I won't." Heyou pushed Solie back, wanting to kiss her but afraid, and stared for an instant at the assembled men, most of them not knowing what he was or what was coming, but all of them willing to fight anyway. It made him glad of what he was about to do for them.

He turned, ran for the edge of the cliff, and leaped off. He heard men shout in surprise and then terror as he changed his shape. Made of smoke and lightning, black wings spread wide, he raced to the attack, screaming his hatred until the plains echoed from it.

Ril shot forward, racing to attack. He could feel the opposing battler, his fear and hatred, his inexperience. The youngster was going to fight back, though, having no other choice.

His foe angled toward him, surely recognizing Mace as being from the same hive line as himself but not recognizing that Mace had orders to kill his master. It was a foolish move, Ril thought. The pup wasn't even fully recovered from their last fight. He'd be terribly easy to kill—and Mace would wipe out everyone on the bluff while Ril did so.

Screaming defiance of the other battler's hate, wings tucked back against his body, Ril dove toward his enemy, ready to make this a quickly won fight indeed.

Mace sprinted for the cliff, his long legs carrying him faster than a horse but not as fast as Ril's wings. He saw the bird shoot by overhead and the young battler on the cliff leap off to fight him. The young sylph didn't have a chance, not against Ril's age and experience.

Mace dipped down in midstride, coming up with a heavy rock. He hefted it, sighted, and threw.

Barely meters away from his foe, Ril braced himself to lash out with a wall of energy. This close, the power would blow through the youngster and probably take out most of the cliff face as well, so he had to be careful. He readied himself, aiming so he would kill his target but no one else. Leon's order matched his own mind: let Mace slaughter the humans and sylphs. He wanted no part of that.

He braced himself . . . and a rock thrown as fast as a lightning bolt speared through his left wing.

"What the hell!" Leon shouted, yanking the spyglass down from his eye.

Jasar smirked at him. "What?"

"Your goddamned battler just attacked Ril!"

Leon was furious. He wanted to kill someone. No, he wanted to maim them and then kill. He could see the dot that was Ril tumbling and the other battler swooping down to finish him off, tiny shadows against the dusk sky. Bringing the spyglass up again, he watched Ril struggle to move his broken wing, flailing at the air and finally just giving up and dropping to avoid the fanged cloud that tried to catch him.

Below, Mace sprinted past small, panicking herds of livestock and leaped at the cliff face. Digging his fingers into the rock, the battler started to climb.

Leon shoved his spyglass into his pocket and pointed at Jasar, who was obviously shocked. "If Ril dies, so do you!" He put his heels to the gray and sent it galloping forward.

Jasar watched in horror as the other man rode off into the fray. After glancing at his distant battler, he grabbed the reins of the packhorse. Turning his steed, he was soon galloping toward safety as fast as he could make them go.

Heyou was so surprised by the sudden attack that he missed his chance to kill the hawk-shaped battler. Screaming in pain, the bird dropped below him, his shattered wing barely able to hold him aloft. He forced it to, though, flipping around and lashing out with a wall of energy. Heyou dodged to one side but was still caught across the mantle. He tumbled himself, and fought to regain control.

Below, the other battler of his hive line was climbing the cliff face with amazing speed, scaling it straight toward an unsuspecting Solie. Heyou's heart surged. This other battler was the one who'd thrown the rock. He was going to protect the queen! Together, they'd be able to defeat the third sylph easily.

The battler was more than two thirds of the way up the cliff, right below where Solie stood. Heyou dove, racing back to his queen's side to join him.

Ril struggled in pain, trying to get his broken wing to work and extremely aware that he was almost helpless. Mace's betrayal was an agony inside him, and in desperation he looked for his master. Leon was galloping across the plains toward the cliff—judging by his emotions, clearly determined to rescue him. For once, Ril was glad of it.

His young foe didn't press the advantage, instead swooping back to the cliff. Ril could see the battler's master standing there, and Mace climbing up from below. In pain and enraged, Ril folded his wings and dove. His orders were simple: kill the battler if he could, or the girl if he couldn't. He was too badly hurt to fight even the young battler now, but the girl was unprotected. Screaming, he attacked.

Solie stood with Devon and the other men of the Community, watching Heyou fight the other battler. She didn't catch the rock hitting the bird, but she did see the hawk fall and Heyou turn back toward her.

"What's he coming back for?" Morgal gasped. "He should finish it!"

A second later, a huge shape appeared at the edge of the cliff, a massive suit of armor with glowing eyes. Solie screamed, even as she felt the creature's joy beneath the hate. Around her, men fell back in a panic. Devon was trying desperately to force himself to protect her, but he couldn't make his body obey him and she couldn't move. The huge battler looked at her . . . and lunged.

Suddenly Heyou was between them, trying to push the larger battler back. He screamed, but the armored creature shoved him aside and rushed at Solie again. Sprawled on the ground, shocked and surprised, Heyou stared in fright at the newcomer. Solie felt the other battler's arms come around her, his metal gauntlets warm against her skin—

"No!" she screamed. "Stop it! Don't hurt me!"

The helm that formed the battler's face was only inches from her own, and Solie blinked as she realized the hate was gone, at least from him. Now it only came from above, from the hawk that was diving to strike her.

The battler threw her to one side and twisted around. Heyou caught her and rolled, pushing her under him and covering her with his body. The armored battler leaped straight up. He caught the diving bird in his huge hands and then landed back on his feet, fighting to hold on. The hawk screamed, digging its claws through his armor, beating one wing at his face. Waves of power were released, but Heyou flared his own energy to shield her. The Community men retreated, shouting, while those who didn't move fast enough were blown off their feet.

The armored battler met the hawk's energy attack with his own. Solie wailed in terror as the pressure in the air increased, both battlers pushing at each other with enough power to vaporize the very stone on which they stood. At last, the bigger sylph slammed the bird into the ground. The hawk went limp, his aura of hate fading. Sprawled on her back beneath Heyou, Solie stared.

Heyou regarded the huge gray battler, too, not sure if he was on their side. Instinct said he was, but for a moment there . . . For a second, he'd been more frightened than ever before in his life. He lay atop his queen and wasn't quite sure what to do.

Mace peered down, truly happy. He hadn't felt that emotion in a very long time, and it was all because of the thin young girl under the badly frightened battler. The child had made a nearly fatal mistake, trusting the instinct that said Mace was part of his hive line. But Jasar's orders had been clear: kill everyone, starting with the girl.

The saving grace was that Mace couldn't kill his own queen. The order Jasar had given him was impossible, even before she ordered him to stop. Now, if only he could tell them that.

The huge gray battler was pleased. Solie swallowed, still frightened by her ability to sense others' emotions, but she tried to focus on him anyway. He felt oddly as if he wanted to tell her something. "What's your name?" she asked at last.

Heyou hugged her and stood, pulling Solie upright and pushing her behind him, glaring at the armored sylph. The big battler only gazed at her, silent.

"His name is Mace," Devon said. He stood a dozen feet away, his face ash white, bloodied and dirty. "He's Lord Jasar Doliard's battler. He doesn't speak."

"He's one of the ones that attacked us," Morgal breathed. "Oh, my god."

"Wh-what?" Solie looked around, wanting someone to take over and tell her what to do. Everyone stared, though, waiting for her to make a decision. It was overwhelming, and finally she had to say something just to break the tension. "You can talk if you want to," she told him.

"Yes, my queen," Mace said.

Everyone gasped. Devon was so surprised that he fell

onto his backside in the dirt, gaping. "You can talk?" he gasped. "But you're forbidden!" Mace ignored him, focused on Solie.

"Um . . ." Solie swallowed hard and leaned against Heyou, needing his warmth. He never took his eyes off the other battler, but his arm moved around her and squeezed reassuringly. That helped. "Why did you talk just now if you're not allowed to?"

"You gave me permission, my queen."

Why did everyone keep calling her that? "How can I be your queen?"

"You carry the pattern of the hive line. Your orders are sacrosanct." He nodded to Heyou. "He feels it, too."

Solie peeked at Heyou, who had started to relax as Mace spoke, his muscles loosening and his attention focusing more on the unconscious bird that dangled from the bigger battler's fist. "Heyou?" she gasped.

He glanced at her and back at Mace. "He's part of the hive. I got scared there for a minute, but it's okay." He glared at the bird. "Can I kill him?"

"No!" Solie gasped.

Galway spoke up. "You might need to." Unlike the others, he wasn't afraid. He just dabbed at a bloody cut he'd received on one cheek and waited to see what would happen now that the battle was over.

Not everyone was so calm. "What's going on?" Morgal demanded. "Someone explain this to me!" He and the other locals were backed well away, gaping at Mace in horror. The huge battler ignored them.

"Can you tell us what's going on?" Solie asked him.

Mace answered immediately. "We were sent to kill you. I was ordered to kill everyone on this bluff, you first, but I can't hurt the queen."

"What?" she whispered, still confused. Heyou leaned against her.

"You're the hive queen," Mace repeated, and pointed at Heyou. "Thanks to him. The imperative to protect and obey you supersedes anything from my master." She gaped at him. "I felt you become the queen. I've been coming to you ever since."

"Coming . . . to me . . . ?" she repeated.

"Yes, my queen."

Solie felt faint. Everything was happening too fast. She had two battlers now? "What about him?" she whimpered, gesturing down at the unconscious bird.

"Ril is from a different hive line, but he has no queen." Mace's eyes glowed. "You can make him yours."

"Mine?" Solie repeated.

"This is insane!" Morgal spoke up, regaining enough of himself to be angry. "We're not going to—"

Mace glared at him, and suddenly the hate was back, thick in the air. Morgal yelped and scrambled backward, most of the others hurrying alongside. Galway was the only one to hold his ground.

Solie stared at the bird. "Why would I do that?" she asked.

Heyou turned and kissed her shoulder. "We'll have to kill him if you don't."

"What do I do?" she whispered. She shuddered.

"Let me project your pattern at him," Mace suggested. "Your right of rule. Without a queen, he'll have no defense." He lifted the bird and shook him.

Solie just shivered and watched.

Ril came awake to confusion and pain. He'd been attacked, tricked, and hurt. Pain flared from his wing, and dazed, he hung upside down. Mace had him, he realized, just as the battler placed a hand around his neck and swung him upright like a throttled chicken. The next thing he saw was a girl, her eyes wide and frightened. She stood before him, staring.

Suddenly Mace focused, taking the pattern of the girl's soul and projecting it. Ril shuddered. She wasn't just a master, this was a queen's mind, a queen's pattern. Only, she wasn't a sylph, but a human who had bound a battler to her and made him recognize her pattern as he would that of a queen. That didn't make her Ril's queen, though, and he screamed, trying to focus his hatred and power.

The girl stepped back, her hands over her mouth, and the young battler put his arms about her, eyes glowing red. Ril raged against them both, against one and all, but Mace forced the queen's pattern onto him even harder. He shoved it down into the cracks in Ril's mind that once, so long ago, had held a queen—one who didn't take him for her mate before Ril crossed the gate for the promise of love and ended up bound to a man. No man could create this kind of pattern, but the girl did, and the harder Mace pushed, the deeper it soaked into Ril, slowly feeling more and more right, and finally he wasn't fighting Mace at all but was helping him. She was his queen, the pattern of obedience in his mind and the focus of his life. Ril shuddered, his energy changing to match hers, and Mace let him go, cradling him in his arms instead. He was a hive mate now, as was everyone on the cliffs and inside the bluff.

He was in a hive, Ril realized dazedly. He'd never have thought that could happen again, and he shook from reaction.

"Um, hi," Solie managed. "I guess, um, you can talk if you want to, and change your shape. If you want."

Oh, it was a good hive. It was a very good hive indeed.

Even with the battle over, the chaos on the bluff continued far into the night. His horse tethered where no one would find it, his cloak left behind as well, Leon made his way through the cold with only a tunic and his pants, his sword strapped to his back and his knife in one hand. Most of the pirates were herded into their tents, making his job even easier. He crept by their guards, all of them starting at shadows so much they couldn't tell when the darkness was actually him. They were amateurs, and there weren't enough of them, so he bypassed them all, easily scaling the back slope.

He had to get to Ril. Careful not to let his worry rush him into any mistakes, Leon followed the link he had to his battler. Most masters couldn't sense their battlers at all beyond the hatred, but Leon had spent years refining his bond, and he could feel where Ril was. A few sylphs in different shapes went past, but none acknowledged his presence, busy with their tasks. Only battlers made good guards.

In the tents, the pirates talked. From the sound of it, at least half of them wanted to pull up stakes and run, but Leon didn't care. It didn't matter to him where they went. All he wanted was Ril back. He heard the word *battler* several times and firmed his lips, honestly not sure what they'd do with their unexpected victory. Could they kill Ril? Mace or the other battler certainly could.

He could feel Ril, felt his pain and weariness nearly as though they were his own, and found himself longing for the sylph's familiar hatred if only because it would mean he was healthy. The battler's emotions were almost the lowest he'd ever felt, almost unrecognizable, and Leon cursed Jasar as he moved forward. How could someone actually lose control of their battle sylph?

The path he took led him to a covered well that bored deep into the bluff with steps circling downward. Leon knelt at the edge and looked. No one was guarding it. Gripping his knife, he started down.

The stairwell was at least eighty steps deep, the air inside surprisingly warm and fresh, the way lit by torches. Leon reached the bottom and found himself in a wide atrium with polished sides, a hundred reflections staring back at him.

Several corridors branched off in different directions, and several doorways had been cut in the walls, but he could feel Ril's presence. As he made his way down that corridor, the walls as reflective as those in the atrium, he started to hear voices as well.

"Are you on our side or not?" a male voice asked, sounding both angry and frightened. "Just answer me!"

"Please," added a woman. "Tell them."

"We obey the queen," a deep voice replied. "If she wants us to protect you, we will."

"I still don't get this," whined a fourth. "What's all this crap about queens?"

Leon crept to an open doorway as another, lighter voice answered the whiner. "We came here for queens, women promised to us that we couldn't get in our hives." Leon peered around the empty door frame and stared in shock. The voice came from Ril, who nested in a red-haired girl's arms. "Only, when we came through, they were killed, leaving us trapped and under the control of men."

"That didn't happen to Heyou," Mace continued, his the deep, booming voice. "Solie lived and bonded to him as his master. They took it further, and she became the queen of any sylph close enough or of the same original hive line. Ril we drew in."

"She's alive," Ril said softly, staring up at the girl. "I went mad when my queen died, but she's alive." He crooned softly.

Leon stared at his battler in horror, forgetting that he was in enemy territory and it meant death if they saw him. Ril. He'd done that to his sylph? Leon thought back to the girl, to that frightened little brown-haired girl with the terrified eyes, and he felt sick. Ril had come for her, not for him, and he'd murdered her.

He staggered back, dropping his knife and gagging. All of Ril's hate over the years seemed to hit him at once. No wonder the sylph had loathed him.

"Outside!" he heard a frightened voice cry.

A shadow fell over him, and Leon looked up to see Mace. The battler's fist came down hard.

Chapter Nineteen

Ril stood in the queen's quarters and changed shape the way a woman changed clothes, trying to find one that he liked.

Sitting on a hay bale brought in to serve as a seat, Solie giggled at him. Heyou lay sprawled across her lap and watched from upside down, while Mace stood silently by the door. The older battler had been happy with the first form he'd changed to—that of a man taller than anyone else, his body heavy with muscle—but Ril couldn't make up his mind. He'd spent so long as a bird, and before that he'd been whatever shape he wished, or more often none at all.

The queen wanted them to fit in, though. Ril looked at his reflection in a strip of mirror-shiny wall and focused. He made himself taller and leaner, his hair blond and short in the back, while bangs hung in his eyes. He looked like one of the heroes in Lizzy's favorite storybook, he thought. His irises were gray, but his eyes were as hard as those he'd had as a bird.

"That one's good," Solie told him helpfully.

Ril looked down and sighed. It didn't really matter. He could have stayed a bird for all the difference it made. Adjusting the loose tunic he'd been wearing over his body while he changed forms inside it, he went to sit next to his queen, leaning back against a sheet that covered the hay. The floor was cold.

The others were content. Solie was pleased with their presence. Mace was as calm as if he'd always been guarding her and wasn't still bound to a master he loathed. Even

Heyou was satisfied, once he managed to convince himself he wouldn't have to share the queen's bed along with her sovereignty. Ril couldn't figure out what was wrong with him. He felt restless somehow, happy to be in a hive with a queen but still feeling that something was lacking. Of course, that had always been his problem. He'd come across the gate because of what he'd been missing.

He glanced at the queen. Whatever it was, it wasn't her problem. She caught his gaze, looking puzzled, so he turned away. No sylph could hide their feelings from a queen for long. He was just lucky that what she could pick up of his unintentional projections was limited. The queen of the hive he'd been hatched into would have felt his emotions like a siren. She just wouldn't have cared.

Solie frowned, obviously not sure of what she was sensing, and looked down at Heyou. He smiled at her happily.

Footsteps sounded in the hallway, and all three battlers tensed, waiting. It was a woman, and Mace opened the door when she knocked, careful to keep his body between the newcomer and the queen. Ril tensed as well, ready to destroy even a female if he must.

"Are you going to get out of my way? At this rate the poor child will have to do everything for herself, since no one else is going to want to get near her. She might not enjoy having only you three for company the rest of her life."

Mace stepped back, peering down in bemusement at a past-middle-aged woman in a black dress. She shoved him aside with one elbow and entered, carrying a covered tray. Bringing it over to the bale, she set it down and glared at Solie.

"Are you planning to sit in here forever?" she snapped, hands on her hips.

Solie blushed, and the three battlers stared at each other, not sure how to handle this. Queens didn't get scolded back home.

"And you," the woman continued, turning on Heyou. "Off! Are you a cat? Her lap is not the proper place for your head!" Grabbing the young battler by the ear, she hauled him into a sitting position, still berating him.

Over by the door, Mace snickered.

Ril went back to watching the woman. She was loud and brash, but most of her bravado was just that. Underneath she was as frightened as the others, if determined not to show it. Still, she smelled female, fertile, and strong. She was no queen, but she was intriguing.

She glared at all three battlers in turn. "It's not polite to stare," she snapped, then turned back to Solie, ignoring them. "Eat your lunch, dear," she said, "and do come outside. You've been in here all day. It's started snowing and it's quite lovely. I can use your help in the kitchen getting the evening meal ready, and these useless slobs can help too. You're absolutely going to ruin your reputation holed up alone with three men."

"They're not really men," Solie pointed out. She sounded uncertain.

"They're lazy, and they're only good for fighting: they're men. At least they don't drink." She patted Solie's head. "I'll expect you in an hour." Turning, she shook her finger at the rest. "And you three, behave yourselves! You're not so big I can't switch you if I have to."

Solie sighed as the older woman swept out and all of the battlers returned their attention to her. "She's right. I think I'm starting to feel trapped," she admitted.

Ril frowned, knowing he was part of the problem, but the bond was still so new, not even a day old! He felt newly hatched again, incapable of even thinking of leaving his queen. She was right, though. She might be a queen, but she was human as well. She'd go mad with them present all the time.

He pushed himself to his feet, announcing, "I'll go stand

guard." As long as one of them was with her, that would be enough, and someone should watch the perimeter anyway.

His tunic brushing his legs—an odd new sensation—he walked down the hallway and up the stairs, one person going so far as to flatten against the wall as he passed. It was snowing outside, and the accumulation drifted down the steps under the awning, but Ril didn't feel it under his bare feet, not really. He shivered a little as he stepped outside. He had fixed his broken wing when he changed shape, but the injury to his form was still there. Not enough to care about, but enough to notice.

Everyone certainly was aware of him. He knew he stood out, walking around in bare feet and a tunic too big for him, and he didn't know what they'd been told about the battle the night before, but he also didn't care. He walked to the edge of the cliff and surveyed the Shale Plain. It wasn't completely covered in white; he could see spears of gray rock throughout. Nothing moved out there, however, and he felt all the life forms on the cliff and below, as well as inside: the other sylphs, their masters, and everyone else. Absolutely everyone. No one felt hostile to him. No one was a threat.

Mace appeared beside him, dressed more completely than Ril with the addition of pants and boots. He stared out over the plain as well.

"If I thought I could, I'd go after my master now," the battler remarked. "He's cold and frightened—he'd be an easy kill. But I don't want to leave the queen that long, or find out that he can still give me an order I have to obey."

"You'd go back to the home hive if you killed him," Ril pointed out. "He's your tie here."

"No. My pattern is tied to the queen now as well. She can hold me here if he dies." Mace looked at him. "Your master is still here, but with the queen to tie you to this world instead, he's no longer necessary, either."

Ril closed his eyes, feeling a hate inside of himself strong enough to taste. It radiated out, and he heard people scream. Reluctantly, he pulled it in. Solie had given her orders: no auras. He could still feel it, though.

"Yes," he breathed.

"I like it here," Mace remarked. "I can guard the hive easily from here."

Ril turned away, knowing the other battler would watch the plains for as long as was necessary, and that Heyou was protecting and nourishing the queen. He turned back to the hive stairs, and he didn't need an aura to frighten the people who saw his eyes.

Heyou watched Solie eat, happy just to be with her, to have other sylphs around, and other battlers. It never would have happened back home, but he was her lover, not the others, and she'd made it clear she would only have him. He'd never felt so loved.

Solie ate some stew and shook her head. "You're staring again," she pointed out.

"Oh, sorry." He looked away, at the room. It was dim, lit only by candles and oil lamps, but was warm and secure. All of the others would move down here when the work was done, if the humans could be convinced to live underground. The dwellings would probably become more appealing once the outside really started to get cold. Heyou liked it. The design was similar to his old hive, if a bit different in shape. Still, if his queen wanted to live out in the snow, he'd be just as happy to go with her.

Solie continued eating her stew, and also the single piece of bread she'd been given. They weren't on severely restricted rations yet, but she savored the bread, knowing it wouldn't last all winter. Finishing, she looked down at her tray. "What happens now?" she wondered aloud.

"Who says anything has to happen?" Heyou asked.

She shrugged. "No one, I guess. I suppose we won. We have three battlers. Who can stop us now?" She made a face and scratched her head. "It's so strange, though. I have a lot to get used to."

Heyou grinned. "Think how Ril and Mace feel." They'd told him a little about their lives since they'd crossed through the gate, and it made him cold inside. This new hive was heaven, even without comparing it to the nightmares they had been forced to endure.

She smiled back at him and twitched her shoulders. "I was thinking. I got you because they did that ritual and the prince didn't kill me. That's how the ritual is supposed to work, isn't it? You get a battle sylph by offering him a woman. What happens if someone else figures that out? Someone who thinks we're an enemy?"

Heyou didn't answer.

"And what about Ril and Mace? They came wanting women." Solie gave a choked laugh. "I'm definitely not sleeping with any of them. They'll get lonely, won't they?"

Heyou shrugged, not sure what to say. "There are a lot of women here," he mused. "Maybe they can find someone."

"You mean, to date?"

"Um. Sort of. Mace said he's been with hundreds of women. We don't have that chance at home. There's only ever one queen in a hive. But we can love any woman. He's already looking at the girls here. He told me."

Solie's eyes got wide. "I never thought a battler would be allowed to have girlfriends. . . ."

"Mace wasn't. He just slept with them."

Her jaw dropped. "He *what*? Wait a minute, you said hundreds?"

"Sure." Heyou shrugged.

Solie closed her mouth and started giggling at an image that was in her mind all too absurd! "The Widow Blackwell is going to be livid! Can you imagine?" She pressed her hands over her mouth, sniggering at the thought of Mace sneaking into the single girls' tents and the widow chasing him out with her spoon.

Heyou laughed along, made happier by Solie's amusement than by the situation. She was the queen and her pattern was primary, but sylphs could absorb as many patterns as they wanted. That was what let them bond to a master in the first place. The others would have to find new masters eventually. In this energy-poor world, they fed from the humans to whom they were bound, and Solie couldn't support three battlers on her own forever.

Of course Ril and Mace couldn't keep their former masters. Solie had ordered them not to take their rage out on men, telling them that human males weren't like those from other hives and therefore enemies. After meeting Galway, Heyou could believe this. But the masters who had enslaved them? They were the worst enemies any sylph could ever imagine. Much better to find a willing woman and see one's former master dead. Surely Solie wouldn't begrudge them that.

The council had never been much, composed as it was of men who'd survived the original battler attack and tried to take charge without much experience or even interest. The fact that those same two battlers were now living among them didn't help any, and the Community teetered on the edge of total collapse, almost everyone wanting to grab their families and run. Seated at a rough table at one end of the largest tent, the council members were nearly swamped by the petitioners gathered before them. Nearly every able-bodied man had come.

"How could you let this happen?" one shouted, his voice rising over the grumbling of the others. "We had flocks and fields, homes of our own. Now we're stuck in some sylph-riddled hole with the very battlers who drove us here!"

Other men shouted in agreement, and Morgal frantically tried to wave them down, truly regretting the deaths of the men who had first led the Community. They were the ones who'd drawn the people together and kept them that way, encouraging others to bind sylphs and to use them to cultivate the harsh ground. They'd had a full harvest in the field to take them through winter . . . until the battlers blew it apart, and the town along with it.

"Calm down!" he shouted. "Please!"

"Make them leave!" a different man shouted, his face filled with fear. "Or kill them!"

Morgal scoffed. "You can't kill battlers!"

Over by the tent flap, Galway watched them argue. Looking down at Devon, he saw the younger man had a hand raised, not trying to get anyone's attention but merely touching his nearly invisible sylph for comfort. He looked exhausted. All of them were. And their weariness and fear were going to cause them problems they might not be able to fix later.

Galway pushed away from the support pole he was leaning against and stepped forward, lifting his own voice. "If you threaten the battlers, you'll put them on the defensive. They're only a danger if they feel they have to fight." When the gathered crowd glared at him with mistrust he added, "Treat them with respect and they'll have no reason to bother anyone."

"You're on their side! You came here with them!" This accusation came from Zem, the man who'd bonded the Community's only healer sylph.

Galway shrugged. "True. And Heyou never laid a hand on me." He waited a moment in the ensuing silence. "Think on this. You say you were driven here by a battler attack. Well, now you have three battlers. They won't let anything happen to this place unless you make them leave, which I doubt you could. They won't desert the girl, and if you threaten her"—he raised a finger—"they'll raze this entire mountain."

A cold shiver ran through the room. Galway just nodded. "Like it or not, they're staying. Why not make the best of it? We've got battlers. That means the next attack that comes won't be so horrible. Think it won't happen? Would you be holing up in a fortress if you didn't?"

The men were all quiet, give or take a few murmurs, before another man stood up. "We've got more to worry about than battlers," he called out. "How are we expected to make it through the winter? There's not enough food, and we can't hunt from here. There's a reason these plains are described as *dead*."

"And what about the prisoner?" someone else cried. "We want to hang him! What's the delay?" Most of the gathered men cheered.

Galway turned away, sighing. He didn't want to hear about any hangings.

Devon followed him. "You make a good point," he remarked as they walked outside.

"What else can I do?" The trapper looked out through the falling white. "I should have left sooner. Unless this snow lets up, and I doubt it will, I'm stuck here. And it won't be nearly so nice with a trio of angry battlers around. I'd rather they didn't think we were a threat."

"You sound so calm about them," Devon remarked, clearly puzzled. "They scare the life out of me. I don't know how you can stand them."

Galway laughed. "Probably helps I've spent my life hunting dangerous animals. They're plenty scary. Heyou's a good kid. *He* doesn't get all worked up that he's a battler, so no reason I should."

"Not everyone is going to agree with that," Devon replied.

"Most of the women will. They know who's going to be

protecting their kids." Galway glanced back toward the council tent, where they could hear arguments still going on, about food and executions and even the battlers again. He'd said his piece. Any more would only serve to undermine his argument.

He had a sudden idea. "Maybe it'll help for them to see the battlers helping with something the people here can't do." Clapping the other man on the shoulder, the trapper set off through the snow.

"Where are you going?" Devon asked.

"To ask a favor."

Chapter Twenty

Leon knelt on the cold floor of a room carved from solid stone, his only light provided by a single fat candle that dripped rivers of wax down its sides. His boots had been taken, along with his weapons, and his hands and ankles were tied behind him. A short rope led between the two, making it so he couldn't stretch from his cramped position. His hands and feet were numb from lack of circulation, and he had a huge knot on his head from where Mace had hit him. His vision was a little fuzzy, and every time he moved he felt nauseous.

He didn't move much, kneeling there in a haze of pain and exhaustion, his head bowed to his chest. Everything he'd ever had faith in had come crashing down, shattering in the instant when he first heard his battler speak. He'd killed that little girl for nothing, murdered her for no reason at all except the order of a king he hadn't respected for years.

Ril had never been his. They'd worked together for fifteen years, lived together, watched Leon's girls grow. All that time, Ril had seemed to hate him a little less than other battlers did their own masters, and Leon had convinced himself that the sylph had some level of affection for him, even that Ril returned a little bit of the love of his master. Now Leon knew just how badly he'd been fooling himself. He was a traitor, a murderer. He'd taken a creature who'd risked everything to come through that gate and betrayed him in a manner beyond comprehension, then turned him into a slave.

Leon's neck and back ached as he knelt there, his knees on fire against the hard stone floor. His mouth was dry but tears leaked down his face and into his beard. All he could do was wait for someone to come and kill him while he remembered every day of the last fifteen years and every second of that girl's death. He didn't know why Mace hadn't already killed him, but it was a cruelty.

The door, a thin slab of perfectly balanced stone, swung open with barely a breath of air. It let blinding light in from the hallway outside, and Leon blinked in pain, peering up. A man stood in the doorway, dressed in a rough tunic that was several sizes too large for him and hung to his bare knees. It was all he wore, and snow peppered his bare legs. He was tall and lean, his short blond hair hanging in front of his eyes.

He looks like one of Lizzy's favorite storybook characters, Leon thought hazily. The eyes, however, were bright with hatred. They were familiar, even though they were gray now instead of gold.

"Ril?" he whispered. The battler's face twisted with rage, and Leon's head dropped again. "Oh, gods."

Ril was suppressing his hatred, not projecting at all, but Leon was still master enough to feel it. He could sense the sylph's loathing and rage, as well as the pain Ril still felt from his wound. And Leon now sensed all of the things that had normally been masked by Ril's aura of hatred, a tempest of emotions he hadn't realized the sylph harbored.

Tasting his turmoil, Leon bowed his head deeper. There was silence. After fifteen years of slavery, his battler apparently didn't know what to say.

Leon spoke first. "I'm sorry."

That broke through. "How dare you say that to me!" Ril shouted. His hate aura flared for a moment, then was just as quickly buried.

"What else am I going to say?"

"You killed her!" Ril screamed. Dropping to his knees before his master, he grabbed Leon by the throat and hauled him upright. "She was helpless, and you killed her!"

Leon found himself choking, and he gasped for air even as he wished the battler would just finish it. "I know. I'm sorry! I'm so sorry!" That girl could have been Lizzie, or any of his daughters.

"You!" Ril squeezed harder, cutting off Leon's air, but finally shoved him back, hard. "I can't kill you! Those damn orders protect you from me!"

Leon lay on the floor, his arms and legs screaming with pain while he gasped for breath. He could only think of one thing that would allow him to live with himself. Or not.

"I release you!" he gasped. "From all of it! Do whatever you want to me!"

Ril stared, feeling the bonds relax. Leon was still his master. He could feed from the man's energy, and he inhaled, drinking deeply. It felt familiar, comfortable, healing. But the rules were gone. Not just the commands never to speak or change his shape that Solie had broken, either. He could do anything now.

He could still feel Leon, though, just as Leon could now clearly feel him. Without the hate aura up, Ril felt the man's remorse and regret, his absolute love for his wife and daughters, and even for Ril himself. The battler told himself that wasn't enough, that his master had to die for every crime he'd ever committed, but he kept remembering Leon stroking him, Leon's gentle touch, the times Leon let his daughters stay and play with him when everyone said he shouldn't, how he'd come here and risked his life to rescue Ril from two battlers after seeing him knocked down. Leon always paid attention to him, which was the very thing Ril had crossed the gate to find: someone's notice.

The battler's face twisted horrifically. "Damn you!" he gasped. "Damn you forever!" Turning, he ran.

Leon lay where he'd been left, weeping quietly from emotions he couldn't name.

Giddy with freedom, Heyou flew high over the plains, his senses tickling the broken land below as he raced against the winds. It was still snowing, but he darted easily through the flakes, headed steadily eastward. He didn't know what lay in that direction, as they'd come from the south, but there had to be something.

Optimistic, he decided to keep going and swooped down, traveling fast enough that he could already see the end of the plains and the ground rising up into more mountains. He swooped through them and over the forests that covered the slopes, darting down valleys in between.

He didn't really see what he was looking for, not in those snow-filled mountain forests. Galway hadn't been terribly specific, other than that he avoid humans and human settlements. Solie had been in agreement when he left her with Mace. It felt strange to be away from her, but good to be trusted with this.

Heyou shot through a canyon and swooped upward in surprise as it opened into a settled valley with pastures of cattle and a full-sized town. No one was outside to see him, cottage-sized and comprised of winged black smoke, but he heard dogs barking. He flew up into the cloud line and kept going, careful not to reveal himself any more than he already had.

There were human habitations everywhere. A road snaked through the first valley and into the next, where more villages stood. Forced to stay high, Heyou followed it, wending his way past the mountains and valleys until they at last ended. Before him now lay a huge expanse of water, any land on the other side too far away to see. Here on the coast, a city with a castle was built along the shore and wharves reached out into the blue, packed thick with ships.

More vessels were out at sea, fishing in the icy water. Intrigued, Heyou swept out past the farthest of the ships and only then dropped in altitude.

The water smelled strange and moved constantly. Barely skimming the waves, Heyou sent out his senses, looking for life . . . and was amazed to find it all around him. Even the water seemed animate, though that wasn't much use for his purposes. He slowed a little and sensed farther, finding schools of fish that darted here and there with a single mind. They didn't help much either.

He finally discovered what he needed farther out, breaching the water in slow arcs. Most of them were more than he could handle, but he did see one or two that were large enough for what Galway intended without being too big to lift. At least, he hoped this was what Galway wanted. The trapper hadn't said anything about great big bodies of water.

Heyou dove, focusing a blast of power strong enough to kill without obliterating. It slammed into his target, blowing the creature right out of the water while its pod mates dove in a panic, and he dug his claws into the carcass before it could fall, yanking it up with him into the air. The weight turned out to be nearly more than he could carry after all. Giving a shriek, Heyou almost ended up plummeting into the waves. Instead he forced himself upward, all of his energy focused on that one task.

Trembling, he started back the way he'd come, his prize dangling below, but this made him somewhat less successful at remaining unnoticed. Heyou saw humans standing in the streets of the city, staring up at him. He tried to gain more altitude, but he wasn't strong enough. Desperate, he created more claws and dug them into the beast, as the ones he had created already were starting to tear through, and sent a plea home along the hive lines. A distant answer came as he struggled onward, slowly making his way back up through the river valleys and mountains, and Ril met him several hours later, appearing as Heyou struggled against shifting air currents he hadn't suffered on his way to the sea.

The older battler had been in a foul mood all day, and he swooped down out of the overhanging clouds as though he expected a fight. He gasped when he saw what Heyou was carrying. It was a third again as big as the youth.

What is that?

I don't know. Galway asked me to get it.

Why?

To eat, I think. Heyou shifted his grip and nearly dropped the thing. *Help?*

Ril shuddered in revulsion, but he moved close, helping to take the weight. Together, they were able to lift the carcass up above the cloud line, where the wind currents weren't so treacherous and no one would be able to see them. Relieved, Heyou headed for home, pleased to be sharing the weight.

Galway *told you to get it?* Ril asked at last, his cloud form flickering in confusion. *Why would you obey a human?*

Heyou considered. *Solie said the men here aren't battlers, and we shouldn't act like they are. She said we have to stop seeing them as enemies.*

Men *are enemies*, Ril replied.

Galway isn't, Heyou argued. *He was kind to me. I would have died without his help.* He paused. *I think I like him. He's a friend. If someone's kind to you, it doesn't matter if they're male or female, does it? They're friends.*

It matters.

But we're *friends*, Heyou pointed out.

Ril lashed a tail of smoke. *We're different. We're from the same hive line.*

So? You weren't originally. We're friends now, though. I want men like Galway to be friends, too.

I don't need to be friends with any man! Ril thundered, and he let go of his end to race away.

Heyou squealed and wrapped himself around his prize, trying not to drop it while descending with barely controlled rapidity. Having just cleared the mountains, he nearly landed on his belly on the plain, and he skimmed that snowy surface, heading slowly and miserably for home. He could see Ril, an angry dot on the horizon, the sylph's hate broadcasting along the hive line if not into the ether, where Solie had banned it.

A distant query came from Mace, asking what was wrong. Heyou just snarled, not understanding it himself. Wrapping as much of his cloud form around the carcass as he could, which didn't prevent blood from dripping onto the snowy ground beneath him, he laboriously continued his quest.

It took him nearly the rest of the day to get home, and he was exhausted by the time he arrived. Too worn out to rise up the cliff face, he flew around back and swept up the slope, startled humans staring at him and his cargo in shock. Children shouted, running after him, but at last Heyou saw Solie coming out of a kitchen tent with a paring knife and a half-peeled potato. She was wide-eyed with surprise and delight.

Mace was just behind her, his face impassive, but shocked men gaped at Heyou from every direction—and at what he carried. For once they weren't afraid. Heyou could even feel a happy relief from them, and the realization of what Galway had intended: that the battlers could provide enough food for the Community to survive the winter.

Heyou floated right up to his queen and dropped his cargo, letting the fifteen-foot whale thud into the snow. Shifting back to human form, he stumbled over to her and fell into her arms, completely worn out. As her energy pulsed out over him, he pressed close, drinking.

"Is this enough meat?" he asked plaintively.

She giggled. "I certainly hope so."

They ate well that night, feasting on thick whale steaks. What parts they couldn't eat were already being smoked and the fat rendered down for candles and oil. Such preparation was disgusting, ugly work, but the Community was happy and confident for the first time in months.

Solie sat at a table with her battlers, and while none of the sylphs was eating, she enjoyed her own meal. There was already talk of them bringing in more food, including fruits and vegetables if possible. That was one task the other sylphs couldn't be used for, as they wouldn't kill anything, not even a plant. Though sylphs helped till the earth and tend the crops, harvesting had to be done by humans. The battlers, naturally, had no such compunctions.

"Do you mind helping get food?" she asked them as she ate. The whale meat was oily but good, and there was more than enough.

Heyou shrugged. "S'long's it's not so big. I think I pulled something."

Ril looked away, but Mace nodded slowly. "As long as this place isn't left unguarded, we don't mind."

Solie smiled at the trio. She still wasn't used to this strange empathy, and she ignored it most of the time, just for the sake of her sanity, but her battle sylphs were hard to block out. Mace felt like a smooth lake, strong and soothing. Heyou was a sparkling fountain, exciting and happy. Ril . . . was a strangled swamp, or a dam about to break.

She looked over at him. The battler was staring out at the gathered families, his aura contained but his mood sour, dragging at her. Something was bothering him, and she wasn't sure what to do about it. Ril was far older than she. Was it her place to invade his privacy? Though he was hers, she barely knew him at all.

Solie sighed, the oiliness of her meal defeating her appetite. She was tired. She had been fatigued since before she came here and the feeling was worse today. She knew the battlers took their energy from her, but it hadn't really occurred to her that she might not have enough. Ril's attitude dragged at her.

As she stared at her plate, Mace leaned over the table and smacked the other sylph across the head. Ril spun, eyes wide with rage, as the bigger battler jerked a thumb at Solie.

"Stop draining her. Heyou took enough today."

Ril glanced at Solie, and suddenly her weariness eased a bit. Heyou leaned against her. "Are you okay?" he asked.

"Yes," she admitted. Her appetite was back and she took another bite.

"Go feed from that master of yours if you're tired," Mace told Ril. "Only one of us should take from Solie."

"I don't see you going to *your* master," Ril growled.

"I'll find someone else," Mace promised calmly. "There are a lot of options here. Maybe you should take one."

As Ril made a face, Heyou smiled at Solie. "Sorry I took so much."

"I don't blame you," she told him. "That thing was huge! And it wasn't that long ago you had that big fight. I can handle it."

"You shouldn't have to handle three," Mace assured her.

At one of the other tables, a family finished dining and started to take their plates up to the front of the tent. Instead of avoiding the battlers, though, they approached the table. The wife addressed the trio.

"Thank you so much," she told them, her eyes shining. "It's the first time we haven't gone hungry in so long." Her children stared worshipfully at the battlers, and even the husband managed to lift his head enough to look at them directly.

"Um, yeah, thanks."

The battlers didn't say anything in return, as none of them was normally inclined to talk to humans. Solie could feel their auras, though. Heyou was pleased by the praise, finding the transition to acceptance of human men relatively easy. Mace was calm—uninterested, but not threatened either. Ril was wound so tight he was ready to lash out. Hesitantly Solie put a hand on his shoulder, and he stiffened before finally forcing himself to relax. His emotions turned apologetic.

The first family started a floodgate, many other people coming up to thank the threesome for feeding them. Solie had known food was short, but it seemed she hadn't realized just how bad things were. Her sylphs had probably saved the Community, and she beamed at them, hoping this was a trend they would be willing and able to continue.

Chapter Twenty-one

Jasar killed one of his horses getting back to the castle, and the survivor was blowing froth and wheezing as it galloped under the main portcullis and into the courtyard. Filthy and frightened, the dandy still managed to look imperiously down at the groom who came to take the animal.

"Alert the king that I've returned," he ordered, dismounting, wincing as all the muscles in his legs and backside protested. That only made him angrier. "I'll need to speak with him privately once I've bathed."

Turning, he swept into the castle proper, servants and courtiers hurrying out of his way. It was humiliating for them to see him like this, but good to be back. He stalked to his apartments and, inside, took a deep breath. He was home, away from the empty roads and cold winds, away from Leon's threats and his own battler's betrayal. The terror he'd felt continuously for the last five days slipped away in the face of renewed comfort, and he snapped his fingers, directing several waiting servants to prepare him a bath and remove his filthy clothes.

Mace's alcove stood empty in one corner of the front room. Jasar glared at the empty space, then turned his back, not wanting to be reminded. The battle had been truly disastrous, and if he wasn't very careful, he was going to end up blamed for this. He could feel his confidence returning, though. Now that he was back on familiar ground, he knew he could survive.

He took an hour to bathe and made servants change the water twice. It would take at least that long before the king would be ready to see him, and Jasar felt positively filthy. Even afterward he didn't feel completely clean, though he was intelligent enough to know that most of his discomfort was internal.

None of the servants spoke to him during his bath—he would have dismissed them immediately if they dared—but it coiled in his gut, the knowledge that they were surely wondering what had happened to Mace. They'd be whispering about it all over the castle. Jasar burned with embarrassment at the very thought. Growling, he slapped one servant across the face who didn't move fast enough, and rising from the tub, held his arms out for a robe. With it belted around him, he went to his dressing room.

They garbed him in satin and silk, with lace at his wrists and neck. Soft boots clad his feet, and he sighed contentedly as they styled his hair and perfumed him. It felt good to be cleaned and again dressed appropriately, the fine material and trappings of power once more a shield against those who might mock or revile him. Tossing a short cloak of ermine over his shoulder, he went at last to face the king.

Alcor awaited him in the same audience chamber he'd used when giving his initial instructions for the quest. Thrall stood behind him in the very same spot, looking down at Jasar impassively.

"What happened?" the king growled as Jasar walked up to the foot of the dais and bowed deeply.

Jasar rose and looked his sovereign straight in the eye. Alcor's directness didn't bother him. He'd have been more worried if the king had asked after his health, which usually meant Alcor planned to alter it. However, the king's bluntness demanded a similar response.

"Your Majesty," he said. "I bring terrible news. Leon Petrule has betrayed you. He's gone over to the side of pirates, and his battler has killed my own."

Alcor was silent for a long moment. Jasar could see his

mind working. He was no fool, the king, but he'd always seen enemies everywhere, and Jasar had encouraged that attitude. He had also always been careful never to directly lie to Alcor, either, who knew it. Someday, Jasar had realized, he'd need that history of honesty. That day had definitely come.

"My head of security defecting and your battler killed by another? How is it you survived?" Alcor's eyes were very narrow as he studied Jasar.

"Mace's sacrifice," was the courtier's smooth reply, and he clasped his hands together before him. "It was the pirate group you sent us to eliminate. I had been led to believe they were all killed, but when we tracked the girl to them, Ril attacked Mace. I apologize that I didn't foresee this betrayal. Leon is definitely working for them, though. He would have killed me if he could."

The king frowned, plucking at his lower lip. "And the girl?"

"She was with them, as was her battler. Mace didn't have a chance against two." He shook his head, his tone deliberately regretful. "Apparently, Leon's assertion that the girl is innocent was a lie. Father Belican was right—she was a plant. The pirates are far more organized and malicious than we thought."

The king sat back, considering. It was a good lie. Even with his panic, Jasar had worked it up over the last few days as he fled, and it was one of his best, shunting all the blame neatly from him to Leon. He could even come out of this with more power and respect than before. He resisted the urge to lick his lips, and waited.

"This is serious," the king said at last, and Jasar was pleased to hear the note of uncertainty in his voice. Alcor believed him. Of course, the lie nearly demanded that he do so. "Gather the council," he ordered the servant who stepped into the room after he sat up and clapped. "We will discuss this."

The king looked at Jasar then. "You've done well to bring us this information," he admitted, and Jasar bowed again, no sign showing on his face of the smirk he felt inside. "You will be rewarded—once the battle is done and you've returned."

"Returned, Your Majesty?"

The king's mouth curled, and Jasar suddenly wondered just how much of his lie Alcor actually believed. His sovereign pronounced, "You know where these pirates are. Someone will have to lead the army and the battlers I send to destroy them. You're familiar with the area. You'll be invaluable."

Jasar's blood ran cold. He had to go back? Back to where Leon wanted him dead and Mace was out of control? No battler had ever disobeyed his master, and he had a sudden, horrible image of the creature coming for him.

"Your Majesty, I couldn't! I—I'd be a target. Leon promised to kill me if I went back, and he still has a battle sylph."

The king languidly waved a hand and looked over his shoulder at Thrall. "Then I suppose we'll have to get you another battler, won't we?" he drawled.

Jasar froze with sudden ambition. Another battler? Someone who would obey him as Mace hadn't? Someone Leon wouldn't be expecting? He smiled and bowed again, deeper than before. "Yes, Your Majesty. Your wish is my command."

They decided not to let the children and teenagers know. None of the Community's youths needed to see such a horrible thing as a hanging. None of them would even know the man had been killed, just as most didn't know he'd even been there.

"May as well let them keep their innocence," Devon murmured quietly. Airi was pressed against his back while he watched earth sylphs grow a stone pole that rose up at the edge of the cliff and then extended out over the drop. A rope lay coiled at the base, ready to be affixed. That rope would go around the prisoner's neck. All they'd have to do was push him off the side, and his own weight would finish the job.

I don't like this, Airi mourned. *Does he have to die?*

Devon shook his head. It wasn't for him to say. Morgal and the others were determined, though. Leon Petrule had caused the deaths of too many people. Ril apparently was going to be excused for his actions, but not the sylph's master. Galway had walked away from Stria and the others creating the scaffold, going to tend his horses, his absence his statement on how he felt. Devon still wasn't sure that he shouldn't have accepted the trapper's quiet offer to join him.

"I can't say as I blame them," he told Airi.

The queen will be unhappy.

"I don't think Solie gets a vote on this."

Devon looked over the crowd gathering at the stairwell leading into the hive. Solie and Heyou were down there now, helping out, as was Mace. More and more of the Community was moving down there to escape the cold and snow, for the place was warm and cozy, if dark in those areas without fire sylphs. The kitchens had moved down there as well, which was where the Widow Blackwell had every youngster working on something to keep them distracted. It was easier to keep them isolated that way, and Devon doubted any of them even knew that their parents were aboveground, gathered on an icy stretch of rock and awaiting an execution. The temperature seemed colder than anything Devon had ever felt, but still no one left.

He peeked behind him. Ril stood a few hundred feet

away, staring out over the plains. It always seemed to be him on guard duty now. Someone had found him a better-fitting tunic and pants, and the sylph didn't really look any different from anyone else—except for the fact that he didn't wear a cloak in the frigid wind and everyone gave him a wide berth.

Odd, how the three battlers had adapted. Heyou was largely accepted by the Community, being cheerful and friendly. Mace seemed to be getting a reputation among the women that had some of the men grinding their teeth and the Widow Blackwell watching him like a hawk whenever he was near her charges. But Ril was the worst. Silent and angry, he made everyone nervous, and Devon hoped he didn't care his old master was about to be hanged. If he knew, he wasn't reacting at all. He wasn't even watching as the scaffold went up.

The crowd gathered, nearly every adult huddled together for warmth and murmuring softly. Their sylphs flickered around them, the air sylphs mostly invisible, those of earth obvious and heavy, water and fire varying between the extremes. They all chattered like children, some of them asking their masters what was happening, and from the look of it not liking the answer.

"You don't have to stay," he told Airi. "I know you don't like death."

I'll stay with you, she answered loyally, which made him smile and hum under his breath for her. She pressed against him, semicorporeal and snuggled against his back.

Nearby the crowd murmured, drawing back, and Devon saw Leon for the first time since his capture. The king's head of security hung limp between two men who dragged him through the snow, a bruise across his forehead obvious against his white skin. His hands and feet were bound, and he was barefoot, not even a cloak wrapped around him.

Devon swallowed, wishing absurdly that this didn't have

to happen. The Community's members were spitting at Leon, though, tossing insults and laughing. Some were weeping. They would all be glad to see him die, and Devon couldn't blame them. Leon Petrule was an extremely dangerous man.

Yet he hoped Leon died quickly. From the look of the setup, he would. King Alcor liked to make his prisoners suffer. Leon would likely die immediately of a broken neck. Devon shuddered, his own neck twitching at the thought. He forced himself to watch, though. He'd had to stay as much as Galway needed to leave—out of respect for both the Community and Leon himself.

He didn't turn away as they bore the doomed man forward. No one did, so no one saw what was happening behind them.

As Ril took his third turn in a row on guard duty, something beneath the skin of his human form itched. He didn't know how to scratch it, or even what it was. The feeling grated at him, though, making Heyou regard him cautiously and Mace keep assigning him guard duty.

He hadn't been in the queen's presence for days. Mace was keeping him away from her, Ril knew, just in case he snapped. He was starting to think it could happen, too. He felt the madness inside him, just as he had when his first human queen died and until Lizzy was born. Thus he was being forced to stay on the outskirts of this new hive, just as he had in the original hive into which he'd been hatched.

Yes, he was falling apart a second time, and he didn't know how to stop it. He kept seeing Leon—saw him killing the brown-haired girl, saw Leon holding out an arm as a place to perch, saw him coming to help after Mace knocked Ril out of the sky. Saw Leon giving him the freedom to do whatever he wanted, including kill him.

He should have killed him. Ril wanted to kill him, but

he could also feel his master's remorse. But that didn't matter. He hated Leon, would always hate him. He was now a battle sylph with a queen who acknowledged his name!

Though . . . he still wanted Lizzy.

Would she hate him if he killed her father? He couldn't. Solie had ordered her battlers to cause no harm, not even if Leon begged. He'd wanted to! Only, Leon had wanted him to as well. How could he give Leon what he wanted when he hated Leon so? Yet how could he let him live? What was happening to him?

Ril shuddered, wanting to run, wanting to fight, wanting to bury his face in Solie's bosom and scream until it all went away. Wanting to go to Lizzy and give himself to her. Wanting to kill Leon. Wanting to throw his master off the cliff and let him fall. Wanting to obey. He hated Leon, and something still held him back, something beyond his queen. Insanity beckoned, the only promise of peace.

The nearby humans were gathered around some strange device. Ril had felt them moving but ignored them. Their emotions were increasing, though, peaking toward rage, and that finally cut through his indifference, far later than it would have for either Mace or Heyou. He turned toward them and blinked as he both spotted and felt his bound master being dragged toward what he suddenly realized was a hangman's scaffold. Leon's emotions were dim, sickly and sad, remorseful and relieved. He saw his own death before him and was glad of it.

Ril saw, too. He froze, his eyes widening and his shape dissipating silently in shock. They were going to kill his master? He couldn't let that happen! Only, Leon had freed him. He *could* let it happen. They would kill Leon for him, free him, leave him to approach Lizzy without interference or guilt. He'd dreamed of this for years.

No, he hadn't. He'd hated Leon—or so he'd told himself—but they'd worked well together, better than any other battler and master. Leon had understood him as well as anyone could through that litany of rules, and the man had given Ril all the freedoms he could. He'd also loved the battler despite his hatred. Ril could feel that love clearly even now. Leon went willingly to his death, hoping to atone for what he'd never meant to do.

A shifting form of black smoke and lightning, Ril wailed up and along the ether, his denial finally abandoned. He loved Leon, too, that emotion somehow sneaking into him over the years, and he *did* want him to live. That was why he couldn't kill him, and why he'd been self-destructing. He loved his master anyway.

He almost went to Leon to save him, but in his epiphany and shock he couldn't focus his shape, let alone his power. He'd kill everyone, including Leon, and Solie's rule was absolute. Harm no one.

Solie! She could stop this.

Wait for me! he broadcast. Then he shot away, angling himself behind the crowd and toward the stairway into the hive. He had to find her before it was too late.

Leon was glad when they finally came for him. He'd known it would happen. It didn't matter how horrible he felt or how much he tried to apologize. He'd still helped kill these people, and he had to die for that. He kept silent instead, trying to make it easier for them.

Though he mourned that he wouldn't see his family again, he was also relieved. What he'd done to Ril . . . The realization of it had torn through him and left him bloody. He couldn't forgive himself. He'd thought himself a man of honor, only to find he had no honor at all. He'd become a murderer and hadn't even realized, blaming Ril, loving Ril, never thinking Ril had a reason for all his unending hatred. He'd even dared think that on some level Ril loved him back. He was such a fool. Now he'd pay for it.

He was dragged from his cell and through the corridors of the underground palace they'd dug, up into a cold that froze his skin and made his teeth chatter. Eyes squeezed shut against the wind, he was heaved through a crowd that roared for his death and to the edge of the cliff. Finally looking up, he saw the stone scaffold from which they'd hang him, the rope already waiting.

Wait for me!

Leon started at the voice even as they pulled him to his bloodless feet and helped him stand. The pirate leader put the noose around his neck and tightened it, saying something about rightful punishment. Leon looked over the crowd, but he couldn't see who had spoken. The words shivered through him and he tried to speak, but no one had given him water since the day before, and his mouth was parched. He had to wait, though, just for a minute. He tried to tell them.

The long-haired leader finished his speech and took a deep breath. "May the gods have mercy on you," he told Leon, and put a firm hand on his chest. The men to either side let go, and he pushed hard.

Leon fell backward off the cliff, the rope leading from his neck twisting in the air. He only had an instant to see a flash of light before everything went black.

Chapter Twenty-two

The children of the Community were making things. Some made candles. Others carded wool or used drop-spindles to spin yarn. Solie had graduated from her usual potato peeling to scraping carrots. As usual, Heyou sat beside her, dumping peels into a bowl with one hand while feeling up her leg beneath the cover of the table with the other.

Solie alternately blushed and giggled, wondering if she could get him back to her room without the widow noticing. The woman couldn't ban her from being with Heyou, but she certainly made such pleasures impossible during the day. Right now, though, the woman wasn't paying her any attention. Mace had come down to the cavernous eating area and was, for lack of a better word, stalking the human girls. Solie could feel his interest.

So could the girls. From where she was sitting, Solie watched Mel and Aneala both gape at him with scarlet faces. Loren winked at him daringly, and the big battler went straight for her. His interest was so strong that it made Solie blush from halfway across the room. The boys watched enviously.

"I didn't know you guys could project *that*," Solie managed to say to Heyou, her face warm.

"Yup." He grinned. "Do you want me to do it to you?"

"Maybe later." When they weren't in public. Solie wasn't so sure Loren cared about decorum, though. The girl's breathless response to Mace's lust was obvious. "I think I better stop him," she said. But she didn't move. Neither did any of the other youngsters, entranced as they were—

though the very young children continued playing obliviously in one corner.

Ignoring all of them, Mace moved around the table toward Loren and reached for her, his eyes glowing.

"Don't you even think about it!" a harsh voice screamed. Shocked out of their trance, everyone turned to see the Widow Blackwell storming toward Loren and Mace, her ever-present spoon in hand. "Loren Malachi! Get yourself into the kitchen this instant, and if I *ever* catch you behaving like some sort of gillie again, I *and* your mother will tan your bottom until it's red!"

Flushing with embarrassment, the girl fled.

The widow turned on Mace. "You! Chasing young girls! Whatever are you thinking?"

"You can't tell?" the battler asked.

The other girls giggled, but the widow shook her spoon at him. "Well, get that thought out of your head! None of these children are available. I don't care how grown-up they think they are, or how all-important you think you are. You won't touch them, do you hear me?"

Mace blinked, and looked deliberately at her chest.

"You won't look at me, either!" she shrieked. "Out! Out!" Brandishing her spoon, she advanced on the battler while the teenagers laughed. He grudgingly allowed himself to be herded toward the door, his emotions amused, Solie noted, and just a little bit disappointed.

Heyou moved his hand farther up her leg, making her shiver. He said smugly, "Guess *he's* out of luck."

Mace walked quietly, the widow smacking him across the back with her spoon and continuing to berate him. As he reached the exit, his emotions changed. He stiffened and suddenly spun, snatching up the widow and leaping out of the path of the door. She screamed. An instant later, Ril blew through the doorway in his natural form.

Everyone started shrieking in panic. Ril's aura was flexing out from his storm cloud despite Solie's orders, the balls of lightning that were his eyes glowing so bright they were nearly white. Solie felt Heyou grab her around the waist and yank her out of the way as the battler flew forward, Ril's emotions so overwhelming they made her head swim.

Ril reached her table and shifted to human form, not bothering to appear inside his clothing. They tumbled to the floor around him as he leaned on the table, naked. "They're going to hang Leon," he told her. "Stop them!"

"What?" she managed.

"My master! They're going to kill my master!" He almost sobbed it, his emotions agonized. Mace stepped up behind him, putting a hand on his shoulder and pulling him away. Heyou was still tense, Solie saw. Both battlers watched Ril, ready to attack.

Solie forced herself to think. Leon was being hanged? No one had told her anything about that. She glanced at Heyou, her heart in her throat. "Go!"

He hesitated for a moment, staring, then he was gone, a flicker of black smoke and wings racing out the door.

Ril stared at her, his eyes wide, and wrenched free of Mace. Turning to smoke himself, he followed Heyou.

Solie lifted her arms. "Help me," she commanded Mace. It was so far to the surface. Too far, she suspected, to arrive in time.

His arms surrounded her, warm and covered in coarse hair thicker than that of Heyou's human form. He lifted her up and changed, became blackness that engulfed, caught, and raised her up. Then she felt them both move.

She couldn't see, and tried not to hold her breath as the battle sylph raced after his fellows. Her position changed from horizontal to vertical and back to horizontal, but finally Mace shifted back, setting her down on snowy ground but keeping the edge of his mantle around her for warmth. Frightened, Solie stared at the scene before her.

"What have you done?"

Heyou shot out of the stairwell at high speed, arcing over the crowd just as Morgal pushed Leon backward off the cliff. Lesser sylphs scattered at the sight of him, and he focused a short sharp wave of destruction that lashed out and hit the scaffold, cleaving through it just as the rope was about to reach its full extension. The entire top of the scaffold broke away with a bright flash and a roar of shattering stone.

Ril shot past, zipping over the crowd and down, catching Leon in his mantle before the man could fall more than a few yards. Heyou followed, not understanding. The other battler was moving toward the bottom of the bluff, Leon fully encased and protected. Hadn't Ril hated him? Why would he want to save his master at all? Or was this why Ril had been acting so unbalanced?

Heyou knew that Mace was worried about Ril's control. Sometimes, Heyou knew, conquered sylphs subsumed into new hives went mad. Both he and Mace shared fears this was happening to Ril, and that they'd have to kill him to protect the hive and Solie. Already neither of them wanted Ril near her, and the young battler suspected Ril knew. He himself couldn't imagine being banned from his queen.

He saw Ril reach the bottom of the cliff and shift, laying his master on the ground. Leon had been bound at the wrists and ankles, and Ril reshaped a finger into a claw. Using this, he cut through the ropes, and the man groaned as his limbs flopped free. Heyou could feel Petrule's pain at the sensation coming back into his hands and feet. Heyou shifted to human form, but Ril ignored him as though he weren't there and focused on his master.

No, Heyou really didn't understand.

* * *

Ril gazed down at Leon, so exhausted he could barely think. Distantly he suspected that he was in shock, that he had been now for a long time. So was Leon, who stared up with wide eyes as Ril loosened the noose around his neck and finally pulled it free with a terrible gentleness.

"I thought you hated me," he whispered.

"I do," Ril said automatically. "I hate you more than anything."

Despite his words, when Leon shivered, Ril partly shifted, draping an edge of his mantle over him. He tried to focus his aura just to prove his hatred, but that wouldn't come. Only relief and confusion. Leon sighed and sat up, trying to rub his wrists with fingers that wouldn't function. He'd been tied so long the tips were gray.

Ril looked up, sending out a call. An answer came almost immediately, in a form flowing gracefully over the side of the cliff and down to them while her master shouted impotently for her to come back. Luck the Healer settled next to them and took on her blurred human form. Glancing first at Ril and then at Leon, she chose the human first after seeing Ril's glare.

She touched Leon's hands and then his feet, restoring life to the strangled limbs, soothing the concussion he'd suffered. Then she reached out for Ril, and the battler sagged as some of the pain in him lifted, the wound Mace had inflicted finally healing. She didn't speak; healers rarely did. She just did her work and went back up the cliff face.

Heyou had watched in silence. He now glanced at Ril and Leon, seemed to make a decision, and followed the healer.

Ril regarded his master. Leon's energy was weak, but it still tasted good to him. Leon rubbed his wrists for a moment and miserably returned his stare. "What do you want?" he asked.

Ril shrugged, too tired to say anything but the truth. "I want the girls. I want to see Lizzy and Betha, Cara, Nali, and Ralad. I want them to come here."

"And me?"

Ril glanced away. "I need to drink energy from somewhere. I can't take it from the queen all the time. She has too many of us."

"I see." Leon seemed to absorb this. "We can bring the girls here, if I'm welcome. I don't know that I will be."

"No one will hurt you," Ril promised.

Leon smiled faintly. Ril felt his old master accept the situation and nearly shuddered, still not sure how to accept it himself. He had to learn, though, or someday soon he suspected Mace *would* put him down. He'd probably welcome it. Only, that would mean he'd never see Lizzy again.

He forced himself to look at Leon, refusing to think of the man as his master ever again. That way lay the madness he no longer wanted to risk. There was nothing else to say.

"We'll go get the girls," Leon remarked. "Bring them all here. I couldn't go back to Eferem anyway. Not now."

Ril nodded, looking down. Again, he felt Leon's shame. "Thank you," he said.

Hesitantly, the human male put a hand on the battler's shoulder, and the sylph lifted a hand to grasp it in his own. Neither of them said anything aloud, but everything was said in silence.

Solie stared at the broken scaffold in horror, her hand pressed to her breast. They'd tried to hang Leon? She had to remind herself that they couldn't feel his regret the way she could. Still, the thought of killing him made her nauseated.

Most of the people didn't pay her any notice, arguing and exclaiming over the prisoner's escape. Solie could see Cal standing close. The carter who'd brought her and Devon to the Community was currently trying to see over the shoulders of others, and everyone was yelling for someone to announce what was happening at the bottom of the cliff. Cal's earth sylph stood nearby, staring at Solie. All of the other sylphs were doing the same, waiting for her to give a command.

Tears filled her eyes. She didn't want this! She didn't want to be in charge of anything, let alone a hive of sylphs and three battlers. Feeling her pain, Mace put a hand on the junction of her neck and shoulder, massaging her gently. He'd do anything for her. He'd do anything *to* her, she realized, and blushed. She didn't want that either.

The one thing she wanted came back over the edge of the cliff, a cloud of thick smoke and lightning with red eyes and wide wings. The humans all backed away and he landed, shifting to his human form. He was hardly bigger than she, forced to look up at all of the men and even most of the women, and he watched her intently. He was waiting, too.

What was she supposed to do? She didn't want anyone to die. But it wasn't her place to say anything to her elders. Only, it was. She was the queen, by right of the sylphs.

Distantly she felt Ril's weariness, but the wrenching turmoil inside him was much less. Whatever had just happened between him and his master, he'd found some measure of peace. He'd lose that if Leon died.

That decided her. If Ril could forgive Leon, she would too. "Nobody dies," she whispered.

Her battlers moved. Heyou turned and slammed a palm against what remained of the hangman's scaffold, which shattered, exploding into dust that blew out over the plains on the glacial wind. Mace stepped in front of Solie, flaring protectively as Ril reappeared at the edge of the cliff, setting Leon down. The king's head of security looked humbled, his regret real as he faced the crowd.

The crowd was unconvinced. They started to push forward, demanding vengeance.

Ril moved in front of Leon. The rest of the sylphs reacted, too, grasping their masters and pulling them back. Solie shivered, seeing the surprise on the human faces. Morgal regarded his fire sylph in stunned horror as she hauled him away, her flame contained so as not to burn him. Even Airi had her suddenly very solid arms around Devon's, keeping them from being raised. The men shouted orders, but the sylphs refused to obey.

"No one dies!" Mace boomed. "The queen has spoken!"

The humans turned to Solie in shock, the men held by their sylphs, the women standing in confusion beside them. All looked at Solie, who wanted to sink into the ground. The Community was full of surprise and growing anger—which made the three battlers growl.

"You can't give the orders here!" Morgal gasped. "You're just a girl."

"She's the queen," Heyou said.

"The queen," the sylphs all echoed.

"The queen."

"The queen."

Men stared in surprise at their sylphs and then at her.

The queen, Airi breathed, holding Devon still.

"Oh, my god," he managed, truly understanding at last.

Leon looked at the crowd that slavered for his execution, and at the dozens of sylphs willing to defend him at the word of a tiny redheaded girl standing half in Mace's warm mantle as if it were some kind of cloak made of darkness. He shivered, feeling the cold, and walked forward, everyone watching as he crossed to her.

Mace's eyes glowed as he approached, but the battler didn't do anything before Leon dropped heavily to one knee and bowed his head. "I am Leon Petrule and I hereby swear my loyalty and allegiance to you, the queen of the sylphs, forsaking all other oaths. I am yours to command, my lady."

Solie swallowed, shaken, while behind the man, Ril gave a strangled little sob. The last of the conflict in him evaporated. She shivered.

"I accept," she whispered, her voice echoing in the silence.

A dozen feet away, Devon looked at her and at Leon, then back at Airi. She was happy, truly happy. He surveyed the amazed crowd, able to understand their horror and confusion. Only a few had realized how things were shifting. Now they all saw how they'd come full circle. Anyone else who wanted to dictate the future of the Community had already lost.

He looked at Airi again. "Let me go, please?"

She smiled and let go, vanishing back into the wind.

Steeling himself, Devon went to kneel beside Leon. "I am Devon Chole," he said, swallowing, trying to remember exactly what the other man had said. "And I hereby swear my loyalty and allegiance to the queen of the sylphs, forsaking all other oaths. I am yours to command as well, my lady." He glanced up and added in a whisper, "Don't screw it up."

Chapter Twenty-three

For the second time in his life, Jasar Doliard of Sialmeadow stood before the altar in the summoning chamber, an ornate knife in his hand. A blonde plucked from the marketplace on a trumped-up charge of witchcraft stared at him in terror, squirming against her bonds and gag. This one had been stripped already and searched so thoroughly it was really doubtful she could even be called a virgin anymore. She had no weapons of any kind.

The priests were chanting. There were far fewer of them now, mostly students raised early in rank and led by the doddering Father Belican. With their chanting, the lines of the circle in which Jasar stood glowed, mirroring another circle that appeared above.

Somewhere behind him, Jasar knew, the king was watching, his presence betrayed by Thrall's aura of hatred. Against all tradition he'd brought the battler with him, and Jasar could see fear on the priests' faces—the sylph's rage interfered with the lines of power they were building. But the king wouldn't risk being unprotected again, and if the holy men didn't like his choice, they kept it to themselves.

Fortunately, despite Thrall's presence, and despite the fact that Jasar still had a battle sylph bound to him, the ceremony was working. Jasar watched the circle widen above him, its interior shifting through a rainbow of colors until it became a nothingness that couldn't be described as any color at all. The blonde girl whined, laid out as an offering and as bait. Jasar adjusted his grip on the knife and waited.

Something shimmered on the other side of the gate, an

awareness peering through. Jasar felt his breath catch in his throat. The last time, he hadn't known what to expect, but now he waited for that pivotal moment when the battler would arrive. It hesitated, but Jasar raised his knife, staring upward.

The battler spotted the girl. Jasar felt it and saw the thing come through, a huge black cloud of smoke and lightning, its eyes ablaze with lust. It came for the girl, and with a yell Jasar drove the knife deep into her breast. Her eyes widened and her body bucked, already dead.

The battler screamed, its hatred shaking the walls as it writhed, unable to go to the girl and unable to return as the gate closed behind it. Jasar let go of the knife, leaving it protruding from the girl's body, and glared up into the creature's maddened eyes.

"Shield!" he shouted. "I name you Shield! I am your master! You will obey me!"

Shield screamed again, named and held, wanting its freedom and Jasar dead, but a thousand years of tradition had yielded an effective litany of slavery.

"You will not harm me!" Jasar shouted, his voice determined and clear. There could be no hesitation here or the battler would kill him and everyone else before vanishing back to its own world. "You will not allow harm to come to me! You will not speak! You will take on the shape I command and stay in it! You will not feed from my energy to the point where I am endangered! You will not attack except to defend me unless I order it! You will do nothing to betray me! You are *my* battler, Shield! I bind you!"

Shield's scream at that was the loudest, shaking the room. Dust fell around Jasar as he glared at the thing. "Look!" he ordered, pointing behind him at a muzzled animal on a leash held by a frightened servant. Last time he had chosen a suit of armor, but this time he wanted something more servile. Other masters described their battlers' shape to them, but Jasar didn't have the patience. It was easier to show them. "Take that shape! I command it. Obey me!"

Shield howled, but he looked at what Jasar wanted him to be and he shifted, shrinking until a burly black dog crouched on the altar over the dead girl, teeth bared.

"Good," Jasar smirked. "Heel, dog."

Shield moved forward, his massive head swinging back to look at the sacrificed maiden. His tongue lapped out toward her, not quite touching; then he jumped down to crouch at his new master's side. Jasar turned, taking a handkerchief from his pocket to wipe the spots of blood off his hand. Shield's hatred was thick, but no worse than that of Mace. It was actually comfortable to feel it again, and Jasar smiled.

The king walked toward him, Thrall a few feet behind. "No problems, I see."

"Of course not, my lord. It's a simple ceremony." He bowed. "When it's not being sabotaged."

The king snorted. "Consider yourself luckier than my son." He turned away. "Ready yourself, Jasar. The air ship leaves in the morning. I'm sending three of my battlers with you. Four against two should be good odds." He strode out of the chamber, Thrall following.

Jasar watched Alcor go, his eyes narrow. The priests followed the king, along with the servant with the dog. Jasar waited until they were all gone before turning to his new battler.

"Listen to me, you piece of shit," he said. Shield's black eyes burned up at him, gleaming with repugnance. "I have one more order for you. Before *everything*, you will protect me. You won't let me get so much as a fly bite, is that understood? You are my shield, and you'd damn well better do a good job of it."

He strode out then, the battler heeling like a well-trained

hound. Jasar didn't look back, but Shield did, barely able to see more than the edge of the dead girl's body atop the altar. The scream inside him didn't feel as if it would ever stop.

Solie's quarters had been expanded, two earth sylphs excavating a passage to another set of apartments beside the chambers she'd already taken to be her sitting room and bedroom. At first she'd been uncertain about the addition, but now she was glad of the extra space, as the second apartment became the residence of the battlers and their new human counterparts. Without it, they'd all have been living right on top of her, and she'd have no privacy at all.

Currently, though, she didn't mind as she sat on the straw bale in the front room, running a comb through her hair. Heyou was out hunting with Ril, while Mace guarded the cliff. Devon was off duty, which left Leon watching her. The former prisoner reclined against the wall by the door, sharpening his sword and glancing at her periodically. It was almost amusing that his oath meant the battlers trusted him to do their work, but they could read what was in his heart. He wouldn't let anything happen to her.

"You know," he pointed out, testing the edge of his blade with his thumb, "you don't have to sit out here with me. I may not be welcome to most of the people here, but I'll hardly die of loneliness."

She frowned and set the comb down, shifting her long hair over her shoulder as she did. "I think I might," she answered softly.

Leon raised an eyebrow and set his whetstone aside. "You're lonely? You've always got at least one of us with you."

She shrugged, struggling with what exactly to say. "Yeah, but, well, you're all guys. I haven't talked to any women since, um . . ."

"Since they tried to hang me?" he supplied. He didn't concern himself with the past too much. It had been two days, and the men and women of the Community still looked at him mistrustfully, but no one could ignore how the sylphs accepted him, including the battlers. Thanks to the food they brought and the protection they offered, Mace and Ril had become popular despite their earlier attack, and Heyou was a local favorite. Leon had hardly been granted the same status, but at least no one was trying to knife him in the back. He could live with that. Trust had to be earned, and he didn't expect it right away. He'd prove himself eventually.

Still, his survival hadn't helped Solie's reputation, and the girl sagged. "Yes. Everyone either hates me or is afraid of me. I can't stand it."

He couldn't blame her. "It's only been two days," he pointed out. "Everyone's had a lot to absorb, and your position has changed pretty dramatically."

"But I don't want it to change."

Leon shook his head. "That doesn't matter." She couldn't be maudlin or afraid. Like it or not, she was in a position of power, and if she didn't use that, someone else would use both it and her—and her battlers, too. "You have to live up to your responsibility. Once you do, you'll find you can have friends again. They won't be like the childhood friends you had before, but they'll still be friends." And with the battlers' empathy, she'd always know if those friendships were real. Few rulers shared such a gift.

"But I don't know how to live up to my position," she protested. "I was born on a farm in a tiny hamlet. It wasn't even big enough to be called a village! My father wanted to marry me off to a man three times my age. That was the only ambition anyone had for me."

"So? I'm the son of a wagon drover. You aren't your origins. You're what you choose to do with your life."

She was quiet a moment, staring at him. "Will you teach me?" she asked at last.

Leon hid a smile. The girl was young, but she wasn't stupid. She knew she needed advisers to train her in the things she'd need to learn. "Of course. Ask Devon too. There are probably things you could learn from him as well. But it's up to you what you do with what we tell you."

She sighed and nodded unhappily.

"Good." Leon stood and sheathed his sword. "It's time to get started."

Leon's first lesson involved sitting in with the half-dozen men who were trying to lead the Community, who stubbornly still met in one of the last tents aboveground, its canvas shaking from the wind and the sides half covered by snow. The interior would have been bitterly cold if not for Morgal's fire sylph. Ash kept the tent warm, but that also resulted in the snow just outside melting underneath the bottom edge. Solie had to walk through mud to make it to the table.

No one quite protested her arrival, though they glared at both her and Leon. She couldn't feel their emotions as clearly as she did around Heyou and the others. She could feel the edges of the men's emotions thanks to the elemental sylphs they'd brought with them, but they didn't seem to have the sensitivity of a battler, and without one of them at her side, she was almost feeling as blind as she'd ever been. Still, she didn't need any empathy to tell they weren't happy about her. They were even less pleased by Leon, but as he pointed out, the meeting wasn't private and he wasn't a prisoner. She could tell they wanted to send her away, but all of them had sylphs who chattered at her happily while bringing her a chair to sit in. It took a while just to quiet them down so the meeting could begin.

Leon sitting in the chair beside her, Solie listened to the men talk, all of them trying to ignore the two interlopers.

She didn't really understand the full implications of what they were debating, but Leon nudged her whenever they got onto a topic of special importance, and she gleaned from that a sense of priorities.

The allocation of rooms in the hive was not important. The earth sylphs could dig many more and were happily doing so. The biggest related problem was in keeping the place from being turned into an unnavigable maze. The piping in of water for drinking and sanitation was also significant, but was under control. So was the food situation, thanks to the battlers, at least when it came to meat. Fruit and vegetables were more problematic. Apparently, these cliffs had only been meant as a rendezvous point in case of disaster, which was what happened. The worst part was that Eferem's attack came just as winter was approaching, and the stored harvests were subsequently lost in the fires. Leon didn't apologize, but he didn't look at anyone during that report, either. Left with only a few livestock herds and the most basic supplies, they'd reached the cliff and realized they had no leaders and nowhere else to go. If the founders of the Community had planned anything further, they hadn't shared it with the survivors.

The bluff wasn't like the sheltered valley in which the Community had first settled. Both areas were covered in dead rock and with the help of sylphs could be turned into arable land, but this cliff was far more exposed to the elements. Harsh northern winds blew down through the mountains and across it, bringing freezing snows that would only get worse. If they hadn't gone underground, they would have frozen to death, even with the sylphs. They needed to clear the vents daily that let in air, and the stairwell leading up to the surface was an icy accident waiting to happen. The council was only aboveground now due to stubbornness. Even the animals were being taken underground as the sylphs dug out huge stables for them at the base of the cliff. Galway was helping with that, not willing to risk trying to get home.

They couldn't stay here long-term, Solie realized. Even with the cliff to live in, the winters were too harsh, the winds so strong they'd blow away any topsoil that was created. This place must have been nearly dead even before the plains were razed. Come spring they would have to move on . . . though where, no one knew. That was the main point of this meeting.

The idea of using the three battlers to conquer land came up.

Solie gasped. "You can't!"

Many men looked at her coldly. Morgal sighed, even though he hadn't been the one to suggest using the battlers. That suggestion had come from a furious-looking Bock. "What do you suggest? Should we stay here until we die?"

"No, but . . ."

"There's nowhere else to go."

"There's nowhere to invade, either," Leon pointed out. He leaned back in his chair, his arms crossed and a boot resting on his opposite knee. "All of you came here from Para Dubh. You left because that was a place oppressive to the lower classes, and because anyone who defies the ruling family is executed by their battlers. They have twelve. The next-closest kingdom is Eferem, where Solie and I come from. King Alcor is paranoid, greedy, and he has eleven battlers left, including his personal one, Thrall."

"So what do we do?" Morgal demanded. His fury had grown along with the humiliation of feeling impotent.

Leon shrugged. "I'd wait for spring and go back to that valley," he said. "You know it's sheltered and you've farmed it once already. You'd have to start over from scratch, but you could resettle there. Better to stay on land no one's using than try to take someone else's. It's a whole lot less dangerous."

"But we were attacked there once already!" Norlud shouted.

"Yes," Bock thundered. "By *you*!"

Leon shrugged again, and Solie watched curiously as he dropped his leg and leaned forward. "So, don't attack air ships. That was a stupid shortcut. If you hadn't done that, Alcor might not have noticed you until you had a kingdom of your own and were sending emissaries. Rebuild the town and the fields, but this time have the sylphs dig a hive underground. You can retreat there in case of attack and use it during the worst part of winter as well. If you *are* attacked, you have Ril, Heyou, and Mace. Even better, you know how to summon battlers now. Keep that a secret and you can soon outnumber any enemy. Do that and sue for peace. Do it right and they'll have no choice but to parley. Give them something worth trading for and they'll even be glad of you. No one claims ownership of these lands. I don't know which one of you figured out that they can be saved using sylphs, but it's brilliant. Claim them yourselves and make your own kingdom."

He sounded passionate. More, he sounded right. The men gaped, but their sylphs looked up from the corner and cheered. Solie smiled. The men weren't so happy at the idea, but the sylphs were ecstatic—and the sylphs had a say in this as much as anyone else. Solie wondered how many of the council had ever thought so far ahead.

She took a deep breath and said, "I think it's a good idea."

Bock sneered. "No one asked you." When his water sylph hissed at him, he started in surprise and his expression turned hateful.

Solie braced herself, her heart pounding. Leon was holding her hand now under the table, and she took strength from it. "He's right, we can't stay here. I say we go back to your valley in the spring." Leon's grip tightened. "I mean . . . I mean *I'll* go there in the spring, and I'm taking the sylphs with me. All of them. The rest of you can come or not, but we're going."

Hard men two or three times her age stared at her in shock, and Leon loosened his grip. Solie had to resist the urge to apologize, but she managed.

"I guess we move then," Morgal pronounced, his face tight. Even with her empathy, Solie wasn't sure if his feelings were of hate, relief, or fear, but she nodded and leaned back in her chair, hoping this was the last time she'd have to offer either an opinion or an order today.

After the meeting, Solie and Leon made their way back toward the hive entrance, both huddled in their cloaks. It really was freezing out. Solie had never felt a winter so bitterly cold, and she shivered massively, slipping on the icy ground. Leon put a hand on her back to steady her. No, they couldn't stay here, not for years on end. No one could, not through winters this harsh.

"I hope Heyou and Ril are okay," she shouted.

"They will be," Leon shouted back. "Battlers don't feel temperature the way we do." He gave a harsh laugh. "They might even have some fun getting tossed around by the wind."

Ahead, Solie saw the edge of the stairwell, nearly invisible in the storm. They would ban everyone from coming to the surface until the weather cleared, she decided, then found herself amazed that she was thinking of orders again.

A wail sounded, the horrified emotions that accompanied it more in her mind than the air, though Leon turned at the cry. Solie did as well, and glimpsed a shape looming out of the blowing snow, arm upraised with a dagger. Screaming, she fell backward, landing on her behind.

Leon roared a warning. Throwing back his cloak, he drew his sword and leaped forward, slashing downward with the weapon. Solie's would-be assassin jerked back with a shriek, tumbling into the snow. Only a few feet behind him, his water sylph gave another wail like the one that had warned Solie, only this one was filled with grief. Her childish face distorted and inhuman, she vanished back into the storm, still screaming.

Without pause, Leon grabbed Solie and pulled her to her feet, rushing with her to the stairs. "Mace!" he shouted. "*Mace!*" The huge battler appeared through the storm as though it had no effect on him, meeting them at the stairs. Together, both males carried the hysterical girl down to her rooms, where Solie couldn't stop shaking until Heyou returned and took her in his arms.

Chapter Twenty-four

The water sylph was named Shore. She huddled in front of Solie's makeshift couch, four feet of swirling water forced into the shape of a small child. She was miserable, torn between the horror of seeing her master die and knowing she'd saved her queen.

"How come she didn't vanish?" Morgal asked uncertainly. For all his dislike of Solie and her battlers, he'd been shaken by the news that Bock tried to kill her. He didn't know how to feel about the fact that it was Leon who was her rescuer. After everything, he didn't dare trust the man.

"She's tied to the queen," Mace told him grudgingly, after a moment of silence and after Solie gave him a curious glance. "All the sylphs here are. If their masters die, their link to her keeps them here."

Standing behind her chair with his arms crossed, Leon leaned over to Ril. "Does that mean if I die you'll be all right?"

Ril considered and nodded. Leon straightened, looking pleased.

"She'll need a new master, though," Mace added. "No one should feed from the energy of the queen."

"Does that include me?" Heyou asked. Solie smiled at him and shook her head. He beamed.

Morgal sighed, looking around at the audience chamber, for lack of a better term. It was now five hours after the attack, and the battlers had been outraged. It had taken everything the redheaded girl had to keep them from killing anyone they even thought might be a threat. He shuddered.

It might have been better if Bock had succeeded. The battlers would have been gone, then, along with all their outlandish ideas.

Across the room, Ril looked straight at him and growled. Terrified, Morgal cringed back, and Leon looked in his direction. The man studied him for a moment before raising an eyebrow. He first pointed a thumb at Solie, and then at himself, then jabbed it discreetly in Ril's direction.

Morgal didn't understand at first; then it came to him. Leon was Ril's master. If Solie died, Ril wouldn't be banished. If Solie had been killed . . . Morgal sagged against the wall and Leon nodded.

"What's wrong?" Solie asked nervously. She could feel his emotions with sylphs around, Morgal remembered, and he shuddered again.

"I think our friend just realized what would have happened to this place if you'd died," Leon spoke up. Solie looked puzzled. "Ril's still tied to me," he explained. "I think he would have been . . . upset."

"I would have turned this bluff into ash," the battler said. There was no trace of humor in his voice at all.

"Ril!" Solie gasped, and Morgal distantly found himself marveling that she was hesitant and uncertain around the council but bossed around the deadliest creatures in the world like children. "You can't do that!"

"Why not?"

"It would be wrong!"

All three battlers looked entirely unconvinced.

Solie puffed out a breath. "No one is turning any bluffs into ash, is that clear?"

"You take all the fun out of it," Heyou sulked.

Solie rolled her eyes and shifted her attention to the little sylph huddled in the center of the room. "Shore? Um, how long had your master been planning to, uh . . . you know."

"Hadn't," the sylph said out loud, her voice bubbling softly. "He just . . . got angry. I—I—I warned. Didn't want him to die! Didn't want you to die! It's so lonely!"

She sounded utterly miserable, and Morgal reached for Ash. The fire sylph pressed against his side, also in the shape of a child, her heat turned down as low as possible. He could feel her relief that her queen was safe. She was much calmer than he himself felt. He'd apologized for the council once he heard about the attack, and Solie had accepted, but it was clear now: no matter what any of them thought, she was in charge. Having never wanted power, Morgal tried to convince himself that he didn't mind, but putting a girl in control felt fundamentally wrong.

Heyou looked at him and hissed. Morgal ducked his head.

"It's okay," Solie told Shore, kneeling on the floor with her hand against the sylph's cheek. "You can have a new master—someone to take energy from who'll pay all the attention to you that you need. Is there someone you'd like?" The water sylph hesitated. "It's okay. You can choose."

Shimmering, Shore became a pool of water and flowed across the floor, leaving the stone behind her dry as she passed over it. Glancing at the battlers, Solie followed. Curious himself and not wanting to stay, Morgal pushed in pursuit.

The hall was crowded, people making their way carefully around in what were still tight quarters. Solie followed the water sylph, Morgal somehow ending up just behind her, and he realized in one terrified moment that he was between her and her battlers. A moment later a red hawk flew over his head and landed on her shoulder, and he breathed a sigh of relief.

They went into the eating area. It was the largest open space in the hive, the high ceiling held up by columns of thick stone and already half-full at the dinner hour. The smell of whale soup and potatoes drifted through, making Morgal realize that he was actually hungry. People eyed the newcomers, nodding at Morgal but watching Solie with uncertainty. They didn't know how to deal with her any more than Morgal did, but no one tried anything as Ril ruffled his wings on her shoulder and the other two moved past Morgal to her side.

Leon followed, his hands clasped behind his back. People gawped at him with real hate, but he either didn't notice or didn't react. Morgal doubted it was the former. No one said anything about the assassination attempt, either. So far, none of them knew.

All of them watched Shore. She flowed into the center of the room and hesitated. There wasn't much for her to choose from, Morgal thought. There were only twenty or so men who didn't have a sylph already, and many had already tried to get one without success. She'd probably have to settle for a youngster.

The water sylph headed away from the men, moving at Solie's encouragement toward a table with teens sitting at it, just as Morgal predicted. He had just realized the teens were all girls, though, when she shaped herself back into a more human form and reached for one. It was fourteen-year-old Loren Malachi. The girl gawked at the water sylph for half a second, and then realized what she had. She gave the biggest grin Morgal had ever seen.

"Damn," he heard, someone else verbalizing his reaction, and he looked over in shared sympathy to find he was staring at Mace—which made him nearly swallow his own tongue in fright. "I wanted that girl for myself," said the battler with regret.

The girls were never going to get to sleep. Every last one of them seemed to be piled on Loren's bed, each trying to become the new best friend of the water sylph. The widow doubted any sylph in the history of the world had ever received so much attention.

"Fifteen minutes!" she bellowed from the doorway. "If you're not in bed in fifteen minutes, I'll tan the backsides of the lot of you!" Giggles echoed back, and she slammed the stone door on them. Fifteen minutes to curfew. They'd better obey, or else.

Turning, she gathered her skirts and stomped toward the boys' quarters. Knowing them, they were all awake complaining about how *they* didn't get a sylph. Still, she admitted with a sigh, it was good they were happy. The last month had been rough. Many of the children had lost their fathers or brothers, and all of them their homes. She understood that pain. It was ten years since she'd lost her husband, and she still thought about him from time to time. The young were resilient, though. She wished she had their resiliency—and their youth. Nowadays, she just felt old and unappreciated. Witch, they called her. She sniffed and walked on.

When she'd been told they were moving all the children belowground, she'd made sure the arranged rooms for the boys and girls were as far apart as possible. She wasn't so foolish as to think none would get together, but she was going to make it as hard as possible. The separate sleep areas were situated so that to get to either, you had to pass through the mess hall, making anyone on a midnight raid sure to be seen. Or so she hoped.

The widow turned a corner and stopped in surprise. "Don't you dare," she snarled. "You are *not* coming in here!" She glanced back toward the girls' chambers.

Mace stared down at her, easily a foot taller, and she was not small. "I wasn't going to. I'm patrolling," he said calmly.

She snorted, not believing that for an instant. Planting her fists on her hips, she advanced, refusing to give in to the fear she felt. "You're not patrolling in there. One sylph is more than enough!"

"I didn't have anything to do with that," he told her. "I wouldn't have given her to the girl."

"Because you're interested in her yourself?"

"Of course."

Over the years of her life, the widow had made many a man cower in fear. Mace didn't even flinch, which she found both intensely irritating and a little intriguing. He just observed her.

"What is so fascinating about Loren?" she asked.

The battler shrugged. "She's strong. I like strong females and I need a master."

She waved a hand dismissively. "I thought you had a master already." And the thought of what the girl Solie was probably doing with those battlers infuriated the widow. The fact that she wasn't permitted to do anything about it drove her mad. It certainly drove her other female wards to giggling distraction.

Mace stepped closer. "Solie is my queen. But I don't want to drain her energy to fuel myself, and she doesn't have time to give me the attention I want. I need a master. Someone who can bind me to this world as she does and from whom I can draw the energy I need to fight. Someone I can be with."

The widow found she was getting warm, and crossed her arms. "You are not draining *anything* out of those girls. Go find some man to be your master. And stay away from my boys!"

"I won't have a man," he said, circling her. The widow started to feel ever so slightly trapped.

"You're not taking a child!"

He leaned in, his face moving close to hers. The hallway was abruptly warmer, tingles running through her entire body. "I should have said I liked strong *women*. Loren's strong. You're stronger."

The widow nearly lost her train of thought. The battler

smelled delicious. But a moment later her eyes narrowed. "What are you doing to me?"

"Seducing you."

He was quite good at it, too, she thought—right before she grabbed his ear and twisted. Mace was so surprised, the aura of lust he'd been filling her with vanished. "Good," she hissed. "Now, you listen to me. I'm not some little trollop you can just turn on and have your way with. Understood?"

"Yes."

She nodded, not letting go of his ear. "Good. Now, are you going to behave yourself?"

"Probably not." He sounded amused but didn't try to extricate himself from her grip.

"Stay away from my girls," she repeated loudly.

"I don't think I want any of them anymore," he replied. His meaning was clear.

The widow was shocked. She let go of his ear, and he straightened. "But I'm old!"

"You're younger than I am."

"I can't have children anymore." She'd lost three to miscarriages.

"Doesn't matter to me. I can't get you with child anyway."

"I'm no virgin."

"I would have fixed that anyway."

She paused, thinking. "You won't use that power of yours on me again?" The question came out with more hesitation than she liked.

"Not if you order me not to."

"Good. Consider yourself ordered." And with that, she took his hand and led him to her bed.

Eventually the girls realized that their fifteen minutes had been greatly extended, but the widow didn't return.

Chapter Twenty-five

The storm that had blown out from the northern mountains finally started to wear out, the wind lessening and the swirling snow finally settling on the bluff and surrounding plains. It was at least five feet deep, but in places smoke curled up from bored-out holes.

In the hive's main stairwell, Leon dug awkwardly, trying not to fall down the steps as he pushed snow out of the way. He was feeling both annoyed at the need and absurdly grateful that the sylph who'd dug the stairs had put an awning over the top. She just needed to add a door. He'd been forced to dig his way through windblown accumulation that blocked the top half of the stairs.

"Well, that settles it," he muttered, looking outside at the distant skyline. Blue was starting to peek through holes in the cloud cover, and the sun shining off the sea of white was painful. "We definitely need to move in the spring." The Community never should have retreated to this place. Doing so showed an enormous lack of foresight on the part of their former leaders. But then, they hadn't taken charge due to their tactical skills. They'd been idealists, not warriors, and they had never really expected to be driven out of their adopted homes.

Their first location had been much better thought out. Leon hadn't seen their whole town, but he remembered the valley. It was at the eastern edge of the Shale Plains, sheltered by the mountains that cut the land off from the ocean. Para Dubh sat on the other side, but they didn't use the Shale Plains any more than Eferem, and were slightly more reasonable. As a kingdom they had battlers to prevent invasion, but were far less insular than Alcor. Their wealth came from trade with countries on the far side of the world, their ships sailing on both the ocean and the air. King Alcor had always been envious of their wealth, but every skirmish with them had been short-lived, with no one willing to engage in a full-blown war. Leon had participated in more than one formalized fight, pitting Ril against battle sylphs from Para Dubh. Ril had always won, but not all of Eferem's battlers could say the same. Ultimately, Para Dubh had more battle sylphs than Alcor wanted to risk fighting against. While it was true, had the Community stayed where they were, either Eferem or Para Dubh would eventually have come to crush or absorb them, now that they had battlers of their own. They wouldn't be so vulnerable when they returned.

Leon glanced over his shoulder at his own battler. Ril hadn't helped him dig up to the surface, but then, Leon hadn't asked. He wasn't sure what his relationship with the sylph was going to be now, but he wanted to be careful that it was a good one. Both of them still had their issues to work through, and Leon didn't want Ril thinking he was viewed as a slave. So Leon did the work himself while the battler watched.

Finally, he set the shovel aside and turned. "Ready?" he asked, rubbing one sore shoulder. The battler shrugged, not quite looking at him, and moved forward. Ril never looked directly at him, Leon noticed with some regret.

The battler let go of his shape as he put his arms around Leon, lifting him up in a whirl of darkness. Unable to see, Leon felt himself rise, and then they were flying on the winds, heading away from the hive. Even blind as he was, Leon gasped at the feel of it all.

What? Ril asked sullenly.

"This is magnificent!" Leon exclaimed. "This is flying?"

Yes, the battler answered, sounding a little mollified.

Leon smiled and settled back, floating in absolute blackness, but warm and comfortable. Even though he knew he was high above the ground, he felt safe.

Ril flew high over the snow-covered plains, Leon held carefully inside his mantle. Time passed and the miles did too, the return trip much faster than the journey to the bluff. What had originally taken nearly a week Ril now guessed would take a little less than a day. Not that he was in any rush. It felt good to fly this way again, to *be* this way. He could change shape, but he wasn't really designed to inhabit any for long periods of time. Staying as a bird for so long had sometimes made him itch until he'd thought he'd go mad, and he stretched now as he flew.

Leon had fallen asleep, Ril noted eventually, worn out by his labor. Though part of him wanted to dump the man into the snow, he instead cradled him more carefully and continued flying. Leon both was and wasn't his master anymore. The man had sworn himself to the queen, and he'd proved his loyalty when he saved her life. And for the sake of his own sanity, Ril had needed to let the hate go. He felt lighter as a result, happier.

Either way, in this, both were of the same mind. With Solie's permission—for Ril couldn't have forced himself to leave the hive without it—together they were headed to collect Leon's family.

Lizzy! All of the girls were precious to him, but Lizzy . . . Ril ached to see her again. She wouldn't be his queen now, and Ril had mourned that even as he gave himself over to Solie. There was only one queen of a hive. But Lizzy could be his master, like Leon. Or more precisely, like the widow, for Mace. Once Lizzy was old enough to share her energy with him, that is. Her energy and her heart.

Below him the plains passed smoothly, eventually replaced by the white snow-covered shapes of the forests they'd traversed before. Finding a ribbon of road, he followed it, flying over the town they'd spent the night in. Awake again, Leon lay patiently inside him, occasionally shifting position but not saying anything. Eventually, he dozed off again.

They flew on, farmlands replacing the forests below and the snow vanishing, the more southern air still a little too warm. Tiny hamlets dotted the fields, with larger keeps on top of bluffs, and finally the great capital of Eferem.

Ril dropped down well clear of the city's outer walls, studying the black flags that hung from the ramparts. The city was in mourning—he supposed for the dead prince—but no one felt upset. Ril could feel their emotions easily as he swept by unseen, finally landing in a copse of trees, where he set Leon on his feet.

"How long did it take us to get here?" the man asked in amazement.

Ril shrugged. "Most of a day." They'd left in midmorning. It was now morning of the next day.

"That's incredible. You're faster than an air ship's sylph."

"That's because I don't have something as heavy to carry," the battler retorted, storming out of the bush. Leon shook his head and followed.

They found a side road that led through a secondary gate into the city and eventually to the keep. Ril walked in the human form he'd adopted, keeping his aura tightly concealed, and Leon put up his hood and hunched his shoulders. He walked a few feet behind the battler, as though he were a servant, following him through the gate. He knew the men who guarded it, and they'd have questions if they recognized him, but they had no reason to stop two ordinary men walking into the city on their own. Depending on what Jasar had reported, the king would probably think of him as an enemy now. Of course, Alcor would expect

Leon to send Ril for any attack, and he'd still expect the battler to be a bird.

Ril strode ahead, ignoring the men around him with a haughtiness only the most potent lord would affect. He did notice the women, but he didn't go after any. Leon had heard rumors about Mace before the sylph ended up with that widow in charge of the youngsters, and he'd seen Heyou with Solie, but Ril didn't show any of the same tendencies. Leon wasn't sure if that was normal or not. Heyou certainly was devoted to Solie. Ril had never done more than look at females, and never for long.

It didn't really matter. Whatever Ril wanted, Leon wasn't going to get in his way. He was just happy that the battler didn't hate him, and more, that he was still willing to work together. That was a gift.

They moved through the city, the residents going about their normal business and their sylphs mostly out of sight, just as usual. Knowing what he did now, Leon regretted them being bound. They had come expecting freedom, but all they got was another type of servitude. The ones within the Community had the right to speak and take whatever shape they wanted, but these others were as trapped as the battlers.

Leon shot a glance at Ril, who walked blithely on. Ril, he figured, didn't ponder overmuch about the plight of others. Free battlers didn't seem predisposed to this. It must have been a simple life for them in their natural dimension—though if it had been that good, Ril would never have crossed over.

Quietly the two of them traversed the city, walking roads that Leon had never taken Ril to as a bird, not wanting to frighten anyone. The battler dropped back beside him as a result, matching Leon's pace. Whenever Leon had business in the city, he'd left the battler with his wife and daughters. Ril therefore knew the way to the castle and the main route from it or Leon's manor to the city's front gate, but that was all. Other battler masters had thought him mad for leaving himself so vulnerable, but Leon was no slouch at defending himself, and crowds made Ril too unhappy to inflict that on him. Or on the crowds.

Or so Leon had thought. Ril didn't react at all to the crowds now, his aura so neatly contained that no one even looked at him. Until Heyou, Leon hadn't even realized the battlers *could* hide their auras. He looked sideways at the blond man. There was a lot he hadn't realized.

Ril's eye darted toward him and his brow furrowed. "What?" he demanded.

"Nothing. Just thinking about what a shit I've been to you."

Ril snorted. "Keep thinking that. Just keep it to yourself. I don't want to feel it."

Leon smiled faintly. "Whatever you say."

Ahead, the road curved toward his manor, the wall high enough to block most of the building from view, and both sped up toward it. The time was past lunch, but not so late that the girls would be down for their naps. They'd probably still be playing in the big back room with the old tapestries on the wall, or finishing their lessons with their mother.

There was a man in a cloak loitering at the front gate, a well-used sword on his hip. Leon didn't need to hear Ril's growl to recognize him as a threat. It seemed Alcor was acting against him, and Leon hoped the presence of the soldier was simply to watch for him, using his family as bait, and did not mean that Betha and the girls had been arrested or harmed. Leading Ril around unseen to another part of the manor's surrounding wall, he pulled a wrought-iron key from his bag, unlocked a small secondary gate that was almost completely hidden by blackberry bushes, and let both himself and Ril in. They found the windows of the manor open to the fresh air, and they both heard female laughter.

The battler behind him, Leon opened the door. "I'm home!" he shouted.

For a moment there was silence, and then he heard the rapid footsteps and squeals of excited girls. Lizzy skidded around the corner first, her knees skinned and dirt on her cheeks, and Leon heard Ril's breath catch behind him as the girl threw herself forward.

"Daddy!" she shrieked. "Welcome home!" A moment later, the two younger girls ran after her around the corner. Betha followed with the baby. Leon grinned, trying to hug all of them at once.

Lizzy pulled away, looking around. "Where's Ril?" she asked.

"Yeah," Cara echoed. "Where Ril?" Nali stuck her thumb in her mouth.

"And who's your friend?" Betha asked.

Leon took a deep breath and straightened, stepping back against the wall so they could all see the battler clearly. "All right, no one be afraid. This is Ril."

Lizzy frowned. "But he's a man."

The other girls stared. Betha looked at the battler, and then at her husband in confusion.

"He can be anything he wants to be," Leon told them. "Right now, he wants to be a man."

"I like him as a bird!" Cara wailed. "Be a bird! Be a bird!" Nali started crying, as did Ralad.

Lizzy walked toward the battler, inspecting him intently. As she neared, he dropped down into a crouch, so she had to look down at him instead. Her brow furrowed with concentration, she reached out a hand and he closed his eyes as she poked the tip of his nose, pushing it in. Then she giggled. "I like it!"

"Thank you," Ril said.

"You can talk!" she shrieked. "When did you start talking?"

Ril looked past her at Leon. "When I was allowed to."

She spun and glared at her father. "You didn't let him talk?"

Leon shook his head. This was not an argument he wanted to get into. "Not now, Lizzy. We have to go."

"Go?" Betha asked, startled. "Go where?"

This was not going to be easy. "Away from here," Leon told his wife. "Right now, and all of us. There are things I've learned since I left, about Ril and myself. We can't stay here anymore. I know it's dangerous for me, and I suspect it's going to become dangerous for you. There's already a guard watching the front gate. I'm surprised he doesn't have a battler." He took a deep breath. "Ril and I have betrayed the king."

Betha's eyes saucered, her skin white. The other girls didn't understand, but Lizzy glanced at him with fright in her eyes, and reached fumblingly to take Ril's hand. He held it gently, still crouching at her side. Leon had never seen his expression so soft.

"You . . . how could you?" Betha wailed, clutching the crying baby to her breast. "What are you saying?" She shook her head frantically, backing away from him.

"He ordered us to kill a girl," Leon told her bluntly, stepping forward to lay his hands on her shoulders. "A girl hardly older than Lizzy. She was supposed to be sacrificed to bind a battler, but instead she bound him instead. The king wanted her killed for that. We failed. But Betha, the things we learned . . . Ril is free now. There are more battlers where we're going, and they're all free. All the sylphs are. Here they're no more than property, and I can't be a part of Ril's slavery anymore. The king will never accept that." He surveyed his wife, his daughters, and finally the battler himself. "None of us are safe."

He let go of his wife and stepped back. "Gather together whatever you can carry, but no more. We can't take much."

Betha's bottom lip trembled, her eyes filling with tears, but a moment later she turned and hurried away, taking the baby with her. Nali waddled in pursuit, still crying.

Lizzy and Cara both stared, dumbfounded. Cara was sucking her thumb in confusion, Lizzy studying the battler. At last she addressed her father. "Where are we going?"

"To a place north of here," he said. "You'll like it—it'll be an adventure. Now go gather your things. Hurry now, and take your sister."

Grasping her sibling's hand, Lizzy walked off, looking back periodically as she did.

Leon approached Ril where the battler had moved to stand at the great windows fronting the manor. The turrets of the castle were visible, along with a huge air ship tethered at the top. Ril crossed his arms and studied the distant ship, his expression pensive.

"What's wrong?" Leon asked. "Has that guard realized we're here?"

Ril shook his head. "There are four battlers on that ship." He regarded his former master evenly. "I want to go now."

Four battlers? No one had sent four battlers to anything less than a major war, and then not for centuries. Leon flushed cold and turned, running back into the hallway. "Girls! Move! Forget everything but a change of clothes. Hurry! We have to leave now!" His daughters yelled in protest, but he turned back into the front room. "Can they sense you?"

"Hidden like this? No." Ril paused. "They will once I change to carry you."

"How much can you lift?"

"Enough," Ril replied. "Unless one of them is in a shape that can fly."

Leon could think of at least three battlers in the king's service with that ability. "Move!" he bellowed again. "We leave in five minutes!"

Despite his order, it took ten before they were downstairs, all the girls crying, save for Lizzy. Betha sobbed in confusion as she tried to bundle her children in cloaks, the baby swaddled in blankets. She was desperate with terror, and the girls picked it up from her. Only Lizzy was unafraid, her eyes shining as she shifted from foot to foot.

"Are we traveling by carriage? I always wanted to travel by carriage."

"Not quite," Ril said. He stood by her side, waiting patiently.

Leon ushered his family out. The afternoon air was cold. It hadn't yet started to snow as it had on the Shale Plains, but he sensed it would soon. Snow was probably falling again where they were going, relentless, and he hoped his wife and family would forgive him. And he hoped the rest of the Community wouldn't make their lives hell just to get back at him.

Likely not, if they thought it would irritate Ril.

"Ready?" he asked the battler. Ril nodded, his eyes on a cloaked shape at the closed front gate who was staring in at them.

"We're not expected to walk, are we?" Betha whimpered, holding the youngest girls close. Ril stepped forward—and suddenly he was changing, surrounding them with smoke and lightning. The girls screamed as the darkness lifted them. Leon felt Ril hesitate, adjusting himself, and then the battler was moving upward, much slower than he had before.

"Ril!" he shouted. "How are you doing?"

You don't have to yell, Ril grumbled in his mind.

Leon felt his way through the darkness, finding his wife's hand and squeezing it. She pressed against him, weeping, and he wrapped his arms around her and the girls, hugging them all close.

"It'll be okay," he promised. "It will."

His family drew close, all except for Lizzy. She squirmed free instead, struggling forward to press her hand against the solid darkness that was her father's battler. He felt warm and solid.

"Are we flying?" she asked.

Yes, he answered, his voice echoing in her mind.

"I want to see!" she demanded.

There was a moment's pause, and then she felt him shift around her, a wave of shadow pushing her forward and up. The darkness parted, and suddenly a strong breeze caught her hair, blowing it back while she squinted into the wind. They were high above the ground, the trees and houses tiny as dollhouses below.

Ril flew through the cold air, his body huge and nearly shapeless, bulbous and dark. His wings were massive, stretched out to either side. Behind them the castle and the city retreated into the distance, while above the sky was a beautiful blue. Distantly Ril sensed the battlers, and something else he hadn't told Leon. Tempest was on that ship: the second-oldest sylph in the kingdom and almost the most powerful, an air sylph who could carry that entire ship faster than Ril had ever flown.

Lizzy squealed in delight, clapping her hands excitedly as she leaned into the wind. Ril held her gently, almost dancing in his own joy as he carried her and her family, pushing himself beyond endurance and fleeing faster than he ever thought he could toward the wasteland, with his love in his embrace.

Chapter Twenty-six

Galway stood at one of the windows the sylphs had made, looking out over the endless snow. It was a wide window, letting in a lot of light but no cold. Some of the fire sylphs had taken and heated sand until it turned hard and clear. This distorted the view in odd ways, but was better than shutters by far. There were so far only a dozen of them on the cliff's sheerest face, but they were popular, and several other people jostled him for the chance to look outside.

He'd waited too long. His curiosity about Heyou and the others had trapped him. He'd have to wait for spring now and leave his family wondering if he'd died. For ten years he'd kept his promise to return before the snow fell. At his home it likely wasn't falling yet, but it would be soon.

Around him, the people suddenly scattered like birds, and Galway straightened, looking at the distorted reflection of a teenage boy behind him. Those who'd been gazing out the window regrouped a short distance away. Heyou was respected, but he wasn't the most frightening of the battlers. They didn't leave completely.

"You left your lady?" Galway asked, turning around.

"Mace is with her." Heyou tilted his head to one side. "You're unhappy, aren't you?"

"You can tell?" He'd gone to pains to hide it. No one else needed the added stress, provided it even mattered to them.

"We can feel emotions. Makes us better guards."

He smiled. "I suppose it would."

"I don't know what you're unhappy about, though. I can't tell that unless you're my master."

Galway shrugged. "I intended to be back with my family by now. Don't think I regret helping you—I don't. But I miss them."

"Why don't you go home?"

The trapper gestured to the window. "The snow out there is too deep. It would take me weeks to get through, and it's dangerous. I might not make it at all."

"Oh." Heyou frowned, considering. "I could take you."

Galway blinked. "What?"

"I could carry you. I could take you home. The horses would probably be upset though."

Galway laughed, the winter suddenly not appearing so bleak. "I'd appreciate that," he admitted. "I really would."

Heyou nodded. He stared out the window, his lip twisting.

"Is there something else?" Galway asked.

"Yeah." The boy grasped his hands behind his back, pulling them away from his body and arching his spine. "Mace says he doesn't want any of us tied to the queen only. He says we should all have someone else to draw on and who can keep us here, just in case. I don't think anything will happen, but he's bigger than I am, and old. It's weird. I'm the lead battler, but everyone else is older than me. I doubt Ril cares, but I think it bothers Mace a bit. He'd like to have Solie, too, but she won't let him. So he's got that widow instead. She kind of makes me nervous, but he likes her bossing him around. Kinda queenlike and all, even if she is just a master."

Galway crossed his arms and leaned against the stone wall. "What are you trying to ask? I assume there's a question in there somewhere?"

"Oh." Heyou let his arms drop. "Mace wants me to get a

master. Someone other than Solie who I can get energy from if I have to and who'll be another link for me to stay here." He frowned. "But if I take you home, I won't be able to get energy from you. You have to be here. I hadn't thought of that."

"You want *me* to be your master?" Galway asked, genuinely surprised.

"Well, sure. You'd still hold me here, even if you went home. And you can come visit us again in the spring." He sounded hopeful.

Galway gaped. Never in his life had he thought he'd gain a sylph. He'd had the childhood dream, of course, as did most boys, but he'd never imagined a battler. Even for the rough boys he'd grown up with, they'd been too frightening. The thought of Heyou asking him now was so ludicrous he almost had to laugh.

"I thought you didn't like men," he said.

Heyou made another face. "I do. I don't. I mean, I don't really like men, but Solie says they're not like battlers. We don't have to fight you all the time like battlers from other hives. And I don't want a woman as a master. I have Solie. It would feel weird to have another woman. I don't want Solie to get jealous or think she might have to. I only want her, so I need a man for a master." He hesitated and regarded Galway directly. "And Mace says to be careful. If you're my master, you can control me. I don't want that. But I . . . trust you."

Galway was silent, moved. There was only one answer he could honestly give to a confession like that. "I'd be honored," he told the boy. "And I swear to you, I'll never take advantage."

Heyou smiled, tension going out of his shoulders. It must have been hard for him to ask, Galway realized, probably alien to everything he was used to. He'd already seen what having a master had meant for the other battlers. But he'd also seen what they were like now. Mace was happy with the widow, presumably, and Ril had deliberately kept the same master. Of course Galway saw how Leon tiptoed around him, even as he manipulated the rest of the Community into doing what was necessary to ensure their survival, but there was affection there on both sides. Galway would have to talk to him about how he managed that sometime, now that he had a battler of his own. Sort of. Heyou wasn't his. He had no delusions about that. He wouldn't allow himself.

"What do I do?"

"We have to do it through Solie," Heyou explained. "We can't just make someone our master on our own." He gestured at the door and Solie came in, accompanied by Mace.

The girl shrugged. "It's okay, Galway. I've done this before—for Loren and the widow." She made a face. "It feels kind of weird."

"Does it?"

Mace stepped forward, dropping his shape to become smoke and lightning, and those people who hadn't left when he arrived gasped. The battler reached out with black tendrils, one to Solie, one to Heyou, and one to Galway himself. It felt like a satin-covered rope, thin but strong, and at its touch the trapper felt something twist inside of him. His senses doubled, and for a brief moment he felt something that was him go into Solie. An essence that he somehow knew was Heyou joined it, and inside her it changed to match his. Galway had a startled moment of feeling as though he'd been duplicated, and then that feeling was replaced by a sudden sensation of concern that the wrong choice had been made, along with an underlying determination to guard and protect Solie that he doubted would ever go away or fade. None of it came from him, though.

Galway's eyes widened. "Am I feeling you?" he asked Heyou.

The battler nodded. "Yeah. A master can almost always feel their sylph, same as we feel all of you. I can tone it down, though, once I figure out how." He looked up at Mace, who returned to his human form. With a nod to Solie, the big sylph went out, having never looked at the man to whom he'd given Heyou. Galway wasn't sure he approved.

Heyou frowned as if wondering the same thing. "Mace said he always hit his master with his hate aura 'cause he hated him, and so that it would drown out his master knowing what he really felt. I won't do that to you, though."

"I'd hope not," Solie said.

"You won't have to." Galway clapped a hand on his shoulder. "You can feed from me now, correct?"

"Yeah. You won't really feel it, though. Leastways, Solie never does. Ril says Leon could tell sometimes, but Leon's weird." Solie made as if she was going to smack him, and Heyou ducked, grinning.

Galway laughed. "Well, you'll have to let me know when you take a nibble, and I'll see if I can feel it." He led both Solie and Heyou out, then, the other people staring curiously as they went. The rumors would be flying, he knew. Heyou hadn't tried to hide what he'd asked, and really there was no reason he should have. The battlers were as much a part of the Community as anyone else.

He'd have to stick around a few more days, Galway decided, now that he knew he could go home after all. He wanted to explore this new relationship and make sure he and Heyou were both comfortable with it before he left. He'd definitely have to come back in the spring, maybe bring the homestead with him, once the Community was moved and his family would be an asset instead of a drain on their resources.

Happy, Heyou walked between him and Solie. Galway

could feel the boy's pleasure and it was nice. A little odd, but good. He was pretty sure he was going to like this.

King Alcor stood watching on the battlements of his castle, Thrall at his back, as the battlers and their masters were boarding the air ship. Jasar went first, his mouth tight and his spine stiff. Shield padded at his side, head low to the ground and snarling. Behind him, three of Alcor's generals followed, each with his own battler. Alcor had never bothered to learn the creatures' names.

One of the sylphs was a hunched thing in a filthy robe, possessed of arms tipped with foot-long claws instead of fingers. Its claws were held up before it like those of a praying mantis, and it started at every sudden noise. Its face was oval, its mouth a round shape overstuffed with fangs jutting out in every direction. The second battler was a golden beast like a great cat, its body sinewy and corded with muscle, its eyes a vividly insane green. The third was a giant spider, walking on a dozen legs instead of six, and with a hundred eyes on its face above its massive fangs.

All three hated, as did Thrall, and their loathing made Alcor's stomach roll and hurt. The pain had been there for years, worse when he was stressed, and no matter how often the healers fixed it, when the stress came back, so did the pain. It had returned when his son was killed, and it was back again now.

The king wasn't sure how much of what Jasar had told him was true, but his inclination was to believe the bulk of his report, though that thought put him in a rage. Leon had betrayed him! How much Jasar had to do with it, Alcor didn't know, but he did know this much was true: his strongest battle-sylph master had turned traitor. And for what? For bribes from a group of pirates he'd been told were dealt with? Apparently they were larger and more organized than Leon had intimated—or that Jasar had seen from his hiding place on the air ship. The courtier's cowardice was the one thing about which Alcor had no doubts. It was part of the reason he'd been willing to give him a battler in the first place. Jasar would never have the intelligence or courage to really use one. He never would have lost Mace if he'd dared stay close enough to see Leon's actions.

The four battlers had their orders, though, and even if Jasar was planning to hide during this fight, that still left three sylphs not bound to cowards. They would kill every last one of those pirates, including the girl. Her battler wouldn't be able to stand up to four, and even if Leon was there, they would still be outnumbered. Ril would be killed and the traitor brought back. Leon would be broken on the rack and whatever was left put in a cage before the castle gates for everyone to watch die. Alcor was in a bad enough mood that he wanted a scapegoat.

Whichever of the generals failed to bring him back would take his place in that cage, and they knew it. Alcor saw the determination on their faces, and he nodded grimly. They wouldn't fail him.

After the battlers boarded, the ordinary soldiers followed. The pirates would likely try to run, and swordsmen and archers would be needed to hunt the last of them down. Battlers were good for mass destruction, but not strategy. As rumors of the betrayal and stolen battler were moving through the castle and city, Alcor must see them all crushed. Then he could focus on his other problems . . . like finding a replacement for his lost heir.

His stomach twisted again, acid eating through it, and he turned before the air ship departed, striding back into the warmth of the castle while shouting for a healer. Thrall followed, as wordless as ever.

He'd never imagined it was possible, but Ril reached the Community just under five hours after he left Leon's manor, cutting a twenty-hour journey by three-quarters. Circumstances demanded he do everything he could in order to gain them time. Lizzy rode on his back all the way, enjoying the wind on her face and the sensations of flight. The others stayed inside him, the younger girls somewhat calmer but still nearly more than their father could handle.

A lot of the heavy snow covering the hive and that which they'd had to dig through was now gone, melted or blown away by sylphs, and Ril saw people outside as dusk approached. They were pointing up at him. He labored up to the cliff, exhausted. Battlers weren't really made to carry loads, and he'd pushed himself beyond endurance to return as fast as he could. Still, he dropped down as lightly as he could, shifting to human form and letting the shrieking girls tumble out onto the ground.

Lizzy rolled, giggling, and rose to her feet as he dropped to his hands and knees, gasping. "Ril!" she shouted. She and her father knelt on either side of him as Betha struggled to round up the younger girls. "Ril," Lizzy wailed, her hands warm on his shoulder. "Are you okay?"

"Go help your mother," Leon ordered. The girl looked at him fearfully and hurried over to Betha. She kept looking back, though—Ril saw it before he had to close his eyes. He was utterly drained.

Leon pulled him close. "Take whatever you need," he said, and lifted him in his arms, carrying him through the cold air to the stairwell. Ril let himself be conveyed, his head resting against Leon's chest as he drank the man's energy—drank deep—and tried to remember that there were no bonds holding him back anymore, and he could kill him by drinking too much. He didn't know where the limit was, though, and finally stopped himself.

He was taken to the queen's audience chamber, the Petrule family either left behind or following, he wasn't sure which. "What happened?" he heard Solie shrill as he was laid upon something soft. Or soft enough—straw poked at him through the blanket covering the bale. He felt the other two battlers close by and relaxed. Everyone was safe.

"He got us here in an afternoon," Leon told the queen. "He shouldn't have flown so fast, but we had to warn you. The king has a ship with four battlers on it. They have to be coming here. We need to be ready."

A small hand stroked Ril's cheek, and Solie whispered his name. "Drink my energy. Please."

Ril blinked at her sleepily and reached up, gently touching her face. Her energy was sweet, light. He drew it in, but he didn't know how much she could spare and forced himself to stop.

"I'm the queen." She smiled. "You can't hurt me."

Leon knelt beside her. "Come on, Ril."

"I don't want to kill either of you," he whispered. "I might."

He was so tired. Even alone he shouldn't have been able to make the trip that fast, but the queen needed him. He would have killed himself for her. Only, that would mean he'd never see Lizzy again. . . .

Mace leaned over him. "You think too often in extremes. Drink. I'll stop you if you start to take too much."

Ril sighed and drank, drawing from both: Solie sweet and light, Leon heavy and warm. They filled and restored him, and finally he was able to rest, sleeping in the queen's chambers while he recovered his strength for the battle to come. Lizzy crept in to sit with him, but he didn't know. He just dreamt of her, and that was enough.

Chapter Twenty-seven

They gathered in one of the larger rooms that hadn't been allocated yet, light provided by a sunset shining through a large window cut into one wall and supplemented by Ash.

The glass in the window was oddly swirled in shape, making the image of the plains outside fluctuate and ripple any time a viewer changed their position. Leon found it nauseating as he sat down at the stone table. Ril had taken more than he ever had, from him and Solie both, and the girl was equally pale as she took her place at the head of the table. Leon hadn't wanted to leave his battler, but Ril needed the sleep, and the rest of them had to plan. Lizzy would watch over him. Leon was sure she would have insisted even if he hadn't suggested it.

The rest of the family was in the eating area, under the care of the Widow Blackwell. He never should have brought them, he decided guiltily—but if he hadn't, they wouldn't have had any warning. Four battlers! The Community had three, but Heyou was young and inexperienced and Ril was exhausted. Mace couldn't take on four alone, even with no limits on his powers. Worse, while the battlers fought, Leon had no doubt that the king's soldiers would move in to deal with the rest of them. There would be hand-to-hand combat in the hallways of the bluff by the end, and almost no one here knew how to use a sword as well as a soldier. Leon knew the abilities of the king's men very well. He'd helped train a great many of them.

"We have to run!" one of the councilmen wailed in fear.

"Where?" Galway asked. "How? We can't outrun an air

ship, and we won't get far in these snows. They'd just follow our tracks, anyway."

"We could scatter," Borish suggested. "While some of us stay behind."

"The same as your former leaders did?" Leon snapped. His head was pounding and all he wanted to do was sleep. He didn't have that luxury. They didn't know how much time they had. Hopefully, that air ship was at least a day behind. "The only ones who can fight battlers are battlers, and we only have two."

"We have three," Morgal corrected.

"Two," he repeated. "The king won't think you're some simple little pirate band now. His generals will have brought fighting men as well. They'll expect our battlers to attack theirs. While they're fighting, soldiers will break in here and kill everyone they find, hoping to get the masters. We can try and hold them off, but they'll have elemental sylphs too. These won't fight, but they'll be able to get the soldiers through the walls. We need to hold one battler back to fight them when they do. I suggest Heyou." He looked at the boy. "You have the least experience. It'll be up to Mace and Ril to defeat the king's battlers. You protect the hive and the queen."

Heyou beamed.

"Two against four?" Morgal gasped. "Can they do it?"

Leon honestly didn't know. He eyed the biggest battler they had. "Mace? Can you?"

The sylph frowned, crossing his arms and looking at the queen. There was no fear in his face, but he was silent for a long time. At last he said, "No," and all the men gave a low gasp of fear. Then the battler added, "I won't wait for them to come here. As soon as Ril is awake, we attack." He tilted his head and regarded Leon, the first time he'd looked any man in the face. "Your plan is good if they arrive before he recovers. Otherwise, we go to them. They're locked into one shape. We're not. We'll destroy the air ship before it reaches the cliff. If we kill their masters, the king's battlers will vanish."

"How long does Ril need?" Devon asked worriedly.

"Until dawn, at least," Leon decided. "I've never seen him this worn out. He made it here in hours carrying my entire family. I still can't believe it." He shook his head in amazement. The attack likely wouldn't come until tomorrow. Ril had bought them a lot of time, time they'd need to ready the hive. The odds weren't in their favor, but things weren't hopeless.

He looked over at Solie, sitting pale and frightened at the head of the table. "These aren't ordinary people trying to make a life for themselves," he told her. "They're soldiers. They'll kill everyone here, and those battlers will turn this bluff into a pile of dust. If you don't give your battlers free rein, they'll lose."

She startled, staring at him. "What?"

He leaned forward, his head still pounding, his legs trembling, and everyone watching as he stared her down. "Lift the restriction that they not kill, and do it now, or everyone in this room will die."

Solie's eyes widened with horror and she glanced at her battlers. Heyou looked with interest, Mace without expression. She turned back to Leon. "Do I have to?"

"Yes," Galway interjected. "This time you do. We're outnumbered as it is." He went over and put a hand on her shoulder. "Just say it."

"And make it an order," Leon added. "Make it clear."

Solie sniffled, wiping tears away as she stared at the table. "Heyou," she choked. "Mace. I order you to do whatever you have to do to protect the Community and everyone in it, even if it means k-killing."

"Ask them if they understand."

"Do you understand?" she whispered.

"Yes, my queen," they said together.

Leon leaned back in his chair. "Give the same order to Ril when he wakes up." He watched her cry for a moment, but Heyou was hugging her, Mace stroking her hair. They'd have to be the ones to comfort her. He still had too much to prepare.

"Now tell me what weapons the rest of you have, and we'll see if we can prepare a defense."

"But we have the battler," Morgal protested.

"Any man who relies only on his battle sylph usually ends up with a sword in his guts." Leon clapped his hands. "Let's get busy. I want a weapons count, a list of names of reliable fighters, and most importantly, I want to know when our enemies will get here." He turned to Devon, who'd stayed silent and was present in the room only because of his oath to Solie. "For that, I want to talk to you."

On the foredeck of the ship, the three generals watched the air-sylph master sing to Tempest, cajoling more speed out of her. Tempest was immense, larger by far than any other sylph on the entire ship, and old. She'd been passed down through ten generations and took the shape of a whirlwind, spinning at the head of the vessel she suspended. Her master sang in a clear, practiced voice, rewarding her efforts.

She traveled immensely fast, other sylphs struggling to keep the winds she created from blowing her passengers off the deck. Her master encouraged this with his song, obviously wanting to impress, and from all accounts they'd arrive at their destination only a few hours after sunset on the day they'd departed.

The generals didn't mind. Each of them were nobles who'd earned their rank before they received their battler, as such creatures were never wasted on men who hadn't already proven themselves. Except for the prince, they were careful not to say, or political threats that needed to be appeased, like Jasar. Or Leon. Of course, Leon was unique, an independent with no noble blood, whom the king used for his subtler work, who'd been given the title King's Head of Security only because it was better than King's Dirty-trick Man. Each of them were secretly pleased that he'd turned traitor. The king would turn more to them now, instead of relegating them to baronies far outside the city, where it would be harder to rebel.

"This shouldn't be a long fight," one of them grunted. He was a heavyset man named Flav, and a veteran of over twenty years. The pirates wouldn't be expecting them. Even if they had a spy at the castle, Tempest could outrun nearly any sylph, even carrying the ship as she was. They could never prepare a defense in time, and they'd be easy to track if they fled.

"We'll definitely be there before midnight," noted a second man. His name was Boradel, and his hair was as red as Solie's—as was his face, weathered from many years of outdoor service. "Tempest has saved us a day's travel. It's too bad."

"Oh?" asked the third, Anderam. "You like this ship that much?"

"Nope. It's just the view won't be so good at night. Claw is eager for this fight. When the king asked who wanted to come, he nearly picked me up and carried me to the castle himself." Boradel laughed. "I've never seen him so excited. The damn thing cowers almost all of the rest of the time."

The other two joined him in laughter. "It's too bad Poison isn't like that," Flav said. "He doesn't give a damn if he fights or not."

"Must be nice," Anderam chuckled. "Yanda will fight his own shadow if he can't find anything else."

"Yanda is crazy," Boradel said.

"Aren't all battlers?"

The generals all laughed again.

A short way distant, Jasar sniffed and pulled his cloak closer around him. The other three had left their battlers farther down the main deck, but Shield crouched at his feet, panting. He knew the other men thought he was a coward, but he didn't care. Battlers or not, he had more power and money than any of them. He looked away, trying not to think how fast they were traveling across the Shale Plains. In another hour, they'd be able to see the cliff where he'd been deserted by his first battler, and where Leon had made his terrible promise. Jasar shuddered and looked down at his new battler. Shield was much better than Mace. He knew his place—as a dog.

It would be over soon, Jasar promised himself. The pirates would be destroyed, the girl killed, Leon would be tortured to death, and he could go back to Eferem and use his new victory to help parlay his way into a marriage with the king's eldest daughter. He only had one thing he needed to be sure of: that none of these men saw Mace and realized he wasn't dead. If they did, it would be simple enough to wait until their three battlers defeated the traitor and then turn Shield loose on them. He'd look very good indeed if he was the only survivor of such a battle. He'd just have to exaggerate what happened a bit. Smirking, he reached down to pat Shield's head, ignoring the creature's heightened loathing.

Suddenly, the battlers roared a warning, and Jasar's eyes widened in panic as he backed toward the stairs leading down into the bowels of the ship. The three generals simultaneously moved forward, searching for the enemy in the growing darkness, and a group of air sylphs raced past, arcing up toward nothing that Jasar could see.

To his shame and disgust, the others saw his fear and laughed again. "Don't worry, my lord. It looks like we have a spy," one of them chuckled.

"Not for long," Flav promised. "Poison!" The massive spider moved forward, passing within feet of Jasar, who flinched, and Flav ordered, "When they drive it above the ship, destroy it."

His heart pounding, Jasar turned and headed downward, no longer interested in what the generals thought of him. His status was higher than theirs anyway, and he'd been given the honor of two battlers. Only, none of theirs had needed a replacement, a treacherous voice whispered inside him. Jasar ignored it and returned to his quarters.

Airi raced across the sky, riding the winds as fast as she could and so terrified that she could barely think. She could feel her master and the hive behind her, but she could distantly feel the hatred of the coming battlers as well. They were far closer than anyone expected.

They must have left the city shortly after Ril and traveled almost as fast. Faintly, Airi could feel the sylph who bore the ship. It was Tempest, one of the oldest of the sylphs here and older than any Airi had known in her original hive. That age gave her power, and the weight of her burden was nothing to her, even as Airi pushed herself to intercept.

She didn't get close. Too close, and the battlers on board would destroy her. She did get close enough to sense the number of people aboard, though, and to search for one very important thing—the one piece of information Leon had asked her to get—along with determining just how close the enemy really was.

It was hard to discern. The ship flew toward her, trailing clouds as it hurtled through the sky. There were dozens of men on board, crew and soldiers both, and the battlers, always the battlers. She felt elemental sylphs as well, among them the air sylphs who kept Tempest's winds from scouring the deck and the earth sylphs who would break into the hive. Before they could detect her, she raced under the ship far closer than she would have preferred, searching even harder.

There were six—no, more than six. She hoped, prayed, and moved ever nearer, desperate to find what she must and get back to the hive to warn them that their leeway was nearly gone. As it was, she didn't know if she could outrun Tempest, even with nothing to carry.

Suddenly she felt it, just as she skimmed below Tempest's winds, and she wanted to cry out in success. There was one on board! But at the same time a roar of hatred sounded, men yelling above her on the ship. Immediately Airi dove, for other air sylphs were racing after her. They were smaller than Tempest, but many were stronger than Airi, and they outnumbered her anyway. They swarmed her, buffeting her with their winds and forcing her up above the ship. They wouldn't kill her—none of them could be ordered to do something like that—but she knew they would bring her up to where the battlers could.

Airi wailed in terror, fighting. She had to get her information back to the others, and she didn't want to die. She screamed as loud as she could, echoing it along the hive line, but none of these sylphs were from her original hive—and even if they had been, they wouldn't be able to help her. They had no choice but to obey their orders, just as she had no choice but to obey hers—though Devon had given her the option of not going.

Desperate, she slammed into the weakest sylph as hard as she could, gaining enough room to twist and dive back beneath the ship before she could be targeted by a battler. Immediately the sylphs dove after her, circling her again and buffeting her upward. They were stronger; there were too many. Airi screamed again and flipped over, tossed upward helplessly toward her death.

Just as she reached the level below the edge of the sails, something arced up through them and caught her, knocking the surrounding air sylphs in every direction and bearing Airi away. Stunned, she felt herself carried down toward the plains and away, incredibly fast. Behind her, the air sylphs reeled, crying out into the sky their pain.

Hold on, Heyou said, his shape condensed to barely bigger than hers, and translucent as well. Clasping her close, he fled back to the hive.

What? she gasped, shocked. She hadn't expected any of the battlers to risk leaving the hive to save her.

I heard you screaming. I had to come. Mace said not to let the men see me.

But the battlers will know you're here!

They knew I was here anyway. Devon would be upset if you died. Then the queen would be upset. Then everyone would be upset. So I came to get you.

He sounded as though he was laughing at her. Always baffled by the minds of battlers, Airi clung to him and let him carry her, not reliant on wind currents but just rocketing through them.

I got the information they wanted, she told him.

Great. You better tell them fast.

Behind them, the king's air vessel raced in pursuit, Tempest putting on even more speed at her master's command.

Flav leaned over the railing, looking down as the ship approached the bluff, its air sylph finally slowing her mad pace. The location was just as Jasar described: a solitary hill over two hundred feet high that had been cleaved down the middle and across the top to leave a sheetlike front. It was lit by moonlight shining off the snow, showing the top bare, save for three figures standing near the edge, staring upward. Pulling out a spyglass, he focused on them.

"Are those people?" Boradel asked.

"Yes. Two men and a boy. They must want to try and negotiate."

Anderam snorted. "As though they have anything we want."

"It might be a trap," Flav said thoughtfully, lowering the glass. The men just stood quietly—they weren't even armed. The boy was grinning, waving.

"Well," Boradel replied. "They'll find we set a trap of our own."

After that sylph escaped earlier, they'd taken some extra precautions—something Leon shouldn't expect, given how badly the generals already outnumbered him. Four sylphs against two? A group of ignorant pirates against seventy armed soldiers? They'd all laughed at the odds. And yet none of them were stupid men, and they knew Leon was a tactical genius.

Flav collapsed the spyglass and put it into a belt pouch, never taking his eyes off the three figures below, none of whom he recognized. There was no sign of Leon, which bothered him.

"Poison!" Hissing, the spider stepped up beside him, glaring at his master. Flav looked at his own reflection mirrored a hundred times in the creature's eyes, and pointed. "Kill them."

Immediately the spider climbed over the railing, clinging to the wood of the ship with his dozen legs as he half-lowered himself over the side facing the three men. He roared, his hatred echoing through the plains, and focused. A wave of shimmering energy blasted out of him, enough to wipe out everything atop that bluff and vaporize the stone itself at least a foot deep.

That didn't happen. Halfway down, the blast wave hit another rising upward and exploded, rocking the ship and setting Tempest to screaming in outrage. Flav grabbed the rail before he could fall over it, gaping down in shock as the two adult men changed form, becoming things he'd only seen on the day he bound Poison. Then their hatred hit him, and he reeled at the impossibility.

"Kill them!" he shrieked at his battler. "Kill them now!"

Behind him, he heard Boradel and Anderam ordering their own battlers to attack, and Poison leaped off the ship, his dozen legs spread as he howled in fury, plummeting toward the oncoming enemy. Claw and Yanda followed a moment later, vanishing over the side.

"Pull the ship back!" Anderam shouted to Tempest's master, and the vessel started to withdraw, pulling them away before they could end up caught in the melee.

"They changed," Boradel gasped, his normally florid face white. "Oh, gods, they *changed*."

There were no controls on those monsters, nothing to stop them. Flav gripped the railing until his knuckles whitened, staring over the side at the fighting. The moon was bright enough for him to make out what was happening, to see the two smoky shapes take on Poison, Yanda, and Claw.

Unbound or not, the pair defending the bluff were still outnumbered, and he began to hope Poison and the others could be victorious after all. He smirked with the same pride he always felt watching his sylph fight. Poison was the finest killer in the kingdom, ruthless and intelligent despite his hate. But a moment later, he saw the last thing he would ever have expected.

"No!" he shouted. Turning, he stared at the other two generals, neither of whom seemed to recognize what had just happened. "We need more battlers!" he shouted, to their surprise. Neither of them had seen. "Where's Jasar?"

The dandy was nowhere in sight. This was unfortunate in a way Flav didn't realize. Jasar, after all, was the only one who had seen before what had just happened, or could have warned them about what it meant.

Chapter Twenty-eight

If they'd had any doubts left, the arrival and escape of Airi convinced the generals that Leon was indeed a traitor, and that he was now leading the pirates' defense. Knowing how good he was at strategy, they had decided to make sure the odds stayed with them, and had thus dispatched their soldiers early. Several miles away, air sylphs carried Alcor's warriors and a team of earth sylphs around to the sloping back of the bluff, where it met the mountains.

As they approached, they'd been able to see the windows cut into the cliff front. The soldier who led the detachment wasn't surprised. In this environment, it really only made sense that the pirates move into the mountain itself. Of course, he and his detachment would drill a few new holes and kill everyone inside while Leon was still expecting a traditional battler fight.

Heyou didn't sense them moving in at the base of the slope so far behind him. He was instead watching Ril and Mace rocket upward to fight the three battlers dropping toward them. He ached to join them, but his orders were clear. He had to defend the hive from the inside. It was frustrating. Regardless, he turned his back on the battle and shifted form, racing as smoke and lightning toward the stairwell.

Cal's earth sylph Stria waited at the top and, once Heyou was past, put a hand on the stone to close it off overhead. Immediately the sounds of explosions and battle were deadened, and Heyou streaked down the steps and along the passageways to the eating area, where everyone was packed except the men and sylphs Leon had set as guards.

He soared over two, both men ducking with yelps of fright, and flitted into the eating area itself, arcing up over the crowd. They shrieked or cheered in response. Heyou ignored all of them, except for giving a quick loop that sent Bevan diving under his seat, then shifted back to human form, landing in a crouch atop the table where Solie sat, his face only inches from hers.

"Are you trying to be dramatic?" she asked.

He leaned in and kissed her roughly. "They're here. Ril and Mace are fighting three battlers. It's wonderful!"

He thought it was fantastic, but there were frightened murmurs all around the mess hall. Heyou could feel the fear, and he looked around in surprise. "What? You think we'll lose?"

Leon leaned over the the table and whispered, "What can you tell me? Which battlers did they bring?"

"Uh, ugly ones?"

Leon clapped a hand over his eyes while the blonde girl standing at his side giggled. Heyou looked desperately at Solie. "Can I go? I really want to kill somebody."

"No." She glared. "You stay here."

"But nobody's gonna get in here!"

As if to prove him wrong, a fire sylph shot into the mess hall, screaming.

"Oh." Heyou launched himself off the table and changed, racing after the hysterical fire sylph. She led him down another staircase to the lowest level of the hive, to the great stables they'd dug there for livestock. As he neared, he started to feel the emotions of all the humans there, including a set he should have felt far sooner, had he not been distracted by excitement.

A half-dozen men fought a losing battle against more than a score in red and black who were pouring through a massive opening at the back melted away by an earth sylph. The invaders were shoving their way past the panicked livestock or even cutting them down. Galway was one of the defenders, his emotions under strict control even as he shouted for the defenders to pull back—and as one of them was run through beside him.

Heyou swooped down over his master and roared, letting loose his hatred. This struck the intruders a second before his force wave blew them apart, vaporizing them into a bloody spray. A second blast took the earth sylph who'd let them in, even before she had a chance to scream. Heyou paused at the ragged entrance for a moment, hovering above the snow, but he felt no life outside. Not anymore.

Close the hole, he sent to Galway, who nodded and gestured to one of the masters of an earth sylph. Heyou left them to seal the gap and raced back up the stairs, returning to the mess hall and his position on top of Solie's table. "I think I get now why you wanted me to stay inside," he said to Leon.

Another sylph appeared, screaming a warning, and he was off again, this time in another direction. They were coming from every side but the front, he realized, and hoped he would be fast enough to stop them all.

Solie eyed Leon fearfully, and then Morgal. Leon's wife was screaming at her husband for bringing them here, and Morgal was sobbing, but Leon's oldest daughter met Solie's gaze with eyes that were frightened but clear. Solie swallowed heavily and nodded. "It'll be all right," she promised.

"I know," Lizzy answered. But as the hive shook, Solie honestly wasn't sure of that at all.

Ril and Mace flew upward, wings spread and lightning-filled mouths gaping. The three hostile battlers dropped toward them, led by that aberration of a giant spider, but Mace could feel a fourth—one still on the ship, being held in reserve. Three was enough, though, maybe more than enough.

Mace flashed into the lead. Three hundred feet above the bluff he slammed into Poison, and the spider drove his clawed feet down, trying to impale him as he also flashed a force wave that Mace blocked with his own. Mace used that same wave to stop the claws before they could rend his mantle, and they both tumbled end over end, locked together.

Ril took the next one, the golden-haired lion, and flinched while blocking repeated blasts from the huge cat. He was still exhausted from his mad flight back to the hive; Mace had dragged him out of sleep when Airi and Heyou returned. But it didn't matter. He would fight with everything he had left for as long as he could.

Darting to one side, able to fly where the lion couldn't, he shifted, part of his mantle forming a bladed whip that lashed out at Yanda. It slammed against the cat's wave shield, knocking him back, and Ril dove after him.

Claw came last, falling directly toward Mace and Poison. His mouth gaped wide, his eyes glowing, and the cloak he wore flapped around him as he landed atop the other two. Overburdened, with only one of them able to fly, they all fell.

Ril flew after the tumbling lion, dodging blasts of power that would have obliterated him if they'd hit directly. He didn't return those attacks, not yet having regained enough strength. He'd have to fight close up to win this. They might have sent Heyou and put him in the hive instead, he considered distantly, but Heyou would have had no way to win. Power meant so much less compared to experience, and this battler was old. Ril was a lot younger than Yanda, but he still had a better chance than Heyou. He had to believe that.

Quickly he shifted again, adopting the hawk form in which he'd spent so many years. He was used to the shape, and it was both smaller and harder to hit. He folded his wings and dove, raking his talons across Yanda's back before sweeping in a different direction.

Yanda's claws ripped a quarter of the feathers out of his tail. It hurt terribly—they were very much a part of his essence. Ril spun out of control for a second before dropping intentionally to avoid another blast. The cat depended on them too much, arching and shrieking as he fell, throwing energy so indiscriminately that holes were blown in the ground and even the left sail of the air ship was destroyed. Ril heard the air sylph holding it up shriek in anger, but he was whirling end over end himself in evasion.

Yanda twisted and landed on the ground, gathered himself, and leaped in the very same motion. Snarling, Ril barrel-rolled, dodging while he created a wall of energy he couldn't really afford that was weak but enough to drive Yanda back a pace and save his life. But without all his tail feathers to help him steer, he cut his next turn too tight, and his trailing wing caught the ground. A moment later he rolled, bouncing up into the air and shifting hard, trying to change shape into something that could fight on the ground.

Pain was everywhere. His mantle screamed in agony where the chunk of feathers had been torn out, and he selected his next-most-familiar form just before he ploughed into the snowy ground again. Flipping over onto his front, he had the breath knocked out of him.

A growl sounded. Washed by the other battler's hatred, Ril rolled fast to his right as Yanda tore into the earth where he'd lain. In human form, Ril jumped to his feet and gasped for breath, staring at the cat only ten feet away. Yanda was cut deeply across his back, energy leaking out of him instead of blood, but Ril knew who was in worse shape. He hadn't been in a fight like this since before he'd left his hive, and even that hadn't been as brutal as this. There, he wouldn't have needed to fight alone, and shape hadn't been so important. Here he was pretty sure shape was the only thing that would save him.

Only, he was running out of the energy he needed to change it. If he was lucky, he had one more blast wave in him, and he already knew it wouldn't be strong enough to cause any damage. Not against a battler this old. Had they known whom they'd be fighting beforehand, Mace would have taken this one. Then Ril could have died trying to fight the other two.

He snarled and moved again to attack.

Filled with far more energy than the younger battler at full strength, Yanda fired another blast. Ril conjured his last wave to block it. The energy that should have vaporized him blew him off his feet instead, and he went tumbling down the slope leading from the cliff, scattering snow-covered stones and yelling. Yanda leaped after him, discharging blasts that exploded all around, throwing Ril up into the air as a cat would toss a mouse.

It was too much. Infuriated, Ril twisted around and landed in a crouch as the cat raced at him, still in human form but with his arm from the elbow down formed into a jagged sword. Yanda dove, sending a haze of snow and rock up behind, and Ril thrust the weapon forward, trying to impale the other battler. The move was fast, incredibly fast, but Yanda rolled, spinning in midair and taking the blow deep along his side and withers—and then he slammed into Ril. Desperate, Ril shifted again, regaining his natural form to try and break away, but the lion rolled right through him, claws and teeth slashing.

Ril screamed, the bottom third of his mantle sliced completely through. It dissolved to nothingness with a reek of ozone, his cry echoing through the hive line to warn the other battlers of his imminent death. The pain was overwhelming, and he bucked upward, trailing energy. Curling around himself instinctually, he tried to hold the last of his life inside and convulsed, falling away.

Yanda roared in triumph and turned toward the hive, his tail lashing and energy pouring from his side. He was hurt, but not enough to kill him, Ril realized. *Leon,* he sent desperately. *I failed. He's coming.* Then, curling into a ball, his injury pressed against his body as tightly as possible, he became the only form he could think of and felt himself hit the frozen ground, just before the darkness took him.

Inside the hive, Leon shouted orders to men and sylphs both, sending them in all directions to keep the lines of communication open so that they would know where the next attack commenced. Heyou flickered into the room again, and Leon pointed him to the northernmost passage, gesturing to a fire sylph, who immediately led him to where the soldiers were reportedly boring through a side wall three levels down.

"I don't like this anymore!" the battler shouted, shifting to human form just long enough to deliver the complaint.

"Tough!" Leon called. "Just keep them out! There can't be more than a dozen left!" The air ship couldn't have held any more. They were spread out and unable to communicate with each other, probably unaware that a battler had been killing each group as it came in.

Heyou vanished, and Leon turned toward Morgal. No matter what the man thought of him personally, there was no doubt in anyone's mind who was now in charge. He had seen a lot of gratitude on the faces of people who'd been shouting for him to be hanged not very long ago. Right now, that didn't matter, just so long as they obeyed. "I want you to—" He stopped, hearing a faint voice in his mind. A faint voice and a horrific, already-fading agony.

"Ril? I . . . Oh, gods . . . Ril!" Leon turned and screamed

it through the stone walls to the Shale Plains before the cliff. "Ril! No! Ril!" Agony tearing through him as surely as it had his battler, he spun toward the northern corridor, wiping tears from his eyes as he drew his sword. "Heyou! Get back here! A battler is coming!" People all around him screamed in terror, and Heyou returned, skidding to a halt in human form.

"What about the soldiers?" he asked.

"I'll deal with the soldiers," Leon said. "You have to take care of the battler."

Heyou nodded and flickered off. Leon gestured at the last of the armed men in the mess hall, Devon and Morgal among them, and he led them toward the northern passage. Behind him he heard his family's screams. He ignored those as much as he did his own pain.

Chapter Twenty-nine

Leaving the dying battler, Yanda galloped toward the cliff, muscles bunching under smooth skin and golden fur. No real conscious thought went through his mind. He had his orders, and attacking other hives was what he had been hatched to do—and all of that had been replaced long ago by madness. The only thing he wanted to do now was kill, and he didn't even feel the deep wounds he'd suffered or how they slowed him down.

The bluff rose ahead, a stronghold reeking of both terror and determination. He wanted to destroy the inhabitants. Dotting the face of the cliff were the dark squares of windows, and while none were low enough to be of any use to a human attacker, Yanda increased his speed, gathering himself and leaping for the nearest, nearly forty feet up. Lashing out with energy, he blasted the window and much of the rock inward.

Landing on the stone floor inside, he skidded across a woven grass carpet into a rope bed and the wall. A water sylph was there, set to watch the window just in case. She screamed in fright and dissolved her form, raining onto the floor and flowing toward the doorway. Yanda pushed himself up and dug his claws into the puddle, cutting into the mantle of energy from which she was truly made. Like the battler outside, she screamed as he tore her apart, ripping her into shreds too small to hold consciousness or life.

Her death smelled sweet. Yanda lapped his tongue across it, savoring the taste even though he couldn't take any nourishment. He purred, but he could sense other life nearby, a few even from his original hive. That didn't matter. He'd kill them all.

He padded out into the passageway, which was dark but full of sound and smells. Another sylph was fleeing down it, racing away from another window. Yanda bounded forward in pursuit, catching her only a few feet farther on. She was an earth sylph, tougher than the first but still helpless against him. She tried to protect herself and he killed her anyway.

There was more life farther ahead, a lot of it grouped together. He sniffed the air, searching the passageways, but where he was now didn't connect directly with the appropriate chamber. He sniffed one stone wall, sure they were just on the other side, milling about and whimpering, and backed up.

The wall erupted inward. In the eating area, men and women screamed, trying to flee the exploding inner wall, many injured or helping others. Yanda dove in and roared, landing in a crouch, flashing his hatred at them. They screamed even more, which excited him, and he leaped for the closest, intending to rip every person present to bloody chunks.

Hysterical air and fire sylphs tried to knock him off his path, but he ignored them; they all looked like children and they were weak. Then a boy slammed into his side, fingers that were suddenly claws biting into the wounds Yanda had already suffered, and he roared as he was scourged by the hatred of another battler who'd hidden himself among the sylphs, using them to camouflage his attack.

It was unthinkable. No battler attacked from ambush! Yanda screamed in outrage, lashing out as the two of them tumbled across the floor, crashing through fleeing humans. Locked together with him, the boy changed into something barbed and clawed, with many mouths. Pain lanced through the cat and he struck out with his energy, only to find it blocked by his enemy.

The strength of the shield was enough to show he was fighting another inferior battler, though this one was not weak but young. Yanda howled gleefully and threw himself into the fight. He'd been attacked by infants before. This one shouldn't take very long to kill.

Mace dropped toward the ground, tangled so effectively with the two other battlers that he couldn't break free to fight. For a moment, neither could either of his foes, and in a strange form of mutual agreement they broke apart just before impact. Still in his natural form, Mace shot to one side, arcing up above as the other two landed, the spider neatly on the dozen legs he'd formed, the cloaked, clawed thing in a low crouch farther down the slope.

For a split second it was a standoff, the spider hissing as it turned, legs shifting the bulbous body delicately toward Mace, putting his back to his partner. Mace stayed where he was, watching and assessing, ready to move in an instant or change his shape. Unlike Ril, he was fresh and rested, older by far than either of his combatants. The cat might have given him problems, but these two were young enough they'd need to take him together.

Apparently they knew it. The spider worked his mandibles furiously, dropping his body low to the ground and letting the other battler move up beside him. They weren't of the same hive—Mace could tell that easily—but they were under orders to work together. All the battlers were under orders to do so when necessary, as he'd worked with Ril to attack the Community before they became hive mates. The spider gave a hissing chuckle, expecting that cooperation now. They could kill him if they worked together.

That didn't happen. The second battler moved up beside

the first, his round mouth wide and the massive tangle of fangs flaring outward. He stepped close to Poison and turned in one motion, slashing the spider across the abdomen with his claws. The spider screamed, hurtling to the side and tumbling over, legs thrashing. Immediately, Claw was after him, as was Mace, changing into the heavy armor form he'd worn for so long and landing on the spider's stomach, driving his feet into that softer body. He punched downward, tearing through the battler's mantle. Claw slashed at the spider again. All of them were screaming, hate rising and power lashing everywhere, the spider's flaring indiscriminately, his killers's blasts focused very deliberately.

Mace's power speared deep, tearing into Poison. It rebounded, throwing both him and Claw back. They caught themselves and crouched to attack again, watching, but it wasn't necessary. Poison made a confused sound, shuddering with his belly gone and his legs curled up over him. His many eyes flared and died. A moment later his body started to break apart, the bits of him falling away and dispersing, crumbling to less than dust and reeking of ozone.

Mace straightened, looking dispassionately at the last specks of the dead battler before turning to the other. Claw stared back with an equal lack of expression, but his emotions were exalted. They were patterned exactly like Mace's—which was no surprise, given how he originally came from the same hive and now belonged to the same queen.

One of the children had been hit by a chunk of flying rock. The toddler screamed despite the fierce battle that raged past her and out through another corridor. Blood poured into her eyes, blinding her and driving her mother nearly to hysteria. Nowhere seemed safe. Explosions and screams from the two struggling battlers echoed up through the corridor, and the hive itself shook, hate pouring out so strongly that the humans could only cower in panic. If the lion sylph returned, there was little they could do.

Gently, Luck reached out a hand and laid it on the wounded girl's forehead, focusing. Immediately the wound closed and the girl stopped crying, blinking up at the healer in confusion. Luck turned away, paying her no more mind. She didn't have time. The wounds in this room were all healed now, and she focused, searching for more pain, more injuries to mend. There were many in the hive, men hurt and bleeding from their melees with the incoming soldiers. She couldn't really distinguish between those of the hive and the attackers, though. Back home, it was easy. Here, it wasn't so simple.

She looked at her terrified master, who was cowering under a table and sobbing. She loved him, but he wouldn't be any help in this. She reached out anyway, touching him and repairing a bit more that thing inside him that couldn't be healed, the hypochondria that had so fascinated her and drawn her away from the wounded battler she'd left her hive to heal. That had been her one moment of freedom, rare indeed. Now she had so much. Before, she'd only left the hive if a sylph was hurt too badly to return but not so badly that the queen abandoned them. Now she could leave anytime she wanted, if she wanted. The knowledge of that was usually enough.

She ached to heal, but she didn't know where to start. She couldn't heal the enemy, but she didn't know who the enemy was. None of the humans smelled like hive. The only hive injury she could sense was . . .

Luck stared out the jagged hole blown in the side wall. It was already being closed by a trio of earth sylphs, while others sealed the passage the battlers had gone down. It was a pathetic gesture, but they had to act, just as she did. To be true to their purpose.

A battler was down, wounded and dying somewhere beyond that hole. Luck knew he was of the hive. Her first instinct was to heal the hive defenders inside, but he was hurt so badly. She could tell he was far gone, farther than she could fully heal, and even if she saved him he'd never be the same, never again be able to serve in the way he was needed. Back home, she'd either leave him to die or help him relax and let his energy bleed out to speed his death. But as she glanced at the queen, crouched under another table with a weeping girl in her arms, Luck remembered the order that no one was to die. The battlers had been given exemption, but not her.

Slowly Luck drifted away from her master, wanting to take him with her but not wanting to put him in danger. He wouldn't be of use anyway. Zem saw her going and screamed, but she was used to ignoring him when instinct was stronger. Picking up speed, she flitted through the hole in the wall before it closed, and raced down the passage on the outside. Barely slowing as she passed the bodies of two sylphs—both were dead—she continued on, flying out the broken window Yanda had entered.

The conflict between Mace and the two other battlers she ignored. Two were of the hive, one was not, so she knew who would win, and she knew the two would protect her from the other. She found Ril lying on a slope of shale, half buried in snow and leaning against a boulder. He'd shifted into the form of an egg in a last attempt to contain the energy pouring out of him. Luck shuddered, feeling how much of him was simply gone, and didn't know if she could help. The queen's order was absolute, though: no one was to die. In her heart, she reveled in the simplicity of that and wrapped herself around Ril, glowing.

She healed him, taking the torn edge of his mantle and sealing it, reflowing the energy he'd contained back into him. He'd lost so much, though, his pattern broken and crippled. She eased him back into the human shape he'd adopted, not sure he'd ever be able to shift form again, and continued her work, close to exhausting herself once more as she struggled to bring him back. Arms and legs akimbo, Ril sprawled under her, his head down lower on the slope than his feet, and she lay along him like a lover, her arms wrapping him in an embrace.

So much was gone, so much lost. But she brought him back to wholeness in form, if not in soul, and rested her own barely corporeal head on his chest, sighing. She'd healed him, true to instinct and order . . . and felt him shiver from the cold as no battler ever should. She'd saved him, and it would be up to him to decide if he'd ever be able to forgive her.

Embracing him again, she hauled him up, carrying him back with her to the light and warmth of the hive.

Heyou squealed as he and Yanda rolled across the huge room, scattering people and angling by some miracle down a passageway on the other side. This battler was older than Ril or even Mace, and Heyou tried not to panic as he remembered what Ril had done to him before—and that Ril was likely dead now from trying to fight this thing.

At least the cat was injured. Heyou dug his claws into those existing wounds and pushed, trying to cause as much damage as possible. That earned him a bite near his eyes, and Heyou shrieked, blasting him in the face. Yanda actually laughed at that, and bit harder, swinging his head to one side and throwing Heyou against the wall. He slammed into it and nearly lost his form, forced to take solid shape just to keep himself from shattering. With a wince he dropped to his hands and knees, wearing the boy form that Solie liked, and Yanda grinned evilly at him, tongue hanging out of his mouth.

Solie . . . , Heyou thought desperately. If he lost she'd be killed, along with Galway and Devon and everyone else. He couldn't just fight this battler, though. He wasn't strong enough. Not unless he waited a few more centuries, and that hadn't helped Ril any. His only real hope was to lead him to Mace—and Mace was busy enough himself.

He also doubted Yanda was that stupid. The cat hunched down and stalked slowly toward him, tail twitching and green eyes glowing. Heyou struggled to his feet and backed away, looking for anything he could use to defend himself.

There was nothing, so he hit the cat with his hate instead, screaming. Yanda matched that scream and returned his own shriek, along with a blast of energy Heyou only blocked by instinct. Propelled backward, he somersaulted down the corridor and crashed to a halt at a T junction. Taking a chance, he scrambled down a side passage, the few water sylphs who'd been hiding there fleeing ahead of him, trailing water. Yanda burst around the corner a moment later, still laughing.

He couldn't keep this up. Running at full speed, the other battler just behind, Heyou breathed a prayer to his queen, gathered himself, and changed. He went to smoke and shot up to the ceiling, condensing just enough that the other battler skidded underneath, slipping on the wet floor.

Dropping back, Heyou fell onto the cat and dug in with every claw he could form while screaming his antipathy, blasting waves of energy downward with everything he had. Yanda shrieked and threw himself straight up, smashing them both against the ceiling before flashing out with his own energy, rocking the hive with it and flattening Heyou against him. Frantic, the young battler dug deeper, fighting to hang on and knowing that the instant he let go he was dead. Yanda kept bucking, hurling them against every surface he could and bombarding him with energy.

In agony, Heyou felt his grip start to slip.

* * *

Mace left Claw behind as he flew up to King Alcor's air ship, the huge vessel retreating with growing desperation and speed. The air sylph was all that held it aloft; the craft canted heavily to one side, and that side's masts were so badly broken, the sails dragged against the ground and dug a trail in the snow.

He'd felt Ril fall, and Claw couldn't come with him. Claw's master was on that ship, and Mace no more wanted to chance him against that general's orders than he himself wanted to risk facing his own master. He could still feel Jasar in the back of his mind, but Mace always pushed all sense of him away, drowning himself instead in the essences of his queen and the widow. The latter was a very vigorous woman, able to please him as much as he did her, despite her stern outward manner. He wanted to go to her after this, and the urge to soothe her fear and anger was much greater than any thought of his old tormentor.

The three battler masters were on the ship deck, the one who'd owned Poison vomiting on the wood from the shock of his sylph's death. Mace recognized them from various visits to the castle, and shifted deliberately to his bound form, wanting them to know who he was.

He landed, and all three gaped at him in shock. Jasar must have been a good liar, he noted dryly. None of them had been expecting him.

"You . . . ," Claw's master gasped. He was shocked but not panicked, which made Mace very glad he'd left the other battler behind. "Jasar lied!"

"You expected any less?" Mace growled, and had the petty satisfaction of seeing all three men's amazement and horror. That was more than enough for him. They weren't like Leon, who'd loved his battler and earned Ril's love in return. He lifted his arm, formed out of something that only looked like metal, and razed the entire top of the deck.

All around him, a dozen or more minor sylphs vanished as their masters died, and he heard the air sylph who held the ship up scream with rage. Her master must be somewhere else, Mace thought idly, and he searched out the stairs that led belowdecks. It was better that way. He was in a foul mood from killing those men, and there was one more battler inside the ship, held there for whatever stupid reason. Mace felt very much like killing the enemy sylph, followed by its master, then killing the rest of the humans who threatened his hive. Once that was done, he was going to go back to the widow and relax in her arms.

Still in his armored form, he stomped toward the stairs.

Heyou didn't know if he could hold on any longer. Hissing and squealing, he gripped with barely a third of the claws he'd formed, the battler beneath him bucking like a maddened horse, throwing them both around as though he didn't care if they were both hurt in the process. He felt more of his claws give way and focused the last of his strength, hoping that he could spike the older battler enough to kill him. He had little hope, but there was nothing else he could think of to do.

Suddenly, the lion froze, gasped, and gave a piercing scream that was nothing but hate and denial. An instant later he vanished, and Heyou fell against the ground, stunned. It took nearly a minute to pull himself together enough to figure out what had happened. The battler's master had died. He'd been sucked back to the hive world, his link to this one broken.

Shivering, Heyou shifted to human form and forced himself to his feet. Wincing in pain, though he didn't look injured, he limped back to Solie, only to find the passageway had been sealed off with rock at least six feet thick.

"Ah, crap," he muttered.

* * *

Terrified, Jasar cowered against the wall in his quarters, Shield standing between him and the door. He'd heard the fighting and felt the hate. Worse, he'd felt the ship being struck by the energy blast. When he and Leon first fought the pirates, the craft had barely been touched, and he'd used his authority to cut the battle short and return home. Now he was desperate to run, but the generals were in charge.

Panic flooded him and he gasped for breath, his chest actually hurting from terror—and from something worse. Being bonded to two sylphs was slowly killing him. He could feel it happening, somewhere deep inside. He shouldn't be here. It wasn't fair.

Before him, Shield shifted, growling, and Jasar tried to take comfort. Shield would protect him. Before anything else, he'd protect him—that order had been made clear. He'd be safe. But such knowledge didn't help Jasar's terror any as heavy footfalls sounded outside, heavier than any human man's had a right to be. Jasar heard metal clinking and blinked at how unnaturally familiar it was. The noises stopped outside the door and it opened.

Shield lunged, mouth gaping wide, and obeyed his orders to the letter. Protect his master. He did—and made no attempt to protect himself from the blast that came through the doorway. He absorbed the attack with his body, and the bolt tore him in half. Shrieking in pain and relief, the battler crashed to the ground and died, his body immediately starting to decay.

Jasar stared in disbelief and horror, letting out a scream. This wasn't what he'd meant! He looked up again as the other battler stepped into the room, and saw a similar shock in the creature's eyes.

Mace.

Chapter Thirty

Mace honestly hadn't expected the battler to sacrifice himself. He'd never thought of doing that himself, but he felt the creature's relief as his servitude ended. Mace understood. He watched the dog die and stepped into the room, intending to kill whatever master his fellow sylph hated so much that he preferred suicide.

Looking up, he saw Jasar and realized his mistake. He'd pushed the man so far out of his thoughts that he hadn't sensed him on the ship. If he had, he would have blown the thing out of the air from a distance. Now it was too late.

Mace bolted for the door, desperate to get free before the man came to any catastrophic realizations.

"Stop!" Jasar screamed, his voice shrill and uncertain.

Mace stopped.

Shaking, Jasar pushed himself off the wall, making his way toward the massive battler. "Turn around and freeze," he grunted. Joints creaking as they would if his armor were real, Mace turned, his bulk blocking the doorway completely. Jasar stared at him and started to grin, but then rage crossed his face and his cheeks burned red. He was nearly insane with anger and humiliation.

"You bastard!" he screeched. "How dare you do that to me! Who do you think you are?"

Mace stared down at his master without any expression, while inside he was screaming. How could he have been so careless? He never would have expected Jasar to come back, but he should have. He should have thought of the possibility, and now it made so much sense. Who else would be able to lead the king's men here directly?

Jasar howled at him incoherently for the next few minutes, froth blowing from his lips while he raved, and Mace held still, not moving, unable to do so without fresh orders. Solie had given him the freedom to speak and to change his shape, but she hadn't ordered him not to obey Jasar again. Neither of them had even thought of it. Now he had no choice but to follow that single order to freeze. He didn't move, he didn't speak, not even to answer Jasar's probably rhetorical questions, but he raged inside, his hate flaring out as always, beating at the man—the hate no master had ever realized could be controlled, the hate that hid his real emotions of terror, despair, and anger that Jasar would otherwise be able to feel.

Meanwhile, he tried desperately to think of a way out. He considered calling for help along the hive line, but he had strict orders to defend Jasar from attack. If any of the others came to his aid, he'd harm them. Such a situation would be horrific.

Jasar had no idea of Mace's thoughts. He was simply outraged at his battler's betrayal and wanted to hurt him. He couldn't, physically. Mace wouldn't feel any blows he delivered, so the courtier decided to humiliate him.

"You are never going to disobey me again," Jasar hissed. "You are never going to move unless I tell you, think unless I tell you, or feel unless I tell you. I am going to figure out a way to hurt you, and once I do, you are going to be in an endless amount of pain, you bastard."

Mace's eyes dimmed slightly, but he was glad at least that he didn't have to admit how badly he'd been hurt already.

Jasar wiped his mouth, looking around nervously. He'd heard and felt the top deck get razed, which was obviously Mace's work. That meant the generals were dead and he was in charge. He was going to turn this wreck of a ship around and fly back to Eferem, and if the king didn't like it, he'd get Mace set on him.

Knowing such a plan was a lie even as he thought it, Jasar eyed the battler angrily, no more afraid of him than he would be of a chained child. Mace had defied him, but he obviously hadn't forgotten who his master was. He couldn't exactly go away with one battler and return with another, though, not when his entire story hinged on the first battler's being dead.

Still, there were ways around even this.

"You saw that dog that was here? Well, you're going to turn into that dog in every detail, and you're going to stay that way and answer to the name Shield. Understood? You're going to be a dog to me and you're going to lick my boots." He lifted his chin. "You're my dog now. My neutered dog."

Mace nearly wept, seeing a lifetime of horror ahead without even the temporary relief he had found before in willing women's bodies. He wailed in despair, his form shifting as the man continued to scream at him. His body condensed, his metal turning to black fur as he hunched forward, falling onto four legs. Soon he was a snarling, slobbering dog with his head hung low.

Suddenly, Claw, who'd climbed up the broken mast and onto the ship when he heard Mace's first scream, leaped through the open doorway straight for Jasar Doliard's throat. The courtier shrieked, retreating in absolute terror, urine staining the front of his pants. Mace watched, knowing that his duty was to defend the man, instantly and without hesitation . . . but Jasar had ordered him not to do anything unless told.

Claw pinned the screaming dandy, his talons slicing into his victim's chest and arms. Jasar's scream turned into a frothy gurgle. Crouched on the floor, Mace felt his master's agony and shock, and watched as Claw lunged forward and latched his nightmarish jaws around the man's head. With a quick jerk, he tore it off.

The bond broke. Mace shuddered, and he almost lost his grip on reality, almost felt himself fade back to the formless world of his first hive, but Solie and the widow's patterns both held him. He shifted back to human form, gasping in reaction. With Jasar dead, all the man's orders were nullified.

Claw regarded him from horrible eyes, claws held before him almost deferentially. His emotions were nervous, beaten.

"Thank you," Mace said, and much of the tension went out of the the other sylph's aura. Still shaking, Mace rose and looked down at the corpse of his master. After all the years of servitude, he didn't feel anything, just a deep loathing and regret that he hadn't killed the man himself. Mostly, he felt disgust.

He turned his back, searching outward with his senses. There was one more battle going on, at the back of the hive where the storage rooms were dug. Mace felt the fear and pain, along with an inescapable sensation of bloodlust. He looked at Claw and they both understood: the hive was still in danger. In tandem they turned and left, neither of them looking at Jasar's body again. He wasn't worth it.

Reaching the top of the shattered ship, which was still hanging in the same place, as the air sylph struggled to manage the unwieldy weight of the crippled vessel, Mace shifted to smoke and lightning. He lifted Claw, carrying him over the bluff to the slope on the other side. Behind them, Tempest's master finally recovered from his shock. He hadn't been harmed, protected throughout the battle in a cocoon of her wind below the hull of the ship. He wasn't a brave man, however, and it took him time to recover his wits—and to start stammering orders of retreat. Still hissing with anger over the insult of the attack, Tempest obeyed, carrying the shattered ship and its few survivors. The two battlers let her go, focused on more immediate threats to the hive, and glad to see the last of the ship that had brought their former masters.

Leon stood in the heart of the conflict, his face a mask of bloody rage as he brought his sword across the neck of one attacker and then turned and thrust it into the unarmored armpit of another. A third man swung at him, but he blocked the blade with a thick chunk of wood. As he fought to keep himself alive, he shouted orders at the men and sylphs of the Community, directing the defense against the soldiers pouring through the gap bored in the empty storage room wall. He did so by instinct, without passion or emotion, but did it so well that Alcor's soldiers fought to kill him first.

Behind him, and clear of the fight for a moment, Devon watched Leon with fear. He'd seen what happened to some men when their sylphs died, and Leon looked almost insane. His skill was undeniable, both at fighting and leadership, but Devon wasn't sure the man would stop once he finished cutting apart the soldiers. He was a man seeking oblivion to vanquish the emptiness his sylph's death had thrust inside him.

Standing next to Devon, Morgal was wild-eyed and pale, but he hadn't run. Ash floated between him and all attackers, barely visible now but ready to flare up as an inferno if anyone came too close. She wouldn't actually hurt anyone, but she'd distracted more than one soldier, who then ended up impaled by her master's sword. Devon could see Airi in front of himself, ready to do the same. She was terrified, as a sword could cut her as easily as any man if she solidified, but most of her fear was for Devon. She wouldn't vanish if he died, thanks both to Solie and her old bond with Devon's father, but she didn't want to leave him. Devon could understand. He didn't want to lose her, either.

Before them, Alcor's soldiers roared, pushing forward as a group. Leon stumbled backward, unhurt but not able to restrain them all. He stopped on the other side of Morgal from Devon, and then they were all three fighting together.

Ash flared, blasting her heat and light, but this blinded friends as well as enemies. A moment later Devon felt Airi grab and push him away from a sword swing that he hadn't even seen. Blinking spots out of his eyes, he fell, but she lifted him upright again, her winds blowing his hair. Leon killed the man who'd attacked, stepping before Morgal to sever the man's head midway through his neck.

Be careful! Airi sent.

"You, too," Devon gasped, and yanked his sword up in time to parry another sword blow, grunting as the shock ran down his arm and into his shoulder. His opponent gritted his teeth, pushing down, but Airi blew into his face, lifting him off his feet. Devon gave a shout and drove his sword under the edge of the man's armor. The soldier screamed, bucking, and suddenly his blood was pouring out over Devon's arms.

Devon swore and jerked back, and Airi dropped the man with a horrified gasp. Nearby he heard Morgal cry out and Ash wail, but he couldn't be sure if his companion was hurt or just terrified. Devon was. Everyone was screaming and killing each other. It was a frenzy of murder.

As Leon shouted for them to pull back and regroup, Devon slipped on the bloody floor. Airi kept him on his feet. At the same time, hatred hit him. It hit everyone, and all the combatants forgot about the battle in exchange for a sudden, bone-deep need to escape. Devon panicked, his terror so overwhelming that he stopped caring who might run him through as long as he was in the process of flight. The only thing that saved him was that the king's men felt the same. The horde forgot their anger and crushed together, each trying to escape through the door that led back to the hive. Some men fell on the slick floor and were trampled in the rush.

The only one who didn't run was Leon. He stood in the center of the room, covered in the blood of other men, staring wearily out the hole that gaped in the side of the hill, and hoping—

Fire and lightning rushed through, flame dancing in the cloud's mouth. It was Mace, who roared again as he released another battler in the shape of a horrible monster, and both sylphs attacked.

None of the men of the hive were touched. The two battlers tore into the invaders instead, ripping men apart and showering the survivors with blood and gore. The defenders of the Community continued to flee, abandoning their weapons behind them. Devon went too, Airi pressed to his side, completely unsure who was still alive. He just knew that he and Airi were, and both of them wanted to get away from the battlers.

In the storage room, Leon wiped blood from his face with his sleeve and watched Mace and the other sylph finish off the last of Alcor's soldiers. He understood that neither was Ril. The part of him where his own battler used to be had gone numb, and he knew that Ril was gone, but still he waited until they finished and the smoke cloud reformed into a human-seeming Mace.

Eyeing the big battler, he sighed regretfully. Mace in turn regarded him, his form as perfect and clean as if he hadn't just slaughtered half a dozen men. Of course, he could take whatever form he wanted, clean or not. Leon just stared, knowing that Mace could feel everything he was suffering and didn't care.

"Why is Claw here?" he asked.

Mace took a moment before he answered—or bothered to answer, Leon corrected. Mace would never care much for men. "He's of the hive," the sylph said at last.

Leon nodded and tossed his sword on the floor. It clattered noisily. "I gather it's over?"

No answer. Claw looked between Mace and Leon uncertainly.

"It's over," Leon decided, and turned to walk back into the hive, shivering from the cold air that came through the hole. It was threatening to snow again, and he made a note that someone would have to come down here to clear away the bodies and bring an earth sylph to close off that hole. There were a lot of holes to close and bodies to bury, and a thousand other things to deal with. He'd be sure to take care of them all, he knew, before he let himself think again. He hoped it took a very long time.

Chapter Thirty-one

Heyou went back to the mess hall the long way, forced nearly the full distance around the outer corridors of the hive before he was able to find a route that hadn't been sealed off. He ran inside, arms spread, and after a startled moment everyone started cheering. As he rushed toward Solie, she leaped up from her seat on the table to meet him, and they slammed together, he lifting her off the ground and kissing her repeatedly. Everyone clapped and roared. She kissed him back, sobbing in relief as he swung her around, laughing.

"Did we win?" she gasped.

"Of course we did," he replied. "We always win."

She started laughing herself and kissed him again.

The exultation of victory was infectious. Grief would come later, when the dead were counted, but for now, everyone celebrated being alive. The fire sylphs danced above the crowd, lighting the underground as bright as day. The earth sylphs reopened every corridor, and the exhausted defenders trooped slowly back to rejoin their weeping families. There were some who didn't return, and family and friends went to search out their bodies, but really the casualties were few. Thanks to Heyou and Leon.

If he sat down, Devon thought, he'd never be able to move again. He stumbled into the mess room, every part of his body aching, especially his arms and shoulders. Someone handed him a mug of beer, and he slumped down on a bench, wincing.

Airi sat too, shimmering into semitranslucence and

smiling up beside him, a glimmer of joy in a childlike form. Able to feel her emotions as clearly as always, Devon sensed happiness about his survival, along with weariness. Wincing, he put his mug down and felt inside his tunic for his flute. Airi's delight increased as he started to play, forcing his fingers to dance along the holes. He played a slow song—he didn't have the energy to manage more than that—and the people nearby fell mostly silent, listening. It wasn't a dirge but a sweet song of winter and a lost summer yet to be reclaimed. Airi closed her eyes, swaying happily back and forth.

Across the hall, Devon saw Galway pushing through the crowd, stopping to drink from his mug while he listened. He was clearly entranced by the music. Devon hadn't known if the trapper even survived the fight in the stables, but the man only had a bandage around his head and looked stronger and healthier than Devon himself felt.

Devon finished his song and put the flute away. Airi sighed, wanting more, but she could wait. She knew that once Devon got some sleep, he'd play entire concertos for her.

As Galway approached, Devon stood. "I'm glad you're alive," he told the trapper.

"And you. It got hairy there. I hear the victory was cinched where you were fighting."

Devon laughed. He and his companions hadn't made the difference. They'd just ended up facing the last of the invaders. If those Eferem soldiers had realized they were the only ones left, they probably would have retreated.

"It's the battlers who made the difference," he admitted. "We wouldn't have lasted much longer if they hadn't shown up." And frightened everyone senseless, he didn't add. The fear of them would always be there, and he looked around uncertainly.

Heyou was nearby, acting no different than any other

lusty teenager, trying to nuzzle Solie even as she walked across the room. Devon wouldn't have seen her at all, but everyone cleared out of her way, giving her passage. They stared at her as if she was their leader now. Leon had lent his assistance and strategy, but she was the one who controlled the battlers. Devon hoped she could handle being queen. She'd have to.

"Have you seen Morgal or any of the other councilmen?" he asked Galway. He hadn't seen Morgal escape the fight below, but he remembered hearing him scream before the battlers arrived.

Galway shook his head. "A few of the others. Morgal? No."

Devon sighed and shook his head. He could see Luck the healer sylph standing near Solie. She was mending the injured, slowly making her way toward the two of them, but she didn't try to go below. Whoever remained down there was beyond her power to heal.

"Damn," he said.

"Yes, Morgal was a good man. We'll raise a tankard to him once we're rested—and to all those who gave themselves protecting our freedom." Galway slapped Devon's shoulder and he winced. "Get some sleep. For me, I think I'll go see to Heyou before he tears that girl's clothes off." He wandered off into the crowd, following Solie and Heyou down the corridor and leaving Devon to sip his drink.

I'm tired, Airi said.

"So am I. I'm going to bed." Pushing himself to his feet, Devon stumbled out and down the corridor that led toward his room. Even a bath could wait until later.

In the opposite direction, Solie followed Mace's mental call into a room that was intended to be the quarters of a family, though none had claimed it yet. The earth sylphs had been happily at work all through the bluff, creating far more chambers than they needed or would ever use before spring, when they'd leave this place. They were happier doing so, though, and she wouldn't argue. Part of freedom was doing what made you happy. There didn't always have to be a reason.

Heyou followed so close that he was nearly a second skin, trying to lick her neck and get his hands under her clothes. Were all battlers so lusty? she wondered, even as she tried to push him back. At the same time, she contemplated leaving everyone for a while to take him back to her room. Would that be rude? She was feeling a little lusty herself.

She couldn't sense exactly how the other battlers were feeling in comparison to Heyou. As queen she could perceive them, just as she could all her sylphs, but they were only a faint buzz in the back of her head. Only Heyou was clear—probably because of the depth of their attachment. It was a good thing. She'd go mad listening to too many voices at once.

They could call to her silently, though, just as any sylph could to its master, and she responded to Mace's request for her to come at once. He hadn't told her why, though, and she stopped short as she entered the chamber. That gave Heyou the chance to get his hand inside her dress and over her breast.

Shrieking, she doubled over, pulling away from him, and smacked him across the head. "Behave yourself!"

"Do I have to?"

Solie glared. Still, part of her thrilled at his attention, glad he was alive, even if he did seem determined to lay with her every chance he got.

She turned to find two battlers. She was relieved to see Mace was the same as ever. Like Heyou, he'd escaped combat with little or no injury, and she grinned at his mild expression of amusement. Beside him, however, was a creature out of nightmare, a hunched form with claws instead of hands, held up before him like a praying mantis's forearms, and a mouth ringed with fangs. Strangely, she could feel him as easily as Mace, and his emotions were extremely . . . neurotic.

"This is Claw," Mace explained. "One of our hive line. He felt you become the queen the same as I did. He was sent to destroy us, but he helped instead. Without Ril . . . he saved us." He paused. "Can you please give him the orders you gave us?"

Solie's head reeled. "Oh, of course," she managed to say. She had four battlers now? Part of her shrieked in fright, but Heyou leaned against her, nearly pushing her over. She braced herself and shoved back, at the same time banishing the momentary feeling of being overwhelmed.

"Claw?" she said. "Any order your master gave you, you don't have to obey. You can take any form you want, and you can speak if you want. All I ask is you don't fight except to protect the Community, and that you don't use your hate aura except to protect the Community. Do you understand?"

Claw shivered, his beady eyes emotionless. "Yes," he squeaked, his voice high and incongruous, with his shape.

Solie nodded, wondering how many more battlers she'd get at this rate. "Can you turn into a human?" she asked. "You're kind of scary like that."

Claw looked down and shimmered, reshaping himself. He transformed into a hunched, nervous-looking young man, eyes bulging and hands still held before him like the forelegs of a praying mantis. His skin was very pale, and his hair, bizarrely, was dark blue. The robes he'd been wearing now hung on him like a tent.

"Better?" he whimpered.

His emotions were primarily those of fear. Solie couldn't really blame him, even as she wondered how any battler could be afraid of anything. What had his former master done to make him like this? Suddenly, the thought of having more battlers wasn't so bad, not if it meant they'd be free.

"Not bad," she told him as cheerfully as she could.

A moment later, a knock came at the door. "Galway," Heyou said without even looking, and he turned around, pulling the door open.

The trapper stuck his head in. "Are you planning to come back anytime soon?" he asked, his appraising eyes on Heyou and Solie as if he'd expected to find them naked and rolling around on the floor.

Solie blushed. "Was someone asking for me?"

He shook his head. "But you're the leader of this place. You're going to have to speak. Leon's probably going to want you, too. He's just coming back."

"Is he all right?" she asked worriedly. She saw a lot of hard years ahead, and she needed his experience. Galway's as well, if she could convince him to stay. She'd need a lot of men willing to train and advise a female monarch.

"Looks like. I can see him coming up the passage. I'll talk to him for a bit, ask him to stop in here before he goes anywhere else. He'll tell you what needs doing." The trapper regarded Heyou sternly, who just grinned back, and withdrew his head from the room. The door closed.

It opened again barely a minute later. Solie glanced up, expecting Leon, but the widow entered instead. She gave Solie the appraising look that always made her want to hang her head and shuffle her feet, but then turned to Mace.

"I see you're not dead," she said.

"No."

"Were you planning to tell me?"

His eyebrows rose. "I thought I did."

Her arms crossed. "No. You sent a whisper in my head summoning me to your august presence. I'm not a dog, you know."

He tilted his head to one side, and Solie felt his emotions soften. "I'm very sorry," he told her honestly. "I need your help with something."

Apparently, the widow felt his contrition as well. Her demeanor softened—if just a bit. Solie felt uncomfortably as though she was spying on them both.

"What is it?" the widow asked.

Mace pointed a thumb. "This is Claw," he told her. The blue-haired battler started, having been happy to fade into the background. "He's a battler of the hive. He's tied to Solie, but none of us are permitted to draw on her energy."

"I am," Heyou chirped.

"You better start drawing from Galway instead, pup," Mace told him flatly, and the youngster made a face. Solie chuckled. She couldn't feel any of them take from her anyway.

"Claw needs a master," Mace continued. "Someone to pattern his energy to as a secondary to Solie. A woman." He looked at her directly. "A woman willing to have sex with him."

Claw perked up.

The widow pursed her lips. "What is it with you battlers and sex?"

"That's what we're for. Fighting and sex."

"Do you realize how many men I've heard say that?" Still, the widow put her hands on her hips. "I'll see if I can find any volunteers. There are a number of widows here who have no children to care for and who are still young enough to have interest in you battlers and your . . . stamina. No children, mind you." She glared over at Solie, who blushed. "I am not handing a mere girl over to a battler's lust. You'll get a woman who's had her children already and has no man, since I doubt you fools will share. Understood?"

Claw blinked. "I get a woman?" He sounded faint with amazement.

"Only if I can find one who wants you." She inspected him, obviously not impressed by what she saw. "Until then, stay away from my girls!" The battler blinked again, nodded shakily when she glared, and seemed relieved when she faced Mace. "As for you, no more silent whispering in my head. If you want something, you'll come up to me and ask politely—got it?"

"Yes, Lily," he answered serenely.

The widow only sniffed and swept out of the room. "I can't believe I've been reduced to pimping," she muttered as she went, holding the door wide for Leon, who came in.

He stopped and stared after her. "Did she just say what I thought she did?"

Solie giggled. "Yes. We have another battler now. Meet Claw."

Leon considered the blue-haired sylph and nodded. He didn't seem surprised at all. "Good. There may be another attack."

Solie went white. "Another one?"

"The air ship escaped," Leon told her. "The king will know what happened. The question is whether he's willing to risk more battlers, when he's already lost six. He only has nine left. Eight, considering he'd never let Thrall leave his side."

Solie imagined eight battlers descending on the Community and felt ill. Heyou put his arms around her.

"I doubt he'll do it," Leon continued. "I would, if I wanted to end us as a threat. The odds are still in his favor but . . . Alcor is paranoid." He smirked. The smile, however, didn't last more than a moment, and it never touched his eyes. "I think he'll pull his tail in and hide, but I can't guarantee it. We'll need all the battlers we can get."

"Where are we supposed to get more?"

"Summon them. Bring a dozen battlers over to willing women, and we'll outnumber him. Keep the secret of how it's done, and we'll never have to worry about an invading army."

Solie stared at him. "Wow."

"Indeed." He looked toward the door. "You should get back out there—let your people see you. They need that sort of recognition now. We'll make all the necessary decisions tomorrow."

There was something terribly sad about him. Solie couldn't feel his emotions very clearly and didn't want to, but she knew the man was somehow drowning in them. "Are you all right?" she asked uncertainly. He had blood on him, but he didn't look hurt.

Leon turned back and smiled at her sadly. "I will be. They say it's hard on the master when a sylph dies. I feel like Ril's still there in my head."

Solie blinked. "Ril's not dead."

Leon stared.

"I just saw him," she blubbered in denial, feeling a wave of horror and sorrow pass over her. "Luck brought him in. He's messed up, but he's alive. Did he die?" She could still feel him, distant and in shock. No, he couldn't be dead! "He was with your family when I—"

She said the last to his back. Leon was already running out the door.

Solie looked up at Mace. "Did you know Ril was still alive?"

The big battler shook his head. "He should have died. That healer didn't do him a favor by saving him. He'll never be what he was."

"That doesn't matter," Solie protested. "He's alive. That's a good thing."

"As you say, my queen," Mace replied, and Heyou tightened his arms around her, his face buried against her neck. Claw just sighed, staring at his hands and thinking about women.

* * *

Leon charged into the mess hall, his heart pounding. He'd felt Ril, felt him the whole time, but he hadn't comprehended. He could feel him even now, but the emotions of the battler were so shattered that he hadn't recognized them. He had thought the numbness and horror were his own emotions. Whatever had just happened, Ril was deep in shock.

He didn't stop for the impromptu party that had broken out, though he was not surprised at all to see it. In the face of such terror and death, people had to let go. Not ready yet to do so himself, he pushed through the crowd, finding himself slapped on the back and having his hand shaken. Once the enemy of these people, now he was tearfully thanked for saving their lives. Leon nodded and kept going, wanting to see both his battler and his family, not sure in truth which he needed to see more.

Ahead, the crowd parted enough for him to see his wife, and the question was answered as he hurried forward, suddenly desperate to get to her. "Betha!" he shouted. She turned to him, eyes wide, and suddenly she was pushing toward him as well, Ralad screaming in her arms. Leon met her near the end of the room and hugged her and the baby both. Betha sobbed in relief, pressing against him even as she struck him with her fist. She screamed at him, holding the baby safe, but he stepped back and cupped her face with both hands, holding her gently still for a deliberate and thorough kiss.

As he finished, Nali waddled up, thumb in her mouth, and regarded her father with great indignation. "Papa, Ril won' turn into a pony," she complained.

Leon stared down at his three-year-old daughter, wanting to pick her up and kiss her, too. "What?"

"A pony! I wan' him to turn into a pony and he won'!"

Leon managed a smile, not aware of the tears that had

started down his cheeks the moment he saw his wife. His family was alive, all of them. "He's not feeling well, Nali. You have to give him some time."

"It's not fair! He's never been a pony!"

Leon kissed his wife again and picked up Nali, kissing her as well despite the child's protests. Setting her down, he moved toward the corner of the room. There Lizzy knelt with Cara, facing a hollow formed between two walls and a table. Ril sat in the hollow with his knees up, wrapped in a blanket. His eyes were heavily shadowed yet blank. He stared straight ahead, shivering but not reacting to anything.

Lizzy acknowledged her father tearfully, barely noting the blood on him. Her priorities had always lain elsewhere. "Daddy, he's sick. Do something!"

Leon dropped to his knees and reached forward to shake his battler. Ril was alive, truly alive, but the gaze the sylph suddenly turned on him was one filled with horror. "I'm crippled," he whispered. "She left me crippled."

"But you're living," Leon told him—and as far as he was concerned, that was all that mattered.

King Alcor Baldorth sat on the throne he'd graced for thirty-two years, staring forward, his crown heavy on his head, and he gripped its arms until his fingers turned white. His gut felt as though he'd swallowed a handful of nails.

Anderam, Boradel, and Flav were all dead. So was Jasar. So were the soldiers he'd sent. All of them. Worst, word was that their battlers weren't gone—they had joined Leon and the girl. That pathetic little girl who should have been dead months ago, instead of his son.

His grip on the armrests tightened, pain starting to flare through his tendons as he stared down at the man who'd brought the news, one of a bare handful to make it back. The fool cowered in terror, afraid of what would be done to him for bearing such bad news. Alcor wanted to kill him—would have if he could—but this was Tempest's master, and he couldn't afford to lose her.

Six battlers lost! Alcor sucked in a deep, shaky breath. Leon had betrayed him so thoroughly and unexpectedly. How long had the man been planning this? How long had the traitor been worming into his graces just so he could plan and pull off this horrendous coup? The man had worked for him for over twenty years, and not once had Alcor ever thought him conspiring.

In the shadows behind his chair, Thrall was laughing. Not out loud—the sylph couldn't make any sound out loud—but his shoulders shook and Alcor could hear his breath hitching. Even worse, his aura of hate was blended with one of delight. Alcor wanted to turn and scream for him to shut up, but that wouldn't stop the amusement. Thrall would only laugh harder.

Alcor licked his lips. "Get out," he whispered. The sylph master kneeling before him cringed in fear. "Get out!" he screamed a second time, and the man ran off, boot heels pounding on the polished floor.

The king finally let go of his throne and put a hand to his forehead, wincing in pain. What was he supposed to do now? He couldn't go after Leon again. He had another eight battlers . . . nine, if he dared go himself with Thrall, but he had no idea of how Leon had done this, how he'd turned battlers against their masters and made them his own. He couldn't risk any more defections. Para Dubh would love for him to leave himself vulnerable. So would the southern kingdoms. So especially would the desert nation of Meridal across the ocean, the people from whom he bought trade goods at such expense. They waited breathlessly to attack with their battlers once he'd spent all of his own.

Alcor returned his grip to the arm of the chair, shuddering. He had to salvage what he could, cover up this disaster before his own people found out, and try to get more battlers. Belican said he was too old to run many more ceremonies. Well, he'd have to train some of those useless children he had left. Alcor needed more battle sylphs—provided he could find men he trusted enough to master them. What if he ended up with another Leon? What if they came after him next?

He sat in his throne room and shook, his mind imagining everything that could go wrong, everything that undoubtedly would go wrong, now that he was weakened so badly. The nightmare surrounded the king, and Thrall held his loyal position . . . and the battler's laughter never stopped.

Epilogue

Spring brought no greenery across the Shale Plains, but pale yellow flowers started to appear on the prickly gray bushes that dotted the landscape, their roots thrust deep into the worn-out soil and showing there was still some life to be found. Life that sylphs set to work together could renew and refresh.

Solie rode at the head of the convoy in a pair of split skirts. Her horse was an ordinary gelding, a little old and its hide gray, but that was enough for her. There were some who believed she should act more regal in view of her new station, but she wasn't so sure. There had been no one like her before. Protocol for the queen of the Community would be whatever she wanted. Right now, it was riding bareback on an old nag.

Heyou was sitting behind her. He claimed this was so he could protect her better, but she knew he just wanted to feel her up under her cloak. No one had threatened her life since Bock, not with so many battlers and every elemental sylph beholden to her. Due to Leon, Galway, and Devon's discreet tutoring, she'd become a leader for real. The position still felt a little odd, like boots that didn't quite fit, but she was wearing them in. Soon enough she'd feel very comfortable indeed.

She looked back over her shoulder at the rest of the convoy, smiling at Heyou as she did. He beamed back. Behind him, the Community stretched out in a line. What horses they had were being ridden or pulling wagons. Other people sat on sheets of stone that earth sylphs flowed along the ground. Air sylphs looped above these, many transporting supplies through the air, and over everything else Mace flew as smoke and lightning, joined by Claw and six others.

With the priest Petr's help, they'd brought over another half-dozen battlers, every one of them drawn to a willing middle-aged woman. Each sylph had come through the gate, taking the female's offer to be their master, but were subsumed into the hive and Solie's pattern before they were allowed any physical consummation. Apparently, the act of love made a female master a queen, but a battler bound to a queen already couldn't turn his lover into one. She'd have to be careful of that, Solie supposed. There were any number of problems tied up in the concept of two queens, not the least of which was the fact that the battlers would go to war over it.

The women chosen for battlers didn't mind not being queen, though, not at all. Solie had grown up in a world where women had little power and few rights. Battlers didn't seem to get that idea, however, and no human man wanted to argue the point. Solie smiled a little. It was very hard to tell a woman she was inferior when she had an irritated battle sylph standing behind her.

It wasn't just their masters they were fond of, either. The battlers protected every woman and female child in the hive—and at Solie's request, the men as well. The women in the Community were the safest in the world, she supposed. There hadn't been a single case of a woman being hurt by a drunken or violent husband since midwinter. The last transgressor had been considered fair game under the "Harm only those who seek to harm the hive" rule, and his widow now had a battler of her own.

Solie looked into the sky. Like her people, her sylphs were happy. Almost playing up there as they watched for danger, the hive's entire complement of battlers was in the air, save two. Heyou sat behind her, his fingers tirelessly searching for a way under her cloak, and there was Ril. She smacked Heyou's hand.

Ril. Glancing back once more, Solie saw that Leon walked a dozen feet behind her, leading two horses. His wife sat on one of them, Ralad tied in a blanket to her breast and Cara arranged before her. Leon's battler rode the other with Lizzy and Nali, Lizzy nearly in his lap. The twelve-year-old was twisted around in her seat and chattering, but the battler barely paid attention, except perhaps to keep her from getting too rambunctious and falling, which was something both girls seemed determined to do.

Ril never looked up at his fellows, Solie noted. He had indeed been crippled in the fight at the bluff. She had heard the battler could still change shape if he really had to, but she hadn't seen him do it and didn't want to ask. He'd lost more than just a third of his energy in that battle, and he observed her with eyes that were almost dead. Still, he kept his arms protectively around both girls.

Heyou breathed in Solie's ear, forcing her to refocus her thoughts. "I think we're nearly there."

They'd been traveling for nearly a week toward the mountains, which had in that time seemed to grow in size until they seemed to fill the world. The group was now heading over a rise that Solie had been told would dip into a valley, one with a river running through it and a lake in the middle of what had once been dead soil. The sylphs had revived the land once, though, and they'd be able to do it again, no matter what had happened there. The Community would be able to rebuild, and this time no one would stop them. There wouldn't be any stupid mistakes—or fewer of them, she hoped.

They cleared the rise and she saw their destination at last. Great gouges had been torn into the earth by Mace and Ril when they'd been ordered to attack. What had once been houses and barns were razed to the ground, and nearly every bit of life had been stripped from the place. But there were spots missed. Solie saw green down there, spreading out over the land, and the dots of flowers that grew on plants more delicate and useful than the scrub bushes that survived in the rest of the plains. The valley was immense as well, more than enough for all of them.

"It's beautiful," she said.

Heyou hugged her, his fingers starting to move again. "Not as much as you," he assured her. "But it's all yours."

No, it was here for all of them. Solie took a deep breath, seeing a lifetime of freedom ahead that she hadn't been able to imagine before she left her parents' cottage. It was good to be home, she thought, but of course as long as Heyou's arms were around her, it didn't matter where that was. She was already there.